Incipience

Sam Silver

Chapter One

"You got that right," Kelly muttered, hurrying past the alleyway's street graffiti while heading through town. That, and the looming storm clouds on the horizon, along with the chill in the air, confirmed that the day was going to hell fast.

She pulled her bag strap higher up her shoulder and adjusted her glasses. Her long blonde hair wavered in the wind as she sighed. She'd time to kill before catching the bus to work, wishing she were at home having breakfast. The usual rice bubbles in front of the TV, but no, not today. She'd been woken extra early by the construction workers across the street, making her swear that it was illegal for them to start work this early, and then making her swear at life in general. Thankfully, they stopped after a while, leaving her to fall asleep on the couch and completely missing breakfast, along with her bus to work. She'd called the office, knowing they'd be annoyed, while being fully aware that she was still on probation. She'd made up a reasonable excuse and they told her to come in later, but she knew they weren't impressed.

Even worse, there was a bus strike. Only a few drivers had shown up to work this morning, meaning limited routes and stops. That left a weary walk across town for her, hopefully with a bite to eat along the way.

She rounded a corner, straight into the path of a strong wind. The air tingled and she stopped dead. There was a storm front moving in so it should be getting colder, she figured. This tingle was warm. Really warm, and deep too, with a prickling resonance. What's more, it was drawing her in, tuning her into its frequency and dancing with her. Yes, it was scary, but at the same time, enticing.

She winced, resisting its engulfing embrace, desperately trying to break free. It wasn't easy and she struggled hard. She pushed on, until finally shaking it off and falling against a brick wall with a loud gasp. Much to her relief, the wind turned cold again, bringing a few raindrops with it.

She shivered, seriously freaked out, swearing she'd felt a presence in the air. No, she concluded logically, it couldn't have been. She was going nuts. That was it. Had to be. Trouble was, who'd believe her? Shaken, she hurried on, desperate to get away.

She hadn't gone far when she saw a café up ahead. She blinked, astonished. She'd walked this path loads of times and was sure it hadn't been here before. The new owners must have swept in and done it up fast, she concluded, and well too. Whatever the case, she was hungry, and the wafting aromas smelt good. More than that. Divine.

She moved in closer. Strangely, a swinging sign was overhead, creaking in the breeze. What is this, she wondered, the old west? She peered at the sign.

'Sanders Café.'

She headed up to the door, pushing it in. Slowly, she entered, peering around.

Everything *seemed* normal at least. Yes, there was a warm presence in here too, only that of a standard café. Everyone was relaxed. No, more than that. Far *too* relaxed, like nobody knew it was a workday, and the exotic coffees and steaming breakfast dishes only added to the holiday atmosphere.

She stared at it, bewildered, and murmured, "Nowhere's this good."

Curiously, she made for the counter.

A cheery voice spoke. "Morning, hon. Haven't seen you here before. Come on in."

The light tone came from a tall woman with long curly, auburn hair, carrying a tray.

Kelly remained cautious. "Nice place."

The woman lowered the tray onto the counter. "Sure is. We cater for everyone, sweetie, and that means you. Take a seat."

"Yeah … uh sure." Kelly sat at the counter. "You new in town?"

"First of our kind," came the response. She pulled out a notepad. "What'll it be …?"

Kelly got the gist of what she was getting at and relented, hesitantly. "Kelly. Kelly Morrison."

"Peachy," the woman replied. "Pleased to meet you, Kelly, Kelly Morrison."

"And you are …?" Kelly found herself prompting, unusually.

"Vanilla," the woman answered, with all the sweetness of a flavoured ice-cream. "Vanilla Pond. What can I get you?"

Kelly cautiously scanned the menu above. "Just a croissant, thanks. Didn't have any breakfast."

"We'll make up for that," came the chirpy reply. "What kind?"

"What have you got? I can't see any options."

"Whatever you want, sweetie."

"You serious?"

"Yep. We've got everything in every way. Try me."

Kelly paused, sure this had to be a setup. Now was her chance to put it to the test, and she was more than ready.

She leaned forward, crossing her arms on the counter. "Okay then. Make it with barbecue sauce, melted cheese dripping off the sides, pasted through with avocado, with a light sprinkling of salt. Not a lot, because that'll put too much edge on it, but not too little either, 'cause that'll be frustrating. A dash of lemon too, for flavour. Oh, and mushrooms. I forgot mushrooms. Olives as well, if you have them. Make the croissant crispy, but not burnt, just crunchy enough so it's toasty, though not too much or that'll ruin it. If you could balance all that, on a croissant, that'd be great."

Vanilla nodded. "Challenge accepted. Might have to fiddle around a bit with an extra big croissant, or maybe I can combine two into one. Doesn't matter. I'll have fun figuring it out. Back in a sec."

She slapped Kelly playfully with her notepad and headed into the kitchen.

Kelly felt a light tingle from the slap. She shook it away, rested one hand under her chin and used the other to flick open a magazine. An article caught her attention. Hollywood gossip, she'd always loved that. She was just getting into it when a good-looking guy pulled out a chair and sat next to her at the counter. She tensed, averting her gaze.

A waitress strode in, picking up the tray that Vanilla had left.

The man glanced at her. "Hey, Skoobie."

"Hey, yourself," came the reply.

"How's things?"

She shrugged coolly. "They're moving everywhere. It's how life works."

"That's very deep."

"The universe *is* very deep."

"Would it provide a cup of coffee?"

"Ask and you shall receive."

"Thanks, Skoob."

"Welcome."

She headed away.

He looked at Kelly.

She shifted nervously, pushing her glasses up.

"Mind if I grab the newspaper?" he asked.

She glanced down, finding her elbow resting on it. "Sure." She handed it to him.

"Gotta see the sports," he said, opening it. "Love the sports."

She focused on her magazine again.

He flicked through the paper noisily. "Cricket, where is it? Basketball, soccer, hockey, where's it gone …?"

Skoobie walked up.

"One existentialist coffee," she said, placing it in front of him.

"That was quick," he noted.

"Time's our relative." She breezed off.

He looked back at the paper. "Now where was I? Football …"

He ruffled it again, unnerving Kelly. She flicked through her magazine just as loudly, trying to show no reaction and failing miserably. He coughed, her hand jerked up, she bumped his coffee, it wobbled violently and spilled on …

"*YAAAAAAAA!*"

He jumped up in agony. She screamed and followed, her hand over her mouth. "Oh my God …!"

She grabbed a towel and moved to dab his trousers, then recoiled when she saw where the spill was.

He cringed painfully. "Ow, ow, ow …!"

"Take your pants off!" Skoobie called.

He undid his belt.

Kelly reacted fast, grabbing a jug of cold water, hurling its contents and drenching him from the waist down. He froze, in more ways than one.

Kelly winced. "Is that better?"

Vanilla lowered her head, hiding her smile, while everyone else watched them curiously.

The man took a deep breath, put his hands on his hips and raised his eyebrows. "If you wanted to make conversation there are easier ways."

Kelly blinked, composing herself. "I … uh … know a good drycleaner down the street."

"I know the one." He grabbed his briefcase, flung his jacket over his shoulder and made for the door. "I'll go myself. It's safer that way."

He headed out and was gone.

Kelly cringed. "I can't believe I just did that." She fell forward onto the counter, face-first into the croissant that Vanilla had put there, then rose startled, covered in food. "Oh, this is great …"

"Yeah," Skoobie quipped, walking past. "You're on a roll."

Vanilla handed Kelly a napkin. "Forget it. Accidents happen, sweetie. Good thing I made you two." She slid over another plate with a croissant on it. "Well, it's the second half, really. Let's just say our challenge was a draw."

She grabbed a cloth to wipe up the mess.

Kelly got ready to leave out of sheer embarrassment, and would have, if the croissant's aroma hadn't stopped her. It smelt divine.

It tasted even better. Her taste buds tingled with delight as she took another mouthful, savouring it, while forgetting about everything that had just happened.

"Oghf! Heaven!"

Despite her stuff-up with Coffee-guy, Kelly found herself relaxing into this place's soothing essence, especially after finishing her superb croissant. She started reading her magazine again, floating into its pages, losing all track of time, and almost drifting into a dream. The world stopped and she loved every moment, at least until she saw an article on workplace relations and suddenly remembered her job.

"Crap!"

She looked at the clock with a start. It was nearly time to grab the bus, leaving her a few minutes or so to reach it. Strangely, she felt like she'd been here all day, and closed the magazine, more relaxed than usual. She blinked, arched back, stretched, and would have yawned if the café door hadn't suddenly flown open and a woman stormed in, wearing a singlet, army pants, and her brown hair tied up in a bun.

A man followed her in, pleading. "Mel, just listen, okay …?"

"Forget it!" She hit the counter. "Hey, where's my service? Service!"

"Right here, sweet Melody," Vanilla said, emerging from the kitchen. She stopped at the sight of the man. "Oh, no. Row time, right?"

"Yuh-huh," the woman replied firmly.

"Places!" Skoobie called. She hurried into the kitchen, peering out through its small, round window. Vanilla ducked behind the counter while everyone else either hid under tables or took cover wherever they could.

Kelly rose from her seat, baffled. "What …?"

The woman, Melody, turned to the man. "You've got one chance …"

He stammered, put on the spot. "Well … I … uh … I …"

"Oh, great start!" she scoffed. "That's all you can say after your work-party? You were on the dance floor with your PA. I saw the snaps. She was drunk as hell and doing the *ho*-down in front of everyone. That aint dancing, deadhead. You had your hand on her butt so tight it was almost up it!"

"It slipped …" he protested.

"And what?" she snapped. "Got stuck there?"

He raised his hand. "Okay Mel, listen. I was mad at you, okay. Your flirting with the postman just got to me …"

"Talking is flirting, is it? Taking the mail and saying, 'thanks,' is flirting?"

"Yeah, but it was the *way* you said it …"

"So what? That allows you a flirty sleaze fest with at least three other bimbos that night, including a rival CEO? She only wanted a leg up in the field by massaging your rising expectations into a strategic merger. How can you not see that she's only a bed diver whose best move is a sweeping backflip? What more's there to say?"

Silence.

An old man stuck his head out from under a table. "You gonna let her get away with that? Sock it to her, Darren!"

Melody turned to him. "Do you wanna get your wrinkly old butt up here and say that?"

"What? You think I'm crazy?" He ducked back down.

Darren beefed himself up. "Mel …"

She turned back to him, bringing herself up to her full height and glaring him straight in the eyes. He returned her gaze defiantly. Slowly, they moved in, until their foreheads almost touched.

Kelly hid her smile. "Enough, already. God, we all *know* you two have the hots for each other."

Melody inhaled sharply, glanced to the side, raised her eyebrows at the sight of Kelly, then looked at Darren. "Okay, how much'd you pay her?"

He frowned, confused. "I've never seen her before."

"Great," she retorted. "Perfect excuse for you to go over and snog her then."

Now, Kelly couldn't help but grin. "Yeah, it's love. He's just got a kid's brain. That's why he freaked out when you talked to the postman. He thought the mother figure in his life didn't love him anymore."

Darren's jaw dropped. "Excuse me?"

Kelly kept her focus on Melody. "He's only attention-seeking to win your approval. Can't you see that?"

Darren was astonished. "Huh?"

Melody tensed, turning red. The silence grew as she glared at Kelly furiously, then threw an arm up. "Well of *course* I can!"

Darren stayed astounded. "Huh?"

"How else do you think I keep him in check?" Melody fumed. "I was trying to bait him for the big reel-in, but you, dimwit, have let him off the hook!"

Darren blinked. "I am?"

"Like hell," she answered. "Now I'll have to tackle things the ol' fashioned way."

He braced himself. "Oh crap …"

Vanilla emerged from behind the counter, went to the front door and opened it.

Smack!

Darren flew outside, hurtling towards the road. A taxi came to a stop by the kerb, a passenger got out from the backseat and hurried away. Darren flew in and the taxi took off, its door wavering as it picked up speed.

"Done and dusted," Melody said, heading to the counter and taking a seat.

Everyone emerged from their hiding places and the relaxed ambiance resumed.

Vanilla returned to the counter, picked up a coffee pot and asked Melody, "The usual?"

"The usual," Melody replied. She patted the empty seat beside her, addressing Kelly. "Wanna join me?"

Kelly was confused. "You're kidding."

"Do I look like I'm kidding?" came the reply. "You stood up to me. I like that. Things came out good, so forget it. Gotta name?"

Kelly spoke without thinking. "Uh, yeah. Kelly. Kelly Morrison."

"Melody Hill. You like sports?"

"Not really."

"Should take you riding sometime."

Kelly was wary. "I haven't ridden a bike in a long time …"

"You'll warm up after the first fifty k's …?"

"Fifty k's …?"

"Yeah. You'll be fine after that."

Vanilla gestured to Melody. "You should listen to her, sweetie; she's a sports freak. Knows every kind there is, back to front and inside out."

"From basic to extreme," Melody confirmed. "Riding's only a base training exercise. You wanna go skysurfing sometime?"

Kelly glanced at the window. A man in a business suit was walking by, reminding her of her job. "I'd better get to work."

"Let me guess," Melody said. "Computers, right?"

Kelly put her bag over her shoulder. "Right. I gotta go."

"It's gonna kill you, sis."

Kelly headed for the door.

"You coming back?" Vanilla called.

"Say yes," Skoobie prompted.

"Computers aren't great company," Vanilla pointed out.

"And you've got a great butt," the old man from the corner added.

Kelly made a face and adjusted her skirt. "I'll think about it. Thanks for breakfast, guys. See ya."

She hurried outside.

She was barely gone when Skoobie nodded, satisfied. "She'll be back."

"Yep," Melody agreed.

"Definitely," Vanilla added.

Melody took a sip of her coffee and flicked open a sports magazine. "Good choice. Kid's got potential."

Kelly hurried down the street, focused on the day ahead. Thankfully, the distant storm clouds had subsided, bringing glimmers of sunlight. She didn't notice it, nor anything else, and was so wound up that she bumped into a man.

"Sorry …" she said quickly.

They tried moving around each other but ended up going the same way. They stepped the other way and the same thing happened. "Sorry, sorry …"

The man spoke smoothly. "We are having fun today, aren't we?"

Kelly looked up, embarrassed. "Oh, no …"

Coffee-guy. With a new pair of pants on.

"Oh yeah," he confirmed. "David, by the way."

"What?" she asked, taken aback.

"David," he repeated. "That's my name."

She nodded. "Kelly. How's your pants?"

"Please, we only just met."

She hid her smile.

He continued. "They're more comfortable without the coffee, thanks. Went home and got another pair."

"I am so sorry …"

"Don't be."

"I'll make it up to you sometime …"

He indicated the café. "Well, you can come inside and we'll try again. Only try to keep things in the cup this time, it's too painful otherwise. We'll sit on opposite sides of a table if it makes you feel better."

She shook her head, unnerved. "I've really got to get to work. I'm late enough as it is."

A bus rounded the corner. She hurried up to the bus stop as it pulled up with a hiss and its doors opened.

"Gotta long ride?" he asked.

"Gordon Street," she answered, moving up the steps.

"But you're coming back?" he prompted.

"We'll see," she replied. "See ya."

She scanned her card, went to the back of the bus and sat by a window.

Coolly, he went over and tapped on it.

She opened it.

"Thought you should know something," he said.

"Yeah?"

"This bus doesn't go anywhere near Gordon Street, and there's a strike on, meaning you'll have a long alternative route and limited stops. This driver gets cranky if you ask him to pull over too, and even if you do get off you'll have to wait ages for another bus. Have fun."

"What …?"

The door closed and she looked around, horrified, as the bus took off.

He smiled and strode for the café, whistling.

Two hours later, the café door swung open and Kelly stormed in, approaching the counter angrily. She threw her bag down and her arms up, exasperated. "Well, I hope you're happy!"

"Always," Skoobie replied, picking up an empty plate and walking away.

Kelly glared at her. "Hey! I was talking to you!"

"Was talking to you too," Skoobie answered, heading for the kitchen. "That's the way it works. Cool, huh?"

She walked out the back.

Kelly banged the bell. "Hey!"

No response.

She banged it several more times.

Vanilla emerged from the kitchen, carrying a plate of food. She placed it before a customer and said, "There you go. One specialty from the specialiser." She saw Kelly's cross look. "Oh, hi sweetie. Welcome back."

"Oh yeah, real smooth!" Kelly retorted. "Do you know what happened to me this morning?"

"We already do," Vanilla said pleasantly. "You came in, had a croissant, read a bit, spilt a drink on David, broke up a fight, then got on the wrong bus for work from what I hear."

"Actually, that was funny," the old man in the corner pointed out. "Thanks for telling us that."

"Welcome," Skoobie replied, emerging from the kitchen.

"I'm glad you think it was funny," Kelly huffed. "Do you know what happened after that?"

Vanilla patted a seat. "No, but why don't you sit down and tell us all about it? Would you like a coffee?"

"Coffee?" Kelly scoffed. "Great! That'll really make up for me losing my freakin' job!"

"Join the club," called another man.

"Yeah, me too," said another. "So what else is new?"

"Coffee's great though, isn't it?" a third added.

Kelly was astounded. "Seriously? You guys are nuts!"

The café door opened and Darren hurried in, heading to Melody in a corner booth.

"Mel …" he began.

Melody lowered her sports magazine with a sigh, rolled her eyes and stood up wearily.

"Row time!" Vanilla called. "Places, everyone!"

All except Kelly dived for cover.

"Oh, no!" she snapped, stepping between Melody and Darren. "This is *my* row time, okay? I've just lost my job because of you lot, so if anyone's gonna row now, it's gonna be me!"

"But …" Darren began.

"Get in line!" Kelly ordered.

He sat down obediently.

"Hey!" Melody cut in, stepping up to her. "Watch your mouth. Only I can treat him like crap."

"Well, you deserve him then!" Kelly shot back.

The whole room gasped, horrified.

"Oh, no …" Vanilla cringed.

Melody's face hardened as she glared at Kelly. "You know something, kid?"

Kelly pushed her glasses up the bridge of her nose. "What?"

"You've got guts," Melody said.

"So what?" Kelly asked.

Melody continued. "You might have what it takes, meaning I'm giving you a ticket to the Flaming Inferno concert tonight. Come along, if you're tough enough."

Kelly was taken aback. "Why would I want anything from you?"

Melody's tone stayed firm. "Great way to unwind. Help you loosen up a bit."

"Well, I might just take it," Kelly retorted. "To spite you."

"Good. I'll meet you there. To spite you!"

"Good!"

"Good!"

"Where's my damn ticket?"

Melody held it up.

Kelly snatched it from her. "See you there!"

"Count on it!"

Kelly strode out the door, storming down the street.

Darren leapt up. "Mel, listen …"

Kelly headed off, huffing, and ignoring Darren as he flew out of the café and into a bus's open doorway, landing on its steps. The door closed with a hiss, trapping his legs and taking him away with it.

Later, much later, when Kelly's temper had eased, she stopped and thought, *Hang on, what have I done?* She'd only seen a couple of Flaming Inferno clips on TV. They were okay. Loud, but okay.

She didn't want to go. She only wanted to sit at her computer and wallow with a pizza whilst pining for her lost job. She would have done exactly that, but there was a message on her answering service when she got home.

"Hey, this is the Skoob tube. Boring message you got there. Could use some sitars."

Kelly seethed, taking her bag off her shoulder. "What do you want?"

"Guess you got a serious mind blank about leaving your purse in the café, huh? How else do you think I got your number?"

Kelly slapped her bag. "Crap!" She opened it and rummaged frantically.

Skoobie continued. *"Don't worry, amigo, happens to me all the time. Pretty cool pic of the Hollywood hunk in it too."*

"You went through my purse?" Kelly cried.

"Pretty dull colour though. I'll fix it for you … "

"No, no, no, no, no …!"

"Yeah, don't worry, you'll get it back at the concert tonight. Meet you out the front at seven. Doesn't matter if you're not on time. None of us have phones but if there's a problem I'll send you a telepathic message, compadre."

"Yeah, and I'll send you one right back …" Kelly muttered.

"Ciao meow," Skoobie finished.

The message ended with a click.

Kelly slumped onto her couch, sighing frustratedly.

Chapter Two

Kelly heard the warm-up act from miles away. She struggled, half-deafened, through the crowded foyer. "S'cuse me, coming through, s'cuse me …"

Two fingers brushed over her shoulder, then four tickets were waved in her face.

Skoobie.

"The universe hath delivered," came the cool tone. "For both of us. Four backstage passes."

"Peachy," Vanilla said, stepping in and taking one.

"Score!" Melody beamed, moving in and taking another. "Thanks, Skoob."

"Thank the universe," came the reply.

"And thanks for coming, sweetie," Vanilla told Kelly.

"I didn't have a choice," Kelly replied, grabbing her purse from Vanilla, "and this really isn't my scene. I've got to get home and start looking for a …"

Melody suddenly slumped over, standing lifeless on her feet with her arms dangling before her.

"… job," Kelly finished. "She okay?"

"Oh yeah," Vanilla answered. "This is just her power nap. She's a little worn out from her triple triathlon this afternoon. She'll be awake in a minute. Come on."

They headed away, with Vanilla leading Melody by the arm. Melody followed in small steps, her arms hanging and her head down as she snored lightly.

Skoobie nimbly plucked a drink from a counter and sipped it as they walked along. Neither the buyer, nor the seller, noticed.

Kelly sighed. "You guys are freaks." She glanced at Vanilla. "You seem pretty normal though."

Vanilla put her hands to her ears, wincing painfully.

"Hey, check this out," a man nearby said to his friends. "Dog whistle."

Vanilla grabbed it crossly and threw it in the bin.

"You guys are freaks," Kelly confirmed.

Kelly blinked amidst the stadium's bright lights and deafening music. The screaming howls of the warm-up act were sheer torture, and the deadhead fans wailing in worship didn't help either. She glanced at Skoobie who was unfazed, as expected, and swaying from side-to-side sipping her drink coolly. Vanilla was closer to Kelly, taking it in her stride and enjoying it. Kelly leaned in, calling to her, "*Hey…!*"

Vanilla recoiled crossly. "*You don't have to shout! I'm not deaf!*"

"*What?*" Kelly yelled.

"*Stop shouting!*" Vanilla yelled back.

"*Your hearing is seriously whacked!*" Kelly cried.

Vanilla looked around. "*Did we lose Mel?*"

Skoobie signalled with a glance.

"*Oh, there she is!*" Vanilla pointed.

Kelly gazed up at the stage. "Oh, this is so not happening!"

Vanilla nodded happily. "Yep. She's up from her power nap."

Kelly watched in horror as Melody air-guitared with the band, leaping up and down seemingly possessed, and loving every second. Much to Kelly's relief, Melody's arm hit a speaker switch, softening the noise a little, not that anyone cared. They were too hyped-up to notice.

Kelly hid her face. "I do not know you; I seriously do not know any of you …"

"Cool, she's junked out," Skoobie said, relaxed as ever.

Kelly tensed. "On what?"

"Adrenalin," Vanilla answered. "She's a *total* adrenalin junkie."

Kelly shook her head.

"Freaks," she muttered again.

Melody was beyond Cloud Nine. The crowd loved her so much that when the warm-up act finished and the actual band came on, everyone kept cheering for her. Her ecstatic air-guitaring annoyed the band until finally, the guitarist threw her offstage. She went with the hurl, stage diving into the crowd who threw her back on. The band tried throwing her off twice more, and twice more she returned. When a large security guard tried hauling her offstage, she threw *him* into the crowd who ran for their lives, letting him land with a thump.

The band were more than happy when she started crowd surfing. Soon, she was sitting on a big man's shoulders. Everyone was so revved up that they failed to notice her fall into a power nap in the middle of it all. Shortly after, she awoke with a start, leapt back on the stage, and was on and off it for the next three songs, doing more than steal the show.

Skoobie, however, swayed with the music, drifting along through the crowd and sipping another drink she'd plucked from someone's hand when they weren't watching. She'd just finished when she saw a gold watch on the floor and picked it up. "Ooooooh, shiny."

A man noticed it. "Nice watch."

She let it dangle from her fingers. "Yours for a twenty."

"That's a pretty good deal."

"Welcome."

He pulled out his wallet, giving her the money. She took it, tossed the watch up lightly and he plucked it out of the air. "Nice doing business with you."

"Likewise," she replied, drifting away.

He looked at the watch, grinning.

Another man grabbed his shoulder. "Hey, man, that's my watch!"

"Yeah right," the first said, "I paid for it!"

"Bulldust, mate! *I* paid for it!"

They collided.

Melody looked up as the house lights came on and the band stopped playing.

"Hey!" she cried from the stage. "What gives?"

Furious yells ignited from a mob in the crowd as several security guards ran in to break up the rising brawl.

Kelly frowned, confused. "What's the deal?"

"Skoobie," Vanilla answered simply. She indicated the brawl with a glance. Skoobie was cruising along its outskirts, picking up fallen trinkets. "Relax, sweetie, happens all the time. She's a charity addict. Just can't help herself helping others."

Kelly pointed at the roaring brawl. "You call that helping?"

A man emerged from the crowd and approached Vanilla. Her lips pursed as he grinned, speaking smoothly. "Scoops."

She ignored him and turned away.

He raised a hand, stopping her. "Relax, I wasn't stalking you. Came here with Cindy." He waved to a blonde in the distance. She grinned and waved back. "Oh, and I forgot to leave these in the car." He reached into his inside pocket, pulling some papers out. "Saw the lawyer before I came. Everything's finished. Sign 'em and the divorce is final. Seal and deal."

She snatched them from him, scanning them over.

"Hey, Andy," Skoobie said, breezing by. "Like the gold watch."

He clasped his hand over it. "Forget it, Skoob. You're not getting another one."

She shrugged. "Whatever whatevers. Hey, where are your kids?"

"Kids?" Kelly asked.

Vanilla's face hardened. "Yeah, Andy, the kids. You remember them, right?"

"Relax," he replied coolly. "They're with Cindy's mother."

Vanilla fumed. "Good to see where your priorities are. You two didn't waste any time moving in together, did you? Where's a darn pen?"

Skoobie held up a silver one that she'd found in the brawl. Vanilla snatched it from her and said to Kelly, "Turn."

"What ...?" Kelly began, then jumped as she was turned around, the papers were placed on her back and signed.

Vanilla stuffed them into Andy's hand. "Beat it."

"Absolutely," he agreed charmingly, and started moving off. He'd barely got anywhere when he bumped into a spinning man who'd been smacked heavily. "Sorry, friend."

The man lashed out fiercely, sending him flying into the crowd.

"Good one," Vanilla said, high fiving the man.

"Likewise," Skoobie chipped in, high fiving him too.

Strangely, Kelly found herself doing the same, but his slap was so hard that she winced and shook her hand. She looked to the stage.

"Oh, that does it!" Melody cried, stage diving into the brawl.

Kelly tensed as the fighting grew closer. This place was freaking her out, big time. "I'm outta here." She made for the exit.

Skoobie stepped back, plucking another drink from a man flying past.

Kelly headed into a small, quiet corridor, glad to be out of the action. This whole scene was insane, she swore, and the weirdos she'd come with were doing her head in. Now that she'd got her purse back from Vanilla, it meant home time. She sighed, turned a corner, and stopped dead.

A body lay on the ground, smack bang out in the open and face down.

She froze in shock. "Crap!"

She trembled, considering what to do. Summoning up her strength, she took a deep breath, before slowly kneeling, reaching out and rolling him over.

"Are you okay …?"

He rolled towards her, then his head sank to the floor, complete with wide-eyed horror, over a hunting knife wedged in his ribcage.

She leapt up, recoiling with a cry, her hand over her mouth, "Holy …!"

"Stupid cow!"

She looked up. A scowling, dark-haired woman stood down the corridor, dressed in jeans and a black singlet. Her scowl grew as she stormed in. "What the hell have you done?"

Kelly braced herself.

"The hit was for midnight!" the woman snapped. "What happened? Did Johnny change plans? Tell me!" She smacked the wall near Kelly's head, making her jump. "Who do you think you are? One of his groupie's playing in the big league? This had to be done right. Look at him!" Her eyes bored into Kelly's. "You've screwed things to hell, babe!"

Smack!

Kelly's head swung sideways from the hard slap. Her cheek stung and her anger boiled. That was it! She'd gone through way too much crap today, sending her sanity plummeting straight to hell. Rage swamped her and she hissed, "You –"

She lashed out, striking the woman square-on, much harder than expected. Dazed, the woman flew back, hit the opposite wall, slid down, landed limply and passed out.

Kelly recoiled, stunned by her outburst. She whimpered, about to let loose, when a security guard rounded the corner. She raised her hands quickly. "This isn't what it looks like …"

He saw the bodies "Stay where you are …"

"Sure," she replied. "I can explain everything. I'm only too happy to help …"

He pulled his gun out, taking aim, "… just so I can get a clear shot …"

"What? No …!"

She ducked, just as the gun fired. The bullet shot past her ear, ricocheted off the wall and whizzed away.

Terrified, she fled, stumbling through an open doorway, into a small room. Another bullet flew by as she staggered to the window, peering out. Down below, several police cars had appeared. Their cops were running in for the rising brawl, spilling out onto the streets.

The security guard ran in, aiming again.

Pure instinct took over as she grabbed a chair, lashing out hard.

Smack!

Her savage impact hurled him into the corridor where his head hit the wall, and he too, slumped to the floor, unconscious.

She shuddered, dropped the battered chair and retreated in disbelief. "Oh … crap!"

Shaken, she returned to the window and looked out. The sheer number of police was growing.

"Double crap!" she quivered.

She bolted, running into the corridor, then bumped into someone and screamed.

Vanilla yelped back. Skoobie stood behind them, sipping her drink, with Melody nearby.

"I didn't do it!" Kelly protested tearfully. "I swear!"

Melody peered into the room. "Yeah, you did. With a chair by the look of it."

"Well, maybe that part …" Kelly said quickly.

"Listen, honey …" Vanilla began.

"But nothing else," Kelly cut in. "You've got to believe me!"

Melody indicated the unconscious woman. "Well somebody gave her a good right hook."

"Yeah, maybe I did that too …"

"So what the hell are you into?"

"I don't know!" Kelly wailed.

Vanilla held her shoulders, staring right at her. "Honey, honey, it's okay. We believe you. All the way …"

Realisation hit Kelly and she broke away. "Why are you here? Were you following me?"

"Nuh," Skoobie answered. She tossed her empty drink cup over her shoulder which spun in mid-air, flew into the room and landed in a bin. "Just the bodies."

"Yeah," Melody added. "So we've got this guy who you hit with the chair, plus the chick down there who you smacked out, so that only leaves knifed-guy. Now since you got two out of three …"

"You think *I* killed him?" Kelly cried. "I *found* the body. Then psycho-hilda rocked up, said a hit was going down tonight and that someone got to knifed-guy first." She glanced at the room shakily. "Might be chair-guy in there."

"Maybe," Melody guessed, "but knifed-guy got stabbed for a reason. Let's see who he is."

Kelly went green. "Seriously?"

"Can we prod him?" Skoobie piped up. "Maybe we can hold his arms up and go, '*yaaaaarrrgh,*' like some scary monster …"

Kelly felt sick.

Vanilla's head perked up. "Police."

Kelly was confused. "Huh?"

Running footsteps rose from some way off.

Kelly shook her head. "What *is* it with your hearing?"

Melody went over to knifed-guy and knelt. "Hey, check this out. Car keys with a remote. All we gotta do is get to the car park and keep pressing this button. A car's gotta respond, then we can find out who he is, and why he was killed."

" … and Kelly can clear her name," Vanilla finished.

"Well yeah, there's that too …" Melody muttered.

Kelly shuddered. "Sounds dodgy. I *really* think we should go to the cops …"

Melody dismissed her. "Waste of time. Let's find the car first. The more stuff we have to clear your sweet little name with, the better."

Kelly relented. "Fine." She sighed reluctantly. "God, I must be insane."

Melody rose. "Car it is. Move out."

They hurried along the corridor.

"Hope we find another body on the way," Skoobie quipped from behind them. "I really wanna play puppet corpse."

Chapter Three

Kelly cringed, crawling through a ventilation shaft on all fours. "I don't believe I'm doing this."

"Trust me, it's a short cut," Melody replied from up ahead.

Kelly shifted uncomfortably, wishing Melody hadn't ushered them down here. They'd barely entered and replaced the grille when several cops ran past. Now, the four girls shuffled along, with Melody leading the way, Vanilla second, then Kelly, and finally Skoobie.

Kelly tensed, "Oh God, what will people think? My parents? My boss …?"

"You got fired," Skoobie reminded her.

Kelly sighed. "Then there's my friends …"

"We're okay with it, really," Vanilla cut in.

"Sure," Skoobie added. "You should be more worried about your butt. That's one big mamma."

Kelly's jaw dropped.

"Relax," Melody said. "We'll have you toned-up soon enough, kid."

"Enough already," Kelly retorted. "I'm on the run from the law here."

"Aren't we all?" Vanilla asked wearily.

"Yeah, but I was the one who decked psycho-mamma and knocked a guy flat out."

"Anger issues," Skoobie concluded. "You need to chill."

Kelly fumed. "It was self-defence."

"Doesn't always work," Vanilla said softly.

Melody stopped.

Vanilla did too.

Kelly bumped into her. "Hey, what gives?"

"You okay," Melody asked.

Kelly got ready to respond.

Vanilla got there first. "Yeah, Mel."

Melody reached back, clasping Vanilla's hand. "Liar."

Vanilla nodded, giving a small sniff. "You're too good, Melody Hill."

Kelly sensed something was up. She lowered her head, giving them a moment.

Silence followed, then Skoobie slapped her leg lightly. "Move it along butt-mamma."

Kelly looked up, seeing Melody and Vanilla crawling ahead. She crawled hurriedly after them, asking, "You alright, Vanilla?"

"Scoops," Melody corrected.

"What?" Kelly wondered.

"It's what we call her," Melody explained. "Scoops. Vanilla ice-cream? Scoops? Get it?"

Kelly considered this. "Doesn't that sound a lot like Skoob?"

"Yeah," she answered, "but by the time *Scoops* and I realised, it was too late."

Skoobie frowned. "Hey, I never noticed that. Why didn't you tell me?"

"Would you have cared?" Melody asked back.

"Not really, no," came the reply. "Gotta point there, babe."

Kelly blinked, baffled. "So are you okay, *Scoops*?"

"Yeah," Vanilla answered sadly. "It's fine. You didn't know."

"Didn't know what?"

"She was in jail," Skoobie piped up.

"What?" Kelly shrieked, stopping in her tracks.

"Big butt up close!" Skoobie cried, crashing into her.

Melody and Vanilla stopped too.

Kelly was stunned. "You were in jail?"

"It's not what you think ..." Vanilla began.

"Well you better tell me 'cause I am seriously freaked out ..."

"So am I by that butt of yours," Skoobie quipped. "So just chill. If you're nervous about something, bring it all back to you, close your eyes and find the real problem within. The external doesn't matter. It's irrelevant. Its only what's inside you that changes everything. So forget about Scoops. She only killed somebody. You're what counts."

Kelly nearly exploded. "What …?"

"Self-defence," Melody cut in. "Just like what you did up top. Pure and simple."

"Yeah," Skoobie added. "There you are. Clean cut. Only hers was literally."

"What …?" Kelly wailed louder.

Vanilla composed herself. "I know this sounds bad …"

"It's *way* beyond bad …" Kelly cut in.

" … but I came home one day and found my new boyfriend about to beat up my son. I ran in to break it up. He started on me, things flew, we struggled, fell and he hit a knife. Next thing I knew he was rolling off me with blood everywhere. I tried to save him. He didn't have a chance."

"Don't know why you bothered," Melody said bitterly. "Guy was a creep. I've told you for years to toughen up. Stop picking deadheads. Shouldn't have been so desperate when you're divorce wasn't done."

"What can I say?" Vanilla asked. "Got sucked in by my smooth-talking divorce lawyer. I was desperate and he played on it. He swore he'd help me see my kids more than once a fortnight, then one thing led to another and we started dating. Wasn't long before he showed his true colours. Things went to hell and then he …"

"Got skewered," Skoobie finished.

Kelly kicked back at her lightly.

"His cronies wanted justice for him …" Vanilla continued.

"Money, more like," Melody said bitterly.

Vanilla spoke on. "Words were twisted, things were said that shouldn't have been, and I got jail time for a few weeks …"

"Until Skoob and I had a little word with the judge …" Melody cut in.

Kelly grimaced.

Vanilla sniffed. "Yeah, but you two could only do so much. Now I'm not allowed to see my children unsupervised. They keep asking when I'm coming home but I don't know what to tell them. At least I can see them now and again, which is better than nothing I suppose."

Kelly bit her lip. "That's awful."

"Worse than awful," Melody huffed. "Damn wrong."

Kelly tensed. "But what if you're found here with me? Oh Scoops, what have I done? What the hell have I done?"

"Hey!" Vanilla cut in, reaching back and grabbing her hand. "You're a friend, and right now I need all the friends I can get. I've got two of the best here that I'd move heaven and earth for, and they'd do the same for me. Could use another."

"Typical," Melody scoffed. "Why do you think she's called Vanilla? It's 'cause she's soft."

"Yeah, and you're the same underneath, Melody Hill," Vanilla replied. "Warm as toast."

"Bite me," Melody grumbled, moving along.

Kelly smiled. "Lead the way, Scoops."

Vanilla smiled back, patted Kelly's hand, and they all crawled along once more.

Melody pushed a grille open, then emerged from the shaft into an underground car park and rose. Vanilla, Kelly and Skoobie all followed and stood up.

"Okay," Melody said, pointing the automatic car key around and pressing the button continually. "Now, where are you?"

No response.

Kelly looked around. "Guess this could take a while."

Melody pulled a screwdriver from her pocket, flipped the key over and unscrewed its back. "There's faster ways of finding a car."

"Oh yeah?"

"Yeah. If I flick this bit, I can set off a three-second car alarm." She fiddled with it.

"Where'd you learn to do this stuff?" Kelly asked.

"Afghanistan," came the reply.

Kelly's eyes nearly popped out of her head. "Seriously?"

"Seriously."

"As a soldier?"

"Nah. Just on holiday."

"You're joking."

Vanilla grinned proudly. "She rode her bike from one end of the country to the other."

Kelly was amazed. "You ride a motorbike?"

"Pushbike," Melody corrected.

"God almighty. So where'd you learn how to work car alarms?"

Melody shrugged. "Got caught up in a few local skirmishes. Here we go …" She pressed a button.

Silence.

Kelly sat back on a car boot. "Didn't work, huh?"

Melody smacked the key against her palm.

The boot suddenly shot to life, making Kelly yelp and leap up.

Melody flicked the alarm off, approached the car and opened the driver's door. "Let's take a look-see."

Kelly turned around. The car was expensive, to say the least.

Vanilla and Skoobie went to opposite doors, opening them.

Kelly peered in. A briefcase sat in the front passenger's side. Scattered papers and folios lay in the back.

"Looks like the business type," Melody observed.

Kelly tensed. "Should we be doing this?"

"Yep," Melody said. "We're trying to get you off the hook, remember?"

"How? By digging me in deeper? Are you in on this, Scoops?"

Vanilla nodded. "All the way."

Skoobie clicked open the briefcase, turned it round and presented it to the others.

Melody grabbed some papers, looking over them. "Okay, so he was a government minister …"

Kelly felt the colour drain from her face.

Vanilla picked up another sheet. " … Called Greg Anderson. Oh, how interesting. He was on *Question Time* last week, trying to get a bill through the Senate."

"Guys, this is so not good …" Kelly said hurriedly.

"What's the bill about?" Melody asked.

Vanilla scanned the paper. "Reforming the education system."

Skoobie put the briefcase down and picked up a red piece of material from the back seat. "Well he sure was practical about it. Look at these mammas!" She held up the large red bra. "Right next to a schoolgirl uniform too."

Kelly stared at it, astounded.

"I'd say she was pretty big and dumb," Skoobie continued. "What's she still doing in school if she's got bazombas that big?"

Vanilla picked up a card. "She's a call girl, Skoob."

"Schoolgirl by day, call girl by night. What a life."

Vanilla flipped the card over. "She's over thirty."

"No wonder he wanted to fix the education system," Skoobie concluded.

Melody reached past the steering wheel, popped the boot, then walked around to it as everyone followed. She raised it and they all looked inside.

Kelly's jaw dropped.

"Cool," Skoobie said.

Lying there, in the trunk, was a young man with glasses. He was bound, gagged, and his eyes were closed.

"Is he ...?" Kelly began.

Skoobie prodded him. His eyes opened in terror and a muffled wail rose.

"Nuh," Skoobie answered. "There goes puppet corpse."

Melody pulled the gag away.

"P-Please," he trembled. "I'll tell you anything you want. Anything!"

Vanilla spoke gently. "We're not here to hurt you. It's okay. Really."

She and Melody unbound him, then helped him out of the car.

His tone was shaky. "Who are you?"

"Ah, we just got caught up in things," Melody answered flippantly.

"Just like you, sweet peach," Vanilla added.

He grinned. "Wow, am I lucky. You're all so hot."

"Ugh, please!" Melody scoffed, turning away.

Skoobie shrugged. "Yeah, we know. You normally hang out in car parks or what?"

He inhaled sharply. "God, no. I met these two guys in a pub ..."

Melody turned back with raised eyebrows.

"Yeah, in a pub," he enforced. "I've been having issues with my mother lately."

"Oh yeah, that explains everything," Melody huffed, turning away again.

"What is it with people?" he continued. "Yes, I have a mother and yes, I live at home. I hate how she's always in my face and never leaves me alone, so I decided enough was enough. I was going to go and ... be a man. Drink, fight, sleep around, sow my wild oats, you know?"

Melody threw her arms up. "God, he even speaks old!"

"Hey, you've got issues too!" he snapped.

"Yeah pal, and you're one of 'em!"

"So what happened, sweetie?" Vanilla prompted.

He paused. "I was at the bar when I heard two guys talking. They were hunched over, whispering, but I could still make out stuff. They said something about a red rose on Yorder Street that's s'posed to bloom tomorrow at midday. I thought they were talking about gardening 'cause I do a lot of that for my mum …"

Melody swore under her breath.

He spoke on. "So I decided to join in, but then this other man came up, flashing a badge and telling me to beat it. Then I might have … sort of … blurted it out … just a little too loudly …"

Melody got ready to blow.

He cut in quickly. "The guys from the bar jumped up, there was a fight, and the next thing I know, these bar-guys are taking me out the back and throwing me into a car boot. I told them to call my mum to explain things but they wouldn't listen …"

"Oh, ya think?" Melody cried. "You stumbled into a stake-out and fell onto the wrong side!"

"I did?" he asked blankly.

"Yeah, genius! Don't you ever watch cop shows? If someone quietly flashes a badge at you in a bar, *don't scream it out!*"

"A red rose on Yorder," Vanilla mused. "Hey, that could be the Red Rose Café."

"Meaning something's going down at midday," Melody concluded.

"But what's that got to do with the hit tonight?" Kelly wondered.

The man went green. "There was a hit? Oh God, was anybody hurt?"

"Got a knife straight through him," Skoobie answered simply.

He whimpered loudly. "Wh-Who did?"

"Eh, government minister," she replied flippantly. "You do know this is a politician's car, right?"

"Oh, what do you think?" he and Melody cried together.

Vanilla put her hands on his shoulders. "We've got to get outta here fast."

"Just not to the cops with all this going down," Melody pointed out. "*We've* gotta get in the clear too."

"For what?" he asked shakily.

Skoobie indicated Kelly. "She decked a psycho-mamma, flattened a guy, and for all we know could have killed the Minster too."

He squealed, inching away from Kelly.

"Gee, thanks, Skoob," she muttered.

"Yep," Skoobie continued. "She's got anger issues."

"You aint seen nothing yet," Kelly mumbled.

"Mel's right," Vanilla said. "Police are off limits. We don't know who we can trust."

"They'll also be annoyed that he screwed their operation," Melody added. "If his Mum doesn't kill him first."

"Not good," he trembled. "You've never seen her blow."

Her fists clenched harder than ever.

"What's your name, honey?" Vanilla cut in.

He shuddered, composing himself. "Irwin, but I had this name in high school and it kinda stuck, so I go by that."

"Which is?"

He shifted uncomfortably. "It's uh … Turbo."

Melody buried her face in her hands, shaking her head, while Kelly covered her mouth, trying not to laugh.

"Cool," Skoobie said.

Vanilla patted his arm. "Come on, sweetie, let's get you outta here …"

Screech!

A black car suddenly veered around the corner, skidding violently and rushing at them.

"Heads up!" Melody yelled, diving on Turbo and throwing them both to the ground behind a parked bike. Vanilla did the same with Kelly. Skoobie merely stepped back, taking it in her stride and watching as the car raced by, skidded hard, and turned to face them.

"Holy crap!" Turbo wailed. "Who's that?"

"Bad guys trying to kill us," Melody quipped, then nodded at the Minister's car. "Get in. Now!"

She rose, pulled him up, pushed him away, tossed the car keys to Vanilla, and ran at the oncoming car.

"What the hell …?" Kelly cried, horrified.

Vanilla plucked the keys out of the air, rose with Kelly and pulled her for the door. "In!"

Everyone dived inside, save for Skoobie who entered coolly. Vanilla sat in the driver's seat, leaving the others in the back, then started the engine.

Melody reached the attacking car, leapt onto the bonnet, scrambled up, and hung onto the roof, swaying from side to side, before being shaken off.

She hit the ground and rolled over, knowing her distraction had brought the others time.

Vanilla lowered her car's window.

Kelly cringed as they took off. "We're screwed, we are so screwed …"

Melody leapt up, diving in through the window with a mighty leap and crawling over Turbo who shrieked awkwardly.

"Hands!" he cried.

"You should be so lucky," she retorted, climbing into the front passenger seat.

The black car swerved around, sweeping in.

Vanilla veered her car to the right. Melody looked back, seeing the black car gain speed as its windows descended, then two hands with submachine guns emerged from either side.

"Incoming fire!" Melody bellowed.

Kelly and Turbo screamed, cowering down. Skoobie casually did the same, before the back window blew in, covering them in glass. Vanilla stayed cool, swerving them out of the car park and onto the street.

Melody pointed ahead. "Go past the café! Get us up on the path!"

Vanilla saw the outdoor tables and chairs. "Through the lot?"

"Through the lot," Melody confirmed. "We want all eyes on us. The more, the better."

Another burst of gunfire erupted. Kelly braced herself as the car rocked violently onto the kerb, crashing through the outdoor setting and sending chairs flying over them as Vanilla beeped the horn rapidly, making people dive for cover.

Melody nimbly reached out the window, clasped a chair, and hurled it back at the black car where it smacked onto its windscreen, bouncing off and bringing her the precious few seconds she needed. Swiftly, she grabbed an umbrella that had flown from an outdoor table. "Gimme some space, Scoops!"

The car lurched into the middle of the road with the umbrella sticking out of its window.

Another round of shots fired.

"Work fast, Mel," Vanilla quipped. "We've got an intersection coming up!"

"I've got my dinner coming up," Turbo cringed.

Melody scrambled in her pockets, pulling out a pocketknife. She flicked it open, used it to rip off the umbrella's material, then cut at the plastic at the pole's bottom. She'd barely finished when she glanced ahead to see an oil tanker moving across the upcoming intersection.

"Ten seconds!" Vanilla called.

"Five seconds!" Turbo also called, indicating his stomach.

The gunfire ignited again. The car veered from side to side before the firing stopped and the gunmen reloaded.

Melody leaned out the window, holding the pole high like a spear. "Left and brake, Scoops!"

Vanilla braked hard, making everyone except Skoobie lurch violently. The other car braked too, skidding towards them.

Skoobie sat up, casually looked back and said, "Three, two, one … now."

Melody rammed the pole's jagged end into the black car's front tyre. The rubber burst and the black car flipped over, exhaust over bonnet, hit the road, landed on its roof and went spinning down the street for the oil tanker.

Melody took her seat quickly. "Suck on that ya …!"

Vanilla sent the car into a screeching, handbrake U-turn, racing back the way they'd come.

The gunmen rolled out of their car, scrambled away and dived for cover as the car shot ahead.

An ear-shattering explosion and blinding flash sent the tanker erupting in a furious blaze of black and gold flames. Several fireballs rushed by Kelly's window, shaking the car and making her and Turbo wail frantically. Heavy clangs followed as large chunks of flaming debris plonked onto the roof, spilling onto the road. Vanilla pulled on the handbrake again, swerving them out of the line of fire and into another violent U-turn before bringing them to a safe stop.

"Casualties?" she asked, as the worst of the blast subsided.

Melody opened the door, stood on the side of the car, and scanned the area. "None."

Skoobie indicated the unconscious Turbo on Kelly's lap. "Second opinion?"

Sirens wailed from afar.

Melody sat back down, slamming the door shut. "Get us outta here, Scoops. Evac One."

Vanilla nodded, hit the accelerator, swung the car around again, and sent them racing away.

"Where we headed?" Kelly called.

"Relax," Melody replied. "We've got a couple'a hideouts for times like this."

"This happens to you guys a lot?"

"It's not an unusual day," Vanilla said.

Kelly was hesitant. "I think we should …"

"No," Melody cut in, holding her hand up. "Evac first, then we focus-group it."

"But …"

"There and then!" she ordered.

Kelly complied, reluctantly. "You're the bosses … clearly."

Chapter Four

Kelly gulped, glued to the TV. They were in an abandoned warehouse that Melody had set up some time ago. There was a TV, a couch, a few tables and chairs, and a fridge.

"CCTV picked up his Ministerial car speeding through the City Centre a few hours ago, evading gunfire from a pursuing car. The conflict culminated in an oil tanker exploding, creating an estimated thirty-five million dollars' worth of damage. Curiously, the Minister himself was absent, and everyone from both cars fled the scene. CCTV detected that the driver of the Minister's car was an unknown woman, accompanied by four passengers. One male, three female. The car was later found torched in bushland …"

Kelly looked at Melody, shaking her head. "There's no way in hell those idiots can find anything, huh?"
Melody folded her arms, looking away with a guilty huff.

The voice continued. *"We're crossing live to our reporter Danni Cooper, who's at the scene of the explosion. Danni, what can you tell us about the latest developments?"*

The image changed to a young woman standing by a fire truck. *"Jodhi, one of the occupants from the Minister's car has now been identified …"*

Everyone except Skoobie gasped in shock.

Vanilla shuddered. "It's gotta be me. I was driving." She trembled. "I'll never see my kids again, will I? I'll be locked up for good and I'll never ever see them again …"

Melody put an arm around her. "Hang in there, Scoops. It's probably me. I was showing off pretty good, remember?"

Kelly shifted uneasily, prepared for the worst.

Danni spoke on. *"The police are currently searching for the whereabouts of this person …"*

The image changed to someone pressed up against the car window, screaming to get out.

"… an IT specialist named Irwin Newcombe, who also goes by the name of Turbo …"

"What … ?" Turbo wailed.

"Oh, thank God," Melody, Vanilla and Kelly said, relieved.

"No!" he cried. "Not good! Not good …!"

"Hey, don't blame us," Melody cut in. "You were the one freaking out."

He cringed. "Okay, so I panicked, but things can't get any worse, right?"

"And here with me tonight, is Mrs Edna Newcombe, his mother …"

"Crap!" Turbo shrieked. "Don't say anything, Mum! Do not say anything …!"

"Irwin! Irwin! Come home! This is your mother talking! Come home!" The lady was pleading directly into the camera. *"I'll make your favourite dinner. Steak just the way you like it. I don't care if you leave crumbs by the toaster – just come home …!"*

"Mrs Newcombe, could you …"

"Here he is!" she cried, holding a baby photo up to the camera.

"Nice butt," Skoobie noted.

"This is who he is! Who he really is! He might be grown up now but he's not a bad boy, only a baby. It's what the world's done to him that's wrong. He doesn't need this. If anyone sees him, please let me know." She stared further into the camera. *"It's okay, Irwin. You just ring me from wherever you are and I'll come and drive you home. Anyone who touches you deals with me!"*

"Mrs Newcombe, if we could just get a word in …"

"Here …" she said, pulling a lady forward. *"This is Elka. His child health nurse from the Daystrom Playgroup. Tell her how good he was, Elka."*

"He was good, he was good," came the fast reply.

"And look, I brought Father Pablo. Say something, Father."

The Priest was pulled in. *"He was a good boy …"*

"See?" she pressed. *"A priest! How can you dispute the word of a sacred man of God? My boy comes from a strong Christian family. We're good people, so why's he being treated like this? Why? Why? WHY …?"*

"Back to our studio …" Danni said quickly.

Kelly, Melody and Vanilla stared at the screen aghast, their jaws dropped in absolute horror. Turbo, meanwhile, had collapsed sideways onto the couch, his hands over his face in sheer anguish.

Melody slowly picked up the remote, turned the TV off and blinked, too shocked to speak. "I … I … I …" she began, trying to get the words out. She ran her hands through her hair and turned away. "God damn!"

Vanilla leaned over Turbo. "Honey, it's okay. Really. Come on, sit up. Come on now …"

She helped him rise.

Silence followed.

Then: "Boy, when you cut loose, you *really* cut loose," Skoobie quipped.

Turbo sprang up and ran screaming for the door.

Melody dived, grabbing him in mid-fall and sending them both crashing to the floor with a thump. "No playing with his mind, Skoob! Grab a rope. We'll tie him up and throw him in the closet!"

Vanilla rose, moving in. "Or maybe we can calm him down. He can help us."

Melody rolled her eyes. "Seriously? How?"

Vanilla helped him up and gently returned him to the couch. "Everyone's useful in every way. Right, Turbo?"

He muttered the barely audible.

"Sorry, what was that?" Melody asked grumpily.

"He says he's good with computers," replied Vanilla, care of her unique hearing. "That's great! He can help clear up this mess."

"Ugh!" Melody mumbled.

"Right?" Vanilla pressed.

Silence.

Vanilla ignored them, focussing on him, "Look, sweet stuff, I'm sorry your mother treats you like that. It's awful, but it happens with older people. It's not what I'd do to my kids."

He looked up at her. "You've got kids?"

"Two," she answered. "Jamie and Sophie. They're in primary school and doing well from what I hear." She paused. "All kids clash with their parents. It's nothing to be ashamed of. I just think that … maybe … you need to get out of the house."

"Uh-huh," Melody confirmed.

Vanilla continued warmly. "Stick with us and you'll be fine. We're all friends."

"We are?" he asked, startled.

"Sure." She smiled. "We are."

Melody shook her head, turning away.

"Guess so," Kelly added. "Hey, I'm new to all this too. These guys are a little weird, but okay."

Vanilla grinned. "Peachy. Welcome to the club, Turbo."

He smiled back, a touch brighter. "Cool. Uh … thanks."

She hugged his shoulders warmly.

Kelly gave him a light punch on the arm.

Vanilla reached up, taking hold of Melody's wrist and smoothly turning her around to face them. Melody sighed reluctantly, tapping his shoulder as lightly as possible. "Yeah, right."

Skoobie, however, came in, grabbed his collar, picked him up, kissed him hard and fast on the lips, then broke away and said, "You needed that."

His eyes widened, gazing at her dreamily. "I'm so in love …"

"Whoa, whoa, whoa," Vanilla cut in quickly. "Calm down. Take a deep breath."

He kept staring at Skoobie.

Melody grabbed his chin, turning his lovestruck gaze to her hard glare. "Now, Romeo!"

He blinked and gulped.

She put her hand on his forehead, pushed herself up and stepped away.

"Great," Vanilla beamed. "So, that's the small stuff done. Next steps. Mel, talk us through 'em."

Melody sparked up, springing into action. "Right! Review 101 people. So what have we got? A dead Minister who wasn't killed the way some Johnny guy wanted."

"Yeah," Kelly agreed. "Psycho-mamma backstage said a hit was s'posed to take place at midnight. Looks like someone got in early."

Melody continued. "Then we've got the security guard, or at least he was dressed as one. There's also a link to the Red Rose Café."

"Tomorrow at midday," Turbo chimed in.

Melody nodded. "We need to check it out, meaning one of us has to be bait while the others are on threat-alert. So, since nerd-boy here's in enough trouble, then the best person for the job's …"

All heads turned except one.

Kelly pushed her glasses up, heading along the street and clutching her bag strap tightly. Despite being surrounded by people, she felt in the spotlight.

"Bad idea, bad idea, bad idea …" she murmured, approaching the Red Rose Café.

She glanced at the hotel across the street. Melody was peering out from an upstairs window, making hand signals to her. Kelly frowned, confused, before shaking her head, walking to an outdoor café table, and sitting nervously.

Two fingers brushed lightly over her shoulder. She jumped and looked up as Skoobie drifted past, searching for a spot to sit. Kelly gulped, though not surprised. Skoobie was keeping a close eye on things, as was the plan, while Melody was across the street, seeing the bigger picture. Vanilla and Turbo were safely tucked away back at base, watching CCTV footage from a laptop, care of Turbo.

There were no more empty tables, and Kelly listened as Skoobie approached a handsome businessman, pulled out a chair and asked, "Mind if I sit here?"

"Well, yeah …" he began.

She ignored him and took a seat. "So now's the time to get over that." She called to the waitress, "Coffee please!" She looked back at him. "So you single or what?"

"No," he answered. "My wife and kids'll be here soon."

"Oh good, they can meet me," came the cruisy reply. "Tell 'em I'm your new friend. More friends make the world a better place, bud."

He smiled. "You're funny, you know that?"

"Who's this?" a haughty voice asked.

He tensed, seeing a woman approach with two children in tow.

"Oh hi, honey," he began. "This is … uh …"

"Skoob-tube," Skoobie beamed delightedly. "His new friend. He thinks I'm funny."

The woman huffed. "Not another one. You're pathetic." She pulled her kids away, storming off.

"No wait, wait …!" he cried, leaping up and running after her.

Kelly watched them all disappear round a corner, impressed by Skoobie's antics, then heard the chair opposite her scrape back. She looked ahead, tensing as Psycho-mamma sat down, wearing sunglasses and as angry as hell.

"Try anything and you're dead," Psycho-mamma scowled. "I got people in the area."

"Yeah, me too," Kelly blurted out nervously.

"What …?" Psycho-mamma snapped.

Kelly cursed herself, summoning up her courage. "You came here to talk, right? So talk."

The woman's face hardened. Kelly grimaced. Finally …

"Name!" the woman ordered.

"Ke-Kelly," came the shaky reply.

"Kelly who?"

"Morrison."

"That your real name?"

Not wanting to argue, Kelly reached into her purse, pulling out her driver's licence. "Wanna check my ID?"

Melody, watching from afar, slapped her forehead.

Psycho-mamma grabbed the card, examined it, then threw it down. "Turbo Newcombe. Where is he?"

Kelly put the licence away. "Safe. From you."

The woman glowered. "From me? You're pretty vicious yourself, kid." She pulled down her sunglasses, showing a black eye. "See?" She put the glasses back on and leaned forward. "So, Kelly Morrison, who you workin' for?"

"I ask the questions," Kelly replied, trying to sound tough. "I hold Turbo, I got the upper hand."

"Oh, please …"

Kelly continued. "I was at the concert with some people. We found the body. His wallet led us to his car. Turbo was in the boot, bad guys tried to kill us, we got away."

The woman sat back. "Fine. I believe you." She opened her coat, revealing a hidden badge. "Name's Vertigo. *Sergeant* Donna Vertigo. I'm a cop."

Kelly was taken aback. "A cop? Seriously?"

"Undercover, and keep your voice down," the woman, Vertigo, hissed. "Turbo blew our sting operation and got caught. We had to find him, along with the Minister, and get them both to safety. My partner on the force, John, dressed it up as a security guard. Sorry he got a little rough on you. He gets carried away."

"A little rough?" Kelly asked, astounded. "He tried to kill me."

"Hey, he thought you killed the Minister," came the reply. "He didn't want Johnny's lot finding out."

Kelly ignored her. "Go on."

Vertigo paused. "We were ready to get the Minister out of the country. 'Course he *had* to stop off at the concert for a goodbye quickie with a groupie, didn't he? Now he's dead and everything's shot to hell."

"I'll bet," Kelly said. "So who got him? The mob?"

"No," Vertigo answered. "No mob involvement."

"So what's the story?" Kelly pressed. "Who's behind the killing? This Johnny guy? Hey, I know about you now. Could tell the bad guys. That gives me leverage."

Vertigo gave a wry smile. "Nice try, kid. You're good. Might be useful." She paused again. "Okay, I'll fill you in." She drew a sharp breath. "I'm part of a special squad, monitoring the Minister's illegal interests. Word on the street was that he'd riled the organised crime networks who were buying a bullet to take him out. My partner and I went undercover as hitmen, putting our names out there. A so-called *businessman* called Johnny placed an order by payphone. He sent one of his hoods, Angelo, to meet us in a bar. Turbo threw a spanner in the works. He screwed things up big time by showing up, shooting his mouth off, and getting taken by the bad guys. My partner and I salvaged things, but only just. Johnny's plan went ahead and we went with it. My buddy and I hoped to get the Minister out of the country last night, but we wanted Johnny and Angelo arrested first. Angelo was meant to meet me here and now and I'd arrest him but …"

" … He split and you've got me instead," Kelly finished.

"Right," Vertigo said. "Things went to hell last night when our dodgy Minister hit the concert and the next thing we know, bam! He gets blown apart, just not by us, or Johnny either. I thought you were the groupie who did it out of revenge but …"

"Excuse me …?" Kelly cut in.

" … That went out the window when we found a card near his body," Vertigo finished. "It was from NUTS."

Kelly was confused. "Well obviously …"

"No, that's their name," Vertigo stated. "They're another group the Minister was blackmailing. There were two hits on him."

Kelly was perplexed. "They're really called NUTS? Well, they must be insane if they're dropping their calling cards by their target …"

"Oh, that was intentional," Vertigo interjected. "They love to advertise."

"What …?"

Vertigo pressed on. "We only found out this morning that the Minister planned to reveal the Delirium's location."

"The huh …?"

"Their headquarters."

Kelly blinked. "You're kidding, right?"

"I wish," came the reply. "NUTS are off the sanity scale. They blow organised crime out of the water. What started off as a prestigious party for weirdos playing dress-ups as serial killers, mad doctors and crazy clowns …"

"I get it …" Kelly cut in.

" … has grown into a secret fraternity, turning deadly. We've heard rumours they're playing dirty by pouring chemicals into their new recruits, brainwashing them. They're outta control."

"So how are they this organised?" Kelly countered. "They must have a leader."

"Sure," came the straight-faced reply. "A man in a black wedding dress."

Kelly almost laughed. "What?"

Vertigo's tone darkened. "He likes to be called the Black Bride. His second in command's the Squirrel, keeper of the NUTS. Their thugs are the Groomsmen. God, the stories I've heard …"

Kelly shivered, wondering if Vertigo was some kind of NUT herself. "Freaky."

"Oh yeah," Vertigo said. "You're in the big league now, little girl." She sat back. "The only thing that might help us find 'em is Turbo. He could have heard something from Johnny's lot that could lead us there. He's a target now, from both sides. So are you."

Kelly glanced across the street, knowing Melody was watching. She felt protected by her new friends, along with their café's golden presence that had risen in her heart once more, keeping her fears at bay. Thanks to it, and those girls, life's odds didn't scare her as much as they would have in the past. Her confidence grew as she said, "No dice."

Vertigo glared at her.

"Nothing'll happen," Kelly continued. "I believe in my … " She drew a deep breath, " … friends."

Vertigo exhaled wearily, flipping a card onto the table. "Your funeral. Take this and call me."

Kelly picked it up. "Thanks." She put it away. "Oh, and there's one more thing."

"Oh yeah?"

"Yeah," Kelly answered. "Vanilla Pond. She works in Sanders Café on the other side of town. A court order's stopping her from seeing her kids. That's a bit harsh. Could you check it out?"

"Only if you help me out too," came the reply." Whatever you find, I want to know about it."

"Deal."

"Thanks." She stood up. "Take care, kid. Watch your back."

Kelly nodded. "You too."

Vertigo headed off.

Kelly shuddered, watching her round the corner. "Okay, that was interesting …"

"Sure was," Skoobie said, turning around from the chair behind her. "Like the sound of that crazy fraternity though."

Kelly gave a wry grin. "I think their Squirrel's missing a nut."

Skoobie stared at her blankly. "Why? Did he have cancer?" She paused. "Oh, wait, I see what you mean …"

Kelly and Skoobie followed Melody back to the warehouse, zigzagging through streets and alleyways to shake off anyone who might be following. Soon, they were all back at base, sitting with Vanilla around a table. Turbo was on the couch with his laptop, analysing the recorded CCTV footage of Kelly and Vertigo.

"So that's it," Kelly finished. "Vertigo was legit, I'm sure of it."

"Totally," Skoobie added.

Kelly pressed on. "So what's our next move? Do we stay hidden or …?"

"Nerd-boy does," Melody answered. "Not us. Though the cops might question Scoops here, thanks to your big mouth …"

"I was only trying to help …"

"Enough," Vanilla cut in. "This isn't about me, remember? We've got to keep cool."

Kelly wasn't convinced. "Won't be easy. We're sandwiched between the cops and the bad guys."

"Sandwiches stick together," Skoobie pointed out.

"They're the ultimate breadwinners," Vanilla added. "Just like us."

"Yeah but …" Kelly began, then stopped. "Okay." She paused. "Who can we trust? Johnny's lot could be anywhere. NUTS too, even among the cops. Then there's your café. For all we know that … David might be one."

"He's not," all three girls replied.

"Really?" Kelly pressed.

The girls glanced at each other.

"Honey," Vanilla said, "when you've been around as long as us, you get to know people. It's no one in the café."

Kelly huffed. "Well, sorry for getting worked up about finding a dead body, being shot at, diving into a car chase, helping blow up a tanker, becoming a fugitive, having the cops find out about me, and learning there's a covert bunch of psychos everywhere. How the hell do I get my life back?"

"What life?" Skoobie asked.

Kelly stared at her.

"Seriously, what life?" Skoobie pressed. "Do you really wanna go back to lonely nights of pizzas and crappy movies?"

"How do you …?" Kelly began, then: "Forget it."

Skoobie continued. "This tops anything you've done so far. Cherish it, amigo."

Kelly was taken aback. "How'd you get so smart?"

"I don't *try* to be anything," Skoobie corrected. "You shouldn't either."

Kelly brushed this off. "Alright, so I *know* you guys have a plan from here on in. Spill."

"Oh yeah," Melody answered eagerly. "Came up with one while you were out there."

"*We* came up with one," Vanilla corrected, glancing at Melody. "Group effort, remember?"

Melody made a face and looked away.

"Why am I not surprised?" Kelly asked. "Go on. What?"

Vanilla looked back at Kelly. "It needs a little refining first. Could use your help."

Kelly's heart rose as the café's spirit returned. The old her would have fought it with a vengeance. Now, she found herself trusting these guys more than anyone.

"Sure," she said. "Got no choice, have I?"

Vanilla smiled.

Kelly returned her smile warmly.

Vanilla addressed Turbo. "Are you in too, sweetie?"

"'Course he is," Melody answered. "We need a tech-head. What else is he gonna do? Go home to his mother?"

Turbo jumped up from the couch, pointing at her and yelling, "Don't take me on … !"

Skoobie reached back without looking, grabbed his shirt and tugged down lightly. He went with her pull, returning to his seat.

"Piece of cake," she quipped.

"Like hell," Turbo seethed.

"No, I'd like one," she corrected, before reaching back again, grabbing his chin and shaking it gently.

He blushed and rose, heading for the kitchen.

"So you're in?" Vanilla called after him.

"I'm in," came the reply.

Melody leapt to her feet, heading for the nearby desk. "Right. I'll get some paper."

"I'll get the ice-cream," Skoobie said, standing up and making for the kitchen.

"Make mine rum and raisin," Vanilla called.

"Gotcha!" Skoobie called back.

Kelly rose to help.

Vanilla grabbed her arm. "Hang on, wait."

Kelly sat down again. "I know. I'm sorry for bringing up your name with the cops. I was only trying to help …"

Vanilla bit her lip. "There aren't many people who'd do that for me. Anyone who helps try and get my kids back is in my heart …" she pressed her hands against her chest, "… forever. You've no idea how much that means to me. No idea. Come here." She wrapped her arms around Kelly, embracing her tightly and saying softly, "I won't forget this. Never." She closed her eyes and whispered, "You're a very good friend, Kelly Morrison. Thank you so much."

Kelly felt like melting inside and hugged her just as tight.

"Hey, you two, quit it," Melody said, returning with a black texta and a large sheet of paper. "Sit down everyone."

Vanilla and Kelly parted. Turbo came over with the cake, while Skoobie returned with a few ice-cream tubs, along with spoons. Soon, they were all seated, save for Melody who stood over them, leaning forward like a general, pointing to various outlines on the paper. Everyone dug heartily into their tubs of ice-cream, mixed with cake, loving every second. Kelly had chocolate, Vanilla, rum and raisin, Skoobie, butterscotch, Turbo, caramel, and Melody eventually took a seat and had portions of everything, plus a strawberry tub all to herself.

There, they talked, ate, and swapped ice-cream long into the night.

Chapter Five

The café door opened and Melody, Vanilla and Skoobie all entered, bright as ever. Kelly followed, sleepy as hell after staying up with them all night. The only one missing was Turbo, who was safely hidden at Skoobie's house. Kelly figured he must have screamed the place down already, since Skoobie had told him to pat the snakes if he got lonely.

Vanilla dropped her bag behind the counter. "Home, sweet home." She went into the kitchen, turning the lights on.

"So who actually owns this place?" Kelly wondered. "Is it you guys?"

"No, the universe," Skoobie answered. "That's why we're open to everybody."

"Sounds cruisy."

"You better believe it." She strode behind the counter.

Kelly frowned, confused. "How does that work, Mel?"

No reply came. She looked back, seeing Melody fast asleep, her face flat on the table.

"Figures," Kelly muttered.

The door opened and Darren walked in.

"Mel …" he began.

Skoobie nodded at Melody.

He turned, saw her, moved over and leaned down. "You should have called. I was worried sick."

"Pfffft," Skoobie scoffed. "Yeah right. Said she wanted to test your loyalty or somethin'."

"I'd better take her home." He pulled her gently out of her seat, lifted her in his arms, and carried her to the door. "Come on, baby."

She snuggled into him dreamily, mumbling, "Don't leave me. Never."

"I won't Mel, I promise."

"Love ya, Darren. Forever and ever, y'know?"

"Love you too." He kissed her forehead. "Let's go home. I've got the day off. We can hit the park this afternoon."

"Roller skating?"

"You know I'm no good at that …"

"Want … roller skating."

"I'll read, you roller skate. Deal?"

"Only … if we can swap … for a while. You need … to live a little."

"While *you* need to slow down, Mel. You're exhausted." He glanced at Kelly. "Thanks for looking after her."

"Hey, she took care of us," Kelly pointed out. "We've gotta lot more planned too."

"I bet. Thanks again."

Kelly went to the door, holding it open. Darren carried Melody through, taking her to his car. Once they were gone, Kelly shrugged and said, "Guess opposites really do attract." She noticed Skoobie. "Aren't you tired?"

"Nuh," came the reply. "I only sleep when I have to."

"And we're opening soon," Vanilla called.

Kelly was baffled. "Are you for real?"

"None of us are," Skoobie quipped. "We're all just frequency spikes of universal dreams on a high energy level."

A crash of pots came from the kitchen.

"So-rry," Skoobie mumbled, turning away.

Kelly dismissed this for the sake of her sanity. "Yeah, well, it's been fun, but I gotta get to work."

Skoobie threw her a tea towel. "Here."

Kelly caught it. "No, I mean my other job."

"Oh right," Skoobie said. "The one you got fired from."

"Damn!" She sighed heavily, knowing that any job was better than nothing. "Oh well, least I get free food, right?"

"Always," Vanilla called again.

"But it's only a fill-in, guys."

"Sure," Skoobie agreed. "Gear up, sis."

Kelly headed to a table. "Might as well enjoy the peace while I can. God knows, things can't get any worse …"

"Over here …!"

"Excuse me, Miss … !"

"Do you have a minute … ?"

"Oh, Miss …"

"Coming, coming, coming …" Kelly said, hurriedly making her way between two tables and almost dropping her plates. She quickly steadied herself, placing the order before a seated family. Her head spun as she struggled to stay on top of things.

"Burger with the lot, side order of chips," she announced.

"Oh, no," the father corrected, "I ordered a steak sandwich with a side order of mushrooms."

"The burger's mine," a man at another table called.

"I have the chips," added a lady in the booth behind him.

Kelly picked up the plates and moved over to them, handing the burger to the man. "There you go …" She placed the chips before the woman, " … and there *you* go."

Burger-guy spoke up. "Oh, Miss, I ordered a burger without sauce …"

"Will my steak sandwich be ready soon?" the father asked.

"Well yes, in a minute …" she replied, flustered.

"Can I have a milkshake?" the child arced up.

"One milkshake," she said quickly. "Where's my notepad?" She pulled it out, fumbled, and dropped it on a table.

The boy grabbed it. "Can I draw on this?"

"No, I need it back," she answered.

"I want a pencil."

Kelly tensed, frustrated. "Give it here!"

"Don't speak to him like that!" his mother retorted. "He just wants to draw."

Burger-guy spoke up. "Miss, there's sauce all over this burger …"

"I'd like some sauce today," Chip-Lady pressed.

"Where's my milkshake?" the child demanded. "I want a pencil too."

"What are you going to do about the sauce?" Burger-guy pushed.

Kelly clenched her fist, then finally snapped, throwing an arm up. "Okay, everyone, listen! This is my first day and there's a *lot* of problems, so please, just wait your turn and …"

"Milkshake!" the boy yelled.

"… *GIVE ME A BREAK OKAY!*"

The boy stared at her, stunned.

So did everyone else.

"Okay?" she pressed wearily.

Silence.

"Fine!" she snapped, tossing her apron off. "You know what? I quit! You guys can all go home and make your own lunches! I've had enough of this place. See ya later." She headed for the door and was barely there when …

"Miss?" Burger-guy called.

She stopped and turned back, exasperated. "Humiliation central. What?"

He spoke gently. "You're not a bad waitress. There's nothing wrong with your skills, just your approach. You need to relax a little."

Her eyes nearly popped out of her head. "What the hell? Lighten up? Are you kidding me? How the crud am I s'posed to do that with you lot yelling like monkeys?"

"Just go with the flow," he answered. "Watch this." He called out, "Yo Skoob!"

Skoobie emerged from the kitchen. "'Sup?"

"I didn't want sauce on my burger," he said.

"And I wanted sauce on my chips," Chip-Lady added.

Skoobie cruised over to the man, picked up the plate, took his burger off and called to Chip-Lady, "Here! Flying saucer." She threw the plate, and then the burger to Chip-Lady who caught both. "Do what you want with the sauce on that. Make a chip burger or somethin'."

Chip-Lady removed the top burger bun, dabbing it over the chips. "Thanks.

The mother spoke up. "My son wanted a pencil and paper. A milkshake too."

"Would he like a blank canvas and a beret as well?" Skoobie quipped. "What have we? A little artist here?"

The boy snickered.

"Moody one, too," she added. "Gimme the pad."

He did so.

She smacked his head lightly with it. "I'll get you some paper in a sec. A milkshake too." She headed to the fridge. "Scoops needs a sec to put her spark in it, so have a soft drink for now. Better behave or the universe'll get ya." She pulled a can from the fridge and swung it behind her back, sending it flying high. The can flipped over a few times before he caught it, opened it quickly, then squealed as the drink sprayed up his nose, making him splutter.

"What'd I tell ya?" she finished.

"Hey, Skoob," another man called. "Where's my coffee? Any chance it'll get here this year?"

"Oh yeah," she replied flippantly. "It's a little hot right now so it's cooling down while hell freezes over."

"Ah, bite me!" he scoffed, returning to his paper.

Kelly stared at the scene in disbelief. "This whole place is …"

"Full," the father pointed out.

Skoobie looked at Kelly. "So you're off then?"

Kelly was taken aback. "Well yeah. No one'll want me here after my hissy fit."

Skoobie raised her eyebrows. "Oh, you're a telepath? Cool. Always wanted to meet one."

"Well, I know what you're thinking," Kelly retorted.

"So spill."

Kelly blinked, feeling the café's golden aura wash over her, illuminating her mind. She frowned, then realisation dawned. "Nothing. You're not thinking anything."

"Never do," Skoobie affirmed. "Neither are they. You're the only one doing it 'round here, and way too much. No more thinking. Live in the moment. Now get back to work."

Kelly was hesitant.

The father smiled. "We're okay with you, really."

Kelly hung her head and, with no other choice, slowly walked to the counter and picked up her apron. She put it on, took her pad from Skoobie, and approached the father.

"What'll it be?" she asked wearily.

Skoobie coughed.

Kelly sighed, emptying her mind and acting on impulse. "What do you want?"

"Steak sandwich," he replied. "I've told you several times."

She let her mouth go. "I probably did hear but my head's clogged up from all your whining and … " She stopped dead, putting a hand to her mouth. "Oh God, I'm sorry."

"No, no, no!" he cut in. "Don't be. You're getting the hang of it."

Kelly was baffled. "What? No. I can't go off at you like that. The customer's always right. We need you to come back to keep the business going."

"Business, pffft," Skoobie scoffed. "We aint about money. Never were. Just want a cruisy place to hang out."

"So how do you survive?" Kelly wondered.

"With a steak sandwich," the father replied. "Can't keep going without food."

"Exactly," Skoobie agreed.

Kelly relented, knowing it was useless to argue. That would only give her more headaches. "Coming right up." She turned, heading to the kitchen.

Vanilla opened the door, passing her a plate. "One steak sandwich."

Kelly went back to the father, put it down and turned to leave.

"Oh sorry," he said. "There's no sauce on this."

Kelly reached to the counter, grabbing a bottle of sauce. Skoobie stepped in, flipping open the top of the sandwich, before Kelly spread the sauce over it and removed the bottle. Skoobie slapped the sandwich back together, then they both grabbed the sandwich, put it in his mouth and high-fived.

The boy giggled.

Kelly stared at her hand, startled by her impulsive high-five. "What … ?"

"Hey!" a big man called. "Where's today's paper?"

A woman spoke up. "What about my salad?"

"I'd like a burger to go …" said another.

Skoobie headed into the kitchen coolly. "Yada, yada, yada …"

"I want, I want, I want …" Kelly found herself mimicking.

Skoobie emerged from the kitchen, dropping a salad dish before the woman. "What are we? Your parents?"

"You guys are so fired," came the grumbling reply.

"Oh, we're fired?" Kelly suddenly retorted.

"Yeah! You're fired!"

Kelly shrugged. "Great. Always wanted to work on a cruise ship."

The entire café, save for Skoobie, burst into loud laughter and rapturous applause.

Salad-Woman smirked over the joyous clapping. "Well done, kid."

"You did it," the father said happily.

"Now you've got it," Burger-Guy added.

Kelly too, smirked, failing to hide it. "Shut up."

Skoobie elbowed her lightly. "Nice work."

Kelly bit her lip, desperately trying to stop blushing. "You know this is only until I get a real job, right?"

"Oh yeah," Skoobie replied, "but I have heard reports from the celestial realm that hell *is* actually freezing over."

Another crash came from the kitchen.

"So-rry," Skoobie mumbled, heading away.

Kelly grinned and got back to work.

Kelly bantered with the customers all morning in what seemed like anything *but* work. The food and laughter flowed freely, embracing her in sheer bliss. She lapped it up, feeling like she'd finally arrived home. Time stopped as she served everyone peacefully, caught in the divine moment of forever.

A lone quip from Burger Guy made her laugh longer than she had in ages, then she strode into the kitchen to grab an order.

Vanilla was looking at a security screen. "Having a good time, sweetie?"

Kelly put an arm around her. "The best." She noted the screen. "Nice system."

Vanilla hugged her back. "Thanks. It was installed this morning."

"By who?" Kelly wondered. "I didn't see anyone come in."

"We work fast," Vanilla answered. "Turbo's linked in it too. You've been doing a good job out there."

"Yeah," Kelly replied cheerfully. "Waitressing's a breeze."

"It's got nothing to do with waitressing," Vanilla corrected. "You didn't even notice you were working by yourself for ages, did you?"

"Well, no ..." Kelly realised.

" ... Meaning you had everyone on camera at one point or another."

Kelly was confused. "What for? You know everyone here, don't you?"

"There's always newbies," Vanilla pointed out. "Skoob and I were out here watching things for a bit. We've never taken measures like this before. I hate spying, but it's essential, and it's paid off. This guy by the window ..." She picked up a pen, tapped the screen, then chewed the pen thoughtfully. "He's been in a couple of times. Sits by the window making notes and not speaking to anyone. Writes an awful lot."

"Of course," Skoobie said, breezing in. "Their NUTS are checking ours out."

Kelly smirked. "Sounds rude."

"I know," Skoobie replied, picking up a plate and walking out.

Vanilla pushed Kelly gently to the door. "Thanks for offering to go talk with him, sweet stuff."

Kelly was startled. "Me? I didn't say anything."

"Not in so many words …"

"What about Skoob?"

"She's in surveillance mode. I need to watch. Cook too. Off you go."

Kelly sighed wearily, recalling her talk with Vertigo. "Why is it always me? Fine." She walked out of the kitchen, across the café, and approached the man by the window. Strangely, he was scribbling notes in his pad, engrossed in his work. Her mind worked rapidly, wondering what to say.

"Hey there …" she began.

He didn't look up.

"Can I get you something?" she offered.

He continued working.

"No coffee?" she pressed. "Cupcakes are good."

His eyes rose slowly and he put his pen down, staring at her darkly and speaking with a clipped English accent. "You don't belong here, do you?"

She blinked, taken aback. "What?"

His tone lowered. "Look at you. Sucked right in." He indicated the surroundings. "What kind of business doesn't care about money? Aren't you the least bit suspicious?"

"Well, yeah," Kelly agreed, "but …"

"Have a seat," he prompted, glancing at the one before him. "Please."

His hypnotic stare made the world fade away and she found herself lowering into the chair, not liking it one bit. His gaze was entrancing. She couldn't figure out why.

He spoke smoothly. "My name is Solomon. Professor Adonias Solomon, to be exact. I'm a behavioural scientist."

Relief overcame her. "Oh! That makes sense. What part of England are you from?"

He ignored her. "This place has swamped you, hasn't it?"

Black shades of doubt rose in her mind. His words rang true, grasping onto her logic, making her sure he was legit.

He continued. "You've lost your job since finding this place, only to be hired here, *and* without meeting an employer. There are no wages. Why haven't you questioned that? *Really* questioned it."

Kelly was about to reply, then stopped. He was right. She'd always been curious, but the cruisy vibe here had buried that.

"Why?" he pressed.

She submitted. "I ... don't know ..."

He spoke on. "I've been in touch with Sergeant Donna Vertigo. She tells me you're involved with these people, and up to all sorts of trouble with the police, I believe."

She shifted uneasily. "I'm not saying anything ..."

"Very wise," he stated. "Considering how dangerous these NUTS in their Delirium are, it's best to ignore her." He leaned in. "Isn't it?"

Laughter flowed from a nearby table, only now it seemed mocking. Her heart missed a beat, then his words kicked in. Her eyes widened as the full horror of what he was implying hit home. "Oh God!"

He nodded, satisfied. "Where else can turn your life upside down like this?" He opened his notepad. "From what I've observed, there's no profit for this company, and no one's ever seen the boss. A perfect profile for the Delirium, wouldn't you say?"

Kelly shook her head, desperately trying to dismiss this. "No, my friends aren't psychos ..."

"You wouldn't know if they were," he pointed out.

Kelly bit her lip, struggling to convince herself otherwise. Logic took over as shades of her old self returned. "How do you know this?"

He tapped his notepad. "My investigations have resulted in findings you wouldn't believe. They're all documented, with sufficient evidence that can't be ignored. I'll show you everything, just not here."

She shook her head. "No. It's too dodgy ..."

"While Vanilla Pond isn't?"

Kelly's temper flickered. "Don't insult her ..."

"A good friend is she?" he interjected. "Well tell me this. What really happened on the night of her boyfriend's murder?" His head rose. "No doubt Melody Hill was involved too. You don't know the real reason she was in Afghanistan, do you? It's bigger than you think." He paused. "Then there's our waitress, Skoobie. At least she doesn't try to hide her psychosis."

His gaze bore right through her, killing the café's touch. Despite this, the faint residue of her friends' faces glimmered in her mind.

"You're in danger," he pushed. "We all are. We need to leave immediately. It's too risky here. A minister died last night, remember? You've been caught in the Delirium. You need help. Please … come with me." He reached in, clutching her hand. "Before it's too late."

Kelly shivered. She pulled her hand back and put it to her head, desperately trying not to believe him, but seeing no other choice. Everything he said made complete and utter sense.

"Okay," she relented, unable to ignore his words. "You got me on this, but I want to see Vertigo first."

"Naturally," he replied. "She's in a meeting right now. I'm due to meet her at the beach in half an hour." He rose from his seat, prompting her. "Coming?"

She rose too, speaking automatically. "Deal."

Vanilla pursed her lips crossly.

He gave a small nod. "Let's go quietly. No need to make a scene." He lifted his hand charmingly. "After you, my dear."

Seriously shaken, she made for the door.

Skoobie threw her notepad onto the kitchen counter.

Vanilla raised her hand. "No, Skoob, forget it. Get Mel. We need to work fast."

"Sure," came the cool reply. "Close up?"

"Close up," Vanilla confirmed. "In ten minutes."

"I'll clear the place in two."

"Ten, Skoob."

"Fine."

Solomon opened the door to his black limousine, politely indicating for Kelly to enter. She did so, not liking it one bit. He followed, somewhat smoothly, closing the door behind him.

The limo took off.

Kelly sat uneasily next to Solomon as they were chauffeured to the beach. They didn't talk, remaining in tense silence for what seemed like forever. Finally, they arrived, and emerged from the limo into the fresh sea breeze. Solomon motioned to the pier and they made their way towards it.

Kelly looked around uneasily. "Where's Vertigo?"

He too, peered around. "On her way. For your sake, dear girl, I hope she hurries. There are good odds that we've been followed. I've never underestimated the tenacity of these psychopaths."

Kelly shivered. "I hope they hurry."

"As do I," he replied. "Chances are we've been followed."

"So why aren't we at the police station?"

"Too risky," he stated. "The Delirium has spies everywhere. Vertigo's the only one who we can trust. She won't be long."

They reached the pier and strode across it, passing a seaside kiosk. Kelly saw a weary waitress carrying two cups of coffee to a seated couple.

"Service doesn't seem as great here," she noted.

"Indeed," Solomon agreed. "It's called real life." He nodded to the waitress who nodded back.

"You know her?" Kelly asked.

"Oh yes," he answered. "I've been here many times. That's Mary. She's under pressure to keep her shop open, which is more realistic than the café, isn't it?"

Kelly concurred. "Sure is."

"YAAAAAAAA …!"

Kelly jumped, whirling around. A man, some way back, dropped to his knees, a knife in his chest. She gasped, putting a hand to her mouth, watching as an athletic female leapt onto the beach, heading for the car park.

Solomon pursed his lips. "Melody Hill. She's got one of my men."

Kelly's eyes welled with tears. "Mel? No way!" She shuddered, horrified. "Mel, how could you?"

"Ruthless," Solomon said bitterly. "This way."

They ran along the pier, into the crowd.

"Hey, amigo! 'Sup?"

Kelly stopped, looking around desperately. Skoobie was nowhere to be seen.

"Yo hopscotch, over here! On the astral plane!"

Solomon stopped too. "Keep moving! Hurry! We need Vertigo."

He started to move, then halted. Kelly gazed ahead and froze. A figure in a black bridal dress was approaching, their face covered by a vale.

Solomon tensed. "Oh hell, it's Vanilla."

"What …?" Kelly cried in disbelief.

The bride moved in, holding a long metal object with a flickering tip.

A flamethrower.

Solomon bolted.

"Scoops, please …!" Kelly whimpered.

A crackly voice spoke from beneath the veil. *That's me, peaches. Come on home now …"*

The weapon rose.

Kelly recoiled in shock, slipping on a puddle, arching backwards and falling over the pier's railings. A flaming stream shot over her head as she tumbled down, dropping into the sea. Her head surfaced and she struggled to stay afloat, fighting against the tide as she was swept beneath the pier to bob amidst the pylons. The flamethrower's rush erupted above, now accompanied by the hideous screams of passers-by.

"Scoops," she spluttered through the salty water. "Mel. Skoob. How could you …?"

She fought against the waves, struggling to reach the beach. Police sirens and running footsteps erupted on the pier above, then a heavy splash breached the water behind her. She glimpsed back, seeing a black veil bobbing in the sea. Sheer terror propelled her to the beach where she staggered out of the water and onto the sand, weighed down by her heavy, wet clothes.

A shadow overcame her, then a confident voice spoke. "Well, this is a first. Usually I'm the one getting soaked when we're together."

She looked up.

David.

He stood over her, unnerved by the pier scene.

She retreated, crying.

He moved in, holding her up. "Hey, hey, hey, I don't know what's going on, but we'll get you out of here."

She broke away from him, sobbing. "No! Can't trust you! Can't trust anyone! You're a freak! From that nuthouse! Get away from me! *Go!"*

She turned, stumbling away, then stopped dead.

Skoobie was in the distance, hands in her pockets, casually heading in.

"No ..." Kelly whispered, falling back.

David caught her.

"It's okay," he said softly. "I've got you now ..."

Darkness swept in and everything went blank.

Chapter Six

Kelly awoke to the gentle crackles of a warm fire. She snuggled dreamily into her blankets, embracing their comfort as she cuddled her pillow.

At least until a wave of horrific memories swept in, swamping her. Her eyes snapped open, the world solidified, and she found herself on the floor by a fireplace. Her heart pounded as she pushed herself up, startled.

"Morning," David said, entering the room. "Or should I say, afternoon since it's just past lunch? Least you had a good rest." He placed a steaming hot mug on the coffee table beside her. "Here, this'll perk you up."

She stared at him, astounded.

"Hot chocolate not your thing?" he asked.

She kept staring. Her voice crackled as she spoke hoarsely. "Let me out of here."

"Sure," he replied. "You can leave when you're ready, though you'll have to go to the police first. What happened on the pier today is all over the news. They want to see you."

"So why am I here?" she pressed.

"You needed a rest," he answered. "You won't think clearly otherwise. You'll have to get your story straight."

She stayed doubtful as hell. "How do I know I can trust you?"

"Don't trust me, trust yourself."

His charm was entrancing. His common sense even more so. She tensed as he indicated the floor. "May I?"

She shifted awkwardly. "Do what you want. You have so far."

He sat before her, keeping his distance, then indicated the dark patch on the left leg of his jeans. "Sorry about the pants. I still can't get your coffee stains out, and they're the only ones I have. It's okay. I've seen you take the wrong bus, lose your job, and then stagger out of the ocean crying. Come to think of it, I've only ever seen you at your worst …"

"Not cheering me up …" she cut in.

"And there we go. That's the real Kelly Morrison. A fighter with guts to spare. Not the wailing wreck you were on the beach. Last time I walked past the café, you were happily serving people, totally in balance. You were really coming into yourself for a while there, weren't you? Well done for coming back."

"Will you stop sucking up …?"

"I don't have enough strength to suck you in."

"Shut up." She sniffed, trying hard to resist him. "I've been through hell. Vanilla tried to kill me. Mel killed a guy and ran off. God, Vanilla was in jail. Mel, Afghanistan. Skoob, god knows where. They're psychos. That whole café. Killers living in a nuthouse …"

"Do you know that for sure?" he asked. "After what you and your friends have done, *together*?"

"Yes!"

"There's no need to be stubborn …"

"I am so gonna kill you …"

"Love it," he said with a grin. "Keep it up."

She made a face.

He continued. "So what changed between happy-café Kelly, and beach-Kelly freefalling past sanity central?"

"I found out the truth!" she shot back.

"From who?"

"From that … Professor …"

She stopped in realisation.

He nodded. "Uh-huh. So you meet him and the world becomes a dark, scary place where all hell breaks loose. That's sure different to a few hours before when you'd never felt better. Did anyone tell you to go meet him?"

Kelly frowned, confused. "Vanilla."

He tossed a log on the fire, brightening it. "So, you're saying that she's so nuts that she wants you to talk to a guy who can tell you the truth about her so she can go ballistic and kill you in public? Not very practical, is it? Did she want you as an ally or dead? She can't have both. The standout factor here is …"

Her lips parted and she spoke in barely a whisper. "Solomon."

"Exactly," he confirmed.

She shook her head, placing a hand on her forehead. No, no! I *saw* Mel knife a guy on the pier …"

"Are you sure it was her?" he pressed.

"Sure," she answered. "She wore the same clothes, and her hair was tied like normal. What more do you want?"

"How close were you? Did you see her face?"

She went silent. Insight kicked in and she ran a hand through her hair, speaking softly. "Miles away."

"*Now* you're getting it," he said.

She sighed, knowing he was right. "Didn't see Vanilla's face either. Bridezilla was speaking through a veil. It was Vanilla's voice though."

He shrugged. "Sure, if you know how to work the tech for it."

A sudden thought struck and she raised her hand. "No! Whoa, wait! I did see Skoob there."

"Correct," he confirmed.

She blinked. "You admit it?"

"Got no choice," he replied simply. "Can't argue with facts. She was checking to see if you were okay. She backed off when she saw I had you, then went to help her friends on the pier save everyone."

Kelly went silent.

"Do you want to go to the police station?" he asked. "I'm happy to take you. Or do you want the cops to come here? I'm fine either way."

Kelly was doubtful. "I don't know about the cops."

"Why?" he queried. "Did that Professor warn you off 'em?"

She exhaled sharply. "You got a point. Vertigo seemed legit. Cop shop it is. You're coming with me though."

He nodded. "Deal."

She rubbed her eyes. "We'll have to stop off at my place first. I need a spare pair of glasses."

"Good that you got 'em," he said.

"Five pairs," she admitted. "Four now."

"Can you see anything?"

"Everything," she replied. "My right eye's a little weak. The left lens is practically glass."

"So why do you wear them?"

"My optometrist says …"

"Don't tell me you're hiding yourself away?"

She tensed. "Look, this is making me jittery. What are you gonna say next? That I'm beautiful without them?"

"Well …"

"Don't you dare."

He backed off, putting his hands up. "Okay. We'll go to the police when you're ready."

She reached up to the coffee table, taking her cup. "After my drink. I like hot chocolate."

"You know what?" He leaned in and whispered. "Me too." He got ready to rise. "I'd better go check on your clothes. They're probably dry by now."

She looked down in shock, finding herself in a flannel shirt and tracksuit bottoms. "What … how … oh my God … did you …?"

"They're mine but relax," he cut in. "You were dead to the world so I had my sister come over and change you. Honest. It's okay, she's a nurse."

She stared at him, stunned.

He indicated the corridor with a glance. "I *was* in the other room."

She covered herself uncomfortably. "Hope she didn't see too much."

He shrugged. "I don't know, but when I came back in, she was holding up your bra, wondering how someone so conservative could be so kinky.'"

"I'll kill her! I'm not conservative!"

He raised his eyebrows.

"David!" she cried, slapping him lightly. "Oh God, I'm sorry!"

"Don't be, I deserved it." He moved to go.

She reached out instinctively, grabbing his arm. She didn't know why, but she felt safe with him, and didn't want him to leave. He was the real deal, and that was all that mattered.

"No," she found herself saying. "You're okay. I'm still freaked out by everything, you know? You … uh … " Her voice lowered shyly, " … don't have to rush off just yet."

He settled back down. "Whatever you wish, Kelly Morrison."

She swallowed hard. "David?"

"Yeah?"

"Thanks for putting up with me."

"Anytime, Kel."

She didn't know why, but she reached out and clasped his hand, trusting him. He clasped hers back, making her insides tingle. She let herself sink into the moment as they sat listening to the crackling fireplace, letting their silence speak for itself.

Much later, they were still sitting in silence, only now in a police interview room. Kelly had changed into an old pair of jeans, having got them from home. Much to her dismay, her tops had all been in the wash, so she'd kept David's.

The door opened and Vertigo entered, dropping her file on the table. "Kelly Morrison, we meet again. Your run-ins with the law are becoming all too frequent these days."

Kelly concurred. "Tell me about it."

Vertigo took a seat. "Oh, I will, believe me. We've reviewed the pier's surveillance footage and spoken to over a dozen witnesses. What you saw there were NUTS in action …"

David smirked.

Vertigo glared at him.

He wiped the smile off his face.

She continued. "Their intent was to cause chaos, suck you in, and get more info on the café. They wanted you *completely* on their side, while having a little fun at the same time. Didn't work. Thanks to you, we've now identified a major player in NUTS's hierarchy. Professor Adonias Solomon, aka Elwyn Gotz. We suspected him for a while, but you've just provided the evidence we need to go after him. Good stuff."

Kelly was taken aback. "Whoa, wait, hang on. It can't be as simple as that."

"Wanna bet?" Vertigo countered. "Your café's security system helped too. What you saw was an illusion of NUTS doing a big show-off."

David smirked again.

Vertigo slapped her folder down in front of him, making both him and Kelly jump.

She spoke on. "We've analysed the pier's footage extensively. A close-up of Melody's face shows that it's not her at all. Surveillance cameras verify her riding her bike down Stanton Street at the time, heading for the beach. Her double stabbed the passer-by on the pier, while another NUT was circling you, playing a recording of Skoobie's voice. A third NUT was impersonating their leader, the Black Bride, who'd never show himself so publicly. Best bet's that he let his deputy, the Squirrel, borrow his wedding dress. Thanks to you we've now got confirmation on Solomon, a lead as to his whereabouts, and a sighting of the Squirrel. Not bad for a day's work. You got a good result. This would have taken us months otherwise. Thanks, kid."

Kelly hid her smile, not wanting Vertigo to see that her faith in her friends was restored.

David patted her hand. "What'd I tell you? It wasn't them."

She pulled her hand away, awkwardly. "I knew it. Always did."

Vertigo continued. "We've also got the groupie who saw the minister at the concert. She confirmed it was Solomon who killed him." She leaned forward. "However, there's a few loose ends needing to be cleared up, and only one person can do that."

Kelly tensed.

Vertigo's voice lowered. "We want Turbo Newcombe."

Kelly couldn't hide her smile at the thought of him, then spoke confidently. "No dice, lady."

Vertigo sat back. "Fine. For now. Since we've got the evidence we need, his story's only standard procedure. The big pain in the butt is his mother who's giving us headaches." She pursed her lips. "Boy, is she giving us headaches." She stood up, went to the door and opened it. "Anyway, there's some people who want to see you. Come in, ladies."

Kelly jumped inwardly and rose, along with David, as Melody, Vanilla and Skoobie all entered. She was relieved to see them, but wouldn't show it, at least until they all got their stories straight.

Vertigo headed past them. "I'll leave you to it."

She closed the door behind her.

Silence followed.

Skoobie broke it. "'Sup?"

Kelly inhaled sharply. "I'm amazed you still want to speak to me after I got sucked right in by the bad guys."

Skoobie was unfazed. "Sure. Why not?"

Kelly frowned. "'Cause I went off with 'em and everything shot to hell."

"You got that right," Melody muttered.

Vanilla nudged her.

Melody grumbled under her breath.

Vanilla spoke gently to Kelly. "Hey, I'm the one who dropped you in it. We all are."

"Hey, yeah …" Kelly suddenly realised.

Melody nudged Vanilla.

"Oh, right," Vanilla said, discouraged.

Kelly was confused. "So where were you guys? How come you didn't send …" She raised her arm, " … Mel in to grab psycho-Professor?"

Melody indicated Vanilla crossly. "I *did* bring that up. Several times."

Vanilla kept her cool. "He already knew about us. We needed …"

"A newbie," Kelly finished. "Someone to throw in the deep end. That was dangerous. They messed with my head. Big time. I could have been hurt."

"Nah, we were looking out for ya," Melody said flippantly.

"Yeah," Skoobie agreed. "That's why we sent David in."

Melody and Vanilla smacked her arms.

Skoobie looked down guiltily. "Ohhhhhhhhhhhh … whoops…"

Kelly's eyes nearly popped out of her head and her jaw dropped. Menacingly, she turned on David. "*You* were in on this?"

He raised his hands protectively. "Now, now wait a minute. You were on edge and things were delicate. You'd flip otherwise …"

"I'd love to flip you right now! There's nothing I'd like *more* than to toss your buns onto a barbeque, hot stuff!"

Skoobie pondered on this, Melody was impressed, and Vanilla gave a small smile at their growing spark.

Kelly glared at him. "So the truth hits home! All that nice guy stuff was just an act to get me back to your house and out of my clothes, was it?"

Skoobie raised her eyebrows. "Really?" She looked Kelly over. "Oh yeah, right. Love the flannel."

"Well, I hate it!" Kelly ripped off the shirt, revealing a white singlet underneath. "Here, have it back!" She threw it at him.

"Everything I said was true …" he confessed.

"I'm not sure about anything anymore …"

"Then go with what you know …" he pushed.

"I know you're a jerk!"

Melody cut in. "Oh, for god's sake, we all know you two have the volcanic rumbles for each other. Snog it up already."

"But only if it feels right," Vanilla warned.

"Totally," Melody agreed. "For someone like junior here, sex is a big step."

Kelly turned to her, horrified. "I … I … I … oh, you're asking for it!"

"Pfffft," Melody scoffed. "Yeah, right."

"That's it!" Kelly took her glasses off, folding them on the chair.

"Oooh, scary!" Melody mocked.

"Get stuffed," Kelly retorted. "You're not a commando, you're a friggin' panda!"

"Pandas are cute," Skoobie pointed out.

Melody nearly blew. "Game on!"

"You said it!" Kelly yelled back.

Melody dived on her and they flew onto the table, struggling fiercely. Kelly winced and Melody growled as they wavered from side to side furiously.

Skoobie observed them curiously. "Y'know this is strangely erotic."

David nodded simply. "I know."

Melody turned Kelly over, laying her face down on the table. "Surrender?"

Kelly grunted, and with an astounding burst of strength she never knew she had, lifted her leg and kicked back, booting Melody into the wall. She rolled over and rose as Melody rebounded, then leapt to the side, letting her fly past. Both turned, facing each other.

"That's it!" Melody yelled, pointing at her. "Now you're gonna die!"

She swept in.

"Skoob!" Vanilla cried. "Intercept!"

Vanilla and Skoobie dived, colliding with Melody, who collided with Kelly, and they all fell to the ground in a heap.

Silence followed.

Finally, Skoobie spoke. "Remind me again how we got into this?"

Kelly tried shifting but was powerless to do anything.

Melody struggled, held fast by Vanilla and Skoobie.

"Mutual surrender?" Vanilla asked.

Kelly sighed, defeated. "Fine."

"Yeah, as if …" Melody began.

Vanilla nudged her.

"Deal," Melody also relented.

More silence.

"You know something?" Kelly asked.

No response.

"I miss this crap."

They all shuffled uncomfortably, embracing each other. Vanilla and Kelly tearfully, Skoobie going with the flow, and Melody reluctantly.

"Once again, strangely erotic," Skoobie mused.

Kelly spoke sadly. "Sorry I doubted you guys. I've been screwed over by so many people for so long. Didn't want it happening again. You've been good to me. Better than anyone in a long time. Losing you would be too much. Hope you can forgive me."

"Hey, Vanilla replied gently. "We hope you can forgive *us*."

"Why, what did we do?" Melody retorted. Vanilla elbowed her. "Ow!"

"We should have been upfront," Vanilla clarified.

Kelly swallowed hard. "Forget it. So we're all good?"

Vanilla smiled. "Yeah. We're good."

They hugged again.

The door opened and Vertigo walked in, holding her coffee. She stopped at the sight of them in a cuddled, huddled heap on the floor.

"Don't ask," David said.

She rolled her eyes and walked out.

Kelly sniffed again. "This is so great. I feel like … like …"

"A coffee?" Vanilla prompted, basking in the aroma of Vertigo's. "I can make one better than that, sweetie."

Kelly grinned. "Yeah. A coffee."

"I know just the place."

They all rolled off each other and sat up, rubbing their shoulders, arms and legs.

Melody wiped her eyes. "God damn. That was tough."

Kelly wiped her own tears away. "Oh yeah. You crying too, Mel?"

Melody smacked her lightly. "Shut up."

The door opened and Vertigo re-entered the room. "You done?"

"Yeah," Kelly replied. "We're done."

"Good," Vertigo said. "NUTS'll be on the warpath now. You'll need police protection."

"God no," Melody scoffed. "That's for wimps."

Vertigo ignored her. "Your funeral, just try not to get anyone killed along the way."

"O-kay," Skoobie replied, "but we can't promise anything."

The four girls rose and moved past her, heading out the door.

Vanilla was the last to go.

Vertigo reached out, stopping her. "Hey, uh, I tried everything. No dice. Your kids are still off limits."

Vanilla bit her lip sadly. "At least you tried. Thanks. It means a lot."

Vertigo nodded. "I can't imagine what you're going through …"

Vanilla nodded back. "Yeah, it's horrific, but I've got the best friends in the world now. They'll see I'm okay. Thanks again." She rubbed Vertigo's shoulder warmly, then headed out the door.

David was the last to go.

"Thank you, Sergeant," he said, walking out after them.

He closed the door behind him.

The door opened and Kelly hurried back in.

"Sorry," she said, making for the chair. "Forgot my glasses." She put them on. "See ya."

She hurried out again, closing the door behind her. It wouldn't shut properly and took a few bangs to get it right, then her loud footsteps headed off.

Vertigo shook her head in disbelief. "You lot are enough to drive anyone nuts."

David quietly slipped away, leaving the four girls to return to the café. There, over numerous servings of ice-cream and cake, they talked long into the evening, and then the night, about anything and everything, leaving the rest of the world to fade away. For what seemed like an eternity, there was only the four of them in this lone café, caring for nothing else except each other, and that was all that mattered.

Chapter Seven

Kelly nodded off at the table shortly before sunrise. Vanilla moved past her, putting a sign on the door saying they were closed for the day. Being enemy targets meant lying low for a while.

Melody had power napped on and off during the night. Now she was raring to go, either for a long swim to a nearby island or to do a three-hundred-kilometre bike ride. Finally, she decided on both, but first had to get Kelly out of the café.

"Where's she live?" she asked, picking Kelly up and hoisting her over her shoulder like a wounded soldier.

Skoobie placed a lollipop in her mouth. "*Mmm-mmm-mmmm,*" came the reply, which translated to: 'I don't know.'

"It's not safe for her at home," Vanilla pointed out, "and David's at work. Better drop her off at Skoob's."

"Fine," Melody said back. "Okay with you, Skoob?"

"*Mmm-mmm ,*" Skoobie answered.

"Cool. Where's my skateboard?"

A few minutes later, Kelly dangled from Melody's shoulders as they flew down the street on the skateboard. They swept down a hill, leapt in the air and sailed over a car, just as Kelly suddenly awoke and screamed. Luckily, she passed out straight away again, leaving Melody to take her to Skoobie's peacefully.

When Kelly opened her eyes again, she found herself on a bed, touched by the glistening sunbeams from a nearby window. She smiled blissfully, then blinked, wondering where she was. For some reason, she recalled a strange dream of flying through the air with Melody.

"Freaks," she muttered, turning over.

A python stared back at her, its long tongue flickering with a soft hiss.

Her mouth opened in a silent scream and she inched away, then looked down to see a frill-necked lizard. She whimpered, inching back, then wailed at the sight of a baby alligator crawling towards her. The alligator smiled back.

"Oh my God!" She smacked her head. "Wake up, wake up, wake up …!"

A growl came from nearby.

She froze, watching in shock as a fully grown tiger slinked past the bed, heading into the bathroom.

She trembled in terror.

"It's okay, he's tame," Skoobie said, walking into the bedroom and over to a fractured mirror. She picked up a multi-coloured hairbrush, stroking her hair. "Like my new brush? Found it at the beach. Pretty funky, huh?"

Kelly was too terrified to move. "Th-This is how you live?"

"Yep," came the reply. "Shouldn't we all? If everything got on well together, there'd be no sickness, right?"

The frill-necked lizard suddenly hissed and leapt onto the dresser, swiping at a bandicoot who squealed and ran.

"I'm still working on those two," Skoobie finished.

Kelly, almost at the point of hysterics, sprang out of the bed, backing up against the wall. "What about diseases? Fleas and stuff?"

Skoobie finished brushing her hair. "The bugs here are friends with everything, including us."

"So why am I here?"

"Frisky parents."

"No, I mean in … zoo-reject central?"

The tiger growled.

Kelly jumped. "Sorry." She steadied herself, then insight hit. "Oh, I get it. Protection from the bad guys, huh?"

"That too," Skoobie answered. She put the brush down, turned, and picked up the python, slinging it around her neck. "No one touches me, or my buddies – right, snookums?" She made a kissing noise at it.

Kelly inched over to the fractured mirror, seeing it surrounded by pictures of Jesus, Buddha, Krishna, Yoda, Superman and Elvis. She shook her head and looked up at the painting on the ceiling, showing a blue sky with fluffy white clouds.

Skoobie looked too. "Cool, huh? Now I don't have to get outta bed to see the sky and the day's always beautiful." She held up a toothbrush. "Wanna brush your teeth? I made the toothpaste myself."

Kelly went green. "Nuh-uh."

"Yeah, good idea, go natural." She indicated the cracked mirror. "Great, huh? Shows your feelings in different colours. That bit up there's happy, that one's peace, there's joy, and over there's excitement. Like it?"

Kelly's gaze lowered to a glow in the lefthand corner. Her reflection shimmered back, bathed in a golden halo. She spoke softly, captivated. "Oh my God!"

Skoobie nodded. "See? You're beautiful."

Kelly was shaken. "Yeah. Guess I am." She indicated another fracture. "Why's my forehead darker there?"

"That's your ego," came the reply. "Needs to lighten up."

"Guess so," Kelly agreed.

Skoobie put her toothbrush down. "Come on, amigo. You can chill with me for a bit. I'm not doing anything."

"Cool."

Silence. Neither of them moved. The silence went on for longer and longer. Finally, Kelly asked, "What are you doing?"

"Oh, you wanna do something more active?" Skoobie asked back.

"That'd be good."

"Okey-dokey." She grabbed Kelly's hand, leading her through a curtain of beads. "In here."

Kelly saw a lounge room covered by …

"Beanbags?" she wondered.

"Funbags," Skoobie replied.

A groan came from one and Turbo sat up, rubbing his eyes and speaking wearily. "Morning." He pushed his laptop away.

Skoobie walked over, dropping into his outstretched arms. "'Sup?"

They hugged warmly.

Kelly nearly exploded. "What? When did this happen? What have you done, Skoob? This is so wrong! Totally!"

"Why?" Skoobie asked.

"Doesn't feel wrong," Turbo added.

"Sure," Kelly scoffed back at him. "Just ditch your mum and shack-up with a free-loving hippie!"

Skoobie stood up crossly, stomped over to Kelly and hissed, "I am not into free love! How could you think that of me?"

Kelly indicated the house. "Duh?"

"So what?" Skoobie asked blankly.

Kelly changed tack. "So you two haven't done anything?"

"Why would I?" came the reply. "I'm not like that, and he's got too many mother issues."

Turbo leapt to his feet, pointing hysterically. "*I do not have mother issues!*"

"See?" Skoobie confirmed. "I'm just helping him out so he doesn't chuck on a chick when one's in his comfort zone. He hasn't been around any who aren't his mum."

"*Enough already!*" he cried.

Skoobie ignored him. "Besides, I'm starting to like the little guy. He's cute."

Turbo blushed bright red.

Kelly made a face. "Ugh!"

Skoobie dismissed this and headed to the rainbow-painted front door. "'Kay, who's for breakfast and a beach walk?"

"Me!" Turbo said eagerly.

Kelly was confused. "Aren't we meant to stay hidden from NUTS?"

"We'll be fine," Skoobie told her. "Let's just say I have friends in very high places."

Kelly didn't want to argue, knowing she'd only get headaches. "Fine, as long as it's a beach breakfast that's café bought."

"Shame," Skoobie said. "You'd have loved my hamster omelette."

Kelly nearly gagged. "You eat hamsters?"

Skoobie made a face. "Devas no! How yuk's that? No, my little buddies just make 'em. Got 'em trained nicely."

Kelly hurried for the door.

Skoobie and Turbo strolled hand in hand past the beach pier. A hood covered Turbo's head so he wouldn't be recognised. Kelly walked nervously behind them, scanning for threats. Skoobie had assured her there were none, but Kelly wasn't convinced. Still, the crashing waves and her friends' banter were comforting.

"See?" Skoobie told Turbo. "Women aren't so frightening, are they?"

"No," he replied, trying to sound tough. "Got the hood, got the chick on my arm …"

"Really?" she asked. "Where?" She paused. "Oh, right."

He clutched her hand tighter, speaking hesitantly. "Skoob, do you think you and I could ever, y'know …?"

She gazed at the sky. "Anything's possible, if you think big enough."

He beamed. "So I'm in with a chance?"

"Uhhhhhhh …"

"Great!" He leaned in close and, much to her discomfort, led her up the slope. Somewhat hesitantly, she let herself go with him, tensing a little.

Kelly slowed down, letting them gain some distance, sensing that Skoobie had got herself in too deep. She may have been trying to help him, but now they were drifting towards each other, amid rising sparks. That left Kelly feeling like an awkward third party and so she stopped, leaned on the wooden railing and gazed out at the sea, feeling alone. Skoobie and Turbo were drifting away, Melody was doing an island swim, and Vanilla was at a legal hearing about her children. She ran a hand through her hair, feeling tired, drained, and a target for …

"Beautiful, isn't it?"

She nearly jumped out of her skin and looked up, feeling worse when she saw who was there.

David, leaning on the railing beside her.

Her heart pounded and she pushed her glasses up nervously, wondering why she was feeling this way. This wasn't like before. Things felt different. He seemed mesmerising. Very much so. "Uh, yeah. So who sent you this time? Mel or Scoops?"

"No one," he answered. "Just finished doing a little work for an animal shelter down the street. Came up for some ice-cream. Wanna join me? Unless you're too busy, that is?"

Kelly found herself tongue-tied. "I … uh … well … I … I … uh …"

"Is that a yes?" he prompted.

"Yes," she said automatically. "No, wait …"

"You have other plans?"

"No."

"You don't like ice-cream?"

"I love it."

"Good. My shout."

She paused, feeling nervous as hell. "Okay."

"Great."

They headed along the path, amid the cawing seagulls. He strode confidently and relaxed, while she walked hesitantly alongside him.

"So what do you like?" he asked. "Butterscotch? Rum and raisin …?"

Fear got the better of her and she blurted out, "Just so you know, I'm not very good at this …"

"Getting ice-cream?" he replied.

"Being one on one with a guy," she revealed, not knowing why her mouth was on autopilot. "Guess I'm just like Turbo over there. Not so hot at … y'know?"

He turned, stopping her in her tracks and making her insides churn. "'Course not, and you know what? That's cute."

She gulped and recoiled, bumping into a man.

"Sorry," she said, inwardly cursing herself.

The man headed off crossly.

David smiled. "There you go again. So what would it take for you to really enjoy an ice-cream with me? Just a guy and a girl enjoying the beach. Nothing major."

Kelly spoke quickly, letting her mouth take over. "Well, first I want a guarantee that it's not going to lead to sex in the short term …"

He frowned. "Okay. Got it."

She felt like jumping into the sea, but her mouth went into overdrive before she could think. "And secondly, we do things my way. Got it?"

"Sure," he replied. "Anything to make you feel comfortable."

"Anything?" she pressed.

"Anything," he confirmed.

"Deal. Let's get this over with."

Kelly glided leisurely down the beach path on a set of rollerblades, holding an ice-cream. David followed, struggling to keep up on his own skates calling, "Hey wait, whoa, whoa, whoa …!"

He nearly toppled over.

Kelly turned to face him, rolling backwards. "Keep up or be out-dated!" She whirled around, gliding off. "Come on, lover boy!"

"Wait up!" he called desperately. "This isn't what I had in mind …"

He regained his balance, picking up speed as they headed down a hill.

She glanced back, failing to notice a dog running by. She only saw it at the last second when, "Oh crap …"

The dog squealed as she hit it, then David hit her and they toppled over together, rolling off the path and tumbling down a sandy slope. They reached the bottom, she opened her eyes and found herself on top of him.

Silence followed.

Finally, he spoke. "Well, this is another first."

The silence grew, before they slowly came together and kissed. An eternity passed, then they stopped, looking at each other tenderly.

He smiled. "I thought you said there was a no-sex policy."

She smiled back. "Yeah, but I didn't say anything about a no-kissing policy."

They kissed again, then parted.

She swallowed hard. "So when did you know?"

"When you spilt coffee on me," he replied. "You?"

"Just now. Up there on the beach."

The cool wind breezed by. They kissed again.

"So where do we go from here, Kelly Morrison?"

She grinned mischievously. "I know just the place."

They were soon back on the path, sailing along again. She was eating another ice-cream, going much slower this time, while he followed on a bike, doing the same.

"So many changes," she said dreamily. "I don't know, it's like I've had the most amazing stuff happen lately. Now I don't have to struggle to fit in or be someone I'm not. I've got real friends who like me for who I am."

"Who love you?" he prompted.

She stumbled a little, then regained her balance. "Let's not go into that. I told you, I'm not good at this …"

"… Yet," he finished for her. "You just think too much. You need to let go and forget yourself. You're okay."

She drifted along awkwardly. "Maybe. So what makes you Mister Perfect?"

"Oh, I'm not perfect, that's for sure. You'll find out soon enough."

She turned to him, rolling backwards once more and raising a hand to her mouth. "Oh God! You're married!"

"No."

"Separated? Divorced?"

"No, and no."

"Struggling with being gay?"

"Not with you in the world.

"David?"

"Never."

She pressed on. "Fugitive?"

"God no."

"Tax exile?"

"I hope not."

"Then what?"

He paused. "I'll tell you one day."

"David …!"

"One day soon. When you're ready to hear it, I promise."

She swirled around, going forwards again. "Let's go down to the beach for a while. We can paddle in the shallows. Get a feel for things, you know?"

"I'd like that," he replied.

A nervous thought hit her. She paused, trying to figure out how to say it. "Hey, uh, can I ask …?"

"Go ahead."

Now that we've kissed, does that mean we're like …?"

"A step forward?"

"Going steady?"

He grinned. "I haven't heard that since high school."

"I'm sorry …"

"Don't be, you're right. We're going steady."

She shifted uncomfortably. "As long as we don't ditch each other for anyone else, 'cause that'd be rude."

"Definitely," he agreed.

She nodded. "Okay. Cool. So now I've got a buh … buh …"

"Boyfriend?"

She staggered on her rollerblades.

He leaned in, balancing her.

"Not used to this," she said uncomfortably. "We'll just take things slow and start off cruisy. Like these bikes and skates, huh?"

"Got it, love of my life."

"Wuuuuuuuhhhhhh …"

She lost her balance, falling to the ground.

He stopped, placed his ice-cream in one hand, leaned to the side and reached down. "You okay?"

She smacked his hand away. "What do you think? Was that slow and cruisy?"

A couple walked past.

"Everything alright?" the man asked.

"Not for him," Kelly grumbled.

"Sorry about that," David told them. "She's just getting used to being my girlfriend."

"David!" she cried, smacking him again.

The woman beamed. "Oh, how cute."

Kelly couldn't hide her embarrassment and blushed. "Thanks."

"You'll be great together," the woman continued. "We'll leave you to it." She headed off, hand in hand with the man.

Kelly groaned, rubbing her thigh, "God, this is embarrassing."

"Would you like me to get you another ice-cream?" David asked. "It'll be your third, but maybe they'll give us a free one if I explain …"

"No, just give me yours."

She grabbed it from him and took his hand. He helped her up and they gently rolled along the footpath again, holding onto each other for balance.

"This is nice," she said. "I … uh … like being with you."

"I like being with you too," he responded.

She wavered shakily.

He held her steady. "It's okay, I got your back."

"Thanks," she replied. "Got yours too." She looked at the ocean. "Hey look! Mel's swimming in for the shore."

They stopped and watched.

Skoobie and Turbo approached them casually.

"So," Skoobie began, "you guys a couple now or what?"

"Yes," Kelly blurted out.

David rubbed her shoulder warmly. "That's right. We are."

"About time," Skoobie said, pulling out a flare gun from her large dress pocket. She fired a shot high over the beach, making everyone jump.

Way off in the ocean, Melody leapt up and down, punching the sky.

Kelly was horrified. "You've got signals for that?"

Skoobie held out her hand to Turbo. "Plus more. Pay up."

He smacked a note into her palm, grumbling.

"You were having bets on us?" Kelly asked, astounded.

"You bet *against* me?" David asked Turbo, equally so.

Turbo looked away guiltily.

Skoobie pocketed the money. "Homeless shelter's a little short right now. Anyway, it was fun."

"Not for me," Turbo muttered.

Kelly sighed. "Doesn't matter. Nothing about you surprises me anymore, Skoob."

"We'll work on that," came the reply.

"Don't you dare!"

"Anyway," Skoobie went on, "we're having a bonfire on the beach tonight. Gonna watch some turtles lay eggs. Wanna come?"

"I'm in," Turbo piped up eagerly. "Let's go together, Skoob."

"When you ask properly," she replied. "Go with the flow, remember?"

"Fine." He took a deep breath. "You're the best thing that's ever happened to me and are my saviour. Will you go with me to the beach tonight to ease my many years of suffering?"

She nodded. "Better."

"Well?"

She shrugged. "Whatever."

Kelly grinned, holding David's hand tightly.

"Wanna go?" he asked her.

"Totally," she replied.

Skoobie and Turbo headed away, making for Melody on the shore.

David pushed a strand of Kelly's hair behind her ear. She bit her lip, stared into his eyes, then kissed him lightly, before they too headed along the path as the ocean waves crashed in the distance.

Kelly snuggled into David, smiling dreamily as he wrapped his blanket over her. The campfire flickered in the cool beach breeze, while the waves gently lapped the shore behind them. It had been the perfect day, Kelly realised. A blissful haven of bicycles, rollerblades, ice-cream, beaches and best friends.

Skoobie and Turbo were next to them. Skoobie was sitting upright, her eyes surfing the waves, while Turbo was lying on his stomach, surfing the net on his laptop. He looked up at her.

"Can we snuggle now?" he pressed.

"No," she replied.

"Come on, we've cuddled a lot. Why not snuggle?"

"Just no."

"Getting too involved are ya, Skoob?" Melody prodded from nearby. "Warned ya." She wrapped a blanket around Darren and herself, then sighed wearily. "God, I'm so bored. Can't we go for a run or something?"

Darren kissed her forehead. "Enjoy the moment, Mel."

"Moment?" she groaned. "It's a friggin' eternity of boredom. Where are those damn turtles already?" She broke away from him and fell back on the beach, her arms in outstretched anguish.

Turbo looked at Skoobie again.

"How 'bout now?" he asked.

"How 'bout no," she replied.

Kelly smirked, then noticed Vanilla. She was huddled in a blanket, looking sadly at a piece of paper.

"You okay, Scoops?" she asked. "You've been staring at that all night."

Vanilla put it down. "Have I? Sorry. Didn't mean to be rude."

"No, it's fine," Kelly said back. "Is everything okay?"

Vanilla bit her lip. "Yes and no. It's my daughter's school report."

Melody sat up quickly. "Oh, geeze …"

"Second highest in the class," Vanilla continued. She put a hand to her mouth, sniffling. "And I'm not there to see it. I should be telling her how proud I am of her and I'm not there …"

Melody scrambled over, pulling the blanket off Darren as she went, and sat next to Vanilla, putting it over them both. Skoobie shifted in with another blanket, sitting on Vanilla's other side and wrapping all three of them up in it.

"Hey, can I have a blanket?" Turbo called. "You guys have got three and I've got none. It's getting cold."

"Huddle with him," Skoobie said, indicating Darren.

Turbo and Darren looked at each other, shuddering.

Melody took the report card from Vanilla. "Let's see here." She scanned it. "Oh, this is good. She's doing real well, Scoops. Sports could be a little better, but the rest is fine."

Vanilla sniffed. "I'm happy, believe me. She keeps asking where I am and when I'll see her again. I've got report cards, photos and everything else, but …"

"Ah, you'll see her soon," Melody cut in. "She and her brother'll come running up to you and that'll be it. There'll be no stopping 'em."

"When's that?" Vanilla countered. "When they're eighteen? I want them now, Mel. While they're still children."

"What about that sergeant?" David pressed. "What's her name? Vertigo. Can she help?"

"She's working on it," Vanilla replied, "just not fast enough." She choked back her tears. "All I want is to take my kids home. It's not asking for much." She bit her lip. "It's asking for … everything." She rested her head on Melody's shoulder, weeping.

Kelly gazed up at a shooting star. Insight kicked in and she focussed on the vital word Vanilla had said. Home. The sheer magic of the café couldn't have come from nowhere. There was more to the origins of these three girls. Much more. She was sure of it.

"So," she began cautiously. "Where *do* you guys come from? Really, I mean. Sure, you've got houses 'round here, but going by what you get up to, there's no way you're locals. So go on, spill. Where *is* home?"

Silence.

David's brow furrowed in thought.

Turbo looked up, interested.

Vanilla wiped her eyes and said to Melody, "She's darn good."

Melody made a face. "I hate that."

Vanilla paused. "You think we should tell her?"

Skoobie shrugged. "Up to you."

Silence.

"Fine," Melody said with a sigh. "Do it."

Vanilla drew a deep breath and addressed Kelly. "Okay, sweetie you got it." She paused again. "Mel, Skoob and I grew up, a long time ago, in a town called …" Her voice lowered and she spoke softly, "Sanders Crossing."

Kelly thought this over. "Oh—" she suddenly realised "—Sanders Crossing, Sanders Café. I get it."

"What's so secret about it?" Turbo piped up. "I can look it up." He patted the laptop.

"You won't find it," Vanilla said.

"Sure, I will," he replied. "I can find anything."

"Fine," Melody stated. "Go ahead. It's your tech's funeral."

He typed eagerly. The laptop whined, then whirred and died with a strange gurgling sound.

"Hey!" he cried. "What gives?"

"Not that," Vanilla answered. "It's not allowed to."

"Universal law," Skoobie added.

Turbo pulled out his phone.

"Do it junior, and it'll go the same way," Melody warned.

He slowly placed it face down on the sand, looking guilty.

"So what's your town's big secret?" Kelly pressed.

"Don't go there," Melody warned again.

Skoobie nodded. "Yeah, it'll blow your mind. For real."

Melody indicated Skoobie. "Look what happened to her and she only got a small blast …" She leaned her head in close to Vanilla's and they both said, " … *Snooping!*"

"Yep," Skoobie agreed. "Got burnt, big time. Mind-wiped too. Can't even remember what I saw. Still, made me what I am. Worth it."

Kelly shifted uncomfortably. "You guys are freaks."

"Hey, believe me, you're freaky to us," Melody retorted.

"Yeah, but this is crazy," Kelly said. "It's just a country town you guys came from, right?"

Vanilla spoke hesitantly. "More of a forest village. Skoob and I were waitresses in the tavern, until we went travelling with Mel, hitting the big wide world. We went home every now and then, but when trouble hit the Crossing we were ordered here."

"Ordered?" Kelly wondered. "By who?"

Vanilla pressed on. "The Crossing's … problem … was dealt with, but we've been asked to stay here."

"Once again, by who?" Kelly pushed.

Skoobie indicated Vanilla. "Café customers for one. They love her cooking."

"Wish they didn't," Melody grumbled. "I'd have kept travelling."

Darren grinned at Melody. "I'm glad you stayed."

Melody nodded back. "Yeah, you gotta point. Me too, babe."

Vanilla continued. "So you could say that we're like … ambassadors. Our home's here now. Along with friends and family."

Darren reached over, clasping Melody's hand. She gave a small smile, clutching his in return.

Vanilla went on. "The café's only part of our village's expansion. There's a few more tendrils out there but …"

"We're the best," Melody cut in. "Meaning the Crossing's coming to you, and you know what?" She beamed. "Here we are!"

"Ta da!" all three girls announced.

Kelly knew she wouldn't get any direct answers. Defeated, she snuggled into David. "Well, wherever your Crossing is, I'm glad you're here. You've changed my life."

Turbo gazed at Skoobie. "Hell, yeah."

Melody nudged her. "Get over there, Skoob."

Skoobie rolled her eyes and crawled over to him. He sat up eagerly as Melody tossed the blanket to Skoobie who put it over them both.

"Hands to yourself," she ordered.

He muttered, frustrated, under his breath.

Vanilla looked at Melody. "You can go back to Darren, if you want."

Melody dismissed this. "Nah, he's fine, aren't you, hon?"

"Sure am," came the reply.

"Besides," Melody continued, "he's there for me if I want him and … hey look! Turtle's here!"

Everyone watched as a large turtle crawled up onto the beach.

Skoobie's eyes widened and she spoke excitedly. "Margaret! It's Margaret!"

"You've met before?" Kelly asked. "Forget it. Why am I not surprised?"

The turtle shuffled along. They all rose and followed, keeping their distance.

Kelly was astounded. "She's the most beautiful thing I've ever seen."

"Yeah, me too," David agreed. "Apart from you that is."

"Oh, shut up." She elbowed him lightly, then stopped, startled. "You think I'm beautiful?"

"Look, she's digging a hole!" Melody said excitedly. "Oh come on, ya wimp! That's not the way. I can do it twice as fast."

"Your arms are twice as big," Kelly pointed out.

Turbo raised his phone. "I'll snap it into history."

"Snap us in too," Melody said eagerly, pulling Kelly and Vanilla into the shot. "Come on, Skoob!"

Skoobie strode in, joining them.

Vanilla beamed. "Everybody say cheesecakes!"

They all leaned in. Melody enthusiastic, Vanilla and Kelly happily, and Skoobie without a care in the world.

The picture snapped.

Turbo looked at the phone's image and grinned. "Perfect."

They all watched as the turtle kept digging. Vanilla and Skoobie were in awe. Kelly held David's hand in wonder. Melody, however, was shaken. She shuddered, filled with fear, before swallowing hard and drawing a trembling breath.

Darren rubbed her shoulders and kissed her forehead. "You okay?"

"Yeah." She looked up at him, nodding with a superficial grin. "Fine. What's up with you?"

"Nothing."

"Same goes. Don't ruin the moment, huh?"

He hugged her warmly. "Right now Mel, I don't think anything could ruin it."

Silence and peace followed.

Then the turtle exploded.

Chapter Eight

A flash illuminated the night. Everyone except Skoobie shielded their eyes as turtle goo flew in all directions, with most splashing on Kelly. As the flash dimmed and a large part of the shell thumped into the sand, they all looked up in stunned silence, too shocked to speak.

Kelly removed her glasses, wiping the slime off her face. "Somebody tell me what just happened."

"Turtle exploded," Skoobie replied.

"I know that, Skoob. Why?"

Melody huffed. "Well it wasn't 'cause it had laid its eggs and wanted to go out with a bang."

Vanilla sighed sadly. "Such a shame. On a perfect night too."

Turbo knelt, examining the shell.

David knelt beside him. "What've you got?"

Turbo shook the shell's remains. A charred metal chip fell out. He dropped the shell and picked up the twisted metal. "Looks like an explosive."

David peered in. "Yeah? How do you know that?"

"Saw it on Hawaii Five-0. The original, I mean."

Vanilla was horrified. "Ghastly! Who'd do a thing like that?"

Melody glanced around, then suddenly cried, "Look!"

Everyone followed her gaze to a ship out at sea, where a light flashed intermittently.

Turbo glanced at his chip. "Our explosive could've come from there. This thing's got a short lifespan once it hits the water so it can't travel a long way. It's a long shot but …"

"Totally worth it," Melody sparked up. "Let's get over there."

"And do what, cowboy?" Kelly countered. "Arrest 'em?"

Skoobie's face hardened. "We take 'em out."

"Agreed," Vanilla said.

"Whoa, whoa, whoa!" Kelly cut in. "I'm not going anywhere."

"You wanna stay here with the boys, be our guest," Melody replied.

"Don't we get a say in this?" Turbo asked.

"No," Melody, Vanilla and Skoobie all answered.

He turned away, grumbling.

"You get used to it," Darren told him. He looked at Melody. "I'll be waiting for you, hon. Be careful, and don't be too rough on the bad guys."

"Yeah right," she scoffed. "See ya soon, babe."

"Sure thing."

They kissed quickly, then she headed along the beach, followed by Vanilla.

Turbo faced Skoobie. "Well, this is it. We might never see each other again."

"Feed my snakes then," she said simply, and headed off as well.

"Don't I get a goodbye kiss?" he called.

"Ask Darren to do it for me," she called back.

Turbo looked at Darren and they both grimaced.

Kelly sighed and called to the others, "Oh hell, wait up for me! Someone's gotta look out for you guys." She headed after them.

"Hey," David said, pulling her back. She was about to respond when he kissed her lovingly on the lips, then broke away. "Take care."

"You're not coming?" she asked blankly, before the shock of his kiss hit her and she recoiled, feeling light-headed. "Whoaaaaaaaa …!"

He leaned in, holding her up.

She blinked and refocused. "Sorry. So you're staying here?"

"I think the four of you make enough magic for all of us," he replied.

She grinned. "Suck up. See you soon." She kissed him quickly and ran after the others.

"That's what I wanted," Turbo grumbled.

David looked at him.

"But not from her," Turbo corrected quickly. "Or you. From Skoob, I mean."

David looked back and watched with Turbo and Darren as the girls headed across the beach, with Melody leading the way.

"So," Kelly said as they strode down a slope, "how are we getting over there? I can't swim like you, Mel. Nobody can."

"No, and it's too slow," Melody replied, and pointed ahead. "We'll check out the shed on that pier. There might be something we can use."

Kelly put her glasses back on, having cleaned off the goo. "Yeah, but it's locked."

Skoobie pulled out a hairpin. "No problem, sis."

"Uh … breaking and entering?" Kelly reminded her.

"Uh … turtle exploded?" Skoobie countered. "Relax. We got this."

Kelly sighed and followed on.

The shed door opened with a long squeak and the four girls entered. Kelly peered into the shadows. Her eyes adjusted and she saw, that in the middle of the shed, bobbing in the ocean, was a speedboat.

Melody hurried over and jumped in eagerly. She searched around, picked up a note by the wheel and held it up. "Check this out."

Vanilla took it. "Good work, Mel."

"What's up?" Kelly asked, moving over.

Vanilla handed it to her. "Look. Counterfeit."

"Seriously?" She took it from her and examined it.

"Any more notes?" Melody asked.

"Not up here, Mel," Vanilla replied. "This isn't random though."

"Nothing is, everything's connected," Skoobie quipped.

Melody turned a knob near the boat's wheel. A static-filled whine rose from its speakers, then she looked at Vanilla. "Scoops?"

Vanilla listened hard. "Radio's tuned into the ship out there. They're both transmitting on the same frequency."

Kelly stared at her astounded. "Are you for real …?"

"Let's rock," Melody cut in, revving the boat.

The speedboat raced across the ocean, bouncing over the waves at full speed. Melody lapped it up excitedly while Kelly went as green as the turtle had been. Finally, they reached their destination and Melody slowed the boat.

"What have we got, Scoops?" she asked.

Vanilla raised her head and listened. "No one on board."

"Goin' in." She moved their boat closer, bringing it alongside it. "Ooooh, this is just like old times. This so brings back memories of Vietnam."

"Vietnam?" Kelly wondered.

"Here we go …"

Clank!

The boat gently hit the ship's side.

Vanilla picked up a rope, binding the two vessels. Melody reached out, grabbed the ship's metal ladder and started climbing. Vanilla went next, followed by Kelly, then finally Skoobie. Soon, they were all on board.

"Looks like a ghost ship," Kelly said.

Skoobie tapped the railing. "No, it's real enough." She paused. "Oh, right."

Melody headed to a metal flight of stairs and descended into the ship's depths, making for the rooms below.

Vanilla moved after her. "Stay on guard, Skoob."

"Yada," came the reply.

"For what?" Kelly wondered. "We're safe, aren't we?"

"Nada," Skoobie said, indicating a ship in the ocean getting steadily closer.

Kelly looked at Vanilla. "Can you hear who's on it?"

"Not with those sharks in the way …" Vanilla replied.

Skoobie's face lit up. "I love sharks!"

"… And it's mating season," Vanilla finished.

Kelly was astounded. "Sharks? Oh, this just gets better and better."

"Their love calls mess with my ears," Vanilla continued. "We'd better get Mel and get out of here."

She moved downstairs.

"One of these days Scoops …" Kelly muttered, then followed.

They reached the bottom, went through a narrow corridor and entered a room filled with large wooden crates. Melody was prying open one with a crowbar, then …

Crack!

She ripped the lid off, looked inside, pushed away the foam and picked up a gun. "Whoa! Check this baby out. Standard issue submachine gun. Ooooh this makes me hot."

Kelly trembled. "What the …?"

"Not as much as this flamethrower will," Vanilla added, picking up another weapon and turning it over. "We've got the works here. Grenades, rocket launchers—it's enough to start a war."

Kelly went white. "Uhhhhhhhhh … guys …"

"One thing's for sure," Melody said. "This isn't a ship; it's an offshore storage hold, meaning …"

Clang!

" … We've got company," she finished.

Vanilla listened. "They're climbing the ladder."

Melody grabbed a grenade.

Kelly shuddered. "You're not gonna use that?"

"Ah, it's just a little insurance if we need a distraction," Melody replied. "We'll take one each. Here, catch!"

She threw it at Kelly who yelped, desperately trying to grab it as it bounced in her hands.

Melody and Vanilla dived in, catching the grenade together and clasping their free hands over her mouth,

"Boy are you gonna suck in a warzone," Melody hissed.

Kelly smacked Melody's hand away, reluctantly put the grenade in her own pocket, and whispered, "What are we gonna do?"

"Relax," Vanilla said. "We've got the best weapon of all on board."

"What? A flamethrower?"

"No. Skoobie."

Skoobie sat on a crate on the top deck, watching as several heavily built men approached. She didn't even blink at the sight of their army pants, tank tops, military berets and Uzi's.

They stopped, then the tallest and broadest man with a dark moustache and beard approached her. He looked her over, then announced, "So, you are early. Welcome. I am Roberto Delasanata Ramirez."

"'Sup?" Skoobie replied.

"You have come alone?" he asked.

She indicated the empty deck. "See anyone else?"

"On behalf of Valtez?" he pressed.

"Looks that way, doesn't it?" She glanced at their guns. "Nice pieces. Won't need 'em here though."

He peered at her curiously. "There's always lying snakes in the grass."

"I prefer to keep 'em," she said simply.

He threw his head back, laughed long and loud, then slapped a hand on another man's shoulder. "I like this one. Her will is of steel. I can tell she is cold-blooded."

"Can tell you are too," Skoobie quipped.

He ignored her. "Your products are waiting in the storage hold. Shall we see them?"

Skoobie shrugged. "Yeah. Sure."

She stood up and they made for the stairs.

Vanilla wrenched the lid off another crate. "This one's empty."

"Get in," Melody ordered.

"There's only enough room for two," Kelly pointed out.

Melody ignored her. "I can take care of myself. Move!"

Kelly and Vanilla climbed in.

Melody hurried out the door and down the corridor.

When Ramirez entered the room with Skoobie and several men, it seemed like nothing had been touched. He strode to a crate.

"Here," he told Skoobie, "are our finest products. Straight from the Middle East. The most effective weapons in ground warfare today. You cannot get higher standards."

"Except peace," Skoobie countered.

They all looked at her.

"Show me what you got," she said.

He opened a crate, pulled out a submachine gun and offered it to her. "Would you like a hold?"

"No," she answered firmly. "How much you charging for that thing?"

"For you, everything here is five million dollars."

"Is that all?"

He grinned slyly. "I'm glad to see that money is no object to you."

"Never has been," she replied truthfully.

He reached over, picked up a small metal box and placed it on a larger one. Proudly, he opened the lid and pulled out a handful of metal squares.

"And here," he continued, "are our latest explosive devices. See how they look like scraps of metal. One inch by one inch, yet they have all the power of a grenade. We threw one into the ocean earlier to test it. A poor turtle gobbled it up. I hate to think where he is now."

He laughed, along with his people.

Skoobie wasn't amused.

"It's not funny to kill animals!" she fumed.

"Exactly," he confirmed. "We must concentrate on killing humans instead." He turned away. "Now, in this crate here …"

He stopped when he saw the lid slightly open. He ripped it off, threw it to one side, and watched as Kelly and Vanilla slowly rose from below.

Several guns targeted them.

"Who are you?" Ramirez snapped.

Vanilla answered, in a put-on accent. "Good evening. Ve are part of your package deal, yuh? Ve are your mail-order bride yummy-yums."

Silence.

Vanilla stamped on Kelly's foot.

Kelly nodded quickly in agreement. "Yah, yah, what she said."

Ramirez looked at Skoobie. "Did you know about this?"

"Nuh," she replied honestly.

He frowned. "So it's possible we have illegal immigrants? Or stowaways, perhaps?"

"Anything's possible," Skoobie agreed, thinking big.

"They are kind of cute, boss," one man said.

"You think I'm cute?" Kelly blurted out.

Vanilla kicked her lightly.

"What happened to your accent?" Ramirez asked.

Kelly spoke hurriedly. "I vas trying to sound more to your liking. You like, ya?"

"Oh, yes." He scanned Vanilla. "This one is perfection." He looked Kelly over. "This one … eh?" He shrugged. "Bit skinny. Not much bouncy-bounce. Looks like a virgin too."

Kelly gasped.

Vanilla kicked her harder.

"However," the man conceded, "I am willing to educate her. Give us a kiss."

"Oh no!" Kelly cut in hastily. "I do not kiss on the first mail order … mmmff!"

She arched back and her eyes widened as he kissed her long and hard on the lips. She struggled wildly against his alcoholic breath and smacked him several times, to no avail. Finally, he broke it off and backed away, leaving her to suck in a huge breath of air.

"Needs experience," the man concluded. "Feels like she'd be lousy in the sack."

Kelly's jaw dropped.

"Is there somewhere ve can freshen up?" Vanilla asked quickly.

Ramirez indicated the corridor. "Quarters are that way. Sanchez! Go with them. Get them undressed. Move!"

"What?" Kelly cried, horrified. "No, wait …"

She yelped as she and Vanilla were pulled out of the crate and pushed into the corridor.

"So," Ramirez said, turning to Skoobie. "Five million is good enough for you?"

"If you say so," she answered.

Clang!

His head rose to the noise from outside.

A man ran in. "Boss, a boat's just pulled up. Valtez has arrived. Says he's come to make a buy."

Ramirez looked at Skoobie. "What is this?"

"Hey, you're running the show," she replied. "I'm just here for the ride."

He grabbed her arm, pulling her out the door.

A short time later, Ramirez, Skoobie and several men arrived on the top deck to find a big bear of a man, flanked by two more, approaching.

Ramirez and his people stopped. "Ah, Valtez. How very good to see you."

The man, Valtez, also stopped. "You too, Ramirez. I have kept our agreement as planned." He nodded at Skoobie. "Who is this?"

"I was hoping you could tell me," Ramirez replied. "She was here when we arrived. Said she was interested in buying our stock."

Skoobie frowned. "Did I? Actually, I'm pretty sure I never said that …"

"What is she doing here then?" Valtez pressed. "Is she an envoy sent by Jack?"

Several guns aimed at Skoobie. "Well?"

Skoobie sighed. "You want the truth?"

"Yes," he ordered. "The truth."

"Okay, here it is …" She took a deep breath and said, "I'm here to investigate an exploding turtle."

Ramirez got ready to blow.

"Clothes off!" Sanchez ordered Kelly and Vanilla.

The two girls stood by a large double bed.

"Look, I think there's been a mistake …" Kelly began, dropping her accent.

"Now!" Sanchez barked.

Kelly indicated her body. "You actually wanna see *this*?"

"He's a guy," Vanilla said, also in her normal voice. "If it's female and it wiggles …"

"Double crap …"

Kelly took her jacket off. An object was caught in it. She shook it quickly.

The grenade dropped to the floor, minus the pin.

Vanilla dived on Kelly, sending them both flying out the door as the grenade exploded.

Ramirez and everyone except Skoobie struggled to keep their balance as the boat rocked.

"What is this?" Valtez snapped. He glanced at Skoobie. "Did she come alone?"

"No," Ramirez answered. "Two mail-order brides are here as well."

"How do we know she is not one?"

"Could be if you wanted," Skoobie replied. "Universe is full of possibilities."

"That doesn't answer the question," Ramirez pressed. "Are you a mail-order bride?"

"As of right now, yes."

"Do not try my patience!"

"Didn't know you had any. Oh, check that out …"

She stepped to the side, entranced by the shark fins out at sea, just as he struck out hard. The swing went wide, hitting Valtez.

"Watch it!" Valtez snapped, returning the smack.

Ramirez smacked him back. "No! You watch it!"

They fell into a struggle, with the mercenaries circling them.

Unseen by anybody, Skoobie put her hands in her pockets and walked away.

Kelly looked into the smoking room where the unconscious Sanchez lay. "Did I kill him?"

Vanilla listened. "No. He's still breathing and his heart's beating."

"Thank God! How's my jacket?"

"Gone."

"Oh, no way …"

"Forget it sweetie, let's get out of here."

They rose to their feet and moved down the corridor.

A mercenary stepped out in front of them, raising his gun.

Smack!

He fell like a stone.

Melody emerged from behind him, brandishing a golf club.

Kelly exhaled, relieved. "Where have you been?"

Melody waved away the grenade's smoke. "Rigging things up to get us out of here. Nice work by the way."

"It was an accident," Kelly said back.

"Uh-huh," Melody and Vanilla replied, heading down the corridor.

"No seriously guys, it was an accident …"

She ran after them.

"Wait, wait, wait!" Valtez cried, still struggling with Ramirez.

Ramirez stopped. "What?"

"The girl? Where is she?"

They looked around, seeing no sign of Skoobie, then quickly untangled themselves and ran across the deck.

Skoobie strode past a cabin door, heading for the ship's rear.

A mercenary rounded the corner, stopped at the sight of her and raised his gun.

She cut in before he could speak. "I think your boss is looking for you. Could be urgent …"

"Right."

He ran past her, headed around the corner and was gone.

" … For him," she finished. "Everyone needs someone in life and he's desperately lonely. You might be good together."

Satisfied, she strode on.

Ramirez, Valtez, and their mercenaries headed to the ship's edge and bumped into the man that Skoobie had just spoken to.

"You wanted to see me, boss?" he asked Ramirez.

Ramirez nearly exploded. "Here is the real buyer!" he snapped, indicating Valtez. "The girl is an imposter. Get her!"

"Right, boss." He was about to turn away when he suddenly cried, "Look!"

Ramirez and Valtez turned to see Melody, Vanilla and Kelly on the opposite side of the deck, ready to climb down the ladder for their speedboat.

Several mercenaries ran over, guns raised.

The girls stopped.

Ramirez and Valtez approached, satisfied.

"Well, well, well," Ramirez said. "So what have we here? Rats trying to desert a sinking ship?"

"It ain't sinking yet," Melody retorted. "Soon will be though. Whole place is rigged." She raised a device. "One press, hotshot. Let us go, or we *all* go. Your choice."

Ramirez sneered.

Melody glared at him. "Drop the guns!"

Silence.

"Do it!"

Ramirez nodded to his men. Slowly, they laid their weapons on the deck.

Melody glanced at Kelly and Vanilla. "Go for it."

Kelly climbed over the ship's edge, needing no further prompting. Vanilla followed, then …

"There is just one thing," Valtez began.

"Really, deadhead?" Melody shot back. "What?"

He lowered his collar, revealing a long scar. "You gave this to me in Turkey."

Melody's face dropped.

He drew himself up to his full height. "My name is Santos Rodrigues Valtez, formerly a sniper for Al-Qaeda …"

"Oh shi …!" She leapt over the side of the ship as he pulled a gun from his pocket and fired. The bullet barely missed her temple as she dropped like a stone, pressing a button on her device as she hit the water.

Vanilla and Kelly leapt off the ladder, plummeting after her.

Bang!

Several sections of the ship exploded, blowing a few men out to sea. The vessel rocked violently as one end dipped, sinking into the water with the men's bodies as blood billowed from their wounds.

Valtez pulled out a hunting knife, put it in his teeth, and dived into the ocean after Melody.

Not far off, one of Valtez's men ran in for Skoobie, growling.

"Don't blame me, blame him," she said, glancing at Ramirez across the sloping deck. "This is his fault."

The man snarled and ran off.

She moved on.

One of Ramirez's men ran up to her, raising his gun.

"Yeah, we don't have time for that," she quipped, indicating Ramirez with a quick nod. "Someone's about to kill your boss."

Ramirez's man looked ahead, then quickly ran off.

Skoobie walked on.

A third man stepped in front of her.

"Valtez or Ramirez?" she asked.

"Valtez," he replied.

"You'd better go," she told him. "Your buddy's in trouble over there."

He bolted away.

Coolly, Skoobie strode off.

Kelly burst up through the water, splashing, spluttering and just managing to grab her sinking glasses. She blinked hard as Vanilla surfaced. Together, they swam desperately for the speedboat and had barely got anywhere when a mercenary suddenly rose from below, wrapping a large arm around Kelly's neck. She struggled wildly, then …

Whoosh!

A massive shape swept by, casting her to the side and grabbing the man. She quickly regained her senses, looked ahead, and shrieked in terror.

A great white shark.

Her body went into overdrive, making for the speedboat.

Melody surfaced behind her and started to follow but was pulled down hard.

Valtez.

Kelly's heart thumped in terror.

High above, several more explosions rocked the ship.

Melody and Valtez struggled beneath the surface, clutching Valtez's knife. The blade pressed against Melody's throat, piercing her skin and causing a trickle of blood.

The shark rushed in.

Summoning up her strength, she kicked him off her and flipped over in a backwards somersault, leaving the shark to sweep between them. She moved hard and fast, making for the surface, and was almost there when another shark surged in.

She arched back, kicking it on the nose and startling it. The beast veered to the side, hitting her on the way. She rolled over in a nauseating spin before regaining her senses and making for the surface again. Finally, she broke through, sucked in a deep breath of air, and saw that the ship had almost sunk. Nearby, Ramirez and his men were clambering onto their own speedboat.

"Mel!" Kelly called from behind Vanilla, now on their speedboat from the boatshed. "Over here!"

Melody swam towards them in long strokes. She was nearly there when Valtez suddenly erupted through the water, grabbed her by the neck and aimed his knife at her chest. Furiously, she grabbed his wrist, twisted it sideways and plunged the knife down, ramming it into his shoulder. He roared as she kicked herself off him and swam for the boat through his blood waves.

"Get on!" Kelly cried.

"Now!" Vanilla yelled.

Melody reached the boat and climbed up the side. She was halfway on when Valtez fiercely leapt out of the sea for her and then …

Smack!

The shark raced off, clutching him in its jaws.

Melody rolled on board. "Go, go, go …!"

Vanilla revved the engine and they sped off.

Kelly knelt before Melody. "You okay?"

Melody panted, gazing at her stomach. "Gotta get to a hospital."

"You hurt?" Kelly asked.

"It's not me I'm worried about …"

"We got company!" Vanilla called, looking back.

Kelly followed her gaze. Ramirez's speedboat was racing after them. Several shots made her and Vanilla duck, then she peered up, seeing that the large ship had now completely sunk.

"Hey," she wondered, "where's Skoob?"

Skoobie sat between two mercenaries at the rear of the pursuing speedboat. Several more were in front of her, while Ramirez steered. She wasn't surprised that no one had noticed her slip on board. They were too focussed on themselves.

She looked to the side, seeing more shark fins rising in the ocean, attracted by the wavering blood.

A man wiped his bloodied brow with a handkerchief, then lowered it, resting his arm on the boat's edge. A sudden jolt sent Skoobie lurching into him, making him drop the handkerchief into the water.

"Whoops," she said.

She rose and moved up to Ramirez, tapping his shoulder.

He glanced at her, spitting, "You!"

A shark breached for the boat. She nodded at it and said, "Turtle's revenge. Karma, babe."

She leapt over the side just as the great white beast dropped directly on him.

Smack!

The boat went under.

Vanilla stopped her speedboat and looked back as the sharks went into a feeding frenzy.

Kelly tensed as a giant fin surged through the water for them, but then frowned when she saw Skoobie holding onto it. The shark swept at the boat, leapt in the air, flew over it and snapped at Kelly who screamed and recoiled.

Skoobie rolled off its back, landing in the boat. "'Sup?"

The shark fell into the sea and swam away.

"Get us outta here!" Melody ordered.

Vanilla nodded and revved the engine.

The boat shot off.

They soon outran the sharks and approached the beach. They were almost at the jetty when a searchlight hit them. The whirring blades of a police chopper followed.

"Freeze! This is the Water Police! You are surrounded! Repeat, you are surrounded! Lower your weapons!"

Melody reached into her pocket, pulling out a grenade she'd pinched from the ship. She failed to notice that the pin had loosened in her undersea struggles with Valtez and tossed it over the side. It hit the sea, the pin came loose and the grenade exploded, sending a torrent of water shooting high.

Kelly cringed. "Oh crap …"

***

Sergeant Donna Vertigo slapped four folders down onto the table of the police interview room. Before her, sat Melody, Vanilla, Kelly and Skoobie. All except Skoobie were looking sombre.

Vertigo was ready to explode.

"Welcome back!" she snapped.

Silence. Then:

"I'm innocent, I swear …!" Kelly began.

"Shut it!" Vertigo growled, pointing at her. "Just shut your mouth or I *will* use police brutality, I swear to God! Rules be damned!"

Kelly shut up.

The tension mounted.

Vertigo rubbed her eyes wearily. "It's three in the morning." She took a deep breath. "Dare I ask what happened?"

It was Skoobie who answered. "Well, this turtle exploded and …"

A file flew over her head, hitting the wall.

"Why does no one believe me when I say that?" Skoobie grumbled.

Vertigo composed herself. "Let's start at the beginning. One derelict ship was sunk …"

"Yeah, that was her," Skoobie said, indicating Melody, "and that's not the beginning, that's the end."

Vertigo continued. "Several mercenaries were caught in a shark-feeding frenzy …"

"That was her," Melody said back, indicating Skoobie.

"On behalf of the turtle," Skoobie pointed out.

Vertigo went on. "All of you tried to evade police capture …"

"Guilty," Vanilla said, raising her hand. "Was only thinking of my kids."

"Not your fault, Scoops," Kelly told her. "I believe Mel's exact words were, 'we can outrun the bastards. They can't do nothing and are useless anyway.'"

Melody huffed, then glared at Vertigo. "So what's yankin' your chain, chief? We did you a favour. Thanks to us, a whole stash of weapons primed for a terrorist attack are now on the ocean floor. Thanks to us, a gang of rogue psychos have either been killed or captured. Thanks to us, lady, there's a ton of people sleeping peacefully in their beds tonight 'cause *we've* just done the job that *you* should have been doing. Right?"

There was a long, long pause, then Vertigo spoke slowly. "That ship, despite being old and tattered, was a sentimental monument. It belonged to the Indonesian President. He regarded it as a treasure because it was the last thing his parents gave him before being brutally slaughtered. You've just sunk it."

Kelly gulped loudly.

"Still doesn't change things," Melody retorted. "There were weapons on board, deals going on, and a good chance that innocent people were going to get hurt, so don't get miffed at us. We've fixed things for you. What's the problem?"

Vertigo opened a file. "Believe it or not, ladies, other agencies were already onto this before you stumbled in. The vessel had been stolen by the Indonesian President's son-in-law. He'd had an argument with his father and rebelled against him by getting involved with the mercenaries."

"So what?" Melody grumbled. "We got there first."

"Uh, no you didn't," Vertigo corrected. "The ship was tracked over thousands of kilometres. Rough weather made our federal authorities lose it, temporarily. Had they not, a raid would have followed and things would have been dealt with quietly and efficiently."

Melody scoffed. "So we miffed a few mercenaries – big deal."

"No, you miffed the CIA," Vertigo countered. "The media's also got wind of it and this thing's gone global."

Kelly put her face in her hands.

Vanilla folded her arms and averted her gaze, looking guilty.

Vertigo continued coldly. "You're sunk deeper than that boat, and to make matters even *worse*, the Indonesian President's son-in-law was a shark victim, care of *you* guys."

"Stop!" Kelly cried tearfully. "Please stop! I don't want to get deported …!"

"Oh, I'm just getting started!" Vertigo snapped. "That shipment of arms you sunk …"

"Oh God …!"

"… was meant for an assassin named Jack who's NUTS's latest recruit. Valtez was going to buy the weapons from Ramirez, and then sell them to Jack for a profit, only Jack was planning on paying in counterfeit notes. Now you've made Jack, and NUTS, even more paranoid by bringing global attention to 'em, so they've sent a message to us, promising to up the stakes of terrorism. I've got a copy of their email from two hours ago. It's alongside all the other messages from the Indonesian government, our own Prime Minister, the CIA Director, and the United States President. All our countries now have strained diplomatic relations and it's *all* thanks to *you* four!"

By now, Kelly was sobbing hysterically. "It was just a poor, innocent little turtle …!"

Vanilla raised her hand again. "Can I just say something?"

Vertigo glared at her. "What?"

"Will this affect my court case?"

Vertigo nearly blew. Keeping her anger in check, she said, "That's up to the CIA. They've got your names."

"Cool, we're famous," Skoobie quipped.

Melody was unfazed. "It's fine – the CIA and I go way back. It'll all be sorted once I get in contact with Mitch Mailstrom."

Vertigo flipped a page over. "Yeah, he thought you might be involved. He's flying in to talk to you personally. You'll be lucky if you're not thrown into Guantanamo Bay for this."

Kelly crumpled over the table, wailing in despair.

Skoobie reached over, patting her head gently.

Melody waved Vertigo away flippantly. "Ah, place is a hotel. Security's terrible. Broke out three times."

Vertigo ignored her. "Lastly, Turbo Newcombe. We still want answers from him. Where is he?"

"Hey yeah," Skoobie realised. "Where is the little guy?"

"Probably ran like hell," Melody muttered.

"We'll get him," Vertigo said. "It also means that anyone linked with you makes 'em a target. Therefore, we've no option but to close your café until further notice."

Melody and Vanilla cried out in horror, while even Skoobie's jaw dropped.

"No way!" Melody protested.

"That's harsh," Vanilla added. "Dangerous too."

"Game's bigger than you think," Skoobie pressed, "and it sure aint in your hands, lady. Never was."

Kelly's head rose, sniffing. "Unemployed again."

"Makes no difference – we weren't gonna pay you anyway," Skoobie said.

Kelly was shocked. "What?"

"We'd have looked after you with food and stuff."

"But I need money!"

"Money, pfffft!" Skoobie scoffed.

"Yeah, we don't work like that, honey," Vanilla said.

Kelly was confused. "But I've seen your account books. I've heard you talk about making it …"

"Yeah, to give to the poor."

"Which gives us reason for a full investigation," Vertigo pressed. "We're going over the place ASAP. Welcome to scrutiny-central, girls."

Melody smacked the table; Vanilla lowered her head and Skoobie pursed her lips.

Kelly rubbed her eyes tearfully. "And to think I nearly had a threesome with a friggin' pirate for this."

"Can it!" Melody snapped. "This is serious."

"Oh, get real!" Kelly sobbed.

"We were trying to until bulldog face here closed the most important place on earth!"

Vertigo made for the door. "Sorry, that's the way it goes. My buddies'll be in shortly. You'll stay out of my way too if you're smart."

She left the room, closing the door loudly.

Kelly choked back the tears. "Jail, Guantanamo Bay, what are my parents gonna think? This is nuts."

"You got that right," Melody huffed. "This *is* NUTS, and we're copping the …"

"Language," Vanilla warned.

"… blame," Melody finished. "We need to go on the offensive. Hey, now that we've got all this free time, I've got a plan …"

"No!" Kelly cried, leaping up. "I'm sick of this crap. Being without a job was bad enough but now this? Forget it!"

"Hey, don't blame us, blame NUTS!" Melody shot back. "They're the bad guys!"

"They didn't get me here!"

"Yeah, in a roundabout way, they did!"

Kelly made for the door. "No! You're bad news. This is wrong. All wrong. I need space. I gotta go. See ya later …"

She opened the door and left.

Silence followed. Then:

"Are we allowed to leave?" Skoobie wondered.

"No," Melody and Vanilla answered.

The door opened, Vertigo threw Kelly back in, slammed the door shut and locked it.

"See?" Kelly wept. "Can't even leave properly." She grabbed a chair, put it in the opposite corner, and sat facing the wall, her arms folded. "Don't anyone come near me."

Skoobie opened her mouth to speak.

"Shut up, Skoob!" Kelly called.

Skoobie's mouth closed.

Melody sighed, defeated. "Better make the most of it I s'pose. Who's in for a power nap?"

"Thrumber?" Vanilla asked.

"Thrumber," Skoobie agreed.

The three stood up, went to the back of the room, sat on the floor and huddled against the wall, with Vanilla in the middle. Melody zonked out instantly. Vanilla placed her head against Melody's, while Skoobie leaned in on Vanilla's shoulder. Soon, all three were sleeping contentedly, with Skoobie letting out strange, whistle-like snores.

Kelly sniffed, looking up at the ceiling.

"What have we done?" she sobbed. "God, what have we done?"

Chapter Nine

Interrogations followed. Details were scrutinised in one-on-one grillings with Kelly, Melody and Vanilla. No one wanted to touch Skoobie. Anyone who tried came out banging their heads against the wall and screaming in frustration. Finally, a hardened CIA marine went in.

"Careful in there," Melody warned him.

"You don't know me," he scoffed.

"You don't know Skoob," she countered.

Four hours later he came out and quit his job altogether.

After countless hours of questioning, all four girls were finally allowed to leave the station. Melody knew it was a ploy for everyone to keep them under surveillance but didn't care. Skoobie even less so. Vanilla's ears, however, were still ringing from her bellowing interrogation, while her thoughts were only on her children.

Kelly's head was also pounding as they glumly walked away from the cop shop, knowing that her three friends could shake any watchers off easily. Despite this, her heart was as heavy as hell and she was more annoyed at them than ever for digging her into this crap. She wiped her eyes and headed off, hugging herself tightly.

"Hey!" Melody called. "Where ya goin'?"

"Away from you!" Kelly shot back.

"It's not safe," Melody warned. "NUTS are on the warpath, remember?"

"Yeah, and now thanks to you I've got the whole world against me!"

"'Course," Skoobie confirmed. "Gravity holds us onto this planet, protecting us from a spatial power vacuum, thereby limiting our abilities, meaning the whole planet literally sucks. That's life."

"Get stuffed!"

"We already are," Skoobie continued. "If we weren't these giant wet walking conscious bags, then we'd be ghosts floating 'round the place, meaning the whole of life really is stuffed ... with stuff."

"Shut up, Skoob!"

"Yeah, we're that too," Skoobie pressed on. "See 'cause we're so limited on this world, we really are shut up in it meaning ..."

Melody and Vanilla smacked her lightly.

Skoobie stared at Melody. "What?"

Melody threw her arm up, annoyed.

Skoobie lowered her head. "Fine. Live in denial."

Vanilla looked at them. "Everybody relax. We need to stick together, now more than ever."

Skoobie opened her mouth to start explaining the chemical makeup of the human body and how everyone really *does* stick together when ...

"Don't start!" Melody warned, holding her finger up.

Skoobie closed it again.

"Exactly," Vanilla agreed. "We need to be here. For Kelly's sake."

Skoobie looked ahead. "Then where is she?"

They followed her gaze. There was no sign of her.

"Oh great!" Melody scoffed. "She's split. I'll go get her ..."

"No," Vanilla cut in, raising her hand. "If we want this to work, she'll need time. She's already proved she can take care of herself. We need to get to the café. I dread to think what the police are doing to it."

"Hang on," Melody interjected. "*I* give the orders. I'm the leader, remember?"

"Yeah, but I'm the oldest, the most mature and I run the café," Vanilla corrected. "Meaning *I'm* the leader."

"Wrong, babes," Skoobie further corrected. "I'm the one who's got a psychic hotline to the head honchos. That makes *me* the boss."

"Oh you ...!" Melody began.

They headed off, arguing.

Kelly went home and lay on her bed for much of the day. She didn't care that NUTS were after her. Let them come, she figured. Her life was a mess anyway.

Sometimes she slept. Mostly she didn't. She'd never felt so alone. Her high school friends were out of town, along with her family. There was no point working on her resume. Why bother when the federal agencies controlled her life, blocking her every move?

After a time, she groggily headed into the kitchen, pulled out a container of ice-cream, took it into the lounge, sat on the couch, and turned on the TV to watch an afternoon soap. She sat there for some time, engrossed in it, and just as the end credits were rolling, there came a knock at the door. She fell sideways with a groan and put her head in her hands, thinking it was Melody, Vanilla and Skoobie.

"Get lost!" she called wearily.

"Sure," David called back. "I'll drop by later."

She sat up, her heart pounding. "Crap! I friggin' forgot I had a friggin' boyfriend!"

She rose in a flash, hurried to the door and opened it.

"Hi," she said softly, at the sight of David.

"Hi," he replied.

Silence.

"You've got ice-cream on your lip," he pointed out. "Just there."

She covered her mouth and reached for a tissue box on the side table. She pulled on the tissue, but it refused to come out. She pulled harder, growing frustrated. Finally, she pulled as hard as she could. Half the tissues came out, the box flew across the room, hit a lamp, and both dropped heavily to the floor.

She waved it away. "I'd offer you ice-cream but I just finished the whole container."

He saw what she was wearing. "I like your Elmo pyjamas too."

"Oh yeah, I'll get changed …"

"No, you're fine like that," he replied, then peered at her. "Then again, you're not fine at all are you, Kelly Morrison?"

"Me?" she retorted. "Oh no, I'm great. No job, criminal record, no one around …"

"I'd like to think I'm still your boyfriend …"

"… Ditzy as hell…"

He smiled. "Would you like to take a ride up the coast? I've got the bike here."

She sighed wearily. "The girls send you after me again?"

"Not this time," he answered. "Honest to God. Though I did hear how bad things are. It's all over the news."

"Must have missed that bit," she grumbled. "God knows how …"

"Things are dangerous too," he warned. "You shouldn't be here."

"Oh, no, not at home, god forbid," she scoffed. "All I wanted was a job and a normal life and look at me. An unemployed ditz who's just annoyed a psycho terrorist group and caused a whole stack of diplomatic tension …"

"In a way, that's funny."

"Glad *you* think so."

"Oh, I do. You can't see it right now, but one day you'll look back on this whole thing and laugh." He paused. "You are so beautiful you know."

"Oh, shut up …"

"No I mean it. Little Kelly Morrison standing in her doorway in her Elmo pyjamas having just wallowed in a ton of ice-cream. It's the most gorgeous thing ever."

She looked away, blushing, then relented. "Alright, let's go for a ride. I'll feel better once I get out of this place."

She headed out the door.

"Don't you want to get changed first?" he asked.

She grabbed his hand, pulling him away. "You know what? I don't think I do. Screw it."

They headed off.

Kelly snuggled into David, holding him tightly as they sat on a grass slope, overlooking the beach. The cool breeze wavered by as they talked. Time passed with the gentle winds and soon she found herself telling him everything, and not just about recent events. She opened up more than she had to anyone, about her childhood, her family dramas, and all the ongoing garbage in her miserable life, as she saw it.

He sat, listening, as she cried herself out, and once her crying was done, she'd never felt more at peace. The sun fell, leaving her to absorb every moment of the heavenly sunset, before she drifted off to sleep in his arms. When she awoke, the sun was rising, and they watched as it ascended over the cool, empty beach.

She clasped his hand warmly.

"Thank you," she said softly. "For being here for me."

He clasped hers back, equally so. "You're welcome. Anything to make you feel better."

She kissed his hand. "God, this is the weirdest time of my whole life." She smiled dreamily. "But also the best."

"Me too."

They kissed tenderly, then slowly parted.

He caught sight of his watch and his face fell. "Damn."

"What is it?" she asked, sitting up.

"I've gotta go to work," he answered.

Her hand rose to her mouth, horrified. "Oh God, I'm sorry. You won't be able to focus …"

"Sure I will," he replied. "Better than ever. This was worth every second and I'd do it again."

"I so do not deserve you." She rubbed his shoulder. "Do what you have to. I'll be waiting."

"I'll look forward to it." He kissed her forehead. "Vanilla lives down the street. House number seven. You'll be safe there."

She nodded. "Yeah. I'll be fine."

He stood up. "Come on, I'll take you over."

"No, it's okay. I'll walk."

"Seriously?"

"Yeah. Seriously."

She rose and they hugged.

"Have a good day, Kelly Morrison."

"You too."

They kissed once more.

"Take care," she said.

"Same goes," he told her.

He turned, walked to his bike and put his helmet on. They gave each other a wave before he revved the bike and headed away.

Now feeling like the weight of the world had been lifted off her shoulders, she walked along the path overlooking the beach, listening to the seagulls squawking above and the waves crashing below. She drifted freely, gazing dreamily out at the morning whilst heading along the path's rising and falling slopes. She went for some way before a police car rolled up, stopping beside her.

"Morning," the policeman said curiously.

"Morning," she replied blissfully. She took a deep breath. "Beautiful day, isn't it?"

"Sure is," he responded. "Where ya headed?"

She gazed at the sky happily. "Oh, wherever the wind takes me …"

"Uh-huh." He opened the door and stepped out of the car, moving beside her. "Are you okay?"

"Sure. Why?"

"Do I have to answer that?"

She turned to him, taken aback. "Uh … yeah. What have I done?"

"Well, when I'm driving along the beach this early in the morning and I see a girl walking dreamily along in her Elmo pyjamas, it kind of gets me thinking …"

Kelly looked down at herself, horrified. "Oh … crap!"

"Are you from the hospital?" he asked. "They're missing a patient this morning … "

Kelly's mouth overtook her mind. "No, it's not like that. My boyfriend drove me here. We were in trouble with the law yesterday …"

"I see …"

"… after that turtle exploded, the pirates attacked and we got a couple of countries mad at us …"

He took her by the arm. "I think you'd better come with me …"

"No, wait," she protested. "I know it sounds bad, but it's true …"

"I'm sure it is. This way please …"

He guided her to his patrol car.

She pulled herself free. "Officer …"

"I'm listening …"

She spoke from the heart. "I've had a really bad couple of days and I just want to go home, okay?"

He stared at her, unimpressed. "Where's that? The moon?"

"No, it's …" She caught sight of the beach house across the road. To her relief, Vanilla was entering through the front gate, pulling a set of keys from her handbag.

"There!" Kelly said hurriedly. "I live there! Come talk to my flatmate. She'll tell you everything."

She broke away from him, hurrying across the street.

"Hey!" he called, following her.

"Scoops!" Kelly cried, running after Vanilla who was climbing the steps to her front door. "Down here!"

Vanilla stopped, turned and smiled at her, then noticed the cop. "Oh, hey sweetie. Who's your friend?"

Kelly spoke quickly. "I just had the best night on the beach with David. God, Scoops, it was so good, but I didn't bother changing. Now this cop thinks I'm totally mental."

"Ah, we're all a little crazy, sweet stuff, don't worry about it."

The officer indicated Kelly to Vanilla. "Does she live here?"

Kelly glanced at Vanilla to indicate yes.

Vanilla submitted, raising her arms happily. "Home is where the heart is."

The officer looked doubtfully at Kelly. "Yeah well, you just behave yourself."

"Thanks," Kelly said relieved. "Hey, are you single?"

He glared at her.

She motioned to Vanilla. "For my friend here."

Vanilla smacked her lightly.

"Kids," he sighed, and walked away.

Vanilla patted her arm warmly. "Come inside, we'll get you changed. You can't stay long though. I've gotta see my lawyer. I'm in more trouble than ever after last night."

Kelly followed her up the steps. "I'm sorry, Scoops."

Vanilla turned to her. "For what?"

"For that and …" She paused. "For going off at you and Mel and Skoob like that. I thought you guys had screwed up my life completely, leaving me with no family or friends." She paused again, feeling her insides tingle. "I was wrong. Guess I got both."

Vanilla squealed and hugged her delightedly. "You got that right." She clutched Kelly's forearm, rubbing it. "You were also a little stirred up with all that terrorist and diplomatic incident stuff, but honestly sweetie, don't worry about it. These things happen. Come on in."

She led her inside.

Kelly found that Vanilla had very little in her beach apartment. It was small and cramped, and everything, though spotless, looked second-hand.

What stood out most were the pictures of her children, along with photocopies of their schoolwork pinned all over the place.

"Sophie got this the other day," Vanilla said proudly, tapping a copy of an English test on the fridge. "Top of the class. Isn't it great?"

"Fantastic," Kelly replied, truthfully.

"Jamie also came third in his running race. He's a little frustrated from what I hear but he'll get there. He just needs that extra push."

Kelly smiled. "You must be really proud of them."

"Oh, I am," Vanilla said back, touching a framed photo of her children. "It's Jamie's birthday next week. Gotta pick up his present tomorrow. I'm paying it off bit by bit, but listen to me rattle on about myself. How are things with you and David?"

"They'd have been better if he didn't have to go to work," Kelly muttered.

"Oh right," Vanilla realised. "You're feeling a little juicy."

Kelly tensed awkwardly. "It's deeper than that, Scoops. I was upset last night. He came by, we spent the night on the beach, and it was heaven."

"Oh, that's wonderful, honey," Vanilla beamed, rubbing her shoulder. "I'm so happy for you. I also think it's great you stayed in your pyjamas. You're really loosening up."

Kelly sighed. "Uh, yeah. Have you got something else I could wear? I don't want to get arrested again."

"Don't worry, sweetie, I've got just the thing …"

Shortly after, Kelly stared at herself in the mirror, horrified. She now wore a long blue dress with flowers and puffed-up shoulder pads, and grimaced as Vanilla gleefully placed a pearl necklace around her neck.

"This looks like something straight out of 1866!" Kelly protested.

"Sorry, but just about everything else is being washed," Vanilla replied, "and you're right. This one belonged to my grandma. You're a year or two out, but that's okay."

Kelly ignored her. "I'll be a laughingstock. This'll get me carted off to the old folks' home for sure. Don't you have anything else I can wear?"

"Only some jeans and an old shirt."

"Great, I'll take those."

Vanilla peered out the window. "Oh, that's my bus coming down the street. Gotta go. Can't turn up to court late, especially after all that's happened. Nice of you to drop by …"

"Scoops …"

Kelly's protests were drowned out as she was bundled out the front door which was quickly locked behind her.

"I hate this dress," Kelly said as they hurried down the steps.

"It'll keep you safe from NUTS," Vanilla said back. "Nice disguise, don't you think?"

"Yeah, 'cause I look like one of 'em. Aren't you worried they'll come here?"

"Not with the security system I have, sweet stuff. It's outta this world."

"For real?"

"No, it's *un*-real. Literally. Best there is."

Kelly dismissed this, knowing she wouldn't get a straight answer. "Sure I can't come with you, Scoops?"

"No, but thanks for thinking of me, sweetie. Really appreciate it." She turned, kissed Kelly on the cheek, then hurried along again. "My little home might be safe but it's awful lonely by yourself. If you need a friend, there's always Skoob."

"Pass."

Vanilla ran up to the bus and flagged it down. "Well Mel's house is in the next street, right at the end on the corner. She's working out at home today. Why not head there?" The bus stopped, its door opened with a hiss and she entered.

The kids on board caught sight of Kelly and snickered. Several more ran to the window to stare at her.

"Hey lady, who's your mum?" one asked Vanilla.

Kelly covered her face, embarrassed.

Vanilla smacked him playfully. "Quiet, you."

An old lady smiled. "I think she looks very nice."

"Yeah –" the kid giggled "– with those fluffy bunny slippers she's got on."

Kelly looked down. "Oh … crap!"

She'd put them on for comfort in Vanilla's house and forgotten to ask about a spare pair of shoes.

Everyone laughed as the door hissed closed.

Vanilla took a seat, giving her a little wave and smile as the bus took off.

Kelly turned and walked away quickly, failing to notice the police officer she'd met earlier, sitting in his car nearby. He sighed and shook his head, deciding it was best to leave her alone.

"Definitely on something," he muttered.

Kelly kept her face covered all the way to Melody's house.

A teenage girl chuckled, riding past. "Everything old is new again, huh?"

Kelly looked away.

A small white bus drove up, stopping beside her. She glanced up, seeing it filled with old people.

"Are you one of ours?" the bus driver asked.

She cringed awkwardly.

"Guess not," he said, and drove off.

She hurried to the small house on the corner. Music blared from inside and the garage door was open. There was hardly any room for a car, she realised, what with the several sets of dumbbells, half a dozen pushbikes, scuba tanks, three skateboards, eight pairs of rollerblades, loads of exercise equipment, and other workout gear she couldn't identify.

"Definitely Mel," she confirmed, knowing there was no way NUTS would come here either. Having out-of-this-world security like Vanilla and Skoobie was one thing, but she knew Melody wouldn't take, nor want it. She'd be more than happy to obliterate the bad guys on her own.

She knocked on the door.

The music grew louder.

Kelly knocked harder, figuring Melody was working out. "Hey! Open up, Mel! It's Kelly! Scoops told me where you live! Open up!"

"Get lost!" a sobbing voice cried back.

"What's up?" Kelly called. "You okay?"

"Ah, what do you care?"

Kelly thumped loudly. "Mel!"

The door swung open, revealing Melody in a black singlet and shorts, staring at her astonished. "What the hell are you wearing?"

"Long story," Kelly replied.

"Scoops?"

"Yeah. Scoops."

Melody huffed. "Yeah, she tricked me into wearing it once too. Didn't work on Skoob though. She was happy about it." She pulled her inside. "Now get in here and cover your face for God's sake; it's embarrassing!"

The door slammed shut.

"Ow!"

Kelly clutched her foot, hopping past the dumbbell and then hobbling through the house. The place was littered with so much workout gear that there was barely room to move.

"So …" Kelly began.

Melody turned to her. "Uh no. Before you talk, you change. Get in there." She bundled her into the bedroom.

Kelly emerged not long after, again embarrassed. Now she wore black skintight pants and a pink exercise bra.

"God, I feel so exposed," she said nervously.

"Yeah well, it's all I've got," Melody replied, turning the music down. "Great for a workout though, and that's what you need. Trim that belly of yours." She slapped it lightly.

"That's just my build," Kelly retorted.

"Excuses, excuses!"

Melody slumped onto the couch, picking up a half-eaten container of chocolate ice-cream.

"You can talk," Kelly scoffed, indicating Melody's binge-fest. "I had one of those last night, hence the belly. What's your story? Slacking off and eating this much isn't your style. So what is it? Men trouble?"

Melody tensed. "Okay, rule number one: do *not* talk to me about men. They are scum! They are *lower* than scum. They are the scum *on* scum times infinity, and now I don't even have the café to dump on 'em anymore."

"You're lucky I'm here then," Kelly said.

"Yeah right. Want some ice-cream?"

"You can never have too much ice-cream."

"Grab a spoon."

Kelly rose eagerly and hurried into the kitchen.

They were soon on the couch, eating from the container.

"So," Kelly began, "what's Darren done now?"

Melody sighed. "He's an idiot. A big, dumb idiot."

"Spill."

Melody shook her head. "I'm not saying. It's too personal." She ate another mouthful.

Kelly also scooped up a spoonful. "Whatever." She put it in her mouth, making her cheeks swell with delight. "Well I just spent last night on the beach with David. We talked about anything and everything, and I do mean *everything*. We really bonded. It's great to know someone, and I mean *really* know them – you know what I mean ..."

"How old is he?" Melody cut in.

Kelly paused. "Uh ..."

"What's he do?"

"Okay, well maybe I didn't find out *everything* ..."

"Where's his family?"

Kelly shook it off. "So I skipped a few details, big deal, but I know he's got a good heart. I've seen it and that's all that matters. He's fantastic, cute, confident, understanding and stable. He's there for me. He puts up with all my garbage and ..."

"Zzzzzzzzzzzzzz ..."

Melody's head slumped into a power nap.

Kelly sighed, then went for another mouthful of ice-cream. A dollop dropped on her top. "Damn! Oh damn! Oh God, I'm sorry, Mel! I'm really, *really* sorry ..."

She put the spoon in the container, placed both on the table, rose and went into the bathroom. She turned on the tap, dabbed her top lightly, looked in the bin and saw ...

"Oh my God ...!"

Melody awoke with a start, leapt up, raced into the bathroom and whirled her around. "You have to *swear* to secrecy!"

"But ... but ..." Kelly stammered.

Melody spoke firmly. "Not Scoops, not David, not Skoobie, and God forbid, if you tell Turbo ..."

Kelly blinked. "So it's true?"

"Says so doesn't it?"

"Then ..."

Melody sighed wearily. "Yes. I'm pregnant."

Kelly squealed and hugged her. "Mel, that's great! That's better than great! That's ... beyond great." She stopped. "But Darren's the father, right?"

"Of course he is!" Melody retorted. "Who else would it be? And why are you so cold and wet?" She pushed her away. "My top!"

"Who cares about your top?" Kelly cried excitedly. "You're going to have a baby! I can't wait to be an aunty." She paused. "I am going to be Aunty Kelly, aren't I?"

"I'm glad you're happy," Melody grumbled.

"You mean you're not?"

Melody gave a little smile. "Yeah, I am. Don't get me wrong, I want this kid. Can't wait to take 'em camping. There'll be canoe rides down the Amazon. Mountain climbs with 'em on my back …"

"It's not even born yet, Mel. Maybe when it's a little older."

"I know, and that's what I hate," Melody moaned. "I'll love my kid more than anything in the world, but I love the world too. I don't want to end up a prisoner in a tiny room with a screaming kid while fun times call. I want to be free."

Kelly laughed. "You'll think differently when you hold them for the first time. Sure, it'll be tough at first, but I can totally see you two jogging through the desert one day."

"If I ever get my body back after being fat and bloated. Stupid Darren!"

"Hey, it takes two to tango, and you tangoed with his fandango …"

"Yeah, and that was a marathon too …"

"I don't want to know," Kelly cut in, holding her hand up, grossed-out by the thought. "More ice-cream?"

"Bring it on."

They went to the couch, sat down, and began eating again.

"So when are you going to tell Darren?" Kelly asked between spoonfuls.

"God, I don't know," came the answer. "I'm not telling anyone until the time's right, that's for sure."

"I won't say a word."

Melody took a deep breath. "I know and … because you're the first one to find out … then that means … oh God …"

"What?" Kelly asked worriedly.

"Oh, just a stupid rule we made up …"

"Go on. Spill."

Melody paused. "Well now you have to … kinda … deliver the kid."

Kelly nearly gagged. "What …?"

"Yeah, you better start practising," Melody warned. "That means classes."

"But … but … me!" Kelly protested. "I'm a klutz! Look, I've just spilt more ice-cream on your top. It's gone on the couch now …"

"Oh this is gonna be fun! You'd better be ready when the time comes, soldier."

Kelly was taken aback. "Who made up this dumb rule?"

"I did," Melody replied. "Gave me an excuse to deliver Scoop's kids. She wanted to return the favour so we set it in stone." She picked up a spoon full of ice-cream. "There's a course down the street. You can sign up there." She put it in her mouth.

"Forget it," Kelly retorted. "I can't sign up for a pregnancy class with all these NUTS targeting my butt."

Melody nearly choked.

"You know what I mean," Kelly finished.

Melody swallowed her mouthful and glared at her.

"Sorry," Kelly said.

Melody sighed. "See all the problems we got? I'm pregnant; Scoops wants her kids and can't have 'em; you have to deliver my kid, and we've got the whole world against us. How the hell can things get better after this?"

Kelly went silent.

"Well say something!" Melody pressed.

"What am I supposed to say?" Kelly asked back.

"Tell me how it'll all be fine in the long run."

"I don't have to because it *will* be fine in the long run."

"Oh shut up – what do you know?" Melody turned away crossly.

Kelly bit her lip. "Guess I'm no good at this. I don't know what to say, Mel. I really don't."

Melody relented. "Forget it. I don't either."

They came together and hugged.

"It'll be okay," Kelly said, squeezing her shoulder. "We'll be here for you. Always."

Melody sniffed. "See, that's what I wanna hear."

"You're a traveller, Mel. Just think of this as the greatest adventure of all."

"Yeah, I know, but …" Her voice lowered to a whisper. "I'm terrified."

"Me too, Mel. Me too."

She rubbed her shoulder warmly.

Kelly stayed with Melody until after lunch, then the landline rang. Melody answered it, listened hard, hung up, then leapt from the couch, springing into action. "Gotta go."

"Where?" Kelly asked.

"The café."

"Thought it was closed."

"To the public, yeah."

"What's up?"

"Got a meeting with the big guns. God, you ask so many questions. Move!"

She pulled Kelly up, bustling her to the door.

"You mean like secret spy stuff?" Kelly pressed.

Melody pulled the door open and pushed her out hurriedly before patting her pockets and saying, "Keys! Where'd I leave my keys?"

"Here!" Kelly said, reaching in and pulling them off the side table.

Melody grabbed them, moved outside and locked the door.

"So why the sudden meeting?" Kelly asked. "Trouble at your … Crossing?"

"You better believe it," came the reply. "Things are serious. NUTS are peanuts compared to what the 'ol Village is up against."

"That bad, huh?"

"Totally," Melody confirmed. "See …" she paused. "The café's like a tree branch bringing in the good stuff. Thing is, if the whole tree falls …"

"I get it. Trouble in paradise."

"Right."

Kelly tensed. "Meaning you guys might have to go home?"

Melody shook her head. "No. Our home's here now. Our job's to monitor things from this end."

"We'd better move then," Kelly said quickly.

Melody held her hand up. "Uh … no. Invites only this time."

Kelly was astounded. "What the hell? When did things get so cliquey?"

"Believe me junior, you aint ready yet. You'll need a couple more stripes before you're allowed to sit in on things."

"Even after the stuff we've been through?" Kelly pressed. "You trust me with knowing about your kid, don't you?"

"Yeah," Melody warned, pointing at her. "Don't blow it." She paused. "Sure, we're … god forbid … friends, but this meeting's about the Crossing, meaning it needs people *from* there, or who've been to it. That includes a kid from 'round here who helped save our Village recently. She's right up there with the best of 'em and'll join us once she closes the arts centre she works at. She'll be coming with our Platinum drawcard." She tapped Kelly's shoulder. "You're not one of the big guns yet kid, but you're getting there. Slowly."

Kelly relented. "Fine. You win. I don't think my head can take much more."

"Good." Melody grabbed a pushbike, wheeling it down the driveway. "Make for David's. You'll be safe there. I'll be in touch."

She leapt on the bike and soared into the street, overtaking several cars, before gliding around a corner and swooping out of sight.

Kelly stood in the driveway, feeling alone. Melody and Skoobie would be at the café, no doubt with Vanilla who'd be pulled out of her lawyer's meeting, while David was at work. There was no choice but to risk it and go home. She'd need to pack if she was going into hiding.

She sighed and made her way along the footpath, heading back for the coast road.

A snicker came from behind her. She turned to see several teenage boys staring happily at her.

"What?" she asked.

Silence.

"What?" she asked again, then looked down at what she was wearing. "Oh … crap!"

Several wolf-whistles came from nearby.

She quickly wrapped her arms around herself, hurrying away. "This is so humiliating …"

The wolf-whistles grew louder.

She turned a corner and stopped.

A familiar policeman was sitting in his car.

"I …" she began.

"Forget it," he said. "Too much paperwork."

He started the engine and drove off.

She watched him go, then hurried down the street, even more humiliated, while trying hard to avoid everyone's stares.

Chapter Ten

Kelly opened her front door wearily. She knew she had to pack fast and get out of the house but was simply too drained. She shut the door, locked it, and automatically headed for the couch. Wearily, she flopped onto it, rolled over and fell into a deep sleep.

It was six in the evening when she awoke. Groggily, she pushed herself up off the couch, looked at the time and her heart leapt, knowing she had to get out of here fast.

She made for the fridge, scoffed down a quick bowl of leftovers, and was just making for her room when …

Smash!

Her window shattered under the impact of a spiked baseball bat which slammed onto her PC in a shower of sparks. She screamed and recoiled as the bat retracted from the broken window before a big man's silhouette strode to her front door.

Crash!

The bat smashed through part of the door, then a heavy, muscular arm reached into the gap, undoing the lock. Kelly cowered back in terror as it opened and the towering man entered, grinning from beneath his brown curly hair under a newsboy hat. She grimaced at the metal studs on his leather jacket that hung over his white singlet and jeans, and trembled as he stepped in, making an air-kiss at her.

"Mwah! You're a cute one, kitten!"

Kelly gulped. "Oh God, you're NUTS!"

He cackled. "More than you could ever know." He loomed in. "You've been a naughty girl. Found it hard to believe meself – but don't worry." He slapped a hand on her shoulder, making her jump. "Ol' Jack'll initiate ya."

She yelped as he grabbed her throat, pinning her against the wall. Her jaw dropped in a silent scream as she stared at him horrified.

He leaned in close, hissing into her face. "Those were *my* guns! My big party poppers, and nobody, *nobody*, stops Jack from getting his shipment!"

She choked, struggling to breathe.

He threw her across the room. She smashed into the bookshelf, tipping it over, before he stepped back, reached through the shattered window and brought in a toolbox, banging it on the side table. The lid flipped up and he pulled out a pair of bolt cutters, testing them with two sharp taps.

"This is gonna be fun …" he sneered, moving in.

Kelly whimpered. "Please … no …"

The cutters rose to her neck.

She froze, bracing for the worst. Somehow, through her sheer terror, she heard an engine whine growing steadily louder. Then …

Smash!

Her front door and part of the wall caved in as a small truck crashed into her house, screeching to a halt. Jack turned to see Melody leap off the truck's trailer, revving a chainsaw. Kelly blinked at the sight of Vanilla in the driver's seat. There was no sign of Skoobie.

Jack glanced at Melody's chainsaw. "Try it, mouse! Dare ya. You aint got the guts."

She revved the chainsaw again, aiming it at his stomach. "So why don't you show me yours?"

He swiped at her with the bolt cutters. She dodged it and swiped back, nipping his arm with the chainsaw's edge and making him recoil. "Ah! F …"

Kelly went into overdrive, leaping to her feet and running to the truck.

Jack swung his bolt cutters fiercely at Melody, hitting her chainsaw and sending sparks flying, then he lunged, shouldering her heavily into the wall.

Kelly climbed into the truck, fumbling over the gear stick whilst pushing Vanilla's leg onto the accelerator. The truck screeched, lurching in for Jack. Melody dived out the way as it hit him hard and kept going. He roared as it rammed him through the wall, into the backyard, over the lawn, through the fence, into the neighbours' yard, then into their pool with a terrific splash.

The truck braked, jolted, and reversed awkwardly over the debris as he rose from the water spluttering.

"What is he, Superman?" Kelly cried.

Melody ran in, leaping into the truck next to her. "Maybe, but he's still as thick as two planks."

Jack emerged from the pool, stomping through a wooden beam and crushing it.

"Yeah, but I needed those planks," Kelly quipped. "Now I'm jobless *and* homeless."

"Better than lifeless," Melody shot back. "Get us out of here, Scoops!"

Jack watched the truck reverse out of the house and onto the street where it swung around and raced away. Growling, he reached to his belt, pulled out a large hunting knife, and strode after them.

The truck veered violently, speeding past several cars and wailing horns. Quickly, it straightened itself out and turned into a side street.

"Please tell me we're making for the cop shop," Kelly quivered.

"Gosh no," Vanilla replied. "That won't stop him."

"They're also a little busy tonight," Melody added, "and we're needed elsewhere."

Kelly's eyes nearly popped out of her head. "Needed? We? When do I get a say in this? I'm kept out of your invites-only meeting but when all crap goes down I'm your numero uno?"

The truck skidded violently to the right.

"You want us to drop you back home?" Melody retorted. "What possessed you to go back there anyway. Didn't I say make for David's?"

"Without stuff? How'd you find me?"

"Heard ya from across town," Vanilla answered.

"How?" Kelly asked baffled.

"You snore loudly," came the reply.

A roaring engine erupted behind them.

Kelly looked back and gasped. Jack was following them on a Harley Davidson, helmetless. The grinning skull between the handlebars made her feel sick.

"Who the hell is this guy?" she wondered. "A bikie hit man?"

"Yep," Melody and Vanilla said together.

"Go figure."

He rode in closer, pulling out his hunting knife.

"We got anything to fight him with?" Kelly pressed. "Please say yes."

"No," they both replied.

He hurled his knife into their back tyre.

Bang!

The tyre exploded, sending the truck flying. It landed heavily, turned on its side, skidded across the ground in a shower of sparks, hit a wall, clanged upside down and lay still.

The three girls groaned.

"Get off me," Melody grumbled, pushing Kelly away.

She kicked the passenger door open and scrambled out. Kelly groggily followed, staggering after her to the truck's other side where Vanilla lay dazed. Together, they reached in, pulling her free.

"Wake up, Scoops," Melody pressed. "Come on, wake up! Rise and shine …"

Vanilla stirred. "Wuuuuuuuuhhhhhh …?"

They lifted her up, wrapping her arms around their shoulders.

Jack's bike ground to a halt behind them. He dismounted, pulling out a heavy chain.

Melody stepped away from Vanilla, leaving Kelly to nearly drop under her weight. "Get her outta here, kid."

Kelly winced and the two staggered off.

Jack stepped in. "Melody, Melody, Melody, let's hear the Melody …"

She turned to face him.

He grinned slyly, then swung his chain hard.

Melody ducked, grabbed a garbage bin lid and hurled it into his stomach. There was little effect, as expected. He lashed out again. She leapt to the side, wincing as the chain's edge clipped her forehead.

"Gettin' slow," he sneered.

"Still alive though," she retorted.

He swung harder.

She dodged the blow, dropped to the ground, scrambled through the gap in his legs and came out the other side. He turned to her, letting loose with another swing. Her arm flashed to the bin lid, holding it up like a shield. The chain hit it with a loud clang, then he struck repeatedly, with growing force. She struggled to hold it as she crawled back with one hand while defending his blows with the other, then saw what lay beside the bin. A cigarette lighter and a few half-drunk bottles of alcohol.

"Good ol' hobo town," she quipped.

She reached over, grabbing a bottle.

The chain crashed down again. She blocked the blow before rapidly crawling backwards, gaining space. A second of freedom was all she needed, and she swigged from the bottle but didn't swallow. Instead, she swished the drink in her mouth, then hurled the bottle at him. His chain smashed through it, shattering the glass and spilling the liquid on himself. She rolled out of the way and scrambled to the cigarette lighter, picking it up. The chain rose high, she held the lighter before her lips, lit it, then spat the alcohol over the flame. The flammable liquid ignited from her mouth, shooting into a long fireball and striking the alcohol on Jack.

Whoosh!

His shirt went up like a bonfire. Startled, he dropped the chain and recoiled.

She grabbed another bottle, hurling it into the leaking petrol tank of the overturned truck with a splintering crash, then turned, leaping into the air as the truck exploded behind her.

Jack stared in horror at the billowing flames sweeping in for him. "Flaming hell …!"

He was cut off by a savage blast, blowing him backwards.

Melody rolled away, dodging the fallen shrapnel. Finally, when everything died down, she raised her head, looking up. There was no sign of Jack.

Satisfied, she rose to her feet, licking her lips.

"Good stuff," she mused about the drink. "Not bad at all …"

Melody found Kelly and Vanilla on the street by an old townhouse. Vanilla sat on the steps, blinking dazedly.

Kelly was concerned. "I think we should get her to a hospital, Mel."

Melody moved in. "Here, let me." She knelt before Vanilla, looked into her eyes and said, "Strawberry cream."

"Orange squash," Vanilla replied.

"She'll be fine," Melody quipped, standing up. "Let's get outta here. We gotta move fast."

"What about psycho rider?" Kelly asked.

"Pfffft! Second-rate try-hard." She helped Vanilla to her feet. "Come on, Scoops."

Kelly helped too, and all three of them headed along the street.

"To the docks," Melody suddenly said.

"What?" Kelly wondered.

"I was answering your question ahead of time," Melody explained. "You were about to ask where we're heading. The answer's, to the docks."

"Oh right," Kelly realised. "Thanks."

"Because that's where it's all going down," Melody continued.

"What's – ?" Kelly began.

" – going down?" they asked together.

Kelly drew a frustrated breath.

"Fine," Melody relented. "As I said, our NUTS have something big going down tonight …"

"That sounds *so* wrong," Kelly muttered.

Melody ignored her. "Digital records recovered from the ship we sunk, thanks to a connected database … and that …" She sighed wearily, " … Turbo … tell us that NUTS are collecting another weapons shipment at the docks tonight. We've contacted Vertigo and she's got a surveillance team there. She hates that we're involved but has got no choice, especially with something this big."

"Where's Skoob?"

"Already at the docks."

"'Cause she's the best there is, right?"

"Right. Let's move."

"Fine," Kelly relented. "Docks it is."

Chapter Eleven

"You took your time!" Vertigo huffed.

Melody, Vanilla and Kelly emerged from the taxi that had pulled into the dockyard, ruffled to the max.

Vertigo stared at them in disbelief. "Crap me out of hell, what have you guys done now?"

"Long story," Kelly answered.

"Never a short one with you, is it?"

"And it'll be even longer if you don't pay this guy," Melody said, indicating the taxi driver.

He held his hand out.

"Forget it," Vertigo retorted.

"Look around you," Melody shot back. She pointed at herself, then Vanilla, then Kelly, then the taxi driver. "I've got no pockets; she's got no job; she's got no job *or* home; he's waiting!"

Vertigo sighed, pulled out some notes, and slapped them into the driver's hand. He counted them quickly.

"No tip?" he asked.

"Get outta here!" Vertigo ordered, pointing away.

He took the handbrake off. "Boy, do you need to get some, lady."

Kelly giggled.

Vertigo shot her a death glance.

Kelly shut up.

The cab drove off.

Vertigo rubbed her eyes. "Dare I ask, what kept you?"

"One big NUT," Melody replied. "Relax, I got him."

"Relax?" Vertigo scoffed. "With you around? It's how much damage you did to get him that worries me." She shook her head. "I'll deal with it later. Surveillance point three's this way. Do not, I repeat, do not even breathe without me saying so. NUTS are here, with Solomon and the Squirrel."

Melody's eyes lit up. "Oh, this is big! I love it!"

"I'm glad you're happy," Kelly muttered.

Melody glanced at Vanilla. "Hear anything, Scoops?"

"What?" Vanilla asked, leaning in.

"Oh great," Melody sighed. "Her hearing's shot from the car roll."

"Double great," Kelly added as they all headed down a path between two warehouses. "This night just gets better and better!"

Shortly after, they were hidden behind an enormous crate overlooking the dockyard. A tanker sat in the water. A gangplank had lowered, and several people were walking into the ship, carrying crates and other cargo. Standing by the entrance, with their face covered by a veil, stood a dark bridal figure.

"The Black Bride," Kelly whispered. "God, he's a freak!"

"You're telling me," Vertigo muttered. "Freak yes, but not one of theirs."

Kelly frowned. "Huh?"

"Look closer."

Kelly did and asked, "So what?"

The figure turned, looking in their direction. Then, unseen by the passing NUTS, they nodded quickly to Kelly as if to say, "'Sup?"

"Holy mother of hell!" Kelly cried.

Melody and Vanilla slapped their hands over her mouth, pulling her down.

Kelly smacked their hands away. "How did she … why didn't they … what's she …?"

"Get a grip!" Melody hissed.

"Seriously?" Kelly retorted. "I didn't think Skoob'd be the type to take out a psycho and go undercover."

Vanilla agreed. "You're right, sweetie. Me too. Skoob doesn't work like this."

"Oh, so you can hear again?"

"Not everything, but yes," came the reply. "Things have settled, slightly." She listened hard. "I'm not hearing the real Black Bride though. Heaven knows where he is."

"So how do we get in?" Kelly asked. "As prisoners?"

"No," Melody corrected. "As cargo."

"Hold it," Vertigo cut in firmly. "Where's my say?"

"Oh, merciful mother of God!" Melody hissed. "Do you want results or not?"

"I don't want another global upset on my hands," Vertigo retorted. "I swore I'd keep an eye on you."

"You were also s'posed to keep an eye on a government minister, remember?"

"Thin ice, Hill, thin ice …"

Melody pushed on. "So, we may have caused a slight diplomatic ruffle, big deal. We still got stuff done. You want to watch us, then do it, from up here."

Vertigo's lips pursed.

"Things'll go to hell whether you're with us or not," Melody pressed. "It's a no-win situation lady, and we need backup."

"You'll be watching us the whole time too," Vanilla added. "No problems. Scouts honour."

"Yeah," Melody said. "We do the groundwork; you cover our butts. Deal?"

Vertigo drew a sharp breath, then relented, seeing no other choice. She raised her finger, speaking through clenched teeth. "Fine, but if things go belly up, so do you!"

Melody beamed. "Great! See ya soon." She headed off.

"Promise," Vanilla said happily, and followed.

"We hope," Kelly finished reluctantly. "Thanks."

"Get outta here," Vertigo ordered.

Kelly crept away, after Vanilla, leaving Vertigo seething and seriously annoyed.

Soon after, two men were carrying a long wooden crate through the dockyard. They barely noticed Melody leap down on either side of them, clasping two crowbars in her hands, pinched from a box above.

Clang!

Clang!

They fell like stones.

"Ouch!" Kelly cringed, emerging from the shadows and climbing down with Vanilla.

Melody dropped one crowbar, raised the other, and pried the crate's lid open. A man in a business suit lay inside, passed out.

"Who's he?" Kelly wondered.

Melody leaned in, sniffed, and made a face. "Drunk business guy from a party by the look of it. He may have been giving 'em headaches for all we know. Still, it's a way on board."

"What do you mean?"

"Don't get too comfortable in there …"

"What?" Kelly's eyes widened in horror. "Oh God, Mel, no …"

She yelped as Melody and Vanilla picked her up and dropped her in.

"No!" Kelly cried, looking up. "No, this is too much! It's gross! Feral! Oh yuck, what if he does something? Guys, this is wrong. So wrong! You've gone too far! I'm gonna gag …"

"Hold your breath," Melody said, raising the lid with Vanilla.

"We won't be long, sweetie, we promise," Vanilla added. "You'll be fine."

The lid was sealed in place and a banging came from within.

Melody and Vanilla dragged the bodies into the shadows, then began undressing the men.

Soon after, they were dressed in black, with their hair bundled under beanies. With the men now sealed in another crate, they lifted Kelly's, carried it to the jetty and went up the ship's gangplank, secretly slapping Skoobie's hand as they boarded.

The crate was set down in a cargo hold. Once the coast was clear, Melody lifted her crowbar, opening the lid.

Kelly's head emerged, looking green, wide-eyed, and horrified.

"I so thought he was going to chuck …" she grimaced.

"Toughened you up, didn't it?" Melody replied, grabbing her by the arm and pulling her out.

"Like hell," Kelly shot back. "You weren't so tough when you found out you were …"

Melody glared at her.

Vanilla looked at Melody curiously.

"... Coming on board," Kelly finished, changing tack. "You were afraid. Yeah, I saw it."

"Bite me," Melody retorted, then: "Down!"

They all ducked behind a crate as two men walked into the cargo hold, picked up a heavy box, and left. Once they were gone, Melody went to another crate and raised the crowbar. "Let's find out what's in these babies. There's gotta be more than guns, here." She opened the lid and cast it aside. "Ah, it's just a bunch of sheets and a wedding dress."

The sheets shifted.

"Then why's it moving?" Kelly asked worriedly.

A gun nozzle rose from under them.

Kelly cringed. "Holy crap!"

Footsteps rose as armed men entered the hold. One pushed Skoobie in, the veil now ripped from her head.

Melody, Vanilla and Kelly watched as the sheets in the crate were pushed aside and Solomon emerged from below, rising smoothly to his feet.

"Great," Melody huffed. "Screwed over!"

Kelly thought this over, then reality hit home and she gasped. "So this whole thing was just a trap to get us here?"

"Yep," Vanilla confirmed.

"And we walked right into it?"

"Yep," Melody and Vanilla said, in unison.

"While I was lumbered with a friggin' drunk guy?"

"Cool," Skoobie quipped.

"Hey, Skoob," Melody said to her.

"'Sup?" came the reply.

Kelly looked at Skoobie. "Let me guess, you walked right up and tried talking your way on board. They saw right through it, fitted you in a wedding dress, and used you as bait to draw us into the picture. I'm guessing we'll be framed next."

"Eh, worth a shot," Skoobie said coolly.

Kelly threw an arm up in disbelief.

Melody glared at Solomon, "So where's the real Black Bride? We know it aint you."

"Unavailable," he answered charmingly. "Oh dear, dear, dear. Watching you young ladies is rather like watching rats in a maze. Predictable and boring."

"Boring?" all four of them said together. "Us?"

"Though I admire your practicality," he continued, "from afar that is. Your invaluable skills will assist me greatly."

"Yeah, we'd rather die first," Melody shot back.

Kelly smacked her arm.

"Figuratively speaking," Melody grumbled.

He smiled. "You four have a knack for causing trouble lately. So much so, that I'm impressed by the scale of it."

"Yeah, so am I," Kelly muttered.

"Now, since you've upped the stakes of global terrorism, we can progress to the next step." He lifted the wedding dress by his leg, smoothed it over, and stepped out of the crate. "This is one of our beloved leader's many garments. He's been having trouble choosing which one to wear for his wedding. Yes, my loves, he is soon to be married, and awaits his groom who goes by the name of darkness. We must ensure that our bride isn't left standing at the altar."

He approached Kelly, raising a hand to caress her cheek.

She stepped back, resisting him.

He studied her carefully. "You're afraid. You've been so for a very long time. You cover it up. That's normal and always has been, for everybody. A sickness on which we all thrive. Magnify that by the billions and what do you have?" He leaned in close and whispered, "Insanity."

Kelly trembled. His frightening stare was drawing her into the swamping clouds of his warped psyche. Her instinct was to scream, to run, to howl. Thankfully, the strong presence of Melody, Vanilla and Skoobie allowed her to stand firm in the face of utter madness, while the café's glow returned tenfold, illuminating her heart. Defiantly, she raised her head, stared right back at him and said, "Get stuffed. I've got one thing you'll never have."

"Oh?" he asked curiously. "Do enlighten me."

Her hands rose, clutching Melody and Vanilla's tightly, while Skoobie leaned in, putting her arms around her shoulders.

"Friends," Kelly finished.

His jaw hardened.

"She's got a point," Skoobie added. "Everybody needs 'em. I got plenty."

"Yet you still failed," Solomon retorted.

Skoobie raised a hand, shuffling her veil around as she fiddled with her ear. "Really? I could have sworn these things had full batteries. Cops get better reception that way." She touched a button.

A piercing, digital whine came from behind a crate, then Vertigo rose, wincing, before ripping off the microphone near her earlobe.

"Quit it!" she snapped at Skoobie.

Skoobie did so.

Several police officers emerged from their hiding places; guns raised.

Solomon merely smiled.

Kelly was unnerved. "Why's he so happy?"

Vanilla listened hard. "Something's up."

"Ah, what's to worry about?" Melody scoffed flippantly, waving them both away. "He can grin all he wants. We got him."

Crash!

Part of the roof burst in.

Melody, Vanilla and Kelly dived to the side, while Skoobie merely stepped back as a rush of debris plummeted past, along with Jack's charred, bloodied form. He thudded heavily onto the floor, landing on his feet and growling.

"He's alive?" Melody cried in disbelief. "Oh, that is total bull …"

Jack roared and thundered in.

"Scuffle!" Melody yelled. She leapt on Solomon, pinning him against the wall. "That's it! Now you're gonna …!"

Jack's big hand clamped on her shoulder.

"Too late," she cringed. "Ah sh …"

He threw her clear across the room.

Solomon dusted himself off, headed to the door and left.

Nearby, Vanilla launched headlong into battle with sweeping high kicks, leaping past Vertigo who spoke rapidly into her microphone.

"This is Sergeant Donna Vertigo requesting immediate assistance, repeat, immediate assistance …"

Kelly saw that Solomon's cronies had all lost their guns in Jack's extreme entrance and watched as one whipped Vertigo's mike away. Vertigo struck out fiercely, dropping him like a stone.

Skoobie turned to face an assailant.

"Yeah right," she said, and turned to face another who raised his fist, ready to strike. She ignored him too and saw a small oil tin on the floor. "Oooh, shiny!"

She leaned down and grabbed it as a fist swung over her head, then rose and walked away, looking curiously at the tin's label. "Damn, thought it was olive oil. Oh well …"

She dropped it, releasing the black liquid over the floor as the men ran in. She barely noticed as they skidded on it, flew high in the air and slammed hard onto the ground. Ignoring them, she casually walked by an open crate and looked in to find a large round magnet the size of her hand. Curiously, she took it, then cruised up to Kelly who cowered before Jack who towered over her like a man mountain.

Nearby, Vanilla kicked a NUT flat-out. He landed by a crate that was bound by a thick rope attached to a pulley system. She glanced at Skoobie who caught her eye, then heaved on the rope. Melody ran in to help and slowly but surely, they hoisted the crate up, all while Skoobie kept Jack's focus.

"'Sup?" she asked him, stepping in.

He glared back at her.

Kelly spoke quickly. "Can't talk your way out of this one, Skoob. He's a deadhead beyond help."

"What?" Jack snapped at her.

"Nothing," Kelly gulped.

He pulled out his hunting knife, snarled, then hurled it at her.

Skoobie's hand flashed up with the magnet, the knife suddenly changed course in mid-air and clunked side-on to it.

Kelly grabbed a gun from the ground and rose, aiming it at Jack.

"Stay back!" she ordered.

He pulled his collar away, showing several bullet wounds. "Whatcha gonna do? Add more to these? Can't do it, mouse. Real killer's just shoot."

He lunged.

She recoiled, slipping on the oil that Skoobie had dropped and …

Bang!

Her shot thudded into his leg, stopping him dead.

"Oh God!" she wailed.

"God damn, she actually did it," Melody said, impressed.

Kelly grimaced in horror.

"Don't worry," Vanilla called to Kelly. "That leg's artificial. It's all metal down there. Didn't you hear the clang?"

"Oh," Kelly realised. "Well in that case …"

She fired again.

Jack screamed and staggered.

"Yeah, that part wasn't metal," Vanilla pointed out.

"Cow!" he roared, then lunged again.

Kelly dived aside, hitting Skoobie whose arm thudded into the wall, loosening her grip on the magnet. Both it and the knife flew at Jack, slapping onto his leg near his groin just as Vanilla and Melody released the rope, dropping the crate hard onto his head. It plonked to one side as he dazedly turned on the spot, staggering dangerously close to a power board. The magnet jerked his leg up, raising it high and clamping it to the board in an awkward position. He raised his hands to push himself away, not seeing a red switch.

"Oh no …" Kelly cringed.

His thumb slipped, flicking the switch. The board came to life and he jolted spasmodically. His arms rose, and to Kelly's sheer astonishment, he used his enormous strength to wrench himself free.

"How the hell …?" she began.

He turned to her with a twisted, painful expression and took a single, heavy step. She stepped back as he stopped dead in his tracks. There was an uneasy silence, before his mouth opened, revealing a wisp of smoke. He looked at her dreamily, a smile spread across his face and he murmured, "Biggest bang of me whole bloody life. Bloody ecstasy."

Kelly jumped as he crashed to the floor, twitched a few times, then was still. She swallowed hard. "Is he dead?"

Vanilla listened. "No sweetie. Heart's still strong."

Kelly looked around. Thankfully, Solomon's people were subdued. Nearby, Vertigo was as dazed as hell, having taken a blow from an assailant.

Kelly stepped towards her. "Are you …?"

"I'll be fine," Vertigo cut in painfully, and indicated the door. "Solomon. Go!"

Kelly nodded. "Thanks." She turned and ran with Melody, Vanilla and Skoobie.

"Your chariot awaits, Professor," the woman in black said, standing by the open door of a small plane.

Solomon nodded back at the woman in the dark jumpsuit and knee-high boots, whose long blonde hair was tied back in a ponytail, while a 'Lone Ranger' mask lay across her eyes.

"Thank you, my dear," he replied, climbing in.

She entered after him, shutting the door.

Melody, Vanilla, Kelly and Skoobie arrived to see the plane heading down a long stretch of road, ready to take off. Helplessly, they watched it go.

"We're too late," Kelly said.

Melody turned to a warehouse behind them and grinned hungrily. "Whoa mamma!"

Skoobie followed her gaze. "Cool."

Vanilla grinned happily. "Oh, that works out well."

Kelly's eyes widened at what lay in there. "Oh no! Nuh-uh …!"

"Come on!" Melody said, pulling her in with Vanilla while Skoobie pushed from behind. "It'll be awesome!"

"No, guys, really, I can't! I'll get sick! I'll die! I can't do it! I won't! No way, no …!"

"I don't wanna goooooooooooo …!"

Kelly wailed, going green as she sat in the backseat of a replica World War I biplane as it roared down the long road, ready to take off. Skoobie sat beside her, while Melody and Vanilla shared the front seat, with Melody piloting. The plane was built to take tourists up, making it slightly bigger than history's original, and could go much faster too, thanks to a larger engine. Melody had discovered, from hidden paperwork in the warehouse, that the business was a cover used by NUTS. Even better, she found to her great delight, that the machine gun at the plane's rear was loaded and operational, having been modified by the bad guys.

Kelly's wails grew louder as the plane veered into the air; banking left smoothly.

"Check out the view!" Melody cried.

Kelly ignored her. "I hate planes! I hate flying! And you guys suck! Big time!"

"Time for you to face your fears, honey!" Vanilla called back.

"Yeah!" Melody added. "Watch this!"

She barrel-rolled the plane.

Kelly's face went even greener as she held on to what she could. The world spiralled several times before the plane levelled off and things returned to focus.

"Keep it steady," she said through gritted teeth, to both herself and Melody.

"Roger that!" Melody replied, then looked back. "We've got choppers on our tail!"

Kelly followed her gaze. "They're police choppers! Vertigo's probably!"

"Yeah, but *they're* not," Skoobie pointed out, indicating the three military helicopters swooping in from the sides. "Luckily we've got this baby." She patted the machine gun behind them.

"Great," Melody said. "Now we're all familiar with air warfare, right?"

"Oh, what do you think?" Kelly shot back.

"Fine, we'll play it by ear."

Two enemy choppers swept in, firing at them. Melody pushed the controls forward, sending their plane nose-diving for the ocean, while the remaining chopper spun on the spot, engaging with the police.

Melody levelled the plane off before flying up. The choppers fired with sharp bursts, making Kelly jump as the bullets flew past her. "Holy crap …!"

The plane weaved from side to side, then barrel-rolled rapidly again, leaving Kelly's head swirling. When things finally steadied, Melody veered the plane away from the savage gunfire bursts as the choppers sailed after them, gliding up and down.

"Okay!" Melody called. "Show 'em we mean business! Shoot back!"

"I don't wanna kill anybody!" Kelly protested.

"I don't either, soldier, but it's either them or us, so fire!"

Kelly braced herself. "Oh, I hate this …"

The choppers soared in.

Kelly cringed and pulled the trigger. The machine gun crackled to life with a thunderous roar, sending violent judders through the whole plane. Thankfully for Kelly, it was enough to divert both choppers, who veered away from each other.

Kelly's whole body hurt from the shots.

Skoobie, on the other hand, was blissed out. "Oh my God, that was better than –"

"Keep firing!" Melody commanded, swinging the plane to the side. "Keep the left chopper moving out!"

Kelly fired again while Skoobie sat beside her, still blissed out among the flying cartridges. Left-Chopper swung further aside, then …

Bang!

"Missile," Skoobie stated.

Melody swerved the plane sideways, letting the missile from Left-Chopper fly past them to explode in mid-air, then they glided smoothly over the black smoke and debris.

"That worked!" Melody called back. "They're gettin' riled."

Kelly was aghast. "That's a good thing?"

"Yeah, mistakes get made! Keep firing at both of 'em."

Kelly tensed. "This is so suck-o-rama …"

She fired, driving Right-Chopper sideways.

Melody steered the plane around in an arc, heading back for the space between the choppers.

Kelly braced herself. "Tell me you have a plan, Mel."

"Kinda," Melody replied.

"Will it kinda work?"

"I kinda hope so."

Whoosh!

Left-Chopper let loose with another missile.

"Incoming!" Vanilla called.

Melody aimed the plane directly upwards.

Kelly felt the missile's heat sweep under them as they shot straight for the moon. The missile roared by and then …

Bang!

Right-Chopper exploded in a mixture of black and gold before its flaming debris dropped into the ocean. Melody straightened the plane and soared away as Left-Chopper pursued them.

Vanilla shifted uncomfortably in her seat, frowned, then pulled out a stick of dynamite from below it. "Hey! Look what I found!"

"I love it when that happens," Skoobie said.

"Light her up," Melody ordered, pulling the controls back.

The plane rose higher, with the chopper racing after them.

Vanilla found a lighter, handed everything to Melody, then took the controls.

Melody lit the dynamite, stood up, turned back to face the chopper, and waited.

Kelly gazed horrified at the explosive. "What the crap are you doing? Get it outta here!"

"Yeah, in a sec," Melody replied.

"Now!" Kelly cried.

"You're probably right."

She hurled the dynamite. It spun through the air, exploding into the chopper's blades and sending the whole thing plummeting into the ocean.

Melody sat down, taking back the controls.

"Done and dusted," she quipped. "Solomon's next."

They soared into the night, leaving the gunfire between the last chopper and the police flaring behind them.

It wasn't long before …

"Over there!" Vanilla called, pointing at the small, white plane below. "It's Solomon!"

"And that's my job," Melody said. "Here, Scoops."

She let Vanilla take the controls, then rose, climbing carefully onto the wing and crawling out. Vanilla steered them in gently as Melody shuffled along. Soon, they reached the plane.

Kelly peered at it suspiciously. "Scoops, wait, has that thing slowed down?"

Melody was caught in the moment. "Okay, I need in!"

Vanilla moved their plane in closer. Strangely, Solomon's didn't attempt to flee.

"Here we go!" Melody cried.

She jumped, landed on the other plane's wing, stretched over and opened the door.

Kelly was unnerved. "Shouldn't they be fighting back more?"

Vanilla's gaze darkened. "That's what worries me …"

Melody climbed into the plane's cabin and closed the door. She quickly steadied herself, then moved over to Solomon, grabbing his arm. It was limp. She put her hand before his mouth. His breaths were shallow, like he'd been drugged.

She looked up as the woman in the pilot's seat put the plane on autopilot, rose, and turned to face her, clasping a gun. Her other hand pulled her collar away, revealing a long scar near her neck, and she grinned, speaking cockily.

"Hola, señorita."

Melody froze, staring at her in shock. "Crap on a stick …!"

Vanilla, now able to hear everything, clenched her fist into a tight ball. "No, no, no, no …!"

Skoobie's face hardened and her head rose. "Spill."

Vanilla spoke darkly. "She's alive, Skoob. Always thought I heard her voice on the wind. Now we know."

Skoobie tensed, then spoke just as darkly. "Yeah. Me too, babe."

"Who …?" Kelly began.

"Not now," Skoobie cut in.

"Skoob …"

"Can it, kid!"

Kelly blinked, startled. Skoobie's gaze, hard as hell, was fixed firmly on the plane.

Melody watched the woman remove her mask. She shuddered deeply, trembled and said, "Oh, tell me you're working undercover …"

The woman shrugged and smiled.

"Are you for real?" Melody asked, horrified.

The woman raised her gun, firing three times into Solomon's body. Melody jumped with each shot and watched, sickened, as he slumped to the floor. Several objects fell from his pocket, including a thumb drive. Melody glanced at it, before the plane jolted, making them both stagger and sending all the trinkets sliding under a seat, hitting a dark metal box.

The woman indicated the body. "I'll miss the old guy, but it was time. His vision was second to none, but he was too good a teacher and paid the price. Now the big boss'll think you killed him. Grade A plan, Mel, and it paid off."

Melody stared at her, shocked. "Who could offer you more than us?"

The woman scoffed. "More than you lot running around like kids? Oh, come on Mel, face facts. You're not an extreme sports junkie. You just wimp off into the world every day 'cause you're too scared to look in the mirror. Scoops, what's she? A struggling waitress who's lost her kids. As for Skoob, she's the nothing beyond nothing and revels in it. Now you're all hanging ten off a cliff with a new loser in your girl group 'cause it's too scary to grow up."

Melody grabbed Solomon's teacup, hurling it at her. The woman dodged it, leaving it to hit the wall and shatter.

"Temper," the woman warned.

"How could anyone offer you more than us?" Melody trembled. "Dammit, we gave you everything! Respect, loyalty, trust …"

"Puppy love," the woman cut in.

"Leaving you as the head bitch!" Melody snapped. "We thought you were dead! We cried our eyes out for days! Now this?" Her lips quivered as a tear trickled down her cheek. "We loved you. We really, *really* loved you. You were the best of the best. Why this, Sandi? Why?"

The woman, Sandi, tapped the parachute on her back. "What's past is past, Mel. World's turning and you're stuck in kidsville. How else could I bait you here?" She pulled out a flashing phone and made for the door. "Welcome to boomtown."

"No!" Melody cried, diving for her.

Sandi's other hand flashed up and …

Bang!

Vanilla jumped in shock.

Melody dropped to the floor, clutching her bleeding shoulder before Sandi's smoking gun.

"Typical," Sandi mocked. "Sayonara babe!"

She opened the door and leapt into the sky, her arms and legs outstretched. Swept away by the wind, she glided over the ocean, before raising her phone and hitting the screen.

Vanilla, knowing exactly what was up, steered her own plane away.

"Scoops …!" Kelly cried, over the roar of the engine.

Melody saw a light flashing below a seat, care of the dark metal box. She leaned down, grabbed the thumb drive beside it, then ran to the door and jumped out, flying into the night. She'd only gone a short way, when Solomon's plane exploded, sending her spiralling. A searing fireball flew over her head as she tumbled into a dark cloud in a flood of tears.

Her stomach tingled, reminding her of her unborn child. She quickly regained her senses, pocketed the thumb drive, zipped it up and rolled over in the freezing air currents, weeping into the wind.

Vanilla struggled with her plane's controls as it swept downward, its left wing ablaze. She ignored its ear-piercing whine as she flew in for Melody.

Finally, she made it. Kelly and Skoobie stretched out, grabbing Melody and pulling her in. Melody collapsed onto Skoobie, hugging her tightly and sobbing, all while Vanilla sniffed tearfully, struggling to level the plane.

Kelly looked down. Parachute-Woman had reached the ocean, landed on a speedboat, and was heading away fast. A sudden jolt from the plane made Kelly lurch sickeningly, knowing it was beyond help and now plummeting in a burning hell-dive.

"Evac One!" Vanilla cried.

"Where the hell too?" Kelly cried back.

"Fine, stay here then," Skoobie quipped. "See ya in the next life, bud." She slapped her shoulder, turned to face outwards and, to Kelly's horror, raised her arms and dived majestically into the sky, with Melody and Vanilla following.

Seeing no other choice, Kelly rose, inching to the plane's edge. Another fierce jolt sent her toppling over the side and plunging into open-air, wailing in terror. The plane dropped with her, before veering to the side and nose-diving hard and fast for the ocean. Seconds later, its flames hit its fuel tank and the whole thing blew in a rip-roaring explosion.

Kelly jumped as a rush of flaming debris swept past her. She was ready to erupt into full-blown hysteria when she suddenly felt someone grab her arm.

Melody.

Skoobie glided in, grabbing hold of her other one and they were soon falling with Vanilla in a tight-knit circle. Much to Kelly's surprise, their speed slowed.

"How the friggin' hell …?" she began, wondering if her friends were controlling their fall. Her arms tingled with their golden presence, making the whole thing feel unreal, then …

Splash!

She hit the ocean hard. The shock of the fall and the sea's icy chill morphed reality into a painful, dizzying blur. Finally, she burst into the night air, sucking in deep breaths. She blinked the water out of her eyes and saw Parachute-Woman's speedboat racing into the distance.

A light cough came from nearby. She turned to see Melody, Vanilla and Skoobie bobbing behind her, watching the boat.

Kelly shivered in the waves. "Sh-she's cleared off. Guess she thinks we're dead."

"Yeah," Melody said glumly. "But unlike us, she won't care a damn."

She choked back the tears, along with Vanilla, and they all huddled into each other for warmth, bobbing through the ocean in silence.

A police boat arrived shortly after, taking them to the hospital. No one spoke. To Kelly, it seemed that a heavy, black cloud had come over her friends, not letting up.

There, they met Vertigo, who, at long last, came face-to-face with Turbo. He'd been hiding out at the library with his laptop and now braved seeing the police to support the girls. Vertigo demanded he be taken to the station for questioning. Flippantly, he told her to can it. At that point, Skoobie beamed delightedly, overjoyed with his progress in life, and cried, "Oh, you make me so happy!" before kissing him long and hard. Vertigo ran a hand through her hair, baffled, wondering if it was worth putting him in police protection after all.

Melody was taken away by a medical team. Her focus was only on her unborn baby, which they assured her was fine. Sandi's shot had gone straight through her shoulder, leaving her arm in a sling. She didn't want it and told the doctor that slings were for wimps, but he insisted. Reluctantly, she complied, intending to take it off ASAP.

Once they'd all been checked over, Melody, Vanilla, Kelly, Skoobie and Turbo, all met in a four-way intersection of a hospital hallway. Skoobie arrived first, with Turbo. The other three approached from separate hallways, meeting in the middle.

Vanilla bit her lip, looking away, while Melody folded her arms.

Skoobie broke the silence. "Shall we go for it?"

Melody nodded. "Yeah. Let's get it over with."

The three of them headed for a supply room. Vanilla and Skoobie entered, while Melody stopped, turning to Turbo. "Oh yeah, there's this." She took out the thumb drive from her pocket. "Check it out, junior." She threw it lightly at him.

He missed the catch and it dropped to the floor.

Melody rubbed her eyes as he scrambled for it, then made for the room again.

Kelly started to follow.

Melody, sensing what she was up to, turned to her and said, "Uh, not you."

"Why?" Kelly asked.

"Private con," came the cold reply. "Sorry."

The door shut in her face.

Kelly frowned. "That was rude."

Turbo held up the thumb drive. "Wanna check this out?"

Kelly shrugged. "Sure."

He sat on a hallway chair, picked up his laptop and plugged in the thumb drive. Kelly sighed and sat next to him as the device activated. A beep followed and Solomon's face appeared on the screen, speaking electronically.

"Naughty, naughty. You didn't enter the security clearance code, did you? Bye-bye."

"Bye-bye?" Turbo wondered.

Kelly pulled the thumb drive out, grabbed the laptop and hurled it down the corridor. It landed with a crash, exploding in a flaming blaze and setting the fire alarms off. As they stood under the sprinklers getting soaked, Turbo raised his finger and said, "Okay, this is going to be a little trickier than I thought …"

Vertigo strode into the corridor with two officers. One grabbed a fire extinguisher and blasted the laptop's remains, while Vertigo stormed up to Kelly and Turbo.

"Right," she snapped. "I've had it with this. Turbo Newcombe?"

"Yes?" he answered.

"You're under arrest." She motioned to the other officer. "Get him out of here."

Turbo yelped as he was pulled away. "Alright, just don't tell my Mum 'bout any of this, okay?"

"Move!" she ordered.

He was bustled around the corner.

Vertigo looked at Kelly. "Where are your friends?"

Kelly nodded at the door.

Vertigo went over, tried the handle and found it locked. She rapped hard. "Open up! Police!"

"We're busy, get lost!" Melody called back.

"That's it!"

Vertigo kicked the door open. It swung in, revealing the three girls sitting cross-legged on a table, having formed a triangle.

Melody looked up tearfully, along with Vanilla.

"What part of 'get lost' don't you understand?" Melody asked bitterly.

"Lives are in danger," Vertigo stated. "You're needed at the station. Now!"

"Yeah, 'cause you're doing a great job so far!" Melody retorted.

"Clearing up your mess?" Vertigo shot back. "Yeah, I think I am! Move!"

Vanilla spoke firmly. "We'll come when we're ready. Not before."

"Yeah," Skoobie added. "Believe it or not, you're not the highest authority round here."

Vertigo motioned to her officers. "Cuff 'em."

They pulled out their handcuffs.

Melody, Vanilla and Skoobie slid off the table and faced them, standing tall.

"We're on your side," Melody stated. "So *back off!*"

An officer looked at Vertigo. "Sarge?"

"Oh, for God's sake I'll do it myself!" she huffed, grabbing one set of handcuffs and walking in.

Skoobie stepped back and opened the laundry chute. Melody and Vanilla worked fast, lunging at Vertigo, grabbing her arms and hurling her down it, hearing her furious yells fade away.

An officer came at them.

Skoobie approached him, grabbed his collar, pulled him towards her, and kissed him hard.

He stopped, dazed.

Melody picked up a chair, knocking him clean out.

"All's fair in love and war," Skoobie said, dropping him and moving past.

The remaining officer retreated.

Skoobie skipped behind him, Melody stepped in front and Vanilla came in from the side.

He raised his hands. "Okay, let's stay calm. I'm sure we'll work something out ..."

Vanilla opened the cupboard door.

He stepped in.

She shut the door and locked it.

Melody brushed her hands off. "Done and dusted."

The three women strode out of the room and down the corridor.

Kelly ran around them, blocking their path. "Hold it."

"Honey, don't start ..." Vanilla began.

"After that?" Kelly retorted. "You guys have been hell-a-rinas since the plane. What's the deal, and don't say it's none of my business."

"It's none of your business," Melody said coldly.

They walked past her.

"I'm making it my business!" Kelly snapped, running in front of them again.

Melody looked at Skoobie. "You're right. She is cute when she tries to be angry."

Kelly seethed, trying hard to control her temper. "Is this about your home? Sanders Crossing, or whatever it's called?"

Melody threw an arm up. "Oh yeah, there's that too! We'd forgotten all about it so thanks for bringing it up! Just so you know, it's falling, care of a Witch who's morphed into the Death Syren, if you're interested."

Vanilla smacked her arm. "Hey! Enough!"

"Oh, what can she do?"

"I can do plenty," Kelly shot back. "So what's the deal with Plane-Woman? How come she's riled you big time?"

Silence.

"She's someone from your village," Kelly concluded. "Isn't she?"

More silence.

Vanilla glanced at Melody and Skoobie. "She's gotta know sometime."

Melody turned away. "Fine!"

"Up to you," Skoobie said.

Vanilla paused, considering how to begin, then looked at Kelly and spoke hesitantly. "Okay sweetie, you got it. Plane-Woman's a NUT, that's for sure, but she and us have … a history. Her name's Sandi and yeah, she's from back home. She was the one who brought us together, as kids I mean." She tensed at the memory. "We went through it all. She'd laugh with us, cry with us, go on quadruple dates with us, you name it. She knew our deepest secrets 'cause we'd share everything with her, even Skoob here who never opens up to anyone." She paused again. "When we got older, we started travelling the world as a team. Sandi was our leader. Gosh, she was so good that she even trained Mel up."

Melody grumbled under her breath. "I never *needed* any training …"

"All in all," Vanilla finished. "Life was one big party with Sandi."

"So what happened?" Kelly asked. "Is she brainwashed?"

"She'd better be," Melody said sourly, "but I don't think so. I saw it in her face. It's her."

"So you guys fell out?" Kelly pressed.

"Kinda," Vanilla answered. "We were in Spain, dealing with a political crisis, and on the run. Sandi was acting weird. She'd been a little distant for a while, but I was the only one to spot it. Mel was caught up in the excitement and Skoob was caught up in the universe so they both missed it. By the time we were scaling that cliff-face by the dam it was too late. She'd scarpered from us and went solo to defuse the bomb, which was way out of character. We saw her fall with the blast and she should be dead but …"

"She's not," Kelly finished. "Maybe the fall triggered something."

"Nah, she just got high and mighty," Melody glowered. "We'd have moved heaven and earth for her, but the backstabber screwed us over!" She smacked the wall. "I loved that cow! I really did!"

Vanilla placed a hand on Melody's shoulder. "I know."

Skoobie nodded in agreement. "We all did. Hell, we even made a tribute to her with blondie here."

Kelly's eyes widened as realisation dawned. "What …!"

Melody and Vanilla glared at Skoobie.

"Good one!" Melody snapped.

Skoobie looked down. "Ohhhhhhhhhhhhh …"

"Oh right!" Kelly cried. "Now I get it! I *finally* get it! After all this time! How could I have been so stupid, but then again that's me isn't it? Stupid Kelly Morrison! Ditz and goof! So that's all I was to you, huh? Someone to make up the numbers in clique central."

"It's not like that …" Vanilla began.

Kelly retreated, her eyes welling with tears. "Go to hell!"

"Already there!" Melody retorted.

Kelly trembled. "You've stuffed me around since we met, but to find out that you used me as a stand-in. You *used* me …!"

"Yeah, and you're a better person for it now, right?"

"Maybe we are too," Vanilla added.

"Oh, bulldust!" Kelly fired back. "You've screwed me over since day one!"

"Hey!" Vanilla said firmly. "We trust each other more than heaven and earth. We trusted Sandi and we trust *you*! It's us who keeps getting screwed over, that's who! Me especially! Look at my life!"

"Look at mine now!" Kelly cried.

"But we never, *ever* lied to you," Vanilla pressed. "Yes, we did need a replacement, and because Sandi was the best, we wanted to replace her *with* the best! You were perfect. You still are, Kelly Morrison. You just don't see it."

"Pfffft!" Kelly scoffed. "You've messed with my head from the start! Who's to say you won't screw each other over next?"

"Because we trust each other more than life itself," Vanilla enforced. "Melody delivered my kids for God's sake!"

"Yeah, well now you can deliver hers 'cause I'm out!"

Vanilla looked at Melody, aghast.

"Cow!" Melody cried. She grabbed a chair, throwing it at Kelly who ducked as it flew over her head, hitting the wall. "I trusted you with that, just like I trusted Sandi with my life! That's it, no more trusting anyone ever again! Period!"

Vanilla was astounded. "How could you not tell me, Mel?"

"How could you not tell she was pregnant?" Skoobie asked back. "Look at those thighs. With someone who works out as much as she does, how can she possibly gain weight? Duh!"

"Whoa, whoa, whoa!" Vanilla cut in. "How come I'm the last to know when I should've been the first?"

"I was saving you that honour," Skoobie said.

"Well how did *you* know?" Melody and Vanilla cried together.

Skoobie shifted awkwardly. "Well Mel's stuff was just like, lying there, so how could I not look?"

Vanilla stared at Melody in disbelief. "Mel, you still told Kelly before you told me."

"I had no choice!" Melody protested. "Junior here rifled through my stuff!"

"See?" Kelly confirmed. "Clique central."

"It's not that," Vanilla said. "Mel gave me the greatest gift of all by delivering my kids. I wanted to return the favour. Now, because of all this snooping, I can't."

Skoobie looked at Vanilla. "Can I just remind everyone about how we knew that *you* had a bun baking away? It was only 'cause Melody broke into your house and …"

"What …?" Vanilla cried at Melody.

Melody picked up another chair and threw it at Skoobie who didn't flinch as it flew past her head, hit the wall and landed next to the first.

Vanilla was stunned. "Breaking into my house, Mel? What the hell did you do?"

"What the hell did *she* do?" Melody cried, pointing at Kelly. "And Skoob? And Sandi? I'm the victim here!"

"Oh, and since I'm the last to know, what does that make me?" Vanilla retorted. She looked at Skoobie crossly. "It's also a bit hard when somebody cheats!"

"It's not cheating, it's pre-emptive compassion," Skoobie corrected.

"Well you know what?" Kelly cut in. "Skoob, you can deliver Mel's baby, then you can all replace me with Turbo."

Skoobie's jaw dropped. "Uhhhhhhhhhhhh …"

"Find someone else!" Kelly snapped. "I'm outta here!" She turned, heading down the corridor.

"Sweetie …!" Vanilla called.

"Get lost!" Kelly shot back. She walked up to a double set of doors, pulled hard, found them locked, and kicked them crossly.

"You can't go that way," Vanilla pointed out. "It's closed for renovation. There's a sign right next to you. See?"

Kelly seethed, turned around, stormed back past them, rounded the corner, and collided straight into a woman pushing a tea trolley.

Melody and Vanilla flinched at the sounds of crashing cups, saucers and cutlery, before seeing some plates rolling down the corridor towards them. They peered round the corner, along with Skoobie, to see Kelly sliding and stumbling on the mess while staggering away as fast as possible.

"And that's why we love her," Vanilla said.

They parted and turned to face each other, listening to the tea trolley woman storming off swearing in Spanish.

"Scoops …" Melody began.

"Save it," Vanilla cut in, raising her hand. "I've had enough. Talk time's over. You'd better run after your friend if you want that kid delivered."

"So what the hell are you then?" Melody shot back.

"Sometimes I wonder Mel, I really do." She lowered her head, turned away and walked off sadly.

"Oh yeah, real mature!" Melody called after her. "That's friendship, huh? Well you know what? I don't need you! Not for a second!"

Vanilla reached the end of the corridor, rounded the corner and was gone.

Melody looked at Skoobie. "And you're not much better. I can't trust you either."

Skoobie stared back at her. "Is that what you think, or what you know? What you *really* know, deep down."

"I don't know what to think anymore."

She too headed off, leaving Skoobie alone in the corridor.

Silence followed, then:

"They'll be right."

She strode away, trying hard to distract herself by whistling.

It didn't work. The pain was too deep this time.

When Vertigo emerged from the laundry chute, looking very much worse for wear, she ordered a hospital-wide search for all four girls but couldn't find any of them, even after tracking Kelly's tea-soaked footprints into the hospital foyer. Angry and frustrated, she stormed to the police station, ready to take her anger out on Turbo.

Chapter Twelve

Kelly miserably walked past an alleyway, bathed in a streetlamp's midnight glow. Several homeless people sat nearby, wallowing amid the flying news pages rolling loosely in the wind. She hugged herself tightly, shivering in the cold night air as she made her way along the desolate street.

Vanilla opened the door of her beach house and tossed her bag onto the counter. She locked the door, sat wearily on the couch, and picked up a framed photo of her children. Her thumb brushed back and forth across their smiling faces as she brought her knees up to her chin, gazing at them tearfully.

Darren found Melody on the beach, looking out at the ocean.

"Thought I might find you here," he said, moving to put a blanket around her.

She smacked his arm away.

"Don't want it," she mumbled.

He put it over her shoulders.

"Yeah, you do," he said, sitting next to her.

"Oh, for God's sake," she huffed. She grabbed his arm, flopped it around her shoulders and snuggled into him.

He lightly brushed her hair behind her ear and kissed her forehead as they watched the waves crashing on the shore.

Skoobie strode through the park, her hands in her pockets. Slowly, she sat on a creaking swing, rocking gently back and forth with only the wind to keep her company.

Knock, knock, knock!

"Just a minute!"

David walked down his hallway and opened the front door.

Kelly stood on the other side, shaken and teary.

"Hey," he said softly.

"Hey," she repeated equally softly. She swallowed hard. "I … uh … I'm in big trouble."

He gave a little smile. "So what else is new?"

She nodded. "Things didn't go well tonight. They've turned out bad. Real bad." She drew a shaky breath. "I've lost everything. My job, my house, the whole lot. I'm wanted by the police and God knows how many psychos out there. Got no family in town. No friends now either. Guess I'm about as big a loser as you can get." She choked, wiping her tears away. "I'm just a toxic person. Everything I do goes so wrong. It's like there's a curse on me or something and I don't know why." She sniffed. "I guess, what I'm trying to say is, that it's unfair for you to be around me. I can't offer you anything but trouble. That's why …" she hesitated "… I came to say goodbye. I'll head back home and live with my parents again. I tried making it on my own. I failed. It sucks, but that's life, hey?" She shuddered. "Besides, you need someone better than me. I'm sorry, David, I really am. I think the world of you but … I'm sorry."

She lowered her head, defeated.

An awkward silence followed.

"Then why aren't you leaving?" he asked gently.

"Oh, I'm sorry; I'll go now …"

"That's not what I meant."

"But you just …"

"You're not leaving because you don't want to," he cut in. "You're crying out for help, only you're too scared to admit it." He smiled again. "So here she is. Kelly Morrison on my doorstep. Ashamed, afraid, alone, taking a last desperate chance on love, yet refusing to give me the satisfaction by admitting it. You're holding desperately onto a glimmer of hope, and you know what? I just might take it."

She was startled. "Seriously?"

He paused. "Let me tell you something. Three years ago, I had a girlfriend. We met at a party, we clicked, we dated, and after a while we moved in together. She was the best thing I could have hoped for. Funny, beautiful, well-off, perfect in every way …"

"Is this supposed to cheer me up …?"

"Just listen. I loved her so much, and after a year I proposed. She accepted and there were parties, lots of parties, with so much laughing and … it was great." He tensed at the memory. "Then … one night … I saw a completely different side to her. I'd seen hints before but couldn't admit it. She rang me, acting weird. Something was up and she was staying the night at her best friend's house. She wanted me to go over there and drop some things off. I couldn't do it. I was exhausted from work and could barely move. She said I was a selfish insensitive pig, as well as a few other things that I don't care to remember. I'd no idea where she was coming from." He bit his lip. "She never came home. She left her stuff at my house and … a week later … she was living with another guy."

"David …"

"She'd been seeing him for months. Him and a several others. She played games, sucking us all in with a picture-perfect performance. She used people, including me, to get what she wanted. She'd seemed unreal, but after that night I saw right through her. To the world she was this fairy-tale princess. To me she was just sad. Once she was out of the picture, I told myself I'd never get involved with a girl like her again." He raised his hand, brushing it gently down Kelly's cheek. "You're the opposite of that, Kelly Morrison. You're honest, you're genuine and you don't try to be something you're not. You can't. You're legit, and that's why I love you."

Kelly blinked. "You still do?"

"Totally," he replied. "You're unique, Kelly. There's no one else in the world like you. No matter what you think about yourself, all I see is … I don't know, I can't describe it. Maybe … the greatest human artwork that evolution's produced."

She grinned. "Are you being serious or are you sucking up again?"

"Mixed in with a slice of heaven, of 'course," he finished. "Though you're probably right. Needs a little work."

"Ya think? No, scratch that. It was pretty cool …"

"See," he pointed out. "You're a fighter. No matter how much goes wrong, whether your house gets trashed …"

"It did …"

"Or you get thrown in jail repeatedly …"

"I have been …"

"Or you nearly start World War Three …"

"I've come close …"

"You push on. Right now you've been dunked by life and are swimming against the tide, but if it's one thing I know about you Kelly Morrison, it's that you'll rise up and see the light again soon. I just hope it's with me. I don't want to lose you."

Her eyes welled with tears. "Do you really love me, David?"

He nodded. "Yes."

"I mean, do you *really* love me?"

"More than anything."

She stared at him in disbelief. "Why?"

He shrugged and smiled warmly. "I don't know."

Her voice quivered. "I-I don't either, David. I'm so confused. I …"

She fell into his arms, letting loose in a blubbering mess of joy and sorrow as her beating heart pressed against his. She choked through her tears, as that very heart took over and she blurted out, "I love you too, David. I don't want you to leave me. I'm so scared. I'm so … so scared."

"It's okay," he said, gently stroking her hair. "Everything's fine, Kelly. Everything's fine."

She blubbered on. "So much changes so fast. I don't know where to go or what to do. Please let me stay. I'm so tired. I just want to sleep."

He kissed her forehead, held her cheeks in his hands, gazed into her eyes and said, "Kelly, you can stay as long as you want. Understand?"

"Yeah," she whispered. "Thanks."

"Anytime."

He guided her inside, shutting the door behind them.

Kelly awoke by the smouldering embers of David's fireplace, wrapped in his arms. Nearby, the first rays of daylight streamed through the window, caressing them gently.

"Morning," David said sleepily. He kissed her cheek.

"Hey," she said back, snuggling into him. "What time is it?"

He glanced at the digital clock nearby. "Five AM."

She frowned. "That's weird. Feels like I slept longer than that."

"You were," he replied. "You were asleep all yesterday."

She grabbed the clock, stared at its date and found he was right. She'd slept for more than twenty-four hours. "Oh my God …!"

"It's fine," he said. "You were tired."

She put the clock down and ran a hand through her hair. "Yeah, no kidding. Anything happen while I was out?"

"Sergeant Vertigo came by," he answered. "We had a talk. I told her you'd see her when you were ready. It took some convincing, but I made her see sense, though she didn't like it. I think you should go to her. It's dangerous out there now."

Kelly paused. "David?"

"Yeah?"

"I'd like to go for a walk first. On my own. Just to clear my head and stretch out for a bit."

He inhaled sharply. "After everything that's happened, I don't know …"

"I won't be long. Trust me."

He relented. "I always do."

She grinned. "David?"

"Yeah?"

"Thanks again."

Kelly walked through the empty streets, her hands in the pockets of one of David's jackets. The early morning breeze was crisp, leaving her feeling fresh amid the golden sunbeams rising steadily towards her.

Soon, she found herself walking towards Sanders Café. The small building that had changed her life completely, now held a sign that read simply, *Closed*.

She took a deep breath. As she exhaled the soft mist, a figure walked around the side of the café, approaching its letterbox.

Vanilla.

Kelly watched her put a key in the small metal box, open it up and take out the mail. With the box cleared, Vanilla locked it again, leafed through the letters, looked up and saw Kelly.

"Hey," Kelly said softly.

"Hey," Vanilla said back. "You're up early."

"Late, more like it," Kelly replied. "Had a good sleep though." She paused. "You opening up?"

"Can't," Vanilla answered, looking at a bill. "The police say no. Besides, big things are going down back home. The Crossing's gone dark and if it falls, it's not just the café that'll be out of business."

"Can I help?"

"I wish you could." She put the mail in her bag.

Running footsteps came from nearby as Melody rounded the corner on an early morning jog. She stopped in her tracks.

"Hey," she said, cautiously.

"Morning," Kelly and Vanilla replied together.

"'Sup?" Skoobie asked, cruising in from across the street.

Silence fell as they turned to face the café's empty shell. The golden presence that had drawn Kelly in from the very beginning, and been magnified tenfold by her friends, was no more, leaving a hollow husk, devoid of life.

Kelly spoke sadly. "Well, here we are. Back at square one."

"My favourite patch," Skoobie said, referring to the concrete slab they stood on. "That's how things start up in life. Always square one."

Kelly nodded. "Such a shame to see this place go. It seemed so … alive."

Vanilla touched the café window, running her hand down it. "More than you could ever know. People became couples here, then married. The unemployed made contacts and got work. The lonely found friends, and all from this one little building tucked away in the street. This place changed lives, big time."

"Yeah," Melody added. "The café's not your standard business. Never was. We're not either."

"Economics!" Skoobie scowled and pretended to spit.

Melody pushed on. "Companies only compete to win in the short term, then struggle to surf the money waves before getting sucked under. We're not like them. Sure, I may be a little competitive at times …"

Vanilla coughed loudly.

"Mamma, you're the walking Olympics," Skoobie pointed out.

"But despite that," Melody continued, "the café's sitting on the stem of a whole different growth."

Skoobie raised her eyebrows. "Impressive, coming from you." She glanced at Kelly. "That growth includes yours."

Kelly watched a man with a paper tucked under his arm walk up to the café door. He pulled on the handle, saw the *Closed* sign, and headed off.

"Small things make a big difference," Skoobie said.

Vanilla caught Kelly's gaze. "Just like you, sweetie."

Kelly's heart missed a beat.

"See," Skoobie began, "life's crap is fertile ground for evolution. You just gotta break out of it and rise up, then you'll find that home was hiding in plain sight all along and you'll grow from it. That's the only way to cross over into a whole new reality."

"Hence the Crossing?" Kelly concluded.

Skoobie was unsure of what to say. "Well … uh …"

"Yeah," Melody and Vanilla finished for her.

"Got it right this time," Skoobie nodded, referring to herself.

Kelly looked up at the café. "Can we reopen this place?"

"Depends," Melody answered. "Things are bad back home and they're not that great here either. If we work on defences from this end, we might have a chance, but we can only do that as a team." Her voice rose excitedly. "One with focus, dedication, leadership, guts, persistence, strength, determination …"

"Yeah, we get it," Kelly and Vanilla cut in.

"We've been pretty good so far," Vanilla said. "Hey, we're not superheroes …"

"Speak for yourself," Melody muttered.

"We just … are," Vanilla continued. "And if it works, why break it?"

"But we *did* break it," Kelly pointed out.

"So what?" Skoobie countered. "You're standing with Sandi going NUTS right now?"

"Well … no."

"So open your eyes, sister. Where are we?"

Kelly smiled. "Standing on a street corner waiting for a café to open."

"Hallelujah, she gets it."

Kelly turned, forming a circle with the rest of them. Summoning up her courage, she asked, "Give it to me straight. Was I just a replacement? A stand-in?"

Melody sighed. "Uh … no. Though you've done real good in stepping up to the plate kid, and you'd be stupid to throw in the towel now. I don't normally say nice stuff to people 'cause mushy stuff's crap but …" She struggled to find the words, "God I hate this … you've done a great job, junior."

Kelly's eyes lit up. "Really?"

"Yeah, don't let it go to your head, sunshine."

Kelly beamed. "So you guys still want me as a friend?"

"Oh, for God's sake, I want to kill you!" Melody cried, lunging in and grabbing her collar.

Kelly recoiled and the jacket ripped. "Damn! That was David's. Oh well, he was shopping for new pants too."

"Geeze, you drive me mad," Melody fumed. "I swear, there are times that I just want to ram your head into a wall to sharpen you up, but I know that no matter how many times I try you'll still keep driving me madder and madder and madder and that's why … why …"

"What?" Kelly pressed.

"WE BLOODY LOVE YOU!" Melody exploded.

Kelly's heart missed a beat. "Did you just say that, Mel?"

Melody tensed awkwardly.

"Might have," she muttered.

"She's right," Vanilla confirmed. "We love you, sweetie."

Skoobie nodded and shrugged. "Mmm-hmm."

"Yeah, yeah, yeah," Melody said flippantly. "Whatever."

Kelly shuddered. "Do you mean it?"

Melody lunged at her again. Vanilla pulled her back.

Kelly's eyes welled with tears as she trembled. "I guess I … luh … love you too. I always have. Always. I …"

"Go with your heart, honey," Vanilla prompted.

"Yeah," Skoobie added. "Logic's crap. I never use it."

Kelly quivered, filled with bubbling joy as soft tears trickled down her cheeks.

Melody braced herself. "Oh no …"

Kelly choked back the tears. "Thanks guys. Thanks so much. Thank you so … so much …"

She swept at Vanilla.

"Hug-a-rama!" Vanilla wailed, sweeping in and embracing her right back as they gently swayed from side to side. Kelly wept on her shoulder, sobbing profusely, while Vanilla stroked her hair lightly. "It's okay, sweetie. Everything's fine. It's okay …"

Melody folded her arms and looked away, fuming, until she finally snapped, "Oh for the love of God!"

She too leapt in, joining them in a three-way hug.

Skoobie stood outside the group, staring at the sky.

"Get in here, Skoob!" Melody called.

"Yeah, take some more time to think it over," Skoobie retorted. She stepped in, playfully pushed Kelly into the centre, then hugged her with Melody and Vanilla.

"No, no, please, no," Kelly cried. "I don't deserve it. No really …"

"You bet, sweetie!" Vanilla laughed.

"Live it up," Skoobie quipped.

"Take a chance," Melody pushed.

They spun her around, whirling her down the street as a group.

A passing council worker shook his head, sighed and walked on.

"Hey!" Kelly sparked up. "Does this mean I still get to deliver Mel's baby?"

"Oh yeah, I forgot!" Vanilla realised, breaking away. "Mel! You're pregnant!"

"Yeah!" Melody beamed.

Vanilla raised her hands and screamed in joy.

Melody screamed right back.

Vanilla screamed again.

Melody did too.

They turned to Kelly who screamed with them, then Vanilla kissed Melody's forehead. "Congratulations, Mel!"

"Yeah congrats," Kelly said, leaning in to kiss her too, but they nearly ended up banging heads.

"Hey!" Melody warned. "Watch it."

"Sorry, I …"

"I'll stay put. Go for the cheek."

Kelly did so, then smirked before pushing Melody into the centre of the circle and sweeping her down the street with the others, whirling her around as they all laughed.

The council worker walked back, carrying a garbage bag.

"Drugs," he muttered, heading off.

Vanilla beamed at Melody. "I'll give you my kids' hand-me-downs!"

Skoobie slapped Melody's shoulder. "I'll tell 'em stories and stuff. They can play with my pets too."

"And I'll… I'll…" Kelly began. "What can I do?"

"You can deliver the thing!" Melody cried.

Kelly blushed and they all embraced again.

Vanilla looked at Kelly. "Sorry about what I said at the hospital. I'll never forgive myself."

"Then we'll have to do it for you," Kelly replied cheekily. "Get in there!"

They pushed Vanilla into the circle and swung her along, laughing.

"Skoob time!" Vanilla called.

Skoobie sighed, failing to hide her smile. "Oh Jehovah …"

She too was pushed into the middle as the others all laughed and spun her along the street. This time she couldn't conceal her joy and giggled somewhat strangely.

"Whoa!" she said, putting her hand over her mouth. "That was weird."

"Bestie's forever!" Vanilla cried.

"Forever!" Kelly cried back. "And no matter what happens, or how many fights we have or whatever junk we have to deal with, it's not the end of the world …"

A dark shadow overcame them.

They all looked up at the rapidly blackening sky.

"On the other hand …" Skoobie said.

Kelly sighed. "Friggin' hell! Why does it never last?"

Chapter Thirteen

The four girls watched as the giant shape, high above, floated slowly over them. Melody frowned angrily, Vanilla frowned sadly, Kelly frowned nervously, while Skoobie pulled out a lollipop, ripped the wrapping paper off, and popped it in her mouth.

For hovering in the sky, was a float of a giant angry-looking squirrel.

Part of it began expanding.

"Is that …?" Kelly started to say.

"Yep," Melody replied.

"Those two lumps underneath …?"

"Yep," Melody said again.

"They're definitely what I think they are?"

"Uh huh," Melody confirmed.

"So why are they growing bigger?" Kelly wondered.

"'Cause that squirrel's about to drop his nuts," Skoobie answered casually.

Bang!

The float exploded with an ear-shattering roar.

Kelly jumped and recoiled as a flood of tree nuts rained over them, dropping heavily. Thankfully, the downpour soon fizzled out, and as the last of the nuts plonked on Kelly's head, Melody said, "Good to see ol' Sandi still likes a laugh." She threw a nut out of her hair. "The cow."

"I don't think that was meant to be funny," Vanilla warned, "which means …"

"Take cover!" Melody cried.

She pulled Kelly back and they all retreated under a balcony as the nuts burst into little fireworks, crackling, jumping and popping up and down the street, ready for painful burns.

Vanilla's top suddenly jiggled. She reached in, pulled out a nut, gulped wide-eyed, and threw it onto the road where it erupted.

To Kelly's astonishment, the streets were still empty, and there were no yells or cries from anywhere.

"Where is everyone?" she wondered. "Shouldn't people be running out and snapping shots by now?'

"Nuh," Skoobie replied. "That's what happens when the world goes NUTS."

The crackles grew, then slowly faded. As the last of them died down, Kelly shook her head and said, "Well, that was weird."

"Not if you're open-minded," Skoobie said, sucking on her lollipop.

"That was just the greeting card," Melody warned. "The actual present'll be a whole lot bigger."

Running footsteps came from around the corner.

Melody leapt in, grabbing the newcomer and throwing them against the wall.

"I give up, I give up!" Turbo wailed, clutching his laptop.

Melody made a face. "You make me sick." She pushed him aside and turned away.

"What are you doing here, sweetie?" Vanilla asked.

Turbo adjusted his collar and glanced at Melody. "I didn't really give up, you know. I could have taken her on ..."

"Just get on with it," Melody said.

He nodded. "The cops let me go and I knew you'd be here." He held up the thumb drive. "I managed to hack into this thing. Now I know exactly what the bad guys are up to."

He smiled proudly.

Silence.

Skoobie continued sucking her lollipop.

"Nobody's impressed," Melody said crossly. "Talk!"

"Right," he replied, indicating the thumb drive. "This thing's cool. See, thumb drives come with a certain amount of memory. Not this one. It's memory's unlimited. I call it the Infinity Drive. You know, after Douglas Adams?"

"Thin ice, junior, thin ice …" Melody seethed.

"Anyway," he continued, "it holds an encoded cyber virus, contained in a digital prison. I've managed to analyse the virus without releasing it, which is quite clever really …"

Melody rolled her eyes.

"If the virus were let loose," he pressed on, "it'd seek out and destroy all cyber barriers globally, thereby allowing the free flow of information into every digital realm."

"Drop the nerd speak and use English," Melody huffed, exasperated.

"I get it," Vanilla realised. "So if we plug this thing into a bank security system, it takes away all the safeguards and allows us to get to the money, right?"

"Worse than that," he said. "If you drop all cyber protection worldwide, you've got access to *everything*. Government files, the CIA, FBI, global defence networks, unlimited finances, along with private medical documents that anyone can exploit. It'd all be up for grabs, leaving no privacy. All secrets would be obsolete."

"Too much repression – that's always been the trouble," Skoobie fumed. "If everyone's sick stuff suddenly bubbles out into the open, there'll be an overflow of guilt, shame, anger, terror and …"

"Insanity," all four girls said together.

Melody tensed. "There'll be killing left, right and centre, leading to complete anarchy. It'll mean the collapse of the world order, maybe even …"

"The end of the world," Vanilla finished.

Silence fell once more.

"Already is for me," Turbo said glumly. "My mum's gonna know about all those sites I've been on."

They all looked at him.

"Elvis sites," he said quickly. "I've been trying to study coolness. Y'know, to be like Elvis."

Melody swore under her breath.

"Then there's your big secret," Kelly told the three girls. "About Sanders Crossing."

Vanilla waved her away. "Oh, don't worry about us, sweetie; we're not even on the net."

"Don't need it when you've got friends in higher places," Skoobie added.

Turbo held up the laptop. "Okay, a signal's coming through. It's broadcasting everywhere. TV, radio, phones – you name it."

"Let's see," Melody said.

He pressed a button and they all moved in to see Sandi's face appear on the screen, speaking cockily.

"Morning, morning, this is your wake-up call. I am your inner voice. The crazy nagging in your head that's slowly risssss-ing." She giggled. *"That's me, and you know what? You people are lucky. Seriously lucky. Your city's now a test site for the ultimate social experiment. See, guinea piggies, I have access to everything. Every single one of your bills, phone sex calls, dodgy credit card transactions, social media secrets, where you've been, what you've done, all your legal documents, hey, I've got it all."*

She grinned proudly.

"You probably think this is some random freak signal or TV show, right? Nuh-uh. I'm the real deal. So now you'll know that the head of your Education Department, Hannah Simkins, has a severe mental disorder. Her buddies have been carrying her workload for weeks. One of them, Marty Ferriman, likes to text teenagers too. We've got the texts. Better not call the police though. Too many corrupt officers. What's more, I can tell you every sting operation in place right now, including one on a lawyer, John Strothers, of 46 Allcott Place. He secretly sees hookers when his wife and boss think he's working late on a Thursday night. He's being monitored by Sergeant Donna Vertigo, when she's not busy having an affair with a married judge …"

"Really?" Kelly asked surprised.

"Sexual frustration," Skoobie confirmed. "Even I could tell that."

"What else have we got? Barry Davison, 54 Sampson Place. Oooh, nice area. Has a drug lab in his cellar. Judging by his texts, he's been selling coke to at least 8 kids in town. Who else have we got? Little Jimmy Dawson, 89 Lilith Terrace – hey, guess what? Your father's not really your father. Got your adoption papers right here. Then we have Irwin Newcombe of 63 Lyall Street. Likes to call himself Turbo. Also likes looking up loads of porn sites too …"

Turbo gulped and went bright red.

Skoobie smacked him.

"So-rry," he said sombrely.

She smacked him again.

Melody, Vanilla and Kelly did too.

"So here's the deal," Sandi continued as long lines of people's details travelled across the bottom of the screen. *"We've released secrets for thirty percent of your city's population. The rest of you can team up with us whenever you're ready. Just head to the City library and we'll go from there. The rest of you can go berserk and kill each other as part of our test before we go global. Try and attack us and we'll release more secrets, and believe me, you 'will' kill each other after that. So in the meantime, keep us entertained and remember…"* she raised her hand into a fist. *"…Go NUTS!"*

The image went dead.

Kelly shuddered. "So what do we do now?"

Vanilla reached over and gently took the laptop from Turbo.

"I think I'll confiscate this for a start," she said, folding the cover over.

"I said I was sorry," he grumbled.

Skoobie slapped him again.

Melody glared at him. "Plan of action, desperado."

He composed himself. "So, what we just saw was a local transmission bouncing off a relay link. There's a couple of places round here where it could've come from."

"Like a TV station?" Kelly suggested.

He dismissed this. "Too open. I ran some checks and figured that the most likely place is a weather station up in the hills."

"Sounds about right," Vanilla said. "Let's get there."

"Totally," Melody agreed, "but first we gotta minimise the damage round town. So, I've got an idea …"

Kelly sighed. "Oh God. What now?"

Kelly shivered at the sounds of distant sirens, steadily rising wails, screams, and gunshots. Much to her relief, she couldn't see any carnage, but sure as hell felt its impact.

She ran a hand through her hair as she sat, unnerved, in the back seat of a car that the girls had 'borrowed' from across town. Turbo sat beside her, engrossed in his laptop, as Vanilla slowly brought the car to a halt.

Melody checked her rucksack.

"This isn't right," Kelly said worriedly. "It's such a bad idea."

"Saving lives is a bad idea?" Melody retorted. "Desperate times call for desperate measures, soldier." She glanced ahead. "Okay, let's do this. Skoob. Clear the area."

"Right," Skoobie replied, opening the car door and getting out.

Kelly tensed. "What are you gonna do, Skoob?"

Skoobie shrugged, sucked on her lollipop, and walked away. Casually, she strode up to a man in a booth by the boom gate.

He spoke.

She spoke.

He looked down at a security camera, there was a pause, then he bolted from the booth and ran inside. Once he was gone, she entered the booth.

Alarm bells rang as a crowd ran from the building, with Skoobie stepping out from the booth and joining them. Strangely, no one came near the car, save for Skoobie who calmly walked over, still sucking her lollipop. Casually, she opened the door and got in.

"Done," she said, sitting down.

"Cameras disabled?" Melody asked.

"Yuh-huh," came the reply.

"Goin' in."

Melody opened the door, leapt from the car and ran into the building, carrying her rucksack.

Kelly grimaced. "I still don't think this is a good idea." She looked over at Skoobie. "What'd you tell him?"

"The truth," Skoobie answered coolly.

"WHAT?" Kelly and Turbo cried.

"Works," Vanilla mused.

"And he believed you?" Kelly asked, astounded.

"Yep," Skoobie replied. "Showed him the security camera zeroed in on our car. Made him zoom in further, then pointed out the wires of the mama bomb sticking out of the rucksack on Mel's lap. Told him what it was, then spilled our plan, give or take a few points."

Kelly gasped. "You're insane …"

Skoobie continued. "Made him get everyone out of the building and away from the car. Also deleted the security camera footage of our involvement. All good."

Kelly shivered. "Oh my God, we are so terrorists."

"This whole situation's NUTS," Vanilla said. "We didn't start it."

"Yeah, but blowing up a power station?"

"Well yeah sweetie, I know it sounds bad …"

"Ya think? Now they'll see us as the bad guys. Booth-Guy'll remember Skoob, and she looks crazy enough for everyone!"

"Cheers," came the reply.

"We cut the power; we save lives," Vanilla reasoned.

"Or cause more panic!" Kelly shot back. "Where'd Mel get the bombs from anyway?"

Vanilla shrugged. "Some freedom fighters in Afghanistan, I think."

Melody came racing out of the complex. "Go, go, go …!"

She dived in through the open car window as Vanilla revved the engine. Kelly lurched sickeningly as the car reversed, skidded around in a screeching U-turn and roared away.

Bang!

Kelly jumped from the deafening roar and covered her ears as a large part of the building exploded. Another blast erupted, then another, then another, before the entire structure imploded in a thundering crash.

Kelly cringed as the car raced down the street. "This is wrong, this is so wrong! How do we know we didn't kill anybody?"

"Casualties nil," Melody reported. "Everyone inside was accounted for. I made sure of it."

"Yeah, but that's them!" Kelly pointed out. "What about the hospitals and emergency wards that now have to go without power? There are people on respirators whose lives are in danger. Did you think of that?"

Melody went white. "Oh crap …"

"They're bound to have generators," Vanilla said. "Ideally …"

Kelly shuddered.

"We are so terrorists," she said again.

Melody glanced ahead. "The weather station, Scoops."

"Right," Vanilla agreed and hit the accelerator.

They drove up into the hills and were soon deep in the bush. After a short drive along a thin path, they arrived at a clearing where a weather tower pointed at the sky, surrounded by several small buildings.

Vanilla brought the car to a halt a short way from a security fence.

"I don't like this," Kelly grimaced, for the third time in five minutes.

Melody sighed wearily. "Right, that's it, you're coming with me. Scoops, you're on standby with Skoob and whiz-kid, here. Hide the car and lie low. I'll head off with little Miss Innocent."

"I'm not that innocent," Kelly grumbled. She unbuckled her seatbelt and left the car with Melody. "See you guys soon, I hope."

The car backed away slowly. Once it was out of sight, Kelly followed Melody up to the gate and watched her climb the fence, flip onto the other side, land smoothly and say, "Your turn."

Kelly pushed the gate open and walked through.

"Wimp," Melody scoffed.

"Show-off," Kelly retorted. "Where is everyone?"

A screech came from nearby.

Kelly turned and froze as a bald white-faced clown ran at them with a spear. Melody dropped to the ground, knocking his legs out from under him, then leaned back, elbowing him hard in the head. He slumped into the dirt and lay still.

A loudspeaker clicked, releasing carnival music.

Kelly tensed. "Not good …"

"Down!" Melody snapped.

Kelly yelped and dropped next to her, shutting her eyes tightly as furious bursts of machine gun fire erupted from an open window, rattling over their heads. Finally, it stopped to reload, allowing them to scramble around the side of a building and stand.

Swish!

Thuk!

A hunting knife flew between them, thudding into the wall.

Melody pulled it out and hurled it back at the masked birdman, striking him in the forehead with its handle. He dropped like a stone.

The girls crept forward. One step, two steps, then …

Click!

Kelly looked down, horrified.

"Mel!" she called.

Melody turned to her and huffed, "Typical!"

Kelly was standing on a landmine.

Melody knelt and examined it. "Old-style. NUTS must be low on funds." She grabbed two rocks, placing them under it. "That should balance things out. Now get off … slowly."

"I …" Kelly began.

Melody jumped up, leaping onto her. Kelly wailed as they flew through the air, hit the ground and rolled over.

The mine stayed intact.

"Quickly does it equally good," Melody quipped, standing up.

A savage dog bark came from nearby. Kelly turned to see a Doberman run in and leap high. She dived one way, Melody dived the other, leaving the dog to fly between them and land on the mine. A deafening explosion followed as she covered her ears, then grimaced as dog goo splattered over her shirt.

She sat up, feeling yuk as all hell while shaking some off her arm.

"Why do animals keep exploding on me?" she grumbled.

"Stay alert," Melody warned, pulling her up and guiding her on. "Trip-wire!"

Kelly stopped dead. "Where?"

"Sunlight's not on it right now. Here, follow me."

Kelly did so, taking long, careful, zigzagging steps across the dirt. Finally, they arrived at a small building. Kelly reached past Melody for the door handle, eager to get inside.

"Ah, no," Melody said. "Back off, big time."

Kelly withdrew her hand.

Another screech came from behind her.

A clown ran at them, carrying a machine gun.

Kelly reacted fast, leaning down, grabbing a rock and hurling it at his head. The shot was direct and he slumped to the ground.

Melody was impressed. "Not bad when you let yourself go." She picked up the gun. "Stand back." She got ready to fire, then paused and examined the weapon. "Oh no, wait. Nice work, Sandman. I'm not gonna fall for that."

"Fall for what?" Kelly asked.

"It's rigged. You fire this thing; it shoots you in the head." She threw it away, pulled out a pocketknife, knelt down and scraped at the dirt. "Now, did I see a mine round here? Oh, there it is." She scraped around a large circle, then slowly reached in and clicked a switch on the mine's side. "I'll delay it by a few seconds and … all done. Get back, kid."

Kelly retreated and watched as Melody swiftly picked up the mine, moved back to a safe distance, then hurled it at the door. The girls shielded their eyes as both it and the door exploded.

"Move in," Melody called.

They made their way through the smoking, shattered doorway, then stopped in their tracks. Standing inside were three figures draped in long, dark robes, wearing grotesque masks, and clutching razor-sharp scythes. One figure bore the curved beak of a bird of prey; another had rat's features; while a third, dressed as a nun, had the face of Richard Nixon. Sandi sat on a chair between two of them, still in her black jumpsuit and mask. She grinned slyly.

"Mel! With a new recruit! You made it!"

Melody's hand flashed up with the pocketknife.

"Do it," Sandi said coolly. "Hey, I'm not afraid to die, but if I go …"

The scythes rose.

"… you do too. So drop it. Drooopppp it …"

Melody threw the knife into the floorboards where it thudded in, sticking fast.

Sandi was satisfied. "Brains, Mel, not impulses. I taught you that, sis."

"You're not my sis," Melody retorted.

"Can't change the past," Sandi quipped. "I know you like a sister and can read you like a book." She looked at Kelly. "So you're the new one, huh?"

Kelly nodded. "Yeah. Guess so."

"Starting at the bottom, as always." She picked up a notepad and glanced over it. "Kelly Morrison. You've been seeing a therapist for over five years …"

"I'm not the one dressed as a squirrel," Kelly countered, holding her ground.

"A therapist who only takes female clients and sleeps with them," Sandi finished.

"He what?" Kelly asked, startled. "No way …"

Sandi tossed the notepad at her. She let it drop to the floor.

"Not you though," Sandi continued. "Seems you weren't unhinged enough for a good screw. Guess he didn't think you were worth it."

Kelly was aghast. "I am so! No wait …"

Sandi ignored her and focussed on Melody. "Let me guess, the others are still scouting around outside, right?"

Melody shrugged. "You know everything: you tell me."

"No biggie," came the reply. "They'll be close and that's all that matters. Cops'll be here soon too. That'll give me enough time to scarper before they get here. Then you can all go down together."

"For what?" Kelly asked. "You're the freaks who broke into a weather station."

"Yeah, and you're the knobs who blew up a power station," Sandi replied cockily. "There was no need to do that."

Kelly's jaw dropped in horror as the truth hit home. "The blackmail threat that Turbo showed us was fake!"

"Yep," Sandi said proudly. "He was always the weak link. He's not the tech genius he likes to think he is. He fell for our fake broadcast. Then it was only a matter of stirring you up with the squirrel float."

"I'll kill him!" Melody seethed. She put her hand to her forehead, astounded.

Sandi flicked a switch on her phone. The screams and gunshots from the street returned, only now much quieter. "See? No threat, just an illusion. It's amazing what one phone can do when plugged into a centralised network. Pump a few drugs into the local water supply to knock everyone out and hey, it's party time." She grinned. "The float, the way this weather station's rigged, the clowns, the guns, the mines, it was all one big act to get you here."

"What the hell for?" Melody cried.

Sandi smirked. "What I said in the broadcast was for real. We need a test site before things go global. That's where the city comes in. We also need to get the authorities off our backs. That's where *you* come in." Her head rose. "See, since you broke the law by blowing up a power station, we've had to call the cops. We've also set this place up so that when they get here, they'll think you're NUTS. That'll keep 'em busy. For a while anyway. The next step's to send a real message to the public, turning 'em into fruit loops, only I won't be the messenger." She indicated Kelly. "You will."

Kelly was astounded. "Me? Why me?"

Sandi shrugged. "What can I say, you look crazy."

"I'll show you crazy …"

"I wish you would."

Kelly shut up.

Sandi continued. "Once we're happy with the city as a test site, the world's ours. NUTS'll sit in the background, watching countries annihilate each other, then claim the glory."

Kelly glared at Melody. "I told you this was a bad idea! Didn't you hear me tell you it was a bad idea? I said it was a *bad idea* …!"

Melody buried her face in her hands, dropped to her knees and doubled over. "Oh shhhhh ..."

Kelly practically saw a black cloud of anguish fall over Melody who slumped to her side in the foetal position.

"Oh crap!" Melody moaned. "Oh crap, oh crap, oh crap ..."

"Now *this* is worth it," Sandi grinned.

"You've so dumped us in it this time, Mel," Kelly huffed.

"Why humiliate us, S?" Melody groaned. "Why not just kill us and get it over with?"

"Hey!" Kelly sparked up.

Sandi's tone lowered. "You want the truth, Mel? Fine." She paused. "Back in the old days, when it was just you, me, Scoops and Skoob doing field work, our methods sucked. We were pushing crap uphill and getting covered in it. The cold hard fact of life is that not everyone *can* be saved. People always die and the world goes the way *it* wants to. Sure, a couple of happy patches break out for a while, then time steps in and all hell breaks loose, despite the efforts of the do-gooders, well-wishers and love prophets because they're all living in denial. Evolution's produced humans as needy animals so *it* can survive. That's reality." She inhaled sharply. "We tried, Mel. The four of us really did, but at the end of the day there's a global psychic scab that needs to be ripped off so everyone can see what they truly are. Totally NUTS."

Kelly dismissed this as clarity took over. "Or maybe that's just you, lady."

"One person's saviour is another's sinner," Sandi said coldly. "Gimme a break, junior, you're not in my league. Time's up." She nodded to the raven. "We're needed elsewhere. Tie and gag 'em!"

The raven put the scythe to one side, picked up a long rope, grabbed Kelly and bound her.

Nun Nixon seized Melody, bringing her up.

"Get off me!" she snapped, pushing him away.

Sandi rose. "I'll tie her. She'll undo any knot you put on her, except one: the forget-me knot. Only I know that."

Nun Nixon stepped aside.

Sandi grabbed a rope and moved in.

"Junior's right," Melody scowled, thinking of what Kelly had said. "What the hell happened to you, S? There's no way you'd go super-feral on us like this."

"Quit it, Mel!" Sandi scowled back. "Turn!"

She grabbed Melody's arm, turned her around and raised the rope. She started with the basics, tying her to a point, then stopped when an engine roar came from outside.

Everyone looked out the window and watched a car drive by.

Kelly froze, then blinked and looked harder. The car had no driver and there was a cord attached to its steering wheel, leading her to guess that a brick had been placed on its accelerator. It jerked awkwardly, lumbering onto the mines and triggering several explosions, before falling onto its side as an empty husk. A final blast made it wobble a few times, then crash into the dirt upside down.

Melody was impressed. "Cool way to get rid of those things, huh S, but it's only the starter spark. The big gun's next."

"Which is?"

Footsteps rose from outside, then a figure entered the doorway, silhouetted in the morning light.

Sandi nodded to the newcomer. "'Sup?"

"'Sup yourself?" Skoobie answered, entering.

"Stayin' cool, Skoob?" Sandi asked.

Skoobie shrugged. "Eh?"

Kelly was astounded. "*That's* the plan?"

"Oh, no plan," Skoobie assured her. She walked over to the window, stood with her back to it, and sat on the ledge. "Gonna spill, S? Tsunami style?"

Sandi dismissed her and motioned to Rat-man. "Gag her. Talking's her greatest weapon."

"Not as great as a bomb," Skoobie said, holding up a liquid-filled jar.

Rat-man stopped dead.

"Homemade," Skoobie continued. "You taught me how to make it – remember, Chief? Said I needed to toughen up. Well, here I am, the aggressive Skoob-tube. Gonna let my buds go?"

Sandi thought this over. "Since when did you become so upfront? You're bluffing."

"Could be," Skoobie agreed.

Sandi raised her gun, taking aim. "Fifty-fifty shot?"

"Sounds good."

"Totally."

Bang!

The jar shot out of Skoobie's hand, flying through the open window and shattering to the ground outside.

"Bluffing," Sandi confirmed.

"Mix-up," Skoobie corrected. "Brought the wrong jam jar. I hate to think what'll happen if someone back at the café tries to spread jam on their toast, 'cause they really will *spread* their toast …"

"Enough!" Sandi snapped. She motioned to the raven. "Shut her up."

He moved in.

Skoobie held her wrists out, ready to be tied.

Sandi frowned. "This is happening just a little too easily …"

She looked to the back of the room.

Kelly and Melody were no longer there. Their severed ropes lay on the ground, along with Melody's pocketknife that had been pulled out of the floorboards. The fallen hairpin nearby confirmed that it could only be the work of one person.

Vanilla.

Sandi seethed and turned to Skoobie. "Good one, Skoob."

"*Muchos gracias*," came the reply. She reached into her pocket and pulled out a grenade. "Oh look, I do have the real stuff here after all." She removed the pin and placed the grenade on the windowsill where it wobbled violently, ready to tip. "See?"

Everyone dived for cover, save for Skoobie who turned and strolled out the doorway with her hands in her pockets, just as the grenade fell. She didn't flinch as the ear-shattering explosion erupted behind her. Coolly, she rounded a corner and was pulled sideways by Vanilla and Turbo.

Sandi, Raven and Nun Nixon staggered from the smoking building, coughing. Rat-man had been knocked clean out by the blast.

Siren wails pierced their ears. Sandi peered up over the hill to see a group of police cars swooping in.

"Nice work," she mused, impressed. "Good job, guys."

The Raven fled, followed by Nun Nixon. They'd only taken a few steps when …

Snap!

A tripwire severed and a powerful blast sent them flying into the side of a building where they hit the dirt and lay still.

Sandi looked at the ground. Several tripwires had been moved, cutting off her escape. Up ahead, a dozen or so cops were running towards her. She wasn't fazed. Instead, she simply said, "Oh well, gym training it is then."

She dropped her gun, ran to the zigzagging tripwires, raised her arms high, and dived. Her hands landed neatly between the glistening lines as she flipped over acrobatically, skilfully making her way through the deadly maze. Finally, she made it to the end, where she flipped up with a double somersault, landing neatly on her feet.

"Show-off," Melody huffed, emerging from her hiding place.

Vanilla, Kelly, Skoobie and Turbo did the same, just as the police ran up behind them.

"Freeze!" Vertigo ordered; her gun aimed at Melody.

Sandi waved happily at the four girls, then turned and ran.

"She's the bad guy!" Melody cried, turning to Vertigo but still pointing back at Sandi. "It's her you want!"

"You blew up a power station!" Vertigo snapped. "We've got footage of you legging it."

Melody buried her face in her hands in sheer despair yet again. "Ahhhhhhh shhhhh …"

"Yeah well," Vanilla cut in quickly to Vertigo, "you're having an affair with a married judge!"

Vertigo's jaw dropped in horror. "Arrest them!"

"Yeah, go ahead," Skoobie piped up. "Just don't step on any mines. Might still be some around."

"This whole place is rigged," Melody said, looking up.

"By who?" Vertigo retorted.

"The masked freaks over there!" Melody pointed. "We were set up!"

"You still blew up a power station," Vertigo pressed.

"Don't knock it," Kelly replied. "Thanks to us, your affair with that judge is staying under the radar, for now anyway."

"Actually, we do know about it," the Officer beside Vertigo said.

Vertigo looked at him, aghast.

"Everyone knows," he continued. "Sam in the canteen said …"

"Would you shut up?" Vertigo snapped. She looked back at the girls. "Somebody better explain and fast."

"Sure," Melody answered.

She and Vanilla grabbed Turbo, pushing him at her.

"He will," they said together.

"Hey!" Turbo protested. "Don't you want me to help catch the bad guys?"

A motorbike engine roared in the distance.

"Looks like Sandi's got wheels," Melody said. She punched Turbo's arm lightly. "Good luck, hey." She turned and ran.

He winced, rubbing it.

Vanilla patted his shoulder and followed Melody. Kelly raised her hand to pat him too, then hesitantly pulled it away and ran after them. Skoobie kissed his cheek and did the same.

He blushed bright red.

"First kiss?" Vertigo asked.

He scowled. "Shut up!"

She motioned to the Officer. "Mouthing off at the police. Cuff him!"

"Oh sh …!"

He turned to bolt.

Several officers leapt in, rugby-tackling him to the ground.

"And somebody call his mother!" she ordered. "We *really* need her off our backs!"

He screamed angrily.

Melody, Vanilla, Kelly and Skoobie rounded a building and stopped. A long road stretched away from the complex where Sandi rode a motorbike into the bush, giving them a little wave as she left.

Melody gave her an angry sign back, then saw what lay past the side gates and beamed. "Check this out!"

Kelly saw what she was getting at and cringed. "Oh God, do we have to?"

Skoobie put both hands on Kelly's back, gently pushing her forward, while Melody and Vanilla grabbed her arms, leading her along.

"Come on," Melody said excitedly. "You'll love it."

Kelly sighed as they took her to the gate.

Vertigo slammed the police car door shut and locked it, blocking off the protesting Turbo's cries. It didn't bring her much relief, for a thunderous roar suddenly rose from nearby.

"Tripwires disabled, Sarge …" the Officer reported.

Vertigo raised her hand. "Ssssssh! What's that?"

He listened. "Well, if I didn't know better, I'd say it sounds like …"

Melody swiftly rounded the corner, riding a black stallion, followed by Skoobie on another and Vanilla on a third. Kelly sat behind Vanilla, holding on tightly.

"Ooooooooohhhhhhh Goooooooooodddddd …!" Kelly wailed, bumping up and down.

Melody, seeing that the tripwires had been removed from up ahead, led them through.

Vertigo looked at the now empty stables.

"Did they just steal those horses?" she asked the Officer.

"Think so, Sarge," he replied.

"You know, we really have to book them one of these days, and I mean, hit 'em hard …"

"But what if they get a good judge?" he countered. "You know, like the one you're seeing?"

She smacked him. "Shut up! That's crap!"

"But at the Christmas party you two were all over each other and …"

"Can it!"

They watched the horses gallop along the path to a small slope at the end. Vanilla, Kelly and Skoobie rode over it, vanishing from sight. Melody, however, stopped, turned to the side, grinned, and waved at the police, all while the horse rose on its hind legs and whinnied, silhouetted against the sun.

"Oh, get stuffed!" Vertigo yelled.

Melody turned away and rode over the hill.

Sighing, Vertigo made for her car, frustrated as hell. "Come on. Let's get after 'em."

"Right, Sarge."

Vertigo pursed her lips. "I can't wait for the day when those dimwits are hit by a landslide from the crap-mountain they cause."

The bellow of hooves suddenly came from the bush again, growing louder.

Vertigo frowned. "What the hell …?"

The galloping rose and then all three horses ran back with Melody, Vanilla and Kelly screaming, "GO, GO, GO! RUN! GET OUT OF THE WAY …!"

A roar of engines erupted as over fifty clowns on motorbikes thundered after them, brandishing axes, hatches, hunting knives, scythes, maces and chainsaws, with Sandi leading the way.

"And there it is," Vertigo said wearily.

Two police cars revved up and came together, creating a blockade. Vertigo and her officers took cover, raising their guns. Turbo screamed from inside one car, trying desperately to open the locked door while banging on the window helplessly. No one took any notice.

Vertigo ducked as Melody's horse flew over her head, then went Skoobie's, followed by Vanilla's with Kelly screaming, "HOOOOOOLLLLLLLYYYYYY CRAAAAAPPPPP …!"

All three horses landed and bolted away.

"Fire!" Vertigo yelled.

Shots rang out as Sandi slowed, letting three bikes zoom past her, shoot up and fly over the blockade. Halfway over, the bikers leapt off them, flew acrobatically into the air, flipped over with skillful grace, and landed behind the cars, leaving their bikes to hit the dirt.

Sandi and several more clowns followed, soaring over the cars and turning upside down on their bikes. Two clowns let go, landing on the car bonnets, while Sandi hung from her bike's handlebars and kicked an officer hard. He crashed to the ground as the bike swung back down, she mounted it once more, landed smoothly and roared off.

A spiked mace slammed onto a police car, while a hunting knife shot through the air, ramming into an officer's chest, sending him flying. A few clowns were felled, but the rest swept off their bikes, swarming over the police with the swinging kicks of martial artists.

The cops didn't stand a chance.

"This way!" Melody ordered, turning her horse off the road and onto a beaten path, leading into the bush. There, they rode down a small slope and entered a grove of trees.

"What's the plan?" Kelly called.

"Relax!" Melody called back. "Don't know why you're so worried. You aint seen nothin' til you've been caught up in Burmese jungle warfare."

"I swear you're making this stuff up," Kelly said.

"She isn't," the other two girls replied in unison.

Kelly let it go. "So you really think that getting back to Mother Nature with a bunch of psycho clowns isn't that bad?"

"If you wanna stick it out in the open with those useless cops then be our guest," Melody quipped.

"Stick what out in the open," Skoobie wondered, then realised what Melody meant. "Oh right."

An engine roar erupted nearby.

Kelly looked back to see a clown on a bike, bobbing through the bush in hot pursuit.

"I got 'em," Skoobie said.

She turned her horse around in an arc.

Kelly frowned, baffled, as she was carried away.

Skoobie remained still as the clown sneered and rushed towards her, his scythe held high. She stared back at him, holding his gaze as he surged in. He was so focused on her that he didn't notice the half-hidden log by a bush. She watched, detached, as his bike hit it, flipped up and went flying. He didn't go far, but when he landed it was on his own scythe.

Satisfied, she turned on her horse and rode after the others.

Kelly jumped as another bike suddenly sprang out of nowhere, having taken a different route. A giggling clown rode it hard over the terrain alongside her and Vanilla.

Vanilla ripped off a long tree branch and passed it back to Kelly. "Here!"

Kelly took it as the clown veered in with a knife and swiped. She yelped and swung out with the branch, missing him completely. A sudden jolt made her drop a little and the branch jabbed into his front wheel, flipping him up and hurling him into a tree.

"Good job, kid!" Melody called, giving a thumbs-up.

Kelly nearly gagged at what she'd done. "I didn't mean it, I swear!"

A bike jumped through the air, landing next to Melody and riding alongside her. She quickly stood up on her horse, jumped through the V-shaped opening of a tree, grabbed onto an overhanging branch, swung in and kicked the clown off his bike. He rolled to the ground, hit his head, and lay still.

She dropped next to him as another bike rushed at her, then picked up a fallen branch and smacked him hard. He flew backwards with his legs flailing high, turned over in mid-air, landed flat on his face and stayed there.

A third bike swept in. She whirled around, smashed the clown into a ditch, then turned back as an acrobat somersaulted out of nowhere, landing in front of her.

"Come on, freak!" she growled, tensing her muscles.

He lashed out. She ducked, then hit him with an uppercut. He let loose with several long kicks, which she dodged, before grabbing one of his legs in mid-kick and using his own weight to smack him into a tree where he passed out. Smoothly, she picked up a rock and hurled it into another clown's head as he raced past. He fell off his bike and slumped to the ground.

She grabbed the bike, leapt on and raced away.

Skoobie rode through a thick clump of branches, feeling their tension. She was barely out when the branches swung back, knocking a rider off his bike and sending him flying.

An engine bellowed and a clown with a chainsaw shot past Vanilla and Kelly to vanish amidst the trees. Moments later, the chainsaw revved loudly from among them, then a tree fell heavily with a splintering crack. Kelly clung tightly onto Vanilla as both horses jumped, sailing over the falling tree. They landed with a solid jolt – completely ruffling Kelly – and galloped on.

Vanilla huffed. "That wasn't environmentally friendly."

The clown with the chainsaw emerged from ahead, riding back at them.

Vanilla ripped a pinecone off a branch and hurled it into another tree. A screech erupted as a flock of birds soared out, engulfing the rider in their flight. He fell to the side, the chainsaw flew high, and Vanilla grabbed its handle as they passed him.

"Here!" she said, handing it to Kelly.

Kelly grimaced and took it.

The horse leapt over a log; she was caught off-balance and dropped it. The blade hit a pursuing bike's tyre, which crashed and exploded, hurling the clown away.

"That helps!" Vanilla quipped.

Kelly felt sick and looked back to see a mass of clowns behind them. "We are so dead!"

"Pretty much," Skoobie said, riding alongside her.

"How can you be so calm?" Kelly asked, astounded.

"I know what's on the other side," came the reply.

"Oh yeah? What's that?"

"Same as here. Just different rules."

The roaring engines grew louder.

Melody bounced through the bush on her bike. She was making good progress until she saw Sandi, sitting on a stationary bike up ahead. She came to a skidding halt, bringing her bike side-on to Sandi's so that they were parallel, but facing opposite ways.

"End of the run, Mel," Sandi said.

Melody wasn't buying it. "I've been in tighter spots, S. You were there, remember?"

"Yeah, but on your side," Sandi corrected. "Things have changed — *remember?* You know …"

"Don't drag this crap out, S, shut up already!"

Melody revved her bike and spun it around, heading away. She didn't go far before a sharp swing brought her back to face Sandi.

Both girls gunned their engines, then surged in for each other with their gazes locked in mutual enmity. They roared in hard and fast, coming closer and closer until the last second, then both leapt up and grabbed a large branch of a giant tree.

The bikes exploded beneath them, sending a billowing fireball shooting by as they struggled up through the leaves and into a sturdier part of the tree. There, they stood on a thick branch, surrounded by the smell of eucalyptus.

Melody raised her fist. Sandi pulled out an object, aimed it at Melody's stomach and flicked a switch. Several parts snapped open, revealing a crossbow.

Melody stopped dead.

Sandi smirked. "You're too reckless to care about your own life, Mel. Oh yeah, the cyber virus has told us a thing or three about you. Do you want your kid or not?"

Melody's face dropped. "You psychotic bi – !"

"Do it!" Sandi snapped, glaring at her.

Melody's jaw clenched as she tightened her fist angrily, then lowered it. "Alright, S, I'm yours, for now, but this isn't over. It'll never be until you're put on trial by the big guns back home."

"Yeah, yeah, yeah, yada, yada, yada, get down there!"

Melody scowled and made her way through the branches.

"Good luck," Vanilla told Kelly as their horse raced on.

"Who me?" Kelly asked.

"Yeah, sweetie," came the reply.

"Why?" Kelly wondered. "What's …?"

Vanilla ducked and Kelly yelped as she was caught by an overhanging tree branch, pulled backwards off the horse and left to dangle in mid-air while Vanilla and Skoobie rode on. Quickly, and painfully, she climbed up the branch and scrambled into a safer part of the tree out of sight. There were only a few small clumps of leaves to hide her, but it was enough. Through a small gap, she watched her two friends head away.

They didn't get far. Three motorbikes emerged up ahead, rounding them off. Vanilla tried dodging one but a smack from a club sent her flying off her horse with a loud cry. She struck the ground hard and rolled over.

Skoobie also tried heading sideways but was forced back by the clowns. The nearest pulled out a skipping rope with demonic handles, hurled it at her, and watched as it spun in, whipped round her arms, and bound them tightly as its handles clipped together. He revved his bike close to her horse, taunting it. The horse bucked and she fell backwards, hitting the ground with a thud. She rose to her feet, still bound, as the bikes closed in and the clowns dismounted.

Vanilla was hoisted up and pushed next to Skoobie.

A clown approached them. Skoobie opened her mouth to speak. He slapped a large strip of masking tape over her lips, sealing them shut.

"Best to take precautions," he growled.

Another clown loomed over Vanilla.

"Where's your friend?" he sneered, referring to Kelly.

"Who, Mel?" Vanilla replied. "No idea."

"The girl on your horse!" he snapped.

Vanilla glanced at the bush. "Out there. She fell off some way back."

He mounted his bike, turned away and roared off.

Kelly watched as the clowns turned Vanilla and Skoobie around and the small group trudged by her tree. Sandi strode up to them, joined by several more clowns and a bound Melody.

"Scoops," Melody said glumly.

"Mel," Vanilla said back, equally glumly.

Skoobie raised her eyebrows and nodded.

Melody sighed. "'Sup, Skoob."

Skoobie did the same again.

Melody frowned and mouthed, "*What?*"

Skoobie repeated her action, moving her head a little to the left.

Vanilla looked up and realised that Skoobie wasn't greeting Melody at all. She was indicating Kelly's hand, which was out in the open.

Vanilla caught Melody's gaze and copied Skoobie's action. Melody's eyes moved up to the tree, she pursed her lips, glared through the leaves directly at Kelly and mouthed, "*Hand!*"

Kelly shifted it slowly into hiding.

Sandi stepped in so that she, Melody, Vanilla and Skoobie were all in a circle.

"Gang's all here," Sandi said. "Just like old times. How ya doin', Scoops?"

Vanilla drew a sharp breath. "Ditch the games, S. You've lost the right to call me that."

"Hey, only trying to help," Sandi quipped. "Better behave if you wanna see your kids again. They're safe at home, for now anyway. What happens to them is up to you."

"Don't you *dare* bring them into this!" Vanilla snapped.

"Plays dirty, doesn't she?" Melody said darkly.

Vanilla composed herself. "I'm giving you one last chance, S. Walk away. Drop everything and go. I don't care where, just lie low. If you don't, I'll …" She paused, " … tell 'em."

Sandi's face hardened.

"Tell us what?" Melody asked.

Skoobie's eyebrows rose quizzically.

Vanilla continued. "We've got a secret haven't we, S? Just the two of us. A deep dark secret that only we know about …"

Sandi scowled. "Shut up, Scoops!"

"And you didn't let me in on it?" Melody said, annoyed.

Skoobie frowned crossly, as if to say, "*Or me?*"

"I couldn't," Vanilla answered, holding Sandi's gaze. "I swore. We made a pact on the banks of the Nile. She broke her word. I can break mine. It's the one thing I hold over her."

Sandi was shaken. "You wouldn't! You'd never sink that low …!"

"Look how low you've sunk!" Melody retorted. "What's the deal, Scoops? How come we're not in the loop?"

"*Mmmmmf!*" Skoobie nodded, translating as, "*Yeah!*"

"She trusted me," Vanilla replied. "I'm the eldest, and the most empathetic. The best one to talk too, isn't that what you said?"

Melody looked away, muttering crossly.

Skoobie did the same, beneath her tape.

Vanilla kept her gaze fixed on Sandi. "You have to end this, S. You need to do what's right."

Sandi spoke softly. "I can't."

"You don't have a choice," Vanilla pressed.

Sandi shook her head. "No. You don't hold the cards here, Scoops. This is my game; my rules …"

"We swore an oath, S. If I say the word, it's game over."

Sandi's jaw clenched.

Silence. Then:

"WILL SOMEBODY PLEASE TELL ME WHAT THE FRIGGIN' HELL'S GOIN' ON!" Melody cried.

Several birds fled from the trees, screeching.

"Mmmmmmf!" Skoobie agreed.

Sandi shuddered. "No way, Scoops. Life's not about looking back. Mel's right. I do play dirty." She brought her face in close to Vanilla's. "You know the deal. My people have orders. Say anything and your kids are gone." She raised her finger menacingly. "We can destroy each other through a few simple words. Have you got the guts to do that?"

Vanilla stayed quiet.

"Have you?" Sandi pressed.

Vanilla's tone lowered. "Don't do this, S."

"Gag her!" Sandi ordered a clown.

Vanilla was pulled back and her mouth was strapped with tape.

"Get 'em outta here," Sandi ordered, turning away. "We've got a job to do."

She walked off.

The clowns pushed the girls forward.

"Mmmmm mmmm mmm mmmm mmmmmf!" Skoobie said from beneath her gag.

Melody was confused. "Why do you want to stop for ice-cream on the way, Skoob?"

"Mmmmmm mmm mmmf mmm?" Skoobie replied.

"Eucalyptus flavour?" Melody wondered. "What the hell?"

"Mmmmm mmm mmm mmmm mmmmmf!"

"No, Skoob," Melody said wearily. "I don't know if there's an ice-cream branch round here that sells eucalyptus flavour."

"*Mmmmmf!*" Vanilla pushed.

Melody looked up to see Kelly's glasses glimmering in the sunlight beneath the leaves.

"Oh right," Melody suddenly realised. "Fine then. I'll *keep an eye out* for it."

Kelly took her glasses off quickly.

"*Mmmmm mmmm mmmm mmmmm mmmmmf?*" Skoobie asked.

"I don't know, Skoob," Melody replied, indicating Vanilla. "Bestie here's got her reasons."

"*Mmmmm mmmm mmmmm,*" Vanilla responded, which translated as: "Sorry, guys, that's the way it goes."

"Yeah right," Melody scoffed.

Sandi sighed. "Why did I ever teach you guys how to do that?" She motioned to her clowns. "Split 'em up."

They were led off in different directions.

"See ya, Scoops!" Melody called.

"*Mmmm mmm mmm 'el!*" Vanilla said back, meaning: "*See ya later, Mel.*"

"*Mmmmm mmm mmmm mmmm mmmmmey,*" Skoobie added, meaning: "*Take it easy, big cheesy.*" She paused in thought, then mused, "*Mmmmm mmm mmmm mmmm mmmm mmmmm,*" translating as: "*I really do wanna try eucalyptus ice-cream though.*"

A clown smacked her.

"*Mmmmmf fff!*"

Soon they were out of sight.

Kelly remained deathly still as the clowns scoured the area. There were many to begin with, but soon their number lessened until finally, there were no more.

She stayed motionless for over an hour, not daring to move in case someone was hiding below. Instead, she listened to the birds and the gentle rustling of the fragrant eucalyptus leaves. Eventually, when she was sure it was safe, she climbed out of the tree and stepped onto the ground. Beaten and weary, she stared into the steadily warming day, then trudged through the bush. "Guess it's all down to me now. Stakes are high this time." She took a deep breath and gazed at the beaten landscape. "Real high."

The day grew warmer as she trudged on, and soon arrived back at the weather station. The place was now empty, save for two wrecked police cars and several bodies.

She wondered if there was a phone around, then figured it wouldn't work anyway. Even stranger was that there were no special ops teams here. Surely they must have been called for, she thought. A few cop cars were gone, having clearly fled the area, but no one had returned. Maybe the cyber virus had kicked in back home, she reasoned, meaning all hell had broken loose.

She was considering what to do next when:

Bang, Bang, Bang!

"Help!"

She jumped and turned to the wrecked police car behind her.

Turbo was inside, banging at the window.

"Sssssh!" Kelly hissed. "We're in freak-central, remember?"

"Get me outta here!" he cried. "I need to go to the bathroom! Hurry!"

She tried opening the door.

It was locked.

She picked up a fallen police gun.

He yelped and ducked.

"Relax," she said, turning it over, "and stay back."

He scrambled away from the window and she swung the gun like a club. The hit was hard, the gun fell from her hand, dropped, flipped over and fired. She jumped as the bullet whizzed past her arm, hitting the window and creating a bullet hole.

"What the hell are you doing?" Turbo wailed, looking up.

"I said to stay back," she warned, before picking up a rock and smashing the window. The glass fell away, and she quickly cleared what was left with the rock and called, "Come on!"

Turbo winced and climbed out through the broken remains. She helped him onto the road.

"Thanks," he said, once clear of the car. "Back in a sec."

He ran off quickly.

A few minutes later, he returned.

"So," Kelly asked, "what's the story?"

"The men's was locked so I had to use the ladies'…" he began.

"Not that!" she huffed. "Where is everyone?"

He glanced into the distance. She followed his gaze to see a black cloud of smoke steadily rising from the city.

"Looks like the cyber virus has kicked off," he said grimly.

Kelly shuddered.

"Street art was right," she murmured, thinking of the graffiti she'd seen in the alleyway by the café. "Acrapolypse Now." She sighed. "God, why did this happen to me? All I wanted was the usual stuff. You know, job, career, family. So what do I get? World War Three!" She headed for an open office. "Well, we gotta try something."

She entered, went to the desk and picked up a mobile. All she got from it was a long tone. The same was true for the landline. The power was out too, meaning the office PC was down.

She returned to the doorway and put her hands on either side of its frame. "Worth a shot, but no luck." She ran a hand through her hair. "God, where do we go from here?"

"The café," Turbo answered simply.

"What?" she asked, confused.

"The café," he repeated. "Skoobie told me in the car while you and Mel were busy dodging traps round here. She said the café was more than just a place to eat, and that it's been growing buds from day one, whatever that means."

"Guess it means us," Kelly replied. "God knows what we can do though. Still, it sounds like we'll find help there, if it hasn't been blown apart that is."

"Uh … no," he countered. "Skoob told me that it's protected against attacks. Something about a psycho-structural firewall that's part of their home insulation scheme."

Kelly blinked, shaking her head.

"Whatever it means," he continued, "she said if worse comes to worst, we'll find help there."

She shrugged. "What other choice do we have? Fine, let's see if we can …"

A gentle clip-clop came from nearby. A snort followed as a horse emerged from the bush. Kelly recognised it as Melody's.

"That'll help," she said. "Though it's kinda weird how it suddenly found us."

"Nah," Turbo said back. "Skoobie probably told it to. She said she speaks to animals all the time, majoring in fluent bull."

Kelly smiled. "I'm not surprised." She approached the horse. "I haven't ridden in a long time. It'll be a bumpy ride."

"What about me?" Turbo asked.

"We'll have to ride together, won't we? Come on, it won't be that bad."

She placed her foot in the stirrup and mounted the horse.

"Your turn," she told him.

He climbed up and sat behind her. Rather uncomfortably, he wrapped his arms around her tummy.

"Hands!" she ordered.

"What?" he asked blankly. "Oh, sorry …"

He adjusted his grip.

"Watch your fingers too," she warned. "I get ticklish."

He did so.

She clicked her tongue and the horse slowly turned in a circle. Trying another tack, she pulled the reins the other way. The horse circled in the opposite direction.

"What are you doing?" Turbo wondered.

"I don't know," she replied. "This thing doesn't have a steering wheel."

"Maybe if you pull this way …" he prompted.

"No, don't do that …" she said back.

"Yeah, yeah …"

"That'll just confuse the horse …"

"It's already confused …"

The reins were pulled from side to side, jerking the horse's head awkwardly, making it snort.

"Will you let me steer?" she asked crossly.

"You're not exactly doing a good job," he countered.

"Oh, you wanna try?"

She raised her arms. He reached under them, grabbing the reins.

"And stop breathing in my ear," she huffed. "Having you there's bad enough, but when you're breathing that heavy …"

"Sorry, I feel a little hoarse," he joked.

She elbowed him lightly.

"You're lucky my stomach was behaving itself there," he said. "Okay, here we go …"

He kicked the horse's side, but a little too hard. The horse bolted with a start towards the bush, making them cry out as they jerked up and down on its back. They quickly pulled on the reins. Much to their relief, their ride slowed somewhat.

"Left, left!" she ordered.

"I am going left!" he said back. "The horse'll go around that tree. It's not stupid."

"Yeah but …" *Crack!* "Ow! There's a branch there!"

Crack!

"I see it," he grumbled sorely.

"Go right," she pressed.

"I am going right," he replied.

"No, you're going into …" *Crack!* "Arggghhh! See? I'm getting a sore head from your steering, and get your hand off my leg. It's icky!"

The horse weaved from side to side, taking them along a path.

"Did I say that riding together wouldn't be that bad?" she sighed. "I was wrong. It's worse!"

The ride was a struggle to begin with. There were protests, swearing and light slapping, along with strained snorting from the horse. After a while, they all calmed down, especially when Kelly made Turbo get off and walk for a bit. Before too long, she felt sorry for him and let him back on, and they continued to the city in relative peace.

Soon, they were heading along a highway. The city wasn't far, but the smoke was growing thicker. Kelly tensed at the sight of it, then saw a farmhouse nearby and wanted to check it out. Turbo didn't like the idea. She dismissed this, they approached the house, dismounted, and she went to the front door.

Thankfully, it was open. Even more thankfully, the place was empty. Its occupants must have left in a hurry, she figured. Luckily, she found a spare set of keys for the truck outside and was soon driving along the barren highway with Turbo by her side, making for the looming spectre of the city ahead.

Sirens wailed as helicopters scoured over the burning skyscrapers, forcing Kelly to slow the truck as they entered the city centre. Nervously, she navigated her way through the angry mobs who were either clashing with the police or attacking each other. She cringed at the sight of the bloodied, splayed-out bodies on the pavement.

"Lying bastards!" one man growled, hurling a rock at an office window, shattering it.

"Criminals!" a large man bellowed. "Let's make *them* afraid!"

A petrol bomb flew into the office, blowing it to smithereens.

Kelly jumped and steered the truck away. She didn't go far and was forced to slow again when a group of youths swept in, banged the bonnet, and ran on.

Clank!

She looked back to see a petrol bomb rolling in the truck's trailer.

"Crap!" Turbo cried, leaping out.

Kelly did the same and they bolted into an alleyway and fell to the ground as the truck exploded behind them in a deafening roar.

Turbo shivered. "What the hell's happening here?"

"Terrorism," Kelly answered darkly. "Only this time *we're* the terrorists. The freaks behind all this don't have to do anything, only sit back and watch us kill each other."

They rose and headed to the end of the alleyway before emerging onto the street.

Screech!

They dropped once more as a car flew by, with machine gun bullets spraying from the uzis' in its windows. The car sped away with the youths laughing inside.

Turbo shuddered. "This is nuts!"

"You said it," Kelly quipped.

They rose again, heading on.

The journey across town was a nightmare as they hurried through several more alleyways, hiding from the violent chaos. Finally, a lone building ahead made Kelly's heart leap out of her chest.

Sanders Café, seemingly untouched.

A few people stood out the front, and with them was …

"David!"

He turned to Kelly's call, then pushed his way through a small group and ran towards her. She ran back at him, just as fast, before leaping into his tight embrace. He caught her, kissed her several times, then placed his hand on the back of her head as she hugged him and wept.

He held her shoulders, leaned down and looked into her eyes.

"You okay?" he asked. "Tell me you are."

She nodded. "Yeah. How 'bout you?"

"As well as can be expected under the circumstances," he answered.

Another man ran up to them.

Darren.

"Kel!" he said quickly. "Glad you're okay. Where's Mel?"

Kelly's face fell. "Uh …"

"Down!" David cried.

They swung themselves round a corner as several gunshots flew by. The couple who'd fired ran away laughing.

"Let's get inside," David said quickly. "We can talk there."

They made for the café door and entered.

Kelly was astonished to find the café as calm and as pristine as ever. Her heart tingled with its familiar, soothing aura, confirming Skoobie's comment to Turbo about it being protected by a real-life firewall, cutting it off from the chaos outside. Despite the clashing in the streets, no crazies out there had noticed the café. To them, she figured, it was seemingly invisible.

What's more, the place was full of people, only now they were looked after in other ways. Medical staff were attending to the wounded, some of whom were lying on mattresses on the floor. Nearby, a small team worked away at laptops on a table.

Turbo's eyes lit up like a Christmas tree at the sight of the tech. "Sanity!"

He hurried over excitedly.

Kelly was impressed. "Wow! Talk about the best service anywhere. The café regulars do this?"

"Uh-huh," he answered. "We call it café-counterterrorism. Serving others is what the café's all about."

"Can I do anything to help?" she found herself asking.

A large military man, with a moustache, approached them.

"You certainly can," the man replied. "Major Kirk, ex-army, retired, up til now that is. Seems I'm back in business."

Kelly was impressed. "A major?"

"Certainly am," he confirmed, then glanced at a man on a laptop. "That's Adam. He's the doctor in charge of the medical team here. Nick behind him, is a damn good engineer. We also have a cook, a few firefighters, mechanical personnel, police officers, and some ex-ones too. Most of us came to the café over the past year because we were burnt out. Now, together, we can stop the city going up in flames." He indicated the laptops. "Many of us have global, political contacts too. We're working on reaching them." His head rose. "We're also hoping you can fill us in."

Kelly beamed, feeling the café's magic tingle inside her.

"Sure," she said proudly.

He motioned to a chair. "Then take a seat, Private Morrison, and tell us everything."

Kelly did so.

Kelly revealed everything that had happened over the last few hours. The Major, David and Darren hung onto every word while Turbo worked busily on his laptop. When she finished, she sat back in her seat.

"So that's it," she said. "It's up to us now. Mel and the others are out of the picture."

David mused thoughtfully. "Sandi'll have 'em locked up, especially Scoops. She won't let her do much."

"Did you know Sandi?" Kelly asked.

He shook his head. "No. She was before my time."

The Major mulled this over. "Keep in mind that the city's only a test site. NUTS wants it to go global, and you know what that means." His voice lowered. "World War Three."

Kelly shivered. "I don't want to think about it. I'm already sick to my stomach."

"Hang on, hang on," David cut in. "If freedom of information's going global and everyone knows everyone's business, then how will NUTS protect themselves? I mean think about it, just think about it. They know all our secrets. Everybody does now, but we know nothing of theirs. They wouldn't go into this without some sort of digital protection, would they? Like a cyber defence system. That's what we need to find."

"How?" Kelly asked.

"By striking the Delirium!" Turbo suddenly sparked up from his laptop.

"Huh?" Kelly wondered.

"Good plan, son," the Major told Turbo, "but we've no idea where the Delirium is."

"Beneath City Hall," he answered.

The man on the next laptop spoke up. "That's good to know. The CIA's been looking for it for years."

Kelly was baffled. "Then how did *he* find it?"

"That's what I was wondering," the Major said.

Turbo grinned and tapped the side of his head. "Easy. Genius."

"I'm gonna throw something at you," Kelly warned.

"Okay, okay." He turned his laptop to face them. "I've been looking at NUTS's video. The real one that is, right after the virus was released. Take a look."

He pressed a button. A paused image of Skoobie's face appeared.

"Skoob?" Kelly said, confused. "Why's she the messenger girl?"

Turbo shrugged. "Hey, she's the best one to speak for a bunch of crazies. This was released a few hours ago. Check it out."

He turned up the volume, pressed play, and they all listened as Skoobie spoke.

"Hey y'all, this is the Skoob Tube. Wow, look at this, huh? I've got my own poco-local channel. It's so cool! I'm everywhere now. TV, radio, computer, phone, you name it, I'm on it." She paused. *"Which makes you lot pretty sad. You're so caught up in your tech that you're missing 'real life'. You could all be doing something useful right now, but you're watching me instead. Well, the dumb ones are anyway."*

Sandi's voice hissed from offscreen, *"Stick to the damn script!"*

Skoobie blinked. *"There's a script?"*

"From the teleprompter!"

"There's a teleprompter?"

"Dammit ...!"

"Oh yeah, right. Take a chill pill, amigo. So, where were we? Oh, there we go. Yeah, the drill is that you've all been hiding behind your tech for so long and have been screwing each other over and there's all this darkness inside of you and, yada, yada, yada. Pause for impact. Oh wait, don't read that bit."

She blinked again and continued.

"So yeah, the cyber virus has been released and the only website that's up and running is ours. Everyone's secrets are now open in a free-for-all and if you wanna look somebody up, go there. Otherwise, you'll get email alerts telling you who your friends and family really are."

She winked at the screen.

"Thing is, the virus does way more than chucking up your sick stuff all over dodgyville. Everything gets unlocked, and that means 'everything.' Bank accounts'll flow freely, turning

them into digital river-banks where all the fishy stuff's up for grabs. Houses and cars'll follow when their systems power-down. I'm just glad that those poor zoo animals'll now have a shot at freedom. Mind you, the prisoners in jail will too, and the name of the game here's fairness and equality. Yep, we're bringing everything out into the open and sending the world totally NUTS. There'll be no barriers. No alarms, clocks, locks, or clouds in your head, and you know what that means? Yes people, the revelation's upon us and it ain't pretty."

She paused and blinked once more.

"And none of this would have happened if you'd stuck with nature to begin with. Simple, wasn't it? No, you had to make waves by surfing round a net that was only there to hook you in. Now you've drowned yourselves in so much digital crap that it's impossible to keep your head above water."

"None of that's in the script!" Sandi hissed.

"Well it should be," Skoobie retorted. *"And why are you guys looking at me like that? Am I'm making terrorism look unprofessional or something?"*

"Yes!" Sandi fumed.

"Please, it was overrated anyway. I prefer 'go-with-it-ism.' She blinked rapidly. *"So … um … everyone, don't panic. You freak-out, you get hurt. Just stay calm and think clearly."*

A gun clicked offscreen.

"Don't go givin' mixed messages!" Sandi warned.

"Mixed messages, what?" Skoobie huffed. *"I don't even get what I'm s'posed to be doing here. I'm just drifting along with whatever my mouth says … "*

"Read the damn last part!"

"Yeah fine, whatever," Skoobie quipped, brushing her off. *"So, you've all got a couple of hours to have a little fun while we let the rest of the world know our plans and watch 'em go berserk. See, our NUTS are getting bigger by the moment … oooh that sounds funny …"*

The gun clicked again.

"Oh yeah, script right?" She cleared her throat and blinked. *"See, we've got new recruits but need more for a global takeover. That means you guys jumping on board the good ship Hellraiser. If you wanna survive this garbage we've got a camp in the hills. Just head there and we'll train you to be on the numero-uno-teamo. Map's coming up soon. Try and attack our little hidey-hole and everyone inside'll be killed."* She paused, blinking, as she thought this over. *"Great, I like camps. They show you how to concentrate on what's really important. They should be called concentration camps. Oh no wait, that's bad. Hey, is this what these are …?"*

The screen went dead.

Kelly was astounded. "That was the dumbest terrorist message I've ever seen!"

Turbo beamed. "There you go, see? They're in the Delirium, under City Hall. We can get in through a ventilation shaft in the southwest block, corridor three. We've just got to disable the security cameras first."

Kelly shook her head in disbelief. "You got that from *that* message?"

"Yep."

He smiled smugly.

She smacked him lightly. "How?"

"Didn't you see her eyes?" he asked. "There were two messages going on at once. One was with her mouth, the other was her blinking. She taught it to me the other day. It's called Skorse code. Her babbling was to keep the bad guys' focus off her face, although a lot of it really *was* babbling."

"You think?" Kelly scoffed. "So Sandi couldn't pick that up?"

"No," he replied happily. "Skoob only made it up a week or so ago when she was in a park staring at the clouds. Said she was bored."

"Genius," David quipped.

"Thanks," Turbo replied. "Oh, you mean her, right?"

"Is she genuine?" the Major asked. "Can we trust her?"

"Totally," Turbo answered. "Now, I've got the building's layout here." He flicked on another screen. "We ready?"

Kelly grinned. "Bring it on."

"Right," the Major said. "Let's get to work."

Chapter Fourteen

Kelly sat silently as the final adjustments were made to her costume. She shifted awkwardly in the dress that had come from the pop-culture store in the next street that she'd raided with the Major and Turbo. Luckily, their journey there and back had been trouble-free.

"I sure hope this works," she said, now fitted as a bloodied bride.

"Sure will," Turbo said back, handing her an axe while dressed as a clown. "We gotta look like nuts to blend in with them."

The Major scratched his moustache and adjusted his wig and skirt, dressed as Dorothy from The Wizard of Oz. He picked up a mask from a table and held it before Kelly. "For your finishing touch, Private Morrison."

Kelly's eyes nearly popped out of her head. "A gorilla? No way."

"It's either that or the apron with a lady's funbags on top," Turbo pointed out.

"I'll take the mask."

She grabbed it.

Turbo brought up a screen on his laptop. "Okay, I've bypassed the cyber-virus mainframe and disabled the security cameras to City Hall. Now we can enter unseen by the big boys. We ready?"

"No," Kelly flat-out answered.

"Good," the Major said. "Move out."

She rose and started to follow him.

David touched her arm, stopping her. "Hey …"

Kelly gave a little smile. "I'm a blood-splattered bride about to go to war, David. Not a good omen."

He smiled back. "You're not an omen, you're a human being. One who's got someone waiting for her. Right here."

"I still don't see why you can't come …"

He stroked her hair behind her ear. "Let's just say that the café's on active service and …"

"You're in charge," she finished.

"Right," he confirmed. "You'll be fine without me. I believe in you."

Kelly felt her insides bubble. "David …"

She was cut off as he took her by the shoulders, pulled her in and kissed her long and lovingly. Caught in the moment, she kissed back.

Slowly, they parted.

He spoke resolutely. "I love you, Kelly Morrison. Don't ever forget that."

Kelly shuddered. "David?"

"Yeah?"

"I love you too."

"Then make sure to come back and tell me."

"Let's go!" the Major called.

"See you soon," David said softly.

Kelly nodded. "See you soon."

They kissed quickly and she turned and headed off.

He smiled, watching her go.

Unable to resist one last look at him, she glanced back lovingly as she walked towards the door.

Their eyes met once again.

Then she walked straight into the doorframe.

"This is ridiculous," Kelly grumbled, holding her sore forehead while following the Major and Turbo down the street. "What did I want to be when I grew up? A ballerina. Now look at me. Stumbling through a sick urban jungle dressed as the bride of King Kong!"

A beer bottle flew at her. She ducked the shot and ran after the others. She couldn't see much through her gorilla mask – not that she wanted to. The surrounding screams were bad enough.

They made it to City Hall unscathed and hurried up the steps. Inside, the place was empty, having been ransacked by the mob.

"This way," Turbo said, leading them along a corridor.

"I hope you know what you're doing," Kelly retorted.

"Quiet!" the Major ordered, listening for threats.

Turbo stopped by a ventilator grille, just big enough for them to squeeze through. He put his hands on it and struggled to pull the cover away.

Nothing happened.

"This'll need a little work," he said. "It seems to be magnetically sealed. Can't see any screws though. If I had my laptop, I could bypass the security grid."

The Major leaned down, placed his hands on the grille and gently pulled it away, with only a touch of strength.

"Oh yeah, right," Turbo muttered.

"Follow me," the Major instructed.

He crawled into the shaft, followed by Kelly and then Turbo. They hadn't gone far when they heard synthesised music coming from up ahead. Its pulsating rhythms brought vibrant colours to the forefront of Kelly's mind. She listened, captivated, to the curious melodies that flowed like a mystical river, entrancing her to the max.

Not knowing why, she crawled faster as her body went into autopilot. The music grew, along with the loud chatter of a large party. Finally, they came to another ventilation grille where an orange halo pulsated from beyond, along with the entrancing harmonies and free-flowing laughter.

The Major removed the grille and crawled through. Kelly and Turbo followed and all three of them emerged under a table with a polka-dot cloth draped over it. They peered out as a strobe light flashed across their faces. When it passed, they gazed in awe at the vibrant spectacle before them that was well and truly …

"Awesome!" Kelly whispered.

For stretched out over an enormous room, was one giant party.

They watched in wonder as two people on stilts walked by, their faces painted white between their dark suits and top hats as they effortlessly juggled several kinds of fruit. High above them were two acrobatic trapeze artists, flying back and forth with athletic aerial feats in time with the music. Nearby, contortionists on podiums posed in the middle of the room, their bodies stretched to painfully awkward angles. Dwarves, lavish costumes, fire-eaters, martial artists, ballet dancers, there were marvels everywhere Kelly looked. To her, this newfound world was nothing short of spectacular.

In the middle of it all, overlooking everyone from the stage, was a bride dressed in black, seated upon a throne. A veil covered their face, while two gloved hands protruded from the dress, resting upon the macabre skulls on the throne's arms. On either side stood four Groomsmen, also dressed in black, with skulls painted over their faces. They stood formally with their arms down in front of them and their hands crossed.

"Can I play too?"

Kelly looked up. The woman who'd spoken wore a top hat and a black business suit, complete with a white tie.

"What are you playing?" the woman asked sweetly.

The Major put a finger to his lips. "Sssssh!"

"Oh, I get it," the woman said happily, and did the same. "Sssssh!"

Acting bizarrely, the Major crawled out from under the table and began sniffing around her legs, like a puppy dog. Kelly also emerged, making ape-noises, while Turbo followed silently.

"Ooooh, you're playing pets!" the woman beamed. "The Apocalypse Party rocks, doesn't it?"

"Apocalypse Party?" Kelly blurted out.

The Major glared at her, then the three of them slowly rose.

"Yeah," the woman replied. "You must be new here."

Kelly opened her mouth to speak.

"Yep," the woman confirmed. "You're newbies. Love it."

Kelly relaxed, if only a little.

The woman continued. "So, welcome to the Apocalypse Party. We're a political movement, but we also need to have fun so, Apocalypse *Party*, get it?"

"Cool," Kelly found herself saying.

"I'm Z by the way. Short for Zianna, and you are …?"

The Major was about to respond when a ballerina suddenly swept in and pulled him away for a dance.

"Whoa!" Z quipped. "Sorry 'bout that? And you are?"

"Turbo Newcombe," Turbo said eagerly.

Kelly stamped on his foot and thought fast. "Turbo Newcombe Aloysius Gonzalez. I'm Gorilla Bridezilla. Call me GB."

"Wanna meet my friends?" Z asked.

"Well …"

"It's okay, they're cool." She looked at Turbo. "Oh, I can tell you like what you see. Tell you what, we'll get together later with a couple of my friends. Free love's all the rage here. Anything goes. Right girls?"

She waved at two blondes walking past. They grinned, kissed the air and waved back.

Turbo went white and recoiled in shock, only to land straight in the arms of a giant older woman who pulled him away.

"I got 'im first," the woman said gruffly.

He looked at her horrified as he was dragged off.

Z pulled Kelly forwards and they both ducked as an acrobat flew over their head.

"The boss is impulsive when grabbing potential," Z said happily. "That's you, chickadee. Come meet my buds." She led her to a small group. "Hey guys, meet our newbie. This is GB, our latest hot rod. GB, these are your new besties. That's Yosemite, Alley-Onda, Nightbird and Charley."

"Hey!" one girl said warmly.

They all stepped in, giving her a group hug.

"Welcome, welcome …"

"Great to see ya!"

"Love the outfit!"

Charley was more casual than the rest, with short dark hair, a pink-striped cotton sweater, black and white tights and a small hat. "How ya goin', GB? Settlin' in?"

"Better than expected," Kelly sparked up.

"Yeah, this place is funky," Charley agreed. "Hey, if you want anything, and I mean *anything*, let us know – we'll get it for you. Where you from?"

Kelly's mind raced. "Uh … Southport."

"Oh yeah? Where abouts?"

Kelly thought harder. "Adelaide Street."

Charley was impressed. "Cool. You'd be right near the park. There's a stall there that sells the *best* hot dogs."

"Better than Jason's?" Yosemite asked, dressed as a slinky black cat.

"*Way* better than Jason's," Charley replied. She pulled Kelly back as a dwarf came past, juggling three animal bones. "Watch out …"

Kelly grimaced and looked away.

"You caught us just at the right time, babe," Charley told Kelly coolly. "We were discussing the socio-economic policies of South-East Asia between

1950 and 1977, but Alley-Alley-Onda here made us stray from the convo and we started talkin' 'bout Shakespeare instead. So it's up to you, GB. Deciding vote. What are we talkin' about?"

"Shakespeare," Kelly replied automatically. "I've always loved Shakespeare."

"Cool," Charley said. "So, guys, best work?"

Nightbird, dressed as a raven, spoke. "I like *Macbeth*."

"Boring, dark and brooding," Charley retorted.

"Seconded," Z agreed.

"Yeah, but it's got all those dark vibes with good lessons thrown in," Nightbird said.

"It's a tragedy," Yosemite said back. "I hate tragedies."

"Go on then, what's your favourite?" Nightbird asked Yosemite.

"*Much Ado About Nothing*," came the reply.

"Nice," Charley mused, "but it really *is* Much Ado About Nothing. Alley-Alley-Onda, your go."

The girl dressed as a fox spoke next. "Well, undoubtedly, *King Lear* was *the* best …"

"Agreed," all except for Kelly said.

"But my favourite's *King Richard the Third*," fox-girl finished.

"*Not* historically accurate …" Charley pointed out.

"Yeah, but such villainy," fox-girl replied. "Z, you're up."

"*Troilus and Cressida*," Z said.

"Ugh!" they all grimaced, making faces.

"Who knows what to make of that?" Nightbird asked, shaking her head.

"Charley, Charley?" Z prompted.

"I like *A Midsummer Night's Dream*," Charley answered.

They all rolled their eyes.

"What?" Charley asked. "I like it."

Z indicated the room around them. "Just a little too close to real life, don't ya think? Okay, GB, your turn. Best or favourite Shakespeare play. Go!"

Kelly thought quickly. "I like … uh … *Romeo and Juliet!*"

"Clichéd!" they all chorused.

"They both end up dead," Yosemite added.

"And she's like, what, fourteen?" Charley scoffed. "That's the teeny-bopper stuff of its day." She started to move away. "I'm gonna grab a drink and then we'll discuss Shakespearean sonnets next, okay?"

"Hang on, hang on," Kelly cut in. "Sorry to do this. I mean, it's great that you're having a good time. This place *is* pretty funky …"

Charley slapped her shoulder. "Welcome to the new world, GB."

"And thanks for letting me in," Kelly replied, "but I've got to ask, why are we partying to the max while people are killing themselves just outside the building?"

"Good point," Z said back.

"Very good point," Charley agreed as the other girls nodded. "People have always partied in the middle of nothing *but* chaos. Outside's the same as usual, only now we can see what our real neighbours are up to as opposed to people on the news in some other country. So what if they're one hundred metres or two thousand kilometres away? Same chaos, right? What's the big diff?"

"Yeah, but it's wrong," Kelly said.

"You only just noticed that now, sweet-cheeks?" Charley asked. "Survival of the fittest isn't fair but that's the way it is. At least the Ev-Rev makes us accept that."

Kelly frowned. "Ev-Rev?"

"Oh yeah, you're new," Charly remembered. "The Evolution Revolution, babe. The dawn of a new age. A new wave's about to swamp the world and it's totally …"

"NUTS!" the other girls cried.

Charley grinned. "Fitting name, ain't it? It shows who we *really* are. See, the world's always been living in denial. Our job's to wake it up and tell everyone not to bother going for sanity. Why not just flow with the chaos and all be …?"

"NUTS!" the girls cried again and laughed.

Kelly stared at them, bewildered.

"Don't think about it too much," Charley told her. "Party. Have fun. Let tomorrow take care of itself."

Z spoke up. "We've got a lot to look forward to. A single society of freedom, parties and no secrets, period. No cliquey-group fights, political power plays or never-ending wars. You'll be free to be yourself, and if people don't like who you are, it's not a hypocritical government's problem, it's yours. You deal with it. When you eventually find out that your attempts to get anywhere in life only lead to futile struggling and then death, you'll realise that the only solution is to forget everything and party. There's nothing else you can do."

Kelly didn't like what she was hearing. "That's not right."

"That's why we're here to discuss it," Charley said. "In all fairness, I don't believe in any kind of wrong or right. That's for the dark ages and the old way of looking at things. You wanna talk ethics, go see Mac, the religious NUT over there. You want evolution, talk to Professor M, the science NUT. You want psychology, go talk to Marsh-Mellow in the corner. It's up to you. Any attempt to control the world is futile because eternity'll obliterate us out of existence in the end. The sooner we accept that and go with the flow for as long as we can, the better."

Kelly was hesitant. "I don't know …"

"Just listen, okay?"

Charley spoke.

Kelly listened as Charley talked for ages, and soon realised that the girls made complete sense. Everything was going to fall away in the end. Why try and fight it? Why not just party and let everyone up top kill each other? There was no solution for anything. Time would always continue, whilst feeding on the whole of her existence to create another for someone else. Fighting back was just futile.

Through it all, Z, Nightbird, Yosemite and Alley-Onda threw in jokes, insights and quips that made Kelly laugh long and loud, feeling like she truly belonged in this surreal kingdom.

Reality faded away as she lived in the moment. Alley-Onda handed her a drink, she downed it, then followed the girls onto the dance floor, passing Turbo on the way. He was still held tightly by the giant woman and couldn't escape.

"I find you very attractive," the woman said.

He grumbled under his breath.

The woman continued. "Why do you have such a strong yearning to escape older women? I bet you had a dominating mother, didn't you?"

He nearly exploded.

Kelly beamed as she stepped onto the dance floor, formed a circle with the girls and started dancing bizarrely as the multi-coloured strobe lights flashed over her. She weaved and wiggled gleefully as the beat consumed her completely, calling her home. Suddenly she understood who and what she truly was, and it felt wonderful to finally wake up and see that. Her view of life was no longer tainted with the storm clouds of struggle. At last, she was cleansed. Free. There were no restraints now and nothing to hold her back.

"Cool ain't it?" Charley called from nearby.

"Chili wah wah!" Kelly called back, sprouting the first thing that came to mind. She looked up. "Hey, I wanna try the trapeze!"

"Go for it, GB!"

She was soon sitting on it, swinging happily back and forth while the party flowed beneath her. She'd always dreamed of flying as a child. Now, she was finally here, blissfully soaring through the Delirium without the horrors of everyday living. There was only the music, the colour, the lights and the freedom.

And that, she reasoned, was all that mattered.

She swung on the trapeze for what seemed like an eternity, loving every minute.

After a time, the Black Bride rose from his throne and the music slowed, softened, and stopped. Kelly slowed too, watching the room go silent.

The Black Bride stepped forward, looming over the crowd. Sandi came up from the party to stand beside him while his four Groomsmen remained near the throne. He raised his arms and spoke in a booming, deep monotone.

"Brethren, beloved brethren, dearest friends, my marriage is upon us. My groom … is on his way!"

The crowd roared with excitement and even Kelly found herself cheering from the trapeze. Down below, she saw Turbo watching entranced, just like the Major.

The Black Bride continued. "For too long, our world has been a toxic cesspool of deception. Beloved's, we no longer have anything to fear. My marriage … is imminent!"

Another roar erupted.

"Humanity's sickness has metastasised into a terminal cancer. Several tumours, working against the purity of our movement, have concluded that we are too big a threat to exist. As we speak, a privately funded army, with weapons supplied by our hypocritical governments, have assigned a bomber, armed with a nuclear warhead, to annihilate this city. It is to leave shortly, intent on our destruction." His hand rose tenderly, stroking the air with his fingers. "My dear's, we have nothing to fear. All is going to plan, as is written by my beloved groom."

The crowd let loose with an explosive cry.

He hushed them and spoke on.

"The bombing will commence shortly. With the city destroyed, we shall release the virus on a global scale, leaving our so-called world leaders to react and fight amongst themselves. Our digital truth serum will see all countries annihilate each other. The fires of hell shall burn, cleansing the earth, while we remain encased in our Delirium. Finally, once the world is purified, we will ascend into a new heaven, a new earth, and a new dawn!"

Celebratory cheers roared to the heights of manic ecstasy, growing to a deafening crescendo, along with cries of:

"Cleansing be upon us!"

"Bring on the hellfire!"

"Praise the Delirium!"

"Glory be to the blessed marriage!"

The excitement rose as the Black Bride stood motionless. Finally, he raised his fist and bellowed, "Let the Apocalypse Party ignite!"

Frenzied euphoria exploded as the crowd's cries thundered to fever pitch.

Kelly found herself screaming too. The room swirled in her vision, growing hazy as the Delirium's colours blurred into one as she sat blissfully on her trapeze in her bridal dress and gorilla mask. She didn't care that a bomber was coming to nuke her city to smithereens. Nothing was real. Life didn't matter. It was only energy. Patterns of light and dark that constantly changed. That was the nature of dreams.

She swung joyously on her trapeze, laughing louder than ever. Then, in sheer bliss, she ripped her mask off and threw it over the crowd, not caring where it landed.

It hit Sandi in the head.

Sandi blinked, looked up, and saw Kelly dreamily swinging away. She smirked and pointed her out to the Black Bride. He nodded to a white-faced dwarf at the side of the room who reached up and pulled a lever on the wall. The trapeze dropped and Kelly fell straight into the arms of a towering muscleman in a hockey mask.

"Dreams come true!" she swooned.

The Black Bride gestured for Muscle-Man to bring her in. The room went quiet as she was carried through the crowd and brought to the stage as a huge dose of reality hit home.

"Oh … crap …"

Muscle-Man dropped her before the Black Bride. She looked guiltily up at him and cringed as he towered over her.

Silence followed, then he spoke softly.

"So, our prodigal daughter has returned."

Kelly gulped. "Hi, guys. I guess Sandi's filled you in on me, right?" She paused. "Hey wait. What do you mean, daughter?"

The Black Bride gave a small nod to a figure in the crowd. A young woman stepped out of it, wearing a beret and glasses.

Kelly stared at her in disbelief. "What the hell …?"

It was like looking into a mirror.

"Uh … hi …" the other girl said nervously. "It's great to finally meet you."

Confused, Kelly asked Sandi, "Who's this?"

The girl before Kelly blinked. "Who am I? Who are you?"

"Kelly Morrison," came the reply.

"You can't be," the girl said back. "I'm Kelly Morrison."

Kelly blinked in shock. "Whaaaaaaaa …?" She looked up at the Black Bride. "You wanna explain this, freakzilla?"

The Black Bride's gloved hand rose, twisting the air.

"The question," he said icily, "is not who she is, but rather, who *you* are."

Kelly stared at the other girl, aghast. "What? You mean, you're me?"

"No," the other girl replied. "You're me."

Kelly struggled to take this in. "So who am I then?"

"I don't know, lady," the girl answered, "but you're not Kelly Morrison. That's me."

Kelly steadied herself against the stage as the world swirled around her.

Sandi placed a hand on Kelly's forehead, feeling for a temperature, then said to the Black Bride, "Not bad. She's almost at fever pitch, and waking up nicely."

"So," the Bride determined, "we can reveal the truth."

He placed his fingers under Kelly's chin and raised it. Her eyes rose to his black veil as she shuddered.

"Please," she whispered. "Who am I?"

He hissed, speaking softly. "Are you ready to accept the truth, beloved?"

"What truth?" she asked shakily.

"Perhaps not," he concluded, "yet it must be told." He paused. "Cherished child, you've never ventured to the outside world. Everything you've ever known has happened within these walls."

Her jaw dropped in horror.

"Your kind's unique," he explained. "You were created as the next stage in human evolutionary warfare. You've no identity, nor were you ever allowed to have one. Instead, you were filled with a personality for us to shape, and peel away, at will."

She stared back at him with wide-eyed shock, absorbing the full brunt of his revelation with every fibre of her being.

"You're what's known as a Vessel," he stated. "We've been working on your kind for many years. I, and many others, developed you in the Incubation Chamber to ensure your success. When we captured the real Kelly Morrison ..." He indicated the girl behind her, "... we left her with you for hours on end, manipulating your mind extensively. Finally, you merged with her psyche and, in time, became her."

She trembled in horror.

"Clearly our work is unfinished," he continued, "yet time is short and you're needed for our cause. Upon my beloved husband's orders, we entered your dreams and woke you up, just on that trapeze over there." He nodded to it, then caressed her cheek gently. "My dear, my poor, pathetic creature, your whole existence has been ... in a Delirium."

She gazed at him pleadingly as tears trickled down her cheek. Slowly, her lips parted and she whispered. "Why?"

"To be the best," he answered simply. "You're a prototype for a servant in the New World Order, created to eliminate all threats in my husband-to-be's sublime vision. You see my darling, you're a scout who's blind to her true nature, meaning others will be too. Your task will be the eradication of all threats to our cause. That makes you the most effective prowler of all. You've been trained successfully my ... daughter."

She trembled in horror. "Trained?"

He raised his hand and pointed. She followed it reluctantly. The room blurred and she saw several figures in the crowd.

The woman closest to the stage gave a little smile. She was dressed in red shorts and a singlet, with her hair in a ponytail.

Melody.

Another woman stood by her, wearing a 1950s dress.

Vanilla.

A third was behind them, dressed in the costume of a bloodied, dead dog. Their arms rose, removing the head slowly, to reveal Skoobie underneath.

The Black Bride touched Kelly's chin, gently turning her focus back to himself.

"Help … me!" she whispered.

"Oh yes," the Bride said, "that's what we're here for. To help you. Waking up is the most painful part. Now it's time to live the dream."

She looked around terrified, then suddenly realised that all the faces in the room were familiar. She saw her mother, father, old friends, and distant relatives. Turbo was there too, no longer a clown, while David stood in the middle of them all, smiling. Even the minister, whose body she'd seen in the boot of a car when all this began, stood there, alive and well. Not only that, everyone she'd met in her whole life was here.

She staggered against the stage, shaking.

The other Kelly stepped up to her. "Say, are you okay? You don't look so good …"

Then everything went blank.

Chapter Fifteen

Time stopped.

There was no past or future, only a plethora of flashing lights, colours and the pulsating synthesised beats of her Delirium. She sat in the middle of the psychotic circus, having morphed into a painted white-faced clown with blood-red lips that rose into a superficial smile. One hand clasped the string of a hovering blood-red balloon. The other held a scowling black-eyed doll. Her hollow gaze stared into nothingness as she remained deathly still, like an empty vessel. She had no thoughts. Feelings. Memories. No sense of past or future. Everything was just … blank.

There she remained, covered in streamers and overlooked by a man dressed as a vulture, seated upon a podium. Finally, his attention was drawn elsewhere, and he leapt up and flew away on a trapeze, leaving her to sit silently.

Charley came in and sat beside her.

"Hey GB," she said, putting an arm around her shoulder. "How ya doin'?"

Her response was a dull monotone. "I've seen the truth."

"Good for you," Charley replied happily. "Sorry my buds and I dropped that little game on you earlier. We were helpin' you wake-up, y'know?"

"No."

Charley gave a little smile. "You're still feelin' lost, right? You just gotta remember that you're a NUT like the rest of us, that's who."

"I have no name," came the blank reply.

"You're not meant to," Charley said. "You're the end result of years of work to perfect the ultimate personality parasite. See, you're a blank human template designed for grafting human identities onto. That means you can impersonate *anybody* anywhere without anyone knowing any better. What's great is that you can work on your own now, so if one self needs changing fast, you can enter another person's mind, devour their sanity, copy it for yourself and completely become them. That's why we call you an *in-person-ate-or*. Well that's the boss's name for you at least. I like the term Sucker better, 'cause you were made for sucking out all opposition. That and because we went through a stage where there was *literally* one born every minute."

She nudged her playfully.

"Trouble was, the mortality rate was high and most of them tanked into oblivion. There was only one we gave a name to, but he was exceptional." Her tone lowered. "Michael Ellis. He was too strong for any of us to control. He went rogue." She shivered. "Ugh, he gives me the chills, but hey, we're talking 'bout you. Do you want a name? What sounds good? Cookie, Jeanie, Marigold? Can you think of one?"

"No," the girl replied. "I am nothing."

Charley shrugged. "Tell you what, we'll call you Zero. How does that sound?"

No response.

"Cool, we'll go by that," Charley said. "Our Bride-Mamma wants to see you, just not yet. Things have to be in place before he sends you to the surface. Hey, it'll be your very first mission. How do you feel about that?"

"Unreal," the girl responded dully.

Charley grinned. "He's finishing-up the details now so he left you here to chill for a bit." Her head perked up suddenly. "Ooooh! Love this song! You won't want to dance, but I can't say no. Take it easy, Z. Back soon."

She beamed, slapped her shoulder and left, leaving the girl with the painted face to sit miserably in the crowd.

The party was relentless.

Its pounding beat consumed her mind utterly. There was only music and laughter. She couldn't think, feel or do anything. Silence had been obliterated. The Delirium was the be-all and end-all, and it should have been all that mattered.

Strangely though, it wasn't. An inkling at the back of her mind kept nudging at her psyche. Small at first, this strange new presence slowly rose like a golden glimmer, resisting the crushing storm of the Delirium. A tingling seed that disliked the music while planting the idea that she should be somewhere else *doing* something else. This spirit was a familiar one of late. She recalled it when she'd first entered a … café? Is that what it was?

Bit by bit, the presence grew, prompting her to rise with it, until finally, as if on autopilot, she stood up.

She didn't know why she did it; she just did. Blankly, she walked through the streamers towards the door. Beside it, stood a large man dressed as a bull. He was called the Gatekeeper and anyone who wanted to leave had to explain why, apparently for their protection. She stopped and watched as he spoke to various people intent on leaving the party. When a small group approached him and were given permission, she found herself following them. Fortunately, the Gatekeeper thought they were all together and didn't even bat a large eyelid.

She headed with these lavishly dressed people down a long tunnel into the darkness. The music faded behind her as they came to a passageway that split into two. She went one way; they went the other, and soon she was walking through the dark depths carrying her balloon and hugging her doll as her painted ghostly smile floated eerily amid the shadows.

After a time, the music faded completely, relieving her from the Delirium's pounding beat. Nevertheless, its residue remained, along with the Black Bride's sick presence that clasped her brain like a hideous spider sucking on her sanity. Thankfully, the café's glistening aura flickered a little, shielding her against the black storm clouds of her mind. Her temples flared as the forces of light and shadows struggled, leaving her caught in the middle as her psyche was squeezed to the extreme.

Somehow, she clung to the light of the café. Its divine essence provided a buffer against the raging horrors in her head, bringing some relief. What's more, it was driving her instinctively to a cell door. Finally, she reached it, and curiously leaned in to look through the small rectangular slit in its centre.

Her eyes widened, for the person inside was familiar. Or was it a delusion? She had to find out.

She raised her hand, turned the handle, and found it unlocked. Slowly, she pulled the door back, opening it with a loud squeak, and entered.

A woman lay inside, strapped to a table. Next to her, was a desk and a metal chair, and on top of that desk was a file. The newcomer stepped closer, observing the file. The name on the page read simply, 'Melody Hill.'

No doubt those who'd done this to her would return soon, the newcomer concluded. Clearly, for an interrogation.

The prisoner looked up, her lips pursed and she snapped, "My God, what the hell have those freaks done to you?"

The newcomer's tone was sombre. "The Mistress said this would happen. You're not real. A delusion of my mind."

"Really, fruitcake?" Table-Girl retorted. "So why are you here? Unless it's another trick to get me to talk. God, I hate this place! Nobody knows what's real and what's bull. Your new buddies think I killed Solomon and now they've gone to get some electrodes to fry my brain with."

"If that is what they wish then so be it," came the dull reply.

"Hey, *this* is reality," Table Girl shot back. "Unlike the sick party you just came from. Looks like they've sucked you into believing that there's nothing else apart from them and their stupid Delirium. Now let's ditch this dump soldier! Hurry!"

The newcomer didn't budge. "I am not the person you think. I am Zero. A Vessel designed for taking personalities. I am nothing."

"You're not nothing; you're a ditz called Kelly Morrison," Table Girl pressed firmly. "They're messing with your mind, deadhead. The beat you were listening to back there – guess what? It's hypnotic. Subliminal messages are pounding through it. I bet you've absorbed all kinds of drugs too. Maybe in the air, or what you drank. I'm tied up 'cause I'm resistant to that crap. Now get me outta here."

The balloon wavered in the newcomer's hand as she stepped back. "I will call the guards. They will prove to me that you're not real."

"Oh, so the café's not real?" Table Girl countered. "What about David, huh? You finally get a boyfriend and live a little and what happens? You wimp out and give in to a bunch of brainwashing crazies! God, you drive me in-sane."

"Insanity is the only way …"

"Dammit …!" Table Girl began, then composed herself. "You're Kelly Morrison. You're a klutz, you're a dummy and, for some reason that I can't fathom in any way, shape or form, you're also good stuff, but I didn't say that …"

"I know," the girl replied.

"Oh shhhhh …!" Table Girl seethed, banging her head against the table. "Okay, I did say that, but if you tell the others I'll rip your arms off. I'm also guessing that an alarm was triggered when you came in here and there's probably a camera on us too, so let's go."

"I can't. You're not real."

"God, give me strength!" Table Girl snapped. "There was nothing more real than you, me, Scoops and Skoob as a team, was there? What we felt was real! The fun, the laughs, the garbage we talked – that's the only thing in your whole damn life that *has* been real. Fine, you want reality; touch my hand. Go on – touch it. Feel it. Your hand'll go right through mine if I'm a ghost. Do it!"

The girl observed her hesitantly. "The mind is powerful."

"Come on."

The girl did so. Her fingers tingled as she touched Table Girl's palm.

"There," Table Girl said. "You see?"

The response was subdued. "It's a delusion."

"Really?" Table Girl retorted. "So, what brought you here? Something ticking at the back of your mind, right? Look, you're strong – I know that. You'd have to be to override the hypnotic junk they poured into you. *You* hauled your butt in here, not them." She drew a sharp breath. "We need to hit the streets up top, and fast. I'll show you what's real. Let's find out for ourselves. You touched my hand, so come to the city where you can smell, taste, see and hear the rest of the world. The *real* world!"

"I …"

"This is our last chance," Table Girl pushed. "If we want this story to have a happy ending, there's no other way. You gotta do it."

Silence.

Slowly, the balloon and doll were dropped, and Table Girl's clips were unbuckled. Once she was free, Table Girl sat up, rubbing her wrists.

"Thanks, kid," she said, throwing her legs over the side, unaffected after being tied up for so long.

Two large men wearing business suits and gorilla masks entered the room.

Table Girl grabbed the metal chair, rushed at them, swirled around in a three-sixty and struck them both in one go. One fell to the ground, unconscious, while the other staggered back. Table Girl dived on him, thumping him out.

"Still think I'm not real?" Table Girl asked, standing up.

"Life is an illusion," came the soft reply.

"Yeah, well I got the perfect remedy for that," Table Girl quipped. "This is reality, Kelly Morrison, and it bloody hurts! You want real?" She grabbed her in a headlock and threw her into the wall. "This is real! So's this …!"

Bang!

"… And this!"

Bang!

"… This too!"

Bang, bang, bang!

"Welcome back to reality."

Smack!

"Life's painful and so's the truth. This is what we call tough love!"

Thud!

"I'll show you a good dose of friggin' reality ya …!"

Bang!

"Cut it out!" Kelly suddenly cried, breaking away from her and reeling back shocked. She watched as Table Girl's face came into focus, along with the sharpening belief that the person who stood before her really *was* Melody Hill.

Kelly's head throbbed like crazy. Her skin tingled as the Delirium's hypnotic effect subsided.

Melody peered at her. "Is that you, kid? You back?"

"Mel …?" Kelly began shakily.

"Yeah, yeah, that's good …"

"Mel …?"

"I'm here, I'm here …"

"Mel, I …?"

"Yeah?"

Kelly inhaled sharply. "I have a sudden craving for a double beef cheeseburger with a side order of fries and an ice-cream sundae."

Melody nodded. "Welcome back, kid."

Kelly smiled, then froze. The bad guys had thrown the doors of her mind wide open, seeing everything, and now it was impossible to close them again. Her long-suppressed fears rose rapidly, ready to consume her, and her eyes welled with tears as she trembled, "Oh God, Mel …"

Melody cringed. "Oh God, no! No, no, no! Stop right there …!"

"Mel …"

"Quit it! I don't wanna deal with this garbage!"

"Oh Mel …!"

"Oh crap …!"

Kelly exploded with a mighty wail, falling against Melody, clasping her tightly and howling in sheer despair as she unleashed *everything*. Melody let loose too, crying at the ickiness of it all.

"I hate it!" Kelly bawled.

"Me too!" Melody bawled back as Kelly's tears flooded over her. "Where the hell's Scoops when you need her?"

Kelly sobbed harder. "What did they do to me? What?"

"I don't know but it sure as hell sucks!"

"It's horrible!"

"Tell me about it. Oh no, hang on, don't! Please God, don't! Seriously, don't …!"

Kelly quivered. "I feel gross! Disgusting!"

"So do I," Melody agreed. "Now get over it and get back at the psychos who did this!"

"How?"

"I don't know. Knee 'em in the …"

Kelly let loose with another cry.

"NUTS!" Melody finished, covering Kelly's mouth and looking out the door. "They'll be here soon. We gotta go."

"No," Kelly wept. "I just wanna die!"

"Right, boot camp 101," Melody snapped, pulling her to the door. "Move, soldier!" She huffed and hauled the whimpering Kelly out into the tunnel. "God, it's like having a kid!" She suddenly gulped, her hand lowered to her stomach, and her eyes widened at the thought of the child in there and what was coming for the rest of her life. "Darren is sooooo dead …"

Seething curses of the inhumanely possible, she led Kelly on.

Kelly was distraught.

She was hardly aware of the nightmarish run with Melody through the labyrinth of tunnels below City Hall. All she felt was the residue of the Delirium's sick beat that made her want to hurl, big time.

They turned a corner, then Melody suddenly pulled her down behind a crate and muffled her sobs as two clowns went past. Once they were gone, the girls rose and headed on.

"Why do I feel so sweaty?" Kelly asked, wiping her forehead. "I remember someone saying I was at fever pitch …"

"That's what the Delirium does," Melody cut in. "It makes you delirious. The fever'll drop once the gunk leaves your system."

Kelly paused. "Were you in your cell the whole time, Mel?"

"And there goes my head." She stopped. "Why?"

"It's just that I saw you in the Delirium," Kelly said. "You and Scoops and David and Skoob, and a whole stack of other people. Me included."

"Yeah, that wasn't us," Melody said back. "Do me a favour. Next time you see your feral twin, smack 'em in the head."

Kelly gave a little smile. "Will do, Mel."

They reached another cell door.

Melody grabbed the handle.

"Careful …" Kelly began.

Melody jiggled it slightly. "Might be alright. I've seen this kind of lock before. Opens from the outside, locked on the in. Takes the pressure off using keys all the time. You're right though. Gotta play this carefully."

She slowly pushed the door open, ready to peer in.

The savage blast of a death metal electric guitar exploded from the sound-proof room, blowing Kelly backwards and hurling her to the ground. Melody kept her balance and struggled through the hideous lyrics of screaming hate, blaring at full volume.

Kelly pushed herself up and peered in to see a room full of speakers revved to the max. She watched as Melody struggled over to one, ripped it off the wall and hurled it outside in a shower of sparks, smacking out a clown who was running in for the cell. He fell backwards, with his legs flailing high in the air and crashed to the ground in a heap. The severing of the speaker cable also affected the other speakers, and the noise died straight away, leaving only silence and a ringing in Kelly's ears.

Trapped in a roomful of bellowing rage at that level would have driven anyone insane, but the figure who sat against the back wall, cross-legged and meditating, merely opened her eyes and said simply, "'Sup?"

Melody knelt and hugged her. "How ya doin'?"

"Fine," Skoobie replied coolly. "You?"

Kelly stood up and entered the room, aghast. "That didn't hurt you at all?"

"Nah," Skoobie answered happily. "I'm always switching my mind … off. See? Cool huh?"

"How'd you learn to do that?" Kelly asked.

"What?" Skoobie asked back.

"How'd you learn to do that?" Kelly repeated.

"What?" Skoobie also repeated.

"I said how'd you learn …?"

"Sorry," Skoobie cut in. "I'm having trouble getting my signal back." She banged the side of her head. "Whoa! That's better." She saw Kelly's clown face complete with trails of tears. "Like the look. Suits you."

Kelly felt her cheeks, saw the white paint smear off on her hands and fumed. "Ooooh, I am so gonna boot some NUTS straight up into the bowels of hell …"

"So, what's the story?" Skoobie asked Melody.

"Not good," Melody answered. "Junior here just saved my bacon from getting fried. Where's Scoops?"

"Down the hall," Skoobie replied. "One of the bad guys said something just after they'd turned the music up and were closing the door on me."

"You heard them through all that?" Kelly asked, baffled. "Didn't you switch your mind off?"

"Parts of it yeah," Skoobie said. "The other parts were busy filtering stuff out."

"You're a freak."

"Sorry, I missed that last word."

"Stop playing around."

Skoobie frowned. "I'm not."

"Scoops is our priority," Melody said firmly. "Come on."

Skoobie rose and they all headed outside.

Two clowns with hatchets turned a corner and strode down the tunnel for them. Melody stepped back into the cell's shadows, unseen, while Kelly shifted uncomfortably.

The clowns approached.

"Why has the prisoner been released?" one asked.

Kelly tried to answer. "Uhhhhhhhhh …"

Skoobie cut in. "Oma dong dong. Merwei jono ski ba ta li ma. Jo jo tong! Nan na hey gusto presto thingo, jo, job, job. Gala time, pub bu, ta dong!"

Kelly indicated her. "She's crazy."

The clowns were satisfied.

"Yep, she's one of us," one confirmed. He gave Kelly a quick nod. "See ya round."

"Yeah bye," Kelly said.

They turned a corner and were gone.

Kelly sighed with relief. "That was sooooo close …"

Melody came out of the cell. "Nice work, Skoob. This way."

They headed through the tunnel.

They soon arrived at another cell door with old-school metal bars. Vanilla sat inside, strapped to a large chair with several electrodes attached to her head. Two men dressed as vultures loomed over her.

Melody leaned into Skoobie and whispered, "You're up."

Skoobie opened the door, walked in, and said, "'S'okay guys, We'll take it from here."

They nodded, turned around, and calmly walked out past a bewildered Kelly. Once they were gone, she looked at Skoobie in awe.

"How do you *do* that?" Kelly wondered.

"Easy," Skoobie answered. "Just told 'em the truth. See, life's a gamble, and to beat the odds you have to act odd. That's my drift."

Kelly stared at her astounded. "How does that even work?"

"Oh no," Skoobie said. "We'll get onto 'even's' later."

Kelly threw a hand up and turned away.

Melody knelt before Vanilla and grabbed her face in her hands. "Scoops? Hey, you okay?"

"Waaaaaaahhhhh …?" came the weary response.

"Strawberry cream?" Melody asked.

"Orange squash," Vanilla answered.

Melody ripped her bonds away and they hugged. "What the hell did they do to you, Scoops?"

"Not a lot," came the reply. "You got here just in time. They were starting a mind-wipe."

Melody checked her over. "Guess S doesn't want you spilling any secrets about her."

"Something's up with Sandi?"

Melody smacked the wall. "Crap!"

"What?" Kelly asked.

"They've rubbed out part of her mind," Melody replied. "We need to find out how much. Skoob?"

"I'm on it," Skoobie said.

Melody moved aside.

Skoobie knelt before Vanilla, held three fingers up and waved them from side to side in front of her eyes.

"How many fingers?" Skoobie asked.

"Three," Vanilla answered.

Skoobie turned her fingers around.

"How many?" she asked again.

"Four," Vanilla replied.

Skoobie waved both hands around and brought them together, like the wings of an outstretched butterfly.

"What colour are the wings?" she prompted.

"Purple," came the answer.

Skoobie turned her hands around. "And now?"

"Deep purple. Slightly red."

Skoobie nodded and spoke to the others. "Not too bad. There's only five per cent missing." She waved her hands rhythmically, then held up three fingers with her nails facing Vanilla. "How many fingers?"

"Four," Vanilla answered.

Skoobie turned them around again and repeated, "How many fingers?"

"Three."

"Snap out of it."

She clicked her fingers.

Vanilla blinked. "Whoa! Okay, what'd I miss?"

"About five per cent of your memory," Melody replied.

"You feel any dark patches in your mind?" Skoobie asked. "Like you're missing something?"

Vanilla shook her head. "No big blanks. Guess I'm okay."

"That's a relief," Kelly said.

Vanilla smiled at her. "Yeah, sure is sweetie. Nice to meet you. And you are ...?"

"And there's our missing five per cent," Melody confirmed.

Kelly stared at Vanilla astounded. "You mean you don't remember *me*?"

Vanilla shrugged. "Can't say that I do. Sorry."

"Five per cent?" Kelly cried, throwing her arms up. "Is that all I'm worth? Five per cent?"

"Don't blame us, blame NUTS," Melody said back.

"Yeah, we'll get to know each other later, honey," Vanilla told Kelly.

Kelly looked away, fuming.

Vanilla ignored her. "Give me an update, Mel. How long's it been since the weather station?"

"Of course she remembers everything else," Kelly grumbled.

Vanilla indicated her to the others and asked, "Is she always like this?"

"Yuh-huh," they both replied.

Kelly made a face.

Melody waved her away. "The station was a while ago, Scoops. Next up …"

"We get the hell outta here?" Kelly cut in.

"Yeah, you go ahead, sweetie," Vanilla replied. "We'll talk again soon – good to meet you though."

Kelly swore under her breath.

Melody pressed on. "So, I've got a few ideas …"

"Me too," Vanilla said back.

"Me three," Skoobie added.

"Lay 'em on me, guys," Melody said.

Kelly tensed. "Why am I expecting the worst?"

Melody spoke quickly. "Here's what we do …"

The Apocalypse Party raged to new heights. Streamers rained over the partygoers dancing ecstatically to the Delirium's pulsating rhythms. High above, the two acrobats swung faster than ever on their trapezes, aerial dancing to the mystical beats of the celebratory glitz.

The Black Bride oversaw it all, seated upon his throne, while Sandi stood by his side, along with the four Groomsmen. All wore hidden nasal filters protecting them from the toxic gases pouring into the room.

One Groomsman checked his phone, then leaned into the Black Bride and whispered. The Black Bride nodded, the Groomsman moved away, and the Bride raised his arms to the crowd and bellowed, "Brethren, our bomber is on its way! Rejoice!"

A delirious cry erupted from the floor.

He continued. "Several countries have condemned our actions. International tensions are at an all-time high. When this city bursts into flames, the next phase of global cleansing can commence, leaving us to reap the remains of another world WAR!"

The room exploded into hysteria as waves of balloons were released to float high into the air while a group of ballerinas leapt by, pursued by masquerade dancers.

"Celebrate!" he roared. "Be Free!"

The maniacal cries rose to heights of sheer insanity, growing louder and louder until …

Whoomph!

The music suddenly died, along with most of the room's power, bringing everyone to a standstill as a hush fell over the crowd. Murmurs followed, until a sole voice called from the floor, "Uh … reality check?"

The Black Bride looked down, glaring at the lone figure who'd dared to defy him.Kelly.

She was back in her own clothes, with the makeup washed off her face, glaring at him defiantly.

He snarled cruelly, then furiously leaned forward and hissed, "So, darling daughter, you resist your mother's will? Who the *hell* do you think you are?"

"Kelly Morrison," she retorted, feeling stronger than ever, "and you're not my mother, father or boss, and even if you were I'd still tell you to get stuffed. You're not God either. You're human, like the rest of us, only you're hiding from reality 'cause you're too scared to face it. What, were you bullied at school so much that you had to form this little hate club here? I'll admit, this place looks like the mother of all parties, but scratch the surface and there's only garbage below. That's you."

"That's life in general!" he shot back.

She looked down and mouthed, *"Crap!"* She quickly composed herself, then looked up again. "Talk all you want, freakzilla, but reality's a lot bigger than your sick ego."

He indicated his minions in the crowd. "Seize her!"

Nobody moved.

"Obey!" he bellowed.

A can flew through the air, hit him in the head and bounced off.

He stood up, enraged. "What is this?"

A voice came over the loudspeakers.

 Fanfare chords played "... I can change the station-ary! No more dream drugs for anyone which means ..."

Another can hit the Black Bride in the head as an angry murmur rose from the crowd.

"This carnival's over," Kelly said firmly.

A small group of people dressed as orangutans raised baseball bats, hitting them into their palms.

Vanilla emerged from them and stood beside her. Fearlessly, she looked up at Sandi and said, "The truth, S. I don't remember much, but one name sure sticks." Her head lowered. "Michaela Brown."

Sandi's jaw dropped in horror. "What? What did you say?"

"Michaela Brown," Vanilla repeated.

Sandi stared at her, shocked.

Kelly leaned into Vanilla and spoke softly. "Who's Michaela Brown?"

Vanilla shrugged. "I don't know, sweetie, it just came to me."

"Shut up!" Sandi snapped. "Keep your damn mouth shut, Scoops!"

"Touched a nerve, have we?" Kelly asked.

Sandi glared at Vanilla furiously. "You swore, Scoops. You swore you'd never tell. That name's bound by our sacred oath!"

"While I'm apparently forgettable," Kelly muttered.

"You're carrying a lot of frustration aren't you, sweetie?" Vanilla asked her.

"Ya think?"

Sandi pulled out a gun, taking aim at Vanilla. "You know the penalty for breaking your promise."

Vanilla froze.

The orangutans ran in, forming a shield around her and Kelly.

"Thanks," Vanilla told them.

One of them pulled a head off, revealing the Major underneath.

"Anything to help," he replied with a small smile.

Sandi promptly put the gun on an amplifier, reached behind it, and pulled out a Tommy gun. "Easy fixed."

"Can never win, can we?" Kelly grumbled.

Sandi aimed. "Lights out, kids …"

Kelly, Vanilla, and the orangutans braced themselves.

A cry came from above.

"*Yaaaaaaaaaa …!*"

Sandi looked up as Melody swung in on a trapeze, let go and dived at her. The two collided with a heavy thud and the gun fired upwards, blowing a strobe light out.

"*Freak-out!*" Skoobie called, both as a rallying cry to the crowd and to the hard blow that Melody had given Sandi, hoping it would knock her out.

No such luck. Sandi's fist rose, smacking Melody backwards, then she dived on her.

Skoobie cranked up the music and the crowd stampeded for the stage.

Kelly did her best to break out of it but to no avail. "No wait! I don't wanna go! Wait …!"

Melody kicked Sandi off her, leapt up, struck a Groomsman so hard that he dropped to the floor and stayed there, then flew at Sandi.

Streamers rained throughout the room as the disco music played and the lights flickered over a full-scale rumble between those free of the Delirium's control and the Black Bride's willing servants. The dark figure himself stepped to the back of the stage with two Groomsmen and observed the madness. The other two Groomsmen stayed up the front, trying to hold the crowd off.

Nearby, Vanilla was pushed out of the chaos and grabbed onto a podium holding a vase for support. The podium wobbled, the vase fell, and she caught it with one hand while holding the podium with the other.

A screaming clown with a knife rushed at her.

She rose, bringing the vase up instinctively.

The clown's head smacked into it and he went out like a light.

"Oh!" she said, surprised.

She turned around, accidentally smacking another clown in the stomach. He doubled over, she tripped backwards, the vase swung up and she knocked him out too.

A third clown ran in.

She clutched the vase with both hands and whacked him on the head. He slumped to the floor and she looked at the vase in disbelief.

"What is this thing?" she wondered.

A man in a pink wig and orange business suit surged in. She recoiled, dropping the vase. It clattered to the floor and rolled under him, tripping him up. His legs flew high before he slammed to the ground with a crunch and lay still.

Curiously, Vanilla reached down and picked up the vase.

"Ooooooh," she said in wide-eyed wonder. "This is powerful …"

Melody and Sandi struggled, flipping each other over the stage, and almost hitting Kelly who stood on the floor, pushed up against the wall.

"Hands!" Kelly yelled to the person crunched up behind her.

"Get me outta here!" Turbo wailed back.

A Groomsman picked him up and threw him screaming over the crowd, before grabbing Kelly and dragging her onto the stage. She broke away from him, whirled around with a sweeping kick and booted him clean out in one go.

"Gym class!" she hissed. "Don't mess with it!" She stopped, horrified. "God, I better not be turning into a raging nutcase." She turned and came face to face with the Black Bride. "Oh crap!"

He pointed at her accusingly. "Yoooooou … must be punished!"

"Ahhhhhhh, bite me!" she shot back.

"Very well!"

He raised his hands to pull his veil away.

She gulped, leapt up and kicked him in the head, hard. To her surprise, he staggered backwards and collapsed onto his throne, which tipped up, making his feet rise high in the air. He quickly gathered himself, rolled over angrily and rose, just as the Major climbed onto the stage.

The Bride sneered, raised a remote and hit a button. A whirr came from above as an enormous hatch in the roof slid back, then he and the Grooms-man pulled out grappling guns, aimed them high and fired.

Swish!

Their lines flew high into the enormous vent above, their hooks hit the top and the four of them shot up into it. They were barely through when the hatch slammed shut under them.

"Wimps!" Kelly yelled.

A dwarf lunged at her with a knife. She recoiled, tripped and hit the ground. He scampered on top of her and they rolled across the stage, struggling furiously as the knife came dangerously close to her throat.

"No …!" she vowed.

She threw him off her with enormous strength and they both rose. He lunged again. She jumped so high that her knees reached her shoulders as she let him run under her, then landed back down and kicked him off the stage.

"Thanks again, gym class," she quipped.

Melody and Sandi staggered to their feet and glared at each other, dishevelled and angry.

"Looks like your boss has split," Melody said, glancing at the hatch above, "but hey, you know who your friends are, right?"

"Rot in hell, Mel, rot in hell," Sandi shot back.

"I'm looking straight into it," Melody snapped.

Sandi scowled, whipped out a phone with one hand and pressed a button, while her other pulled out a grappling hook. The hatch opened, she fired, the hook shot out, hit the vent's roof and she flew up.

Melody grabbed onto her leg and rose with her until she was kicked off and hit the stage. Helplessly, she watched Sandi enter the vent before the hatch shut and she was gone.

Vanilla smacked another freak out with the vase, then turned to see Skoobie walking coolly through the crowd.

Vanilla waved. "Hey, Skoob!"

Several men flew past Skoobie in a brawl, almost crashing into her. She barely noticed them as she approached Vanilla and saw the vase. "Hey yourself. Whatcha got?"

"Vase of Power. Wanna try it?"

"Sure." Skoobie took it and felt its weight. "Hey, there's some serious cosmic vibes in this baby. Can feel it big time."

"Yeah," Vanilla agreed. "Try doing something with it. Anything."

A woman in a catsuit landed before them, claws outstretched.

Skoobie tossed the vase high, letting it fly and not bothering to look where it would end up. It spun over, thumped on the woman's head, knocked her out, then hit the floor, rolled away and tripped another man up. He slammed into a circus freak, their heads cracked together and they both crashed down and were still.

Vanilla and Skoobie scrambled through the crowd and picked up the Vase in wide-eyed awe.

"Whoooooooaaaa …!" they breathed.

Kelly retreated into a corner, away from the fighting, then saw Charley whimpering on the floor. She knelt beside her and said, "Reality hit home, huh?"

Charley put a hand to her forehead, tearfully. "All I remember is some guy buying me a drink at a club. We went for a walk and I passed out. Everything since has been a nightmare."

She shuddered and ran a hand through her hair.

"Yeah, it's sick," Kelly agreed, "but don't freak. We'll get you outta here."

"Why?" Charley asked glumly. "There's no point. If what I dreamed was real, then a nuclear bomber's on its way to blow us all to hell."

"What about psycho-bride and his freaks?" Kelly asked. "Where are they headed?"

"To an IT company," came the reply. "There's been a change of plans. They now want the virus to go global *before* the nukes hit."

"Guess it's up to us to save the world then."

Charley whimpered. "What the hell are you talking about? Us?"

"Yeah," Kelly confirmed. "Us. Now move."

The party music suddenly changed.

Its hypnotic undercurrents morphed as an automatic setting took over, turning it into …

"Bony M!" Skoobie cried excitedly. "Is that Bony M?"

"Oh good, that helps," Vanilla said.

Kelly and Charley ran up.

Kelly indicated Skoobie to Vanilla and asked, "What's up with her?"

"Bony M," Vanilla replied. "She goes berserk when she hears them."

Skoobie jumped up and down ecstatically. "Bony M!"

"And that's what we need," Melody quipped, smacking a clown out. "Scoops, Skoob, let's go 'Clubbing.' Floor it!"

"Bony M!" Skoobie wailed.

She ran onto the dance floor, with Melody following.

"Here," Vanilla said, handing Kelly the Vase. "Guard this with your life. Don't lose it, whatever you do."

"What is it?" Kelly asked.

"Vase of Power," Vanilla replied, running after the others.

Kelly looked at it baffled. "Vase of what?"

Charley was just as confused. "What are they up to?"

Kelly sighed. "I dread to think …"

Melody, Vanilla and Skoobie hit the dance floor as the music grew louder.

Streamers fell past them as they formed a circle, linked arms, faced outwards and spun with the beat. Skoobie was the most into it, jumping joyously as they picked up speed, twirling faster and faster.

Three NUTS dressed as grandma's ran in.

Melody kicked the first in the head, booting him into the NUT behind him, then Vanilla swung up and, supported by her friends, kicked the third freak back with both legs before turning head over heels in a three-sixty and landing upright.

More NUTS surged in.

Energised, the girls broke the circle and faced them, now filled by the power they'd generated.

"Bony M!" Skoobie cried, leaping up and headbutting a man out cold.

Melody and Vanilla danced in long, graceful slides, flowing in unison. As two NUTS lunged, the girls let loose with the music's beat, punching them both in their stomachs. Two more beats, two strong uppercuts, and the NUTS went flying.

A giant of a man ran at Melody. She and Vanilla linked arms back-to-back. Melody kicked the man hard, rolled over Vanilla's back and jumped away, leaving Vanilla to kick the man in the stomach, again in time with the music. He doubled over with a savage grunt before Skoobie jumped in, headbutting him clean out.

"Bony M!" she wailed.

He slumped to the floor as the three girls formed a line, moving as one and clubbing down anyone who came near them.

Kelly watched them in disbelief.

She shook her head and turned to find herself face to face with the other Kelly Morrison, her double. It was like looking into a mirror.

"Well," they both said at once. "This is awkward."

Kelly frowned.

So did the other one.

They circled each other.

"Who do you think you are?" they both asked. "You're not me! I'm me! Stop it! Would you stop it? Cut it out!"

They both stopped, and Kelly saw her double's neck. Part of the skin had peeled away, revealing a mask.

"Gotcha!" Kelly snapped.

She lashed out hard. Her double slumped like a stone.

"Good advice, Mel," she said, relieved, and then grinned. "I'm so glad to be me." She looked around at the chaos. "I think …"

Melody and Vanilla struck down several more NUTS with sweeping blows and high kicks as they clubbed to the max. Skoobie preferred headbutting as opposed to the others, but also swung her arms widely to floor her opponents. Bodies flew to the left, right and centre, yet it was clear to everyone that the girls' priority was dancing, especially Skoobie who, lost in her own delirium, screamed, "Bony M!"

Someone picked Turbo up and he also screamed as he flew over everyone's heads and across the room again, also in perfect time with the music, all while the NUTS fell by the dozens, dropping like stones.

Soon, only two were left.

Melody came in between Vanilla and Skoobie and bent her legs. Vanilla jumped up and stood on one of Melody's thighs and Skoobie did the same on the other. Both held Melody's arms tightly, waiting for the music's final beat, then Vanilla and Skoobie kicked out hard, silencing the last two freaks.

With the song ended and all the NUTS floored, the only response from the people left standing was silence. Now free of the brainwashing, they stared at the girls astonished.

"You're welcome!" Melody said, as Vanilla and Skoobie leapt down.

The Major approached them. "Well done. A magnificent performance, I must say."

"You should have seen us in Ibiza," Vanilla said proudly.

"I need a cigarette," Skoobie panted.

"You don't smoke," Vanilla pointed out.

"I need a cigarette," Skoobie repeated.

"The police are on their way," the Major said, holding up a mobile that he'd pulled off a man on the floor.

"Good," Melody said back. "To a point. All hell's ready to break loose, globally. We'd better move."

"To where?" the Major asked.

"Forty-three Quirk Street," Kelly answered, coming in to join them, along with Charley. "Charley here tells me it's a skyscraper still under construction, but it's also got NUTS's tech base. On the surface it's an 'official' IT company called Silent Futures Incorporated Technologies, or SI-FI Tech. Unofficially, NUTS are using it as a cover, calling it the Nuthouse."

"There's a satellite dish on top of the building," Charley explained. "I don't recall much from the gunk they poured into me, but I do know that they've modified the dish. Now it's strong enough to boost the cyber virus beyond the city, and without the effects of the geo-proximity bug too."

"Geo-proxima what?" Kelly asked.

Charley spoke quickly. "A NUT who tried to defect put a digital bug into the virus so it couldn't travel far, leaving it confined to the city. *That's* the real reason why NUTS are using the city as a test site. If the virus goes beyond it, it dies. Now they've figured out a way to fix things, but only in the past hour. They've still gotta put some fail-safes in, so it'll still take a little time before they're ready to transmit."

"Gotcha," Melody said. "But what they didn't count on was us, right?"

"Or this," Skoobie added, grabbing the Vase from Kelly.

"And that," Melody said, perplexed. "What is that?"

"Vase of Power!" Vanilla and Skoobie answered proudly.

"Let's see." She grabbed it from them, her hand slipped and it dropped, landing on the head of a NUT dressed as a beaver who was just waking up. He slumped back down and lay still.

"See," Vanilla and Skoobie said.

Melody picked the Vase up. "You know this thing does feel weird. It's got vibes."

"Told ya," Skoobie quipped.

"Can we get moving?" Kelly pressed.

"Sure," Melody answered, tossing the Vase lightly at Vanilla who caught it. "Let's hit the streets."

They headed for the door.

Kelly looked up.

"And?" she prompted.

Melody rolled her eyes. "And somebody get Turbo off the fan."

He groaned from above as he slowly turned with it.

Chapter Sixteen

Several police cars and vans came to a screeching halt outside City Hall.

Vertigo emerged from her car and took a sharp breath of the crisp morning air as a SWAT team ran around her. Her face was bruised, the result of the battle in the hills, which she'd barely escaped with her life.

She raised her walkie-talkie. "All units …"

She stopped dead as part of the pavement near the building's steps slid back and an enormous wave of red balloons billowed out, ascending into the sky. A cry ignited as a crowd of colourful people spewed up from below, dressed to the extreme as they ran out onto the street like an outrageous costume party that stood out wildly against the smoke, flames and bleak backdrop.

Vertigo watched the spectacle in disbelief. "What the bloody hell …?"

Her lips pursed as the four girls and Turbo ran up to her. "I should have known."

"SI-FI Tech!" Melody said, slapping her on the shoulder. "Also known as the Nuthouse."

"Join the party," Vanilla added. "Oh, and see that ute over there? We're just gonna borrow it, but we'll bring it back soon – we promise."

"Catch ya," Skoobie said.

They started to move off.

"Hold it!" Vertigo snapped.

They all stopped.

"Sexual frustration," Skoobie confirmed.

Melody turned to Vertigo crossly. "You can scream all you want lady, but right now *we're* the only ones who can save you and the whole damn world. That means you gotta trust us. So what is it? A flaming city or your flaming ego? Your choice."

Vertigo glared at her.

"Ask a stupid question," Melody grumbled.

Vertigo didn't move, then finally she said, "You know what? Fine! *Fine!* No questions. Go! Just go. Get outta here before my sanity comes back."

Vanilla grinned. "Thanks so much. We won't let you down. See you soon."

"Later," Skoobie added.

Kelly walked past, holding the Vase.

Vertigo stopped her, pointing at it. "What's that?"

"Vase of Power," Skoobie answered. "Careful. That's strong stuff."

Vertigo's eyes nearly popped out of her head. "That's the damn Mongolian artefact stolen from the museum last year. The amount of time and manpower we've spent searching for it and you … you … that thing's priceless!"

Skoobie nodded. "Yeah, we know."

Vertigo tried grabbing it, then her hand recoiled from a sharp tinge of static electricity. "Arrrrgh!"

"Holy crap!" Melody breathed.

"Told ya," Skoobie said. "Vase of Power!"

Melody indicated Kelly. "All the more reason why junior here should take it. She needs all the power she can get."

"It's just a damn vase …" Kelly began.

"Ssssh!" Skoobie hissed. "It's listening."

Kelly sighed and tossed it at Melody who caught it.

"No, no, no, no …!" Melody cried, throwing it back at Kelly.

It brushed past Vertigo on the way, giving her another static shock and making her flinch again. "Quit it!"

"Don't mess with it," Skoobie warned Vertigo.

Kelly caught the Vase without a reaction. "I can't lug this thing around, guys."

Vanilla reached into the open door of Vertigo's police car. "Look, there's a rucksack here …"

"… Which is mine by the way," Vertigo pointed out.

Vanilla ignored her and said to Kelly, "You just put it on like this …" She placed it over Kelly's shoulder, then walked behind her, took the Vase and put it inside. "Then you just seal our new friend in here like this, zip it up, and there we go."

"Cool," Melody quipped. "Let's move. We're missing the party, people." She threw her arm up at the crowd. "Come on guys!"

A yell went up as the four girls ran off with Turbo, followed by a flood of people.

Vertigo sighed and let them go.

"Idiots," she said with a small smile.

It wasn't long before the four girls and Turbo were in a ute, leading the crowd through the city streets as they all headed for the skyscraper. Melody had told everyone exactly what was going down before they'd left the Delirium, and now they were all eager to help out.

Others in the street, entranced by the sight, ran to join them. More people emerged from the buildings they'd been hiding in and went with the flow as they sensed hope in the air, along with the police helicopter overhead.

Vanilla drove the ute while Skoobie and Turbo sat next to her. Melody stood in the trailer, fully in her element as she lapped up the crowd's glory while calling for them to follow her.

Kelly stood beside her, grateful that she wasn't a Vessel from the Delirium and that everything that the Black Bride had told her was a straight out lie. The pounding in her head had gone too and she could think clearly again. She was Kelly Morrison, and the world wasn't a nuclear wasteland… yet. Not if she could help it.

Melody cried out triumphantly, having pulled the Vase from Kelly's rucksack to hold it high with one hand while punching the sky with the other.

"You always overdo it, don't you?" Kelly muttered.

Melody beamed to high heaven and howled delightedly.

The truck came to a halt in a cul-de-sac, overlooked by the half-finished skyscraper towering over them. Kelly saw that much of the building was incomplete. Large parts of it, including the top left-hand quarter, were a mass of skeletal pipes, beams and scaffolding exposed to open air, reminding her of a giant climbing frame. She grimaced, knowing that the Nuthouse would be high up in what little there was of the completed section.

Melody handed the Vase to Kelly as the crowd started moving in. Kelly was about to speak when several bursts of machine gun fire erupted from above. The crowd scattered, taking cover, while Melody and Kelly ducked behind the ute's roof. Kelly had gone down fast, leaving the Vase standing on the roof with her hands around it. A bullet hit the Vase, bounced off, and rebounded back up into the gunner's arm.

"Mother of Mercy!" Melody whispered.

Kelly pulled the Vase down, shocked. "How come it didn't break?"

"'Cause it's made of tough stuff," Melody answered. "Just like us. Move."

They leapt off the ute and scrambled behind it where Vanilla, Skoobie and Turbo joined them.

"We need to get in the building and fast," Melody said. "What's the status on the nuke bomber, Scoops?"

Vanilla listened hard before replying, "Point Beach."

Kelly looked at her, amazed. "How do you do that?"

"I've always been a good listener," Vanilla replied.

"Of course you have," Kelly scoffed, throwing an arm up. A bullet whizzed past her hand, making her yelp and bring it back down.

Melody peered at the gunners. "Gotta get past those guards first."

"How?" Kelly asked.

"Relax," Skoobie said. "We planned it all in the truck."

Kelly cringed. "Oh no …"

They pulled her away.

Soon after, Kelly found herself sneaking with the girls and Turbo around the side of the building.

Melody looked at Turbo. "Status report. How are things coming along?"

He glanced at Skoobie. "We haven't really had much to say to each other since meeting up again …"

"Not that!" Melody snapped. "Hacking."

"Keep your voice down!" Kelly hissed.

Melody grumbled under her breath.

Turbo spoke. "It's getting there but taking way too long. You guys need to get on top of things and fast."

"Like, how?" Kelly wondered,

"My boy here'll take care of that," Skoobie said, pushing Turbo's shoulder lightly. "Good luck, hey."

He pushed hers back, just as lightly. "You too."

"Why not just kiss?" Kelly asked.

"Need him conscious," Skoobie answered.

Turbo ran off.

The four girls stood in silence.

The silence grew, along with Kelly's frustration. Finally, she asked, "So what's he up to?"

"All part of the plan, sweetie," Vanilla replied.

Kelly looked at Melody. "Did you know about this plan?"

"We're all on the same wavelength so I kinda guessed," came the reply.

"Care to fill me in?"

"No," they all said.

"Waste of time, babe," Skoobie quipped.

"You'd only make a fuss," Vanilla pointed out.

"And it'd give me headaches," Melody finished.

"Then count me out," Kelly said firmly, stepping back.

Melody and Vanilla grabbed her arms.

Kelly struggled. "Hey!"

A whirr came from above as a long metal construction beam descended.

A beam attached to a cable, attached to a crane.

A crane with Turbo at the controls.

"No, no, no, no, no …!" Kelly cried.

"Get her on before she blows!" Melody ordered.

They hauled her over to the beam, clamped her hands onto it, and held them tightly.

Kelly trembled. "I hate heights."

"Well, now's your chance to get over it," Melody replied. "If you see a freak below and your stomach blows, aim for him."

"Guys, this isn't safe," Kelly said worriedly. "What if we fall?"

"As I said, aim for him."

Skoobie gave a thumbs-up sign to Turbo who gave one back.

Kelly shivered. "This is so not a good idea …"

"I'm more worried about nerd boy at the controls," Melody muttered.

Vanilla shot her a glance.

"Oh, yeah right," Melody mumbled.

Vanilla squeezed Kelly's hand warmly. "It'll be okay, sweetie. Just hold tight and think of ice-cream."

Melody looked up. "Here we go."

The beam jolted and Kelly's arms were nearly wrenched from their sockets as she was lifted off the ground. She shut her eyes tightly as they all ascended, dangling from the beam. They rose at a steady pace, and all was going well until Kelly opened her eyes, caught a glimpse of the ground far below and wailed.

"Hold it, soldier!" Melody ordered.

Kelly quivered. "The ground! The trucks! They're so far down …!"

Skoobie took one hand off the beam and scratched her cheek.

Kelly gasped in horror.

Skoobie raised her hand and did a half-shrug. "What?"

Kelly shuddered and closed her eyes. "I can't hold on!"

"Only a couple more floors," Vanilla said gently. "You're doing great. Hang in there, sweetie."

"What else can I do?" Kelly whimpered. "My arms are about to go!"

"Your arms aren't the issue, it's your butt," Skoobie told her, putting her hand back on the beam. "Look at that mamma. That whopper's a sagger."

"Can it Skoob, I've been dieting for years," Kelly replied painfully.

"On what? Mudcakes?"

"Okay, so I'm not perfect …"

"Got that right," Melody agreed. "You'd look a million bucks with a little discipline."

"You're not that great either …"

"Yeah, but she's got personality," Skoobie countered. "You got nothin.'"

"Skoob …"

"And we're here," Vanilla announced.

They were lowered into a part of the building exposed to open air and landed on a thin surface. Kelly let go of the beam, winced, and rubbed her arms.

"Made it," Melody said. "Good one, Skoob."

They high-fived.

Kelly steadied herself on a beam amidst the chilly wind. "That was so wrong, and it's the last time you pull the bull over my eyes, Skoob."

Skoobie noted Kelly's rear and frowned. "Well …"

Now it was her turn to receive a death glare from Vanilla.

Skoobie submitted and nodded to Kelly. "Sure."

Melody strode ahead. "Kicking the bad guys' butts is all I care about. We've gotta stop that cyber virus from getting out, no matter what."

"And to save ourselves from being nuked," Vanilla added.

"Well yeah, there is that too …" Melody muttered.

"While getting the right spiel out to the rest of the world," Kelly said grimly. "That's if they believe us."

"Well, hopefully they will," Vanilla said back.

"Hopefully?" Kelly asked in disbelief. "Guys, we're the last line of defence on planet Earth. We don't even have a plan and you're giving us a *'hopefully?'*"

"Oh, there's a plan for *you* …" Skoobie began.

Vanilla glared at her again.

"Oh yeah, right," Skoobie mumbled.

"Hey, why not up the stakes?" Kelly retorted. "What else could they throw at us?"

"Contortionists," Skoobie replied.

"Yeah, random quips don't help, Skoob …"

"Tell them that."

Skoobie indicated ahead and Kelly looked. Two contortionists in skin-tight lycra were creeping towards them, stretched into a ball with their feet on their hands and their heads poking out from between their knees.

"Skoob," Melody began, "take junior here and go find the big bad. We'll take on Contortionist Freak Central."

"CFC's," Skoobie mused. "Well they are toxic. Like it. Have fun." She pulled Kelly through a doorway and down a corridor.

Melody stood poised for battle as a CFC unravelled himself, rose to his full height and walked towards her.

"Come on, you …" she seethed.

She threw a punch. He flipped backwards, kicking her in the face. She swung out angrily. Her punch went wide as he arched back, with his palms and feet on the ground, before his foot lashed up, kicking her in the head. She recoiled as he formed into a ball once more.

"This is garbage!" she snapped.

She ran in to boot him but missed as he rolled away, rose again, and threw a long kick that she caught. Nimbly, he swung himself around her whole body, brought himself back-to-back with her, linked his arms and legs through hers and pulled solidly, stretching her limbs to the max. She winced and leapt backwards, body-slamming him face down into the floor. Swiftly, she rolled to the side, elbowed him hard, and moved to scamper. He arched up and lunged on top of her.

"Crud!" she sighed.

Vanilla picked up a wooden beam and swiped at the other CFC. He dodged her smack, then evaded several more by weaving around her expertly. Finally, he grabbed the end of the beam, kicked her away, threw the beam aside, curled up into a wheel and rolled at her, fast. She quickly regained her balance and called, "Hey you know what?" She jumped high and flipped over him. "Had a few classes myself."

He stopped, stood up and ran at her.

She flipped back, kicking him in the head, then whirled around and belted him with an uppercut, sending him reeling. He regained his balance, rolled back in, uncurled himself, leapt up and grabbed her in a headlock.

"'Course, I may have missed a class or two," she winced.

Melody, nearby, lay flat on her back, struggling with her CFC. She lashed out with several swings as his head swayed from side to side, dodging each one, before his hands formed a single club, smashing down on her shoulder and making her growl. Slyly, he leaned in and whispered, "Let's see how well you do the twist …"

He hissed delightedly as he grabbed one of her arms, then her leg, and turned both at an awkward angle. She cried out painfully, before swivelling onto her back with enormous strength, lurching off the ground and slamming him into the floor, loosening his hold on her. She rolled away but barely got anywhere when he leapt onto her hard and fast, pushing her into the floor-boards.

"Scoops!" she called.

Vanilla broke out of her headlock and recoiled. Her CFC lunged, grabbing her wrists.

Melody booted her own freak heavily. He resisted the pain and still held on as his arms stretched out obscenely, clutching her wrists. Defiantly, she rose to her feet.

"Double-slammer dizzy-wizzy!" she called to Vanilla. "One … two …"

The girls clutched their CFCs' arms tightly, stayed close to the ground, and began whirling on the spot. The CFCs' held on easily, going with it.

The girls picked up speed, swirling so hard that the CFCs' holds became lighter and lighter until a swift kick from each girl sent them flying into each other with a resounding crack. The two rolled into a ball, tumbled over the edge of the building and were gone.

Melody and Vanilla stopped spinning and staggered around dazedly as the world came into focus.

"High-five!" Melody said breathlessly.

They raised their hands, slapped out and missed. Now seriously out of breath, they steadied themselves on each other, looking green.

"Gimme a minute," Vanilla puffed.

"Gimme ten," Melody puffed back.

Vanilla blinked hard. "We used to be able to do that all day."

"Yeah, when we were kids in the playground, Scoops."

Vanilla looked to the building's edge, panting. "You think we got 'em?"

"Nah, they're probably climbing back up," came the reply. "We'd better move."

"Yeah, we'd better."

They took a few staggering steps, then collapsed to the floor with their vision swirling again.

"Boy, do we suck!" Melody sighed.

Skoobie led Kelly towards an open door at the end of a corridor. Through it, Kelly saw Sandi, two Groomsmen and the towering Black Bride, all facing away from them.

Skoobie pulled Kelly away from the doorway and whispered, "Not you. He's too strong."

Kelly nodded. "No argument there, Skoob. You want me to snoop around?"

"Yep," Skoobie answered. "On the roof."

Kelly looked up. "But that's not finished."

"That's the fun part," came the reply. "The Turbster showed us a layout of this place on his laptop."

"When the hell was that?" Kelly asked, bewildered.

"In the truck on the way here," Skoobie replied. "So, listen up. On the very tip of this joint, and the hardest part to get to …"

"Of course …"

"… is a satellite dish. That's what's gonna boost the cyber virus when it goes radio-*active*. You gotta disable it, amigo. I believe in you." She slapped Kelly's shoulder and turned to leave.

"Whoa, whoa, whoa!" Kelly said, pulling her back. "*I've* gotta disable it? What am I? An electrician?"

"If you get any probs, use your phone and call the Turbster. Chill, will ya?"

"What phone?"

"Oh yeah, this one." She pulled it out and slapped it into Kelly's hand. "His number's in there, somewhere."

"Just how much did you guys' plan in that truck?" Kelly wondered. "Okay, whatever, fine. The world depends on me."

"Yep," Skoobie agreed. "You're our last resort." She opened the door to their right and pushed her through it. "Have fun."

"Wish me luck," Kelly said grimly.

"You won't need it," Skoobie replied. "You've always been … well … walking good luck."

"Oh, Skoob!" Kelly's heart melted as she came in and hugged her warmly. "That's the nicest thing anyone's ever said to me." She paused. "I guess … uh … I've always thought the same about you guys too."

Skoobie nodded. "Cheers."

"I won't let you down Skoob, I promise. See ya soon."

"Catch ya."

Kelly smiled, then turned and headed through the door.

Once it was closed, Skoobie cruised away.

"Walking good luck," she mused thoughtfully. "I wonder if I really do think that about her?" She mulled it over and shrugged. "Whatever."

Kelly headed to the room's window. She struggled with it for a bit, opened it and looked down.

"Mother of hell …!"

The cars on the ground were mere specks.

She took a deep breath, composed herself, and climbed outside, inching along the small ledge. Construction beams were nearby. They weren't too far to reach. Once there, she could scale the building.

"Well …" she cringed "… life begins at fifty feet up."

She grimaced.

"Let's hope it doesn't end there."

Skoobie placed her hands in her pockets and stepped into the small room where the Black Bride and two Groomsmen were poised over a laptop while Sandi stood at a nearby terminal. Nobody noticed Skoobie.

Sandi spoke. "Power grid drained by forty per cent. Give it another few minutes and we'll have enough fuel for a global metastasis. The geo-proximity bug should have burnt out by then." She moved in and joined them, looking at the laptop.

Skoobie did the same, staring curiously at the small screen.

The Black Bride's head rose, entranced. "So begins the dawn of a new age."

"Totally," Sandi agreed. "We just need to inject the virus now. Once it's up and running, it'll spread like digital wildfire, destroying all global fail-safes."

"Can any more be put in place?" Skoobie piped up.

"No," the Black Bride replied crossly.

Skoobie mused thoughtfully. "So what's protecting NUTS' stuff?"

"Our Immunity Circuit," he retorted. "Final tests show that it's the only element resistant to the cyber virus."

"Is the Circuit safe?" Skoobie pressed.

"I have it here."

He tapped a small pouch near his chest, then stopped dead. There was a long, long pause, before he turned his head menacingly towards her, as did the others.

"'Sup?" Skoobie asked.

He growled as his hand shot up, ready to lash out.

"No!" Sandi ordered, raising her own hand and blocking off his strike. "She's too strong. Our friends have sent in the big guns first."

"No, that's still coming," Skoobie quipped, nodding at a monitor showing Vertigo and her squad clashing with the NUTS near the building's entrance and winning. "Look at that. The cops are just walkin' all over your lot." She addressed the Black Bride and indicated Sandi. "Just like you're doing with her."

Sandi smirked. "Cheap shot, Skoob, but you're not turning us against each other. We know your game. Besides, another party's on its way." She pressed a button on the laptop. The screen changed to show a riot squad approaching the colourful crowd from behind. "A few politicians have declared martial law. Politicians working for us, that is."

"Talk about NUTS in high places," Skoobie mused.

Sandi ignored her and pressed on. "Their 'unofficial' orders are for the riot squad to slaughter everyone in this place, cops included. What do you think of democratic freedom now?"

Skoobie shrugged. "Same as dictatorships. Garbage and hypocritical."

The Black Bride grabbed her by the back of the neck and pulled her face up to his. She peered into his dark veil, unable to see his eyes but firmly holding his gaze, refusing to submit. He turned his head to one side, examining her.

"Beloved," he said observantly, "you were born to stand by our side. If we can awaken her …" He indicated Sandi, "Then you have no hope. You never did." He caressed her cheek. "Dearest child, you've always been wavering on the brink of sanity, forever unbalanced. With a little push, we can tip you into your destiny." He paused. "Therefore, we must eradicate your defiance and replace it with unshakeable guilt."

He uncurled his hand to reveal an electronic chip.

"Your mind," he said, pressing his thumb on her forehead. "Your finger …" he reached down and opened her palm. "… And a lone piece of metal." He placed the chip in her hand and rolled it up. "My cherished darling, both you and the world shall embrace your destinies as one. That means, beloved, that my gift to you is the honour of activating our virus, so that you may evolve together. The world's blood shall pour from your hands. From your …" He clutched her fingers "… precious fingertips."

Skoobie nodded happily. "Cool. Let's do it."

Sandi spoke, addressing the Bride. "Hold it. She's here as a decoy. Look." She glanced at a terminal screen showing an image of Kelly climbing up the building's side, followed by several NUTS dressed as bats. "The kid's making for our dish up top. Doesn't matter. Our Acro-Bats are hot on her tail." She looked back at Skoobie. "More are making for Mel and Scoops. None of 'em stand a chance."

The Black Bride's gaze didn't waver from Skoobie. "How ironic that the self-proclaimed, apathetic neutral child ends up being the world's destroyer." He chuckled from beneath his veil.

Skoobie was unfazed. "Okay sure. Which button do I press, or do you want to rant some more?"

Sandi frowned.

Skoobie noticed it. "Yeah, I'm legit. Only way to test it is to let me press the ol' button, then we can sit back and warm our hands by the world's flames." She sighed, frustrated. "Look, why are we waiting? We're all ready. Search me for weapons. I haven't got any. You can hold me as I work your gadgets, for which I doubt there's a fail-safe. I'm not gonna fight you. I barely know how to turn on a computer, let alone destroy a cyber virus. How can you lose? I'm the real deal. Come on, the cops'll be here soon. Let's start."

The Black Bride paused. "Your acceptance comes too easily."

Sandi agreed. "She's playing with our heads. The more we try and figure her out, the more time she buys."

"Then we must work quickly," the Black Bride confirmed.

"That's what I said," Skoobie pressed. "Let's go for it."

"Reverse psychology doesn't work, Skoob," Sandi pointed out.

"Yeah, but I'm doing reverse-reverse psychology," Skoobie replied.

"As in … going forwards?"

"Yep, you got it."

"So why not call it telling the truth?"

"I did."

"Delay no longer!" the Black Bride snapped. He motioned to Sandi. "Find her friends. Break them."

"You shouldn't be alone with her," Sandi warned. "That might be her plan too. She'll sway you more easily without me here."

"Hey, that's a good idea – thanks," Skoobie said. "Oh, did I say that out loud?"

"See?" Sandi stated. "She's screwing with our heads."

"Screwing, what?" Skoobie retorted. "I'm just going with the flow."

"The best thing's to shoot her now," Sandi pressed.

"Go ahead," Skoobie told her. "Oh sorry, am I confusing you with that reverse-psychology stuff again?"

Sandi raised her gun menacingly.

"Go!" the Black Bride ordered. "She riles you, but not I. All will go according to plan. Leave!"

"Yeah," Skoobie agreed. "Get outta here; we're trying to work."

Sandi pursed her lips. "Your funeral."

She turned and left the room with the Groomsmen.

The Black Bride clasped Skoobie's shoulder with a heavy hand.

"You will learn," he said softly. He pushed her into the chair before the laptop, leaned over her, and typed away.

"Yeah, I know," she replied. "Just make sure it doesn't take too long, huh? I get bored easily."

He continued typing.

Chapter Seventeen

Kelly shivered in the freezing winds as she put her foot into the nexus of two metal beams that crossed like an 'X.' She reached up to grab another beam. It was a long stretch and she just made it. Slowly but surely, she pulled herself up, trying not to think about the ground, which was getting further and further away.

A pigeon swept past her, leading a small flock. She recoiled in fright, falling out into open air and just managing to grab a pole on a hinge. She wailed in terror as the pole swung outwards, making her face the open sky as she dangled in mid-air high over the city by one hand while getting a full view of the horizon. Frantically, she put her free hand back on the beam as it swung in again, then quickly climbed onto the building and regained her balance.

She took a few shallow breaths, composed herself, and began scaling the skyscraper again. High above, she saw the satellite dish on the building's peak. There was still a good way to go.

"Okay," she said shakily. "Not far now. Things can't get much worse."

A bullet ricocheted off the Vase on her back, making her jump. She looked down to see several Acro-Bats swinging effortlessly over the structural beams, rising with spectacular aerial feats. A surge of adrenalin hit her hard, making her bolt up the steelwork faster than she ever thought possible.

"Damn Murphy's Law, damn karma, damn Skoobie, damn God …"

A bullet whizzed past her.

"Sorry, God."

She kept climbing.

Some way below, Melody and Vanilla watched Kelly through the scaffolding, seeing the Acro-Bats gaining on her.

"Looks like somebody could use a little help ..." Melody began.

Bang!

A bullet whizzed between them, hitting the wall.

"Uh-uh, BFFs," Sandi announced, walking into the room. "Just us now. I've called everyone else off."

Melody hurled a wooden plank at her, then leapt sideways as Sandi fired. The plank hit Sandi's hand, just as Melody hoped, sending the gun flying.

"Fine," Sandi said. "We'll do this the old-fashioned way."

She raised her arms above her head, flipped over, kicked Melody to the floor, then lashed out with a sweeping ground kick, sending Vanilla reeling. Melody growled and kicked out, flooring Sandi who fell hard. Melody rolled over, booted her in the stomach, and came in for a second kick. Sandi was faster, grabbing Melody's leg and twisting it fiercely, making her wince in agony.

Vanilla scrambled in to help as the floorboards creaked under her. She dived at Sandi, was backhanded, and sent flying again.

Melody freed her foot, kicked back at Sandi, turned over and leapt on her. A massive creak erupted, the floor gave way and they all fell through it, crashing into the building's next level in a bundle of arms, legs, dust and debris.

Melody and Sandi struggled to their feet.

Vanilla blinked dazedly.

Sandi sneered. "You're a little rusty, M. Guess that's what happens when I'm not around to train you, huh?"

Melody scowled. "Roll over and die!"

She threw a punch. Sandi blocked it and threw another one back. Melody deflected it and let loose with several more. Sandi smacked each one away, then backhanded Melody, sending her reeling and hitting the ground.

Sandi stepped up and placed her foot on Melody's stomach. "Say goodbye to your kid, Mel ..."

"No ...!"

"I remember!" Vanilla suddenly called.

Melody winced, pushing against Sandi's foot. "That's great, Scoops! Get over here!"

"No need," Vanilla replied. "I remember everything about Michaela Brown."

Sandi stopped dead. "What?"

Melody growled and twisted Sandi's ankle.

Sandi crashed to the floor, wrenched off her feet.

Melody rolled over and staggered up. "Guess that fall knocked some sense into you, Scoops."

Vanilla blinked again. "What fall?"

"Or out of you," Melody corrected. "Seems your memory's still a little hazy."

"There's a problem with my memory?"

"Oh boy …"

Sandi stood up.

"But you still remember Michaela Brown, right?" Melody asked quickly.

"Oh yeah," came the reply. "Every last detail. I think it's time for a little therapy session, don't you, S?"

Sandi was shaken. "No! No way …!"

"You've run for too long, sweetie," Vanilla said. "Let it go. Please!"

Sandi whimpered. "No …!"

Vanilla ignored her. "You can't hide forever. It's time to stop fighting …"

"Screw you, Scoops!"

"Who's Michaela?" Melody asked.

"She …" Vanilla began.

Sandi hurled a chunk of rubble at them. They both leaned out as it flew between them, then watched Sandi run furiously to a locked door, leap in the air, smash through it, scramble to a window, and climb outside onto the scaffolding.

"Looks like she's gonna hit blondie," Melody quipped, referring to Kelly. "Let's join the party, Scoops."

"Sure," Vanilla agreed, "but be careful Mel. S is more unstable than ever."

They headed after her.

The Acro-Bats came in hard and fast.

Kelly was no match for their speed. One grabbed her ankle. She kicked him in the face, he arched back, lost his grip and fell for some way before grabbing a beam and scrambling up again.

Another lunged at her with a knife.

She leapt instinctively, landing on an outstretched pole attached to a hinge, then swung out wide over the city once more, cringing in sheer terror. Much to her relief, the pole swiftly brought her back to the building where she grabbed hold of a strong beam and booted the pole hard into an Acro-Bat's face. He wailed and went flying.

She didn't see where he went.

Summoning up her courage, she climbed higher, fighting against the pummelling winds until reaching a slope of pipes, poles and beams, all leading to a satellite dish. The dish itself wasn't that big – only slightly larger than herself – but was clearly enough to bring down the whole world.

The path ahead was covered by wooden planks over small patches of scaffolding, making things slightly easier. Carefully, she headed up it, climbing the gently ascending slope for the building's peak. Bit by bit, she made her way up the wonky path until finally, she reached the dish.

"Made it," she puffed.

She pulled a panel back to find a complex mass of circuitry underneath.

"Now what?" she muttered.

Down below, Melody and Vanilla were now scaling the building while clashing with the Acro-Bats. Among them all was Sandi, climbing after Kelly as fast as she could.

An Acro-Bat dived for Melody. She sprang to the side, swung around a pole and kicked him over the edge.

Nearby, Vanilla, pursued by another Acro-Bat, leapt through the air, grabbed a long horizontal pole, circled it, and rose in a frozen handstand. With astounding strength, she waited for just the right moment, before swinging down and completing her three-sixty by kicking him over the edge. His arms flailed wildly and he was gone.

Propelled by sheer momentum, she skilfully let go of the pole and sailed gracefully over the building in an outstretched ballerina leap. An Acro-Bat did the same, flying at her while slashing his knife at her throat. Her top half arched back nimbly as she glided to a beam, sailed around it, landed, and steadied herself on a plank.

Not far below, Melody scrambled over a path of thin wooden scaffolding. An Acro-Bat landed before her and swiped with a hunting knife. She ducked, his knife swished over her head and she recoiled as a weak board creaked beneath her feet.

He lunged.

She put her hands by her sides and jumped down with all her weight, crashing through the board. A sharp piece of wood angled up, ripping into his leg as she fell for some way, before grabbing another pole, booting an Acro-Bat out into oblivion and looking up.

High above, Vanilla was scrambling up after Sandi.

"Finish her, Scoops," Melody hissed.

She kicked hard, booting another Acro-Bat in the face. A savage uppercut followed, sending him flying off the building.

Kelly put her phone on speaker and listened for the ringtone.

Then: *"Turbo here."*

She spoke quickly. "I'm at the dish. What now?"

"I'll just bring the layout back up on my laptop," he replied. *"There, got it. Are you at the primary board?"*

"How should I know?" Kelly retorted. "I just opened what opened."

"Guess you are then. Now, there should be a large, red wire in front of you."

"Yeah, like a dozen …"

"Not in the top left-hand corner," he said. *"It's the thickest one. There's a small insignia on its side."*

"I see it."

"So cut it."

"With what?"

"The wire cutters in your jacket pocket."

"What?" She unzipped it and pulled the cutters out. "How'd they get in there?"

"Skoob snuck 'em in. It was all part of the plan."

Kelly was gobsmacked. "How much more of this plan should I know about?"

"Would you relax?"

"Relax?" Kelly scoffed, looking around. "Duh!"

"Cut it out already. The wire, I mean."

She did so. A sharp jolt sent her reeling back with a yelp and tumbling rapidly to the building's edge. Somehow, she managed to reach out and grab a pole with one hand while holding the phone and cutters with the other. Crossly, she steadied herself and asked bitterly into the phone, "What was that?"

"*Sorry*," he replied. "*We forgot to disconnect the safety switch first. We'll do that next.*"

"Now he remembers ...!"

"*So snip the small green wire near the bottom right-hand corner ...*"

"Let me get back up there first ..."

He ignored her. "*That's the safety switch. Then cut the red, blue and green, and in that order, near the top. After that there should only be one wire left, and that's the most important. There are several coloured wires in the middle, but if the wrong one's cut, we're screwed. The vital one is the ...*"

A cry erupted as Sandi lunged over the side of the building and grabbed her leg. Kelly yelped and dropped the phone which tumbled into the sky with Turbo saying, "*I'm losing your signal ...*"

Kelly swiped with the wire cutters, going for Sandi's shoulder and missing. Sandi leapt, throwing her against the scaffolding and seizing her neck with both hands. Kelly pushed back in a futile attempt before dizziness hit her. Just as it became unbearable, Vanilla bounded up over the side of the building, swept in and kicked Sandi away.

Kelly sucked in a sharp breath as the air returned to her lungs.

"Get out of here, sweetie," Vanilla ordered. She glanced at the satellite dish. "Get up there."

Kelly coughed and gave a small nod before scrambling back up the skeletal structure of poles, beams, pipes and platforms, making for the dish.

Sandi started to follow Kelly. Vanilla dived into her and they both tumbled down the slope to the building's edge in a swirling roll, then dropped into the sky, turned over through a small cloud and ...

Thud!

Thud!

They landed on the long broad metal beam still attached to the crane line that Turbo had hoisted the four girls up in. The beam dangled solidly in mid-air as they pulled themselves up onto opposite sides of the cable and sat facing each other with their legs dangling high above the city.

"Enough already!" Vanilla called over the wind. "It's over, S!"

Sandi pulled out a knife. "Shut up, Scoops!"

She hurled it at Vanilla's head.

Vanilla dodged it, letting it fly past. "Can't live in the Delirium anymore, S! Gotta come out and face the world sometime. You've gotta let go and it's gonna hurt."

Sandi trembled. "What the hell do you know? I took you and Mel and Skoob and I made you! You guys were nothin' without me. Two-bit losers — that's all!"

"And you know what, honey?" Vanilla asked. "You're nothing without us. You need friends, especially after everything with Mickey."

The beam rocked in the breeze.

"She loved you," Vanilla continued. "You were her hero. Just like you were ours."

Sandi sniffed. "I–I messed up. She ended up screwed 'cause of me. I let her down, just like I've done w-with … with you … dammit!" She shook, trying to hold off her tears but to no avail. Her lips quivered as she stammered, "Mic … Mic … Mickey …"

Her grief exploded as she fell forward onto the beam, feeling her heart erupt into a furious burn as she wailed from the depths of her soul. Her long streams of tears trickled into the clouds, plummeting into the howling winds and then the city streets far below as the dark veil in her mind swirled furiously, revealing the black anguish within.

Vanilla watched sadly, wiping the tears from her own eyes before looking away, feeling every moment of Sandi's pain but holding her nerve.

Sandi choked hard and then coughed, staring out into the sky with a hollow gaze. Silence followed. Finally, she spoke in a crackly voice that was sombre and lifeless.

"M-M-Michaela Brown. Mickey. God, I wish I'd told you everything on the Nile Scoops, but I couldn't. I just couldn't …"

Vanilla looked back at her. "I'm listening."

Sandi shuddered. "I can still see the morning when I first met her. In the forest at the edge of the Crossing. God, she was so full of life. We were only kids. We played. Had adventures. Knights and castles was fun but superheroes was the best. We wanted them to become real so badly." She quivered. "The urge became too much and we left the Crossing to do just that. We travelled the world, bound for glory. Before you and Mel and Skoob, there was S and Mickey. What we started, is what the four of you now have. Don't you see? You're all here because of us."

The icy winds grew. She ignored them and continued.

"We never should have taken the Mahdi on. We got cocky in Saudi, but he was too strong and drove us right back to the Crossing. Then came the war and …" Longer streams of tears trickled over her cheeks " … Mickey's whole family was killed." She wiped her face quickly. "Them, and so many others, died because of us. The whole Crossing took a battering, and that's not even the worst part." She bit her lip and gazed sadly up at the sky. "I was too ashamed to face the Judges of Old but hey, she faced 'em for me. I lied, let her take the rap, and she was exiled for good." She took a deep breath. "Mickey left the Crossing, hating my guts. She went AWOL and I had no chance of finding her on my own. I needed help."

Vanilla bit her lip thoughtfully. "So that's where Mel, Skoob and I came in, wasn't it?"

Sandi nodded. "Yeah, Scoops. It was." She paused. "I made our first meeting by the Cerberus Rock that day seem like an accident. I roped you all in and we were outta there. Soaring into the big wide world in search of fun, as well as to avoid those old fuddy-duddies back at the Crossing."

"It's the Crossing we're talking about, S," Vanilla pointed out. "They'd have understood."

"Yeah right!"

"It's *you* who can't forgive you," Vanilla stressed. "You should have let us in, with everything."

Sandi shook her head. "I never told you, Scoops, the real reason why I spilled my guts to you on the Nile that day. It was because … because …" She tensed. "I'd found Mickey that morning, wasted in an alleyway. A pathetic drug addict, scrounging in the middle of nowhere. She didn't recognise me. Everything that made her special was shot to hell. I begged her to come with me. It took a while, but she finally remembered who I was, and you know what happened?" She sobbed tearfully. "She slapped me, Scoops. Hard. It hurt. God, it hurt. Then she ran."

Vanilla paused, thinking deeply, then drew a sharp breath and said, "S?"

"What?" Sandi retorted.

"I found Mickey too."

"Oh, you did, huh?" Sandi asked bitterly.

"I tracked her down after you split," Vanilla said gently. "She was in New York, and still in a bad way. She didn't want to talk to me and ran. That was a few months ago. I haven't seen her since."

Sandi sniffed loudly. "NUTS were the only ones who made sense. I found 'em soon after. They dulled the pain and made things easier. The Black Bride understood. He knew the truth. We're all NUTS, Scoops; that's the law of life …"

"That's the law of garbage …"

"They helped me find Mickey again. Only a couple of weeks ago now. I was recruiting for them and really thought there'd be hope for her. I knew that if she joined NUTS, she'd see the light." She trembled. "I was too late. She's dead, Scoops. She's gone."

Vanilla sighed sadly. "I'm sorry."

Sandi shivered. "Look at me now. A damn mess. You and the others thought I was a hero before we met up again. The truth is, I'm a liar."

Vanilla dismissed this. "No, you just made mistakes and tried to cover them up, like a lot of people. The trouble is, secrets are like bubbles. The more you try to push 'em down, the bigger they get, until they explode to the surface. You and Mickey only wanted to have fun and make a real difference in the world. You're not the enemy. The Mahdi was and the Black Bride is. That's *real* insanity. Now do the right thing. Come back and face the Judges of Old."

"I can't …"

"No S, you're just scared. Anyone would be, but I'll be there. The Judges know more than you think. They're not stupid."

"Scoops, you don't understand — I *can't* go. Not now. Not ever." She reached in, took hold of the cable and stood up on the beam.

"You can't run forever," Vanilla warned.

"Sorry, Scoops. Life sucks, doesn't it?"

"S …"

She was cut off as Sandi swung around the cable and leapt on her, sending them both falling onto the beam, before grabbing her throat.

Vanilla struggled back, choking, "Mickey wouldn't want this …!"

"She was a dumb idiot who didn't know *what* she wanted!" Sandi hissed. "You're the same …"

"Get off me!"

Vanilla punched her cheek with a resounding crack. Sandi fell back with a cry, hitting the cable and making the beam waver violently. She slid onto its metal surface, shook her head, grabbed the cable and rose.

Vanilla sat up.

Sandi scowled. "You wanna do this the hard way, Scoops? Fine by me." She lunged.

A figure swept through the air, slamming into Sandi and sending her rolling off the beam to dangle from it by one arm. She quickly pulled herself up onto the other side of the cable and scrambled back from Melody, who'd landed between her and Vanilla.

"So what have you two been chatting about?" Melody quipped, holding the cable.

Neither of them spoke.

Melody looked at Vanilla. "Is it over?"

Vanilla eyed Sandi. "Yeah. It's over."

"Fine," Melody said. "The NUTS back there are all dealt with and blondie's at the dish. I'll take it from here, Scoops. Go."

Vanilla wasn't going to argue. She looked sadly at Sandi and said, "See ya soon, S." She rose, took hold of the cable, and climbed up it with muscular athletic pulls. When she was some way up, Melody glared at Sandi. "Just you an' me now, S."

Sandi stood up, balancing on the beam without support. "I taught you all your moves, remember?"

"I'm younger, remember?"

"So die pretty!"

She lashed out.

Melody stepped off the beam, dropped, grabbed onto it at head height, swung up and kicked her. Sandi growled as she fell back onto the beam, then rose as Melody scrambled onto it. Sandi tensed, before flipping across it, kicking out, and sending Melody falling back and rolling off the side to dangle over the city once more.

Sandi moved in, raising her leg for a savage kick, but Melody was faster. She launched her legs up, booted her in the stomach and sent her falling onto the beam.

High above, Vanilla struggled to pull herself up the cable. She fought to stay steady as the wind wrenched her line violently, along with the clashing below. She didn't have far to reach the crane's tip, but she was tiring.

Melody pulled herself onto the beam again, smacked Sandi back onto it, turned her over, dug her knee into her spine, twisted her arm at a painful angle and hissed, "Game over, S! You lose!"

Sandi struggled to break free. Melody held her tightly and she tried struggling harder but found it futile. Finally, she whimpered, sobbed, then let loose, howling like a spoilt child.

"Ah, quit your crap!" Melody retorted. "It's time to face the Judges of Old, and some serious shrinks." She looked up to see Vanilla reach the crane's skeletal structure and descend it. Satisfied, she turned her attention back to Sandi. "Scoops'll be in the driver's seat in a second, then we can all go down nice and easy."

Sandi wailed louder than ever, kicking the beam repeatedly but unable to break free of Melody's grip. With a savage cry she yelled, "I hate you, Mel! I hate you!"

"Oh, I know you do, baby. The feeling's mutual."

She dug her knee in harder while twisting Sandi's arm up higher behind her back, leaving her to scream helplessly into the wind.

Kelly stared at the wires of the satellite dish in disbelief, desperately trying to recall Turbo's instructions. She'd cut everything he'd told her to. Now there was only one wire to go. The vital one to shut everything down, but if she was wrong, it was World War Three. One simple snip could either save the world or destroy it.

Red, green, blue, black, gold or white. Which to choose?

"Friggin' hell," she murmured. "Why me?"

Despite the acrobatic chaos rampant all over the building, and the high global stakes involved, Skoobie sat coolly before the Black Bride's laptop as he loomed over her.

"So what's this mean, bad buddy?" she asked, indicating the screen. "We in?"

He nodded. "Yes, little one, we are. The geo-proximity bug is no more. All that remains is the single press of a button and the virus shall go global."

"Gotcha," Skoobie said. She watched as he opened a slot on the laptop, took out a chip and pocketed it. "So we don't need the chip in there anymore?" She patted the laptop. "The virus is on both, right?"

"Exactly," he replied.

"Cool," she said back. "Can I set our bug off globally now, or what?"

"I did select you for this task ..."

"Yeah, I thought you might've had a change of ego and wanted to do the honours yourself. You know, all power and glory to you …"

"Do it!" he ordered.

"Fine by me." Her finger moved to a button.

"Freeze!"

Vertigo stepped into the room with several armed cops.

Skoobie waved her away flippantly. "Yeah, not now, we're busy. Come back in five."

"Whose side are you on?" Vertigo snapped.

"No one's," Skoobie answered. "I'm just havin' fun."

The Bride sneered. "It's futile to play games you don't know the rules to. Oh yes, I understand your frustration only too well …"

"Shut up!" she bellowed.

"There's a bomb in this room," he cut in.

Vertigo tensed.

He patted Skoobie's shoulder gently, raised a mobile and pressed a button. A beep came from below the chair.

Skoobie leaned over, looked down and raised her eyebrows, impressed.

"Oh right," she realised. "*That's* what that hunk-a-junk down there is."

He continued. "Our blessed bomb is now primed. Two things can deactivate it. A mere press of a button on this phone, or one from the laptop. Of course pressing either means that the cyber virus is released." He snarled. "What's it to be, Sergeant? Fight, run, join me or die?" He chuckled cruelly. "You can't win. Should worse come to worst, the satellite dish on the roof can also release our digital plague." He chuckled cruelly. "You lose in every way, but then again, you've been doing that for so very long, haven't you?"

"You sick …"

"Choose!" the Black Bride snapped.

Vertigo's jaw clenched. "You're forgetting one thing, you freak."

"Fire away," Skoobie said.

Vertigo ignored her. "What's to stop me from killing you and taking my chances?"

"As I said, fire away," Skoobie pressed.

Vertigo agreed and pulled the trigger, letting loose with several shots.

Skoobie stayed calm as they whizzed past her head, hit him in the chest and sent him staggering back without a trace of blood. Caught off balance, his arms flew up, throwing the phone high as he recoiled. Everyone could see, from the impact, that he wore a …

"Bulletproof bra," Skoobie noted. "Impressive."

He roared as he slammed through a thin wall and dropped out into the open air. The phone followed as he fell over the city, flailing as a billowing mass that plummeted for the ground far below. Over and over he rolled, like a churning black ball, until he pressed a button on his arm, igniting two burning thrusters from beneath his dress.

"A jetpack?" Vertigo said in disbelief. "Oh, that's just bull …"

Her swear word was cut off as he flew up, grabbed his falling phone and shot past her, making for the building's peak like an ascending dark angel.

Vertigo thumped the wall angrily. "Bastard's still got his phone." She turned to Skoobie who was musing over the computer. "Run!"

Skoobie looked up at her. "Why?"

Vertigo was astounded. "There's a bomb under your butt, sweetcheeks!"

"Hey, not for the first time," Skoobie quipped. "But that's okay now. I've pressed the enter key."

Vertigo nearly exploded. "You did *what* …?"

Skoobie spoke happily. "Pressed the ol' button here, turned off the bomb and saved your cute pa-ta-ta."

"But that's what he wanted!" Vertigo cried. "You've set things off globally!"

"Yep," Skoobie said proudly.

Vertigo was aghast. "You've killed us all!"

Skoobie frowned. "Hope not."

"What the hell are you on about?"

"See I …"

Her chair beeped.

"What's that?" Vertigo asked, cutting her off.

Skoobie looked down. "Oh, seems we can't trust the bad guy after all. Bomb's still going off. Mamma, look at that counter fall …"

"Move!" Vertigo ordered.

She and her team bolted from the room.

Skoobie rose, put her hands in her pockets and walked after them, whistling coolly. She'd only gone a short distance when the room exploded behind her.

She walked on, unfazed.

The Black Bride flew rapidly to the roof, glancing at his phone.

He smirked at the results, grateful that Skoobie had pressed the enter key. Trouble was, things had stalled in the satellite dish up top, thanks to some young, blonde interference he could see in the distance.

He snarled and hit a button on his phone, activating the dish, while rapidly ascending.

Kelly gasped as the dish hummed loudly. A small screen told her that a burst of power from below had bypassed the wires she'd severed.

She looked worriedly at the ones still left, having no idea where to make the final cut. The dish hummed louder, and she knew that every second she hesitated was one closer to global war.

"Cut the wires and I'm screwed, do nothing and I'm just as screwed," she said worriedly. "Hell, what would Mel, Scoops or Skoob do? Something logical." She paused. "No, *illogical.*" She pulled the satchel off her back. "I don't believe I'm doing this …"

She took out the Vase and held it high.

"One shot to save the world, Kelly Morrison. That's all you got. One shot, one shot, one friggin' sh …"

She slammed it down hard. It hit the dish with an almighty crash and strangely, didn't break. She struck out again and again, battering it until part of the dish unhinged with several small sparks, then fell to one side, dangling from a few remaining bolts. She watched as its hum lowered and its power faded, if only a little, buying her some time.

She stared at the Vase in awe. "Whoa! Maybe you guys were right about this thing." She knelt before the wires. "Now to shut it off for good. Blue, green, red – which one? Oh, this is killing me! What could be worse?"

A roar erupted and she whirled around as the Black Bride rose behind her, his arms outstretched like an angry spectre of death. His jetpack shut off as he stepped onto a small platform, towered over her and scowled, "Looking for a wire to cut? I prefer black. It has a shorter fuse!"

Kelly held the cutters close to the gold wire. "Game over, loser."

He was unmoved. "If your faith is that strong, cut it. Are you a true believer?"

"Yes," Kelly answered automatically.

"You lie," he mocked. "Your mouth says one thing, your face another."

"Damn," she muttered. "Always lost at poker too."

"Not that it matters one iota," he mocked. "The dish may be damaged, yet all is not lost." He indicated a socket on it and raised his phone. "Move!"

Kelly pocketed the cutters and glared at him defiantly. "Get stuffed!"

"I shall," he replied. "On your blood!'

He lashed out. She recoiled as his fist flew over her head, then yelped as she rolled down the skeletal structure with the world blurring wildly. She reached the building's edge and instinctively grabbed a pole where she clung on for dear life, somehow still holding the Vase.

The Bride ignored her and turned to the dish. He flicked several switches, severed the white wire, then plugged his mobile in and delicately returned the dish to its original position.

It hummed back to life, becoming louder.

Down below, Turbo looked up from his phone in horror. "Crap! The virus is airborne!"

His hands flickered over the keyboard.

"Let's see if I can slow things a bit ..."

He peered in and frowned.

"Oh, that's weird ..."

The Black Bride, satisfied with his progress, raised his arms high, as if in a spiritual embrace.

"Now, my beloved," he whispered. "Consume me!"

The distant bomber grew louder.

Kelly spoke defiantly. "You do know that all *your* secrets will be a free-for-all when the virus kicks in, right?"

He sneered cruelly. "Not with my most precious gift. An Immunity Circuit." He pulled it from his dress, ready to plug it into the dish. He held it up, looked at it closely and stopped dead.

"What? This isn't ... how? No ...!"

He threw his head back and roared.

His cries were so loud that Vertigo heard them clearly as she went down the stairs with Skoobie.

"Oh," Skoobie said surprised. "That worked."

"What's up with him?" Vertigo asked.

"Sounds like he found out about my little switcheroo," Skoobie replied.

"Switcheroo?"

"Yep. Used my eyes to distract him while my hands did all the work. I swapped the cyber virus chip with that other Circuit, so what he's transmitting now is digital contrareception. Means the cyber virus'll drop dead wherever it goes, leaving the whole world immune. He's screwed."

Vertigo blinked, took this in, then stared at her aghast. "You're a genius – you know that?"

Skoobie shrugged. "I know."

She cruised down the stairs.

Vertigo shook her head with a smile and followed.

The Black Bride hurled the cyber virus chip into the sky, knowing it was no good to him now. Fiercely, he gazed up at the clouds.

"The bombs," he hissed. "They still come! This whole wretched city will be annihilated." He looked down at Kelly. "But not before you!"

He clenched his fists, then surged down the slope, sweeping in for her.

Instinct took over and she threw the Vase at him, hitting him in the head. He recoiled, the Vase rebounded into her grasp, then she hurled it again. He turned sideways to protect himself, the Vase hit his jetpack, set it off, and sent him flying headfirst into the base of the satellite dish, ramming him into it in a shower of sparks. He jolted wildly and then, to Kelly's sheer disbelief, placed his hands on its side and wrenched himself free.

"What the hell?" she cried.

He growled and turned to her, stepping on a loose board that sent the Vase rolling down the building's slope and flying over the side, into the clouds.

She started to rise but barely got anywhere when he surged at her once more. She yelped, fell back down and rolled sideways, evading his fierce stomp, then rolled the other way, dodging another.

"A wretch like you disrupts my wedding," he snarled. "You shall die for this!"

She kicked up, booting him in the stomach. The effect was minimal. She tried kicking his legs out from under him. They refused to budge.

Furiously, he reached in, picked her up by the neck with both hands and held her over the edge of the building. "So perish all enemies of the Queen!"

"You're … forgetting one thing," she choked back.

"Oh?"

"Gym class!"

She clasped his wrists tightly, brought her legs up, stretched one around his back and tapped the side of the hidden jetpack. A small burst of fire ignited, propelling them both up the building's peak to the dish and dropping them beside it.

He started to rise.

She was faster, picking herself up and diving on his back.

"I haven't won at a lot of things," she hissed. "No job. Never had a real boyfriend until now. My life's sucked and you know why? I figured it out. It's not me. I'm fine. It's cause of sick freaks like you always dumping on me." She pulled out her wire cutters and snipped a strap of his jetpack. "Say goodbye to your cheat sheet!"

He roared and threw her backwards. She tumbled away as he rose to his feet, with his jetpack half hanging off him, and menacingly came for her. She also rose, struggling to keep her balance.

"This is my wedding day!" he growled. "Mine!"

He swung at her. She ducked to the side and lashed out with her cutters, smacking his head. He staggered back against the dish where his elbow hit a button on his dangling jetpack. A savage blast erupted, then he was wrenched off the building at full speed, striking her on the way. She tumbled down onto the roof's edge, grabbed a pole, turned over and watched as his jetpack shot him to the ground as a fiery speck. One hand was tangled in a strap. The other was too far away to reach it, leaving him unable to fight against the wind's savage forces.

Faster and faster he went until …

"Crap!"

Turbo grabbed his phone and ran from the ute as the flaming Black Bride spiralled in, headfirst. With a mighty leap, Turbo toppled into a dumpster as the Bride hit the truck and exploded.

Skoobie emerged from the building with Vertigo.

Melody and Vanilla approached them, with Melody pushing a handcuffed Sandi along.

"Here," Melody said, throwing Sandi at Vertigo. "Keep an eye on her, at least until we can get her back home." She nodded at Skoobie. "Hey, Skoob."

"Hey, yourself," came the reply.

Vertigo threw Sandi into a police van and locked it.

Nearby, the tension was at boiling point, with the riot squad closing in on the Delirium's survivors, all overlooked by a news helicopter.

Vertigo formed a circle with Melody, Vanilla and Skoobie, facing outwards.

"Stay close," Melody warned.

"Yeah," Vertigo quipped, "this could get ugly."

"Hope not," Skoobie said. "That'd mean we're not doing a good job at the café."

"The café?" Vertigo wondered, confused. "What the hell's the café got to do with this?"

"Where's your phone?" Melody asked her.

Vertigo pulled one out and held it up. "I can trust you guys, right?"

Melody grabbed it. "Always." She keyed in a number. "I hate these things." She listened. Then: "Yo, Chief. We need the Hellfreeze. Stat."

A faint voice spoke from the other end. "*Roger that.*"

Melody ended the call and handed the phone back.

"Who was that?" Vertigo asked.

Melody looked up at the plane. "A General in the US army."

Vertigo was baffled. "How do you know him?"

"He comes into the café whenever he's in town," came the reply.

"Likes choc milk," Skoobie added.

"Our café attracts all kinds," Vanilla said. "That's what it's there for."

Vertigo gazed out at the crowd, nervous as hell.

"Stand firm!"

The Riot Squad Commander flinched, raising his shield to deflect a pelting missile. He tensed as he led his squad in, cautious about his orders from up top. He'd been told, from his superiors linked to the government, to massacre the crowd. An order he was holding off from and didn't like one bit.

A scratchy voice came through his headset. Not from his immediate superiors, but from someone much higher up. A General, who he'd only met once but always had respect for. He listened as the message was not only relayed to him, but the whole squad.

"Yes, sir?" he asked. He pressed his hand against his ear, listening hard. "What's that?" He frowned. "You can't be … yes, yes … yes sir. I understand." He took a deep breath, grateful that his orders had been changed, though not knowing if it was a good thing or a bad one.

He pursed his lips and addressed the squad through his mike, "Okay, you heard the man. On the count of three. One, two …"

Vertigo braced herself, ready for gunfire.

"Three!"

Everyone in the riot squad threw their batons and shields down before raising their guns, unclipping their magazines and emptying their bullets onto the street. The crowd slowed, watching the squad remove their helmets and toss them away.

One of the Squad spoke nervously to the Commander. "What the hell are we doing?"

"Changing the rules," came the reply. "There's always a bigger picture. People just need to see it." He took a deep breath and called to the crowd, "You win! It's over!"

The crowd stopped, somewhat surprised.

"Take the most serious by hand," the Commander ordered into his mike. "As for everyone else, stay back."

Nearby, Vertigo gave a wry smile and glanced at the three girls.

"Cows," she whispered admiringly.

Washington

The United States President sat watching the chaos from a large screen in the Oval Office. The riot's squad's actions were hopeful, he determined, but not enough to stop the bomber that was about to nuke the city of one of America's greatest allies. Even worse, he couldn't get through to the bomber and cursed himself for his stupidity. He'd never wanted it sent in. The whole thing was unofficial, channelled through a private company in Saigon, and he'd regretted dealing with it ever since. Trouble was, he'd been desperate and needed the money for a wider political picture, not only to fend off political rivals but also for the greater good of helping the needy, and he'd been torn to all hell about it. How he'd been so blind as to give so much control to this company was beyond him. Now they'd blocked him out of everything, leaving him powerless.

The Secretary of State watched the scene with the riot squad in disbelief, then spoke with a thick Texan accent. "What the hell are they up to?"

"Refusing to fight," came the cool reply.

"They're insane," the Secretary said, horrified.

"Just the opposite," the President corrected. "Whatever leads to peace always is. That was always the end game." He shook his head. "How on earth did I ever let myself get talked into working with that nutcase from Saigon?" He inhaled sharply. "Well I won't be making that mistake again." He shook his head. "Keep trying to get through to that bomber. We need to reach it, stat."

"Sir."

He watched the screen closely.

"Quite a move," Vertigo said, seeing the reports on her phone. "Or a really dumb one. It'll be a long shot if it works," She glanced at the bomber ahead, "and a single shot if it doesn't."

Vanilla too, gazed at the plane. "Everyone has to lay down their arms together, to make a real difference. That can only happen in a crisis."

"All or nothing, babe," Skoobie added.

Vertigo stared at the sky grimly.

Saigon
The FIRE-ARM Corporation
Illegal Weapons Dealer

The CEO sat in his dimly lit office. Like the American President, he also watched a large screen showing the bomber moving into the city.

His subordinate, on the phone beside him, ended his call and said, "Sir, the White House have confirmed that the cyber virus wasn't released. Reliable sources from several global networks back this up. Seems some kind of digital immunity bug was sent out instead. We're in the clear."

The CEO paused, then spoke darkly. "We're never in the clear, Mister Mergrave. We haven't found the source of our cyber virus, have we? All we know is that it came from that one little city. Who knows what else is hiding in there?" He paused and sat back. "We either cover our butts or the crap hits the fan." His head rose. "Take 'em out."

Kelly watched the bomber close in. The sheer size of its military build told her exactly what it was. She gulped loudly. Even more so when its undercarriage opened, revealing a bomb below.

"Hell-Suck 101 …"

Vanilla put a hand to her ear, listening nervously. "No, no, no, no …"

"'Sup?" Skoobie asked, darkly.

Vanilla tensed. "Hold tight guys, this one's close."

"Bastards!" Melody hissed.

"All or nothing, huh?" Vertigo snapped, knowing what they were getting at. "What happened to your friends in high places?"

"Hey, not everyone comes to the café," Melody retorted.

"We'll have to work on our menu," Vanilla muttered.

Vertigo waved them away and went to join her cops.

Vanilla wrapped her arms around Melody and Skoobie, pulling them in, holding them tightly as they gazed up at the skyscraper, knowing Kelly was up there.

Kelly bit her lip worriedly, glancing between the bomber on one side of her and the rising news helicopter on the other. There was no chance of the chopper grabbing her and fleeing. Hell, she reasoned, it didn't have time to escape on its own anyway.

She let loose with a shuddering breath, wondering what to do.

"Gotta be something," she murmured.

Going with her gut instinct, she ripped her shirt off, revealing a white singlet underneath, then grabbed a long pole, pulled it free with a few sharp tugs, knelt, and tied her shirt sleeves to the end of it.

The bomber loomed closer.

She rose with the pole and held it high as the shirt flapped wildly in the wind. Praying like hell that this would work, she fiercely swung it in wide circles.

"Come on," she murmured. "Take a look. Just one …"

The news helicopter zeroed in on her.

"Guys!" Turbo called, running in and holding up his phone. "Check it out."

Melody and Vanilla grimaced at the smell of him.

"Whatcha got?" Skoobie asked.

"Local news," he answered. "Take a look."

The three girls peered at the screen.

"Is that …?" Melody began.

"Yep," Turbo replied.

They all stared at the image showing Kelly on top of the building, swinging her pole with her shirt on the end.

Vanilla grinned. "She's beautiful, isn't she?"

The bomber pilot looked down from his cockpit, seeing Kelly on the skyscraper's peak, swirling her pole. Nearby, the news chopper hovered steadily, observing the scene. No doubt it was zeroing in on his plane and the bomb in the undercarriage.

His finger remained poised on the trigger as he thought hard.

The CEO's harsh tone came through his helmet. *"Problem, Commander?"*

He steered his plane past Kelly, changing direction. "New factor, sir. We've been sighted by a news chopper and our target's surrendered. The whole thing's broadcast on live TV. We're compromised."

"Not we," came the reply. *"You. There's only one way to buy yourself time. Blow the city and let the big boys figure out who's responsible. We'll see you're looked after. Of course I can also ensure you're not. I have contacts everywhere. Think of your family."*

The pilot considered this. "So drop the bomb and I'm screwed. Do nothing and …"

" … You're family's dead," he finished.

"Sir, I repeat, they've surrendered …"

"You know you're orders."

"With all due respect sir, this is nuclear war that we … no … I'm about to ignite."

"Your family's life or theirs. Take it or leave it."

Washington

The Secretary of State listened hard on his phone, then put his hand on the receiver and looked up.

"We're through to the plane," he stated. "Text-wise anyway."

The Bomber

A beep came from the pilot's flight screen. He glanced at it quickly.

"Just received a message from the White House, sir. The cyber virus is dead."

"*Makes no difference,*" came the cold reply. "*All traces of its origins must be destroyed so drop the damn bomb!*"

He clutched his controls tightly, veering back for Kelly.

Far below, a cry went up from the Delirium's survivors, knowing what was coming.

The pilot's finger hovered over the trigger once more. He paused, momentarily, then saw Kelly again.

Suddenly everything made sense. There was only one way to end this garbage, and that was not to go with it and do the exact opposite by showing everyone the bigger picture. The blonde girl below had done just that, and her bravery confirmed his resolve.

He spoke firmly. "Sir, if you want the nuke dropped, then you can haul your butt up here and do it yourself on live TV."

He hit a switch.

Outside, the bomb rose back up into its hatch which shut over it.

The bomber's thrusters flared brightly as it turned and soared away.

Kelly dropped the pole and fell back on the roof, astonished as hell.

Washington

The Secretary of State looked up from his phone. "Our pilot's just sent a message. He's standing down and the bomber's retreating. All looks good."

The President leaned onto his desk, his face in his hands. "Looks like we picked the right pilot to send to Saigon." He paused, then raised his head and sat wearily back in his chair, thinking of the short, blonde-haired woman with sunglasses who'd suggested that very pilot for him. "Still takes a lot out of you though. A hell of a lot."

"You got that right," came the reply.

The Secretary continued listening into his phone.

The Bomber

"Got a thing for young girls, have you?" the CEO sneered.

The pilot didn't react to his harsh tone. "No, sir, just a daughter like her. I want her to remember that her daddy was the one who didn't nuke the world when he had the chance. She's gonna see me a hell of a lot better than your kids'll see you."

"You won't be around for the glory …" came the snarl.

"Maybe, but I'll last longer than you. I've just leaked your details to the world media. They'll be on your doorstep shortly. I'll be leading the charge. See you soon."

He severed the connection and changed the frequency to contact the choppers behind him.

Saigon

Click!

The CEO looked up at his subordinate, now holding a gun on him. "What the hell do you think you're doing?"

The only response was a cold stare.

"You're in this as deep as I am," the CEO pushed.

"That's business sir," the younger man stated. "You taught me that, remember? I'll need to get my story straight for when all hell ignites, meaning you're a liability so …"

Bang!

The CEO slumped onto his desk, filling it with blood.

"… I have to go out with a bang *and* a whimper," came the sneer. "Namely, yours."

Coldly, he put his gun away and strode from the room.

The bomber flew into the horizon, leaving a celebratory cry from the people below as the only thing to explode in the streets.

"I don't believe it," Kelly said, astounded. "I've saved the friggin' world!"

One person, however, was not so happy.

"That should be me up there," grumbled Melody.

"She's good, isn't she?" Vanilla beamed, indicating Kelly on Turbo's phone. "What's her name again?"

"Kelly," Turbo said.

Vanilla looked up at the skyscraper and chanted, "Ke-lly, Ke-lly, Ke-lly …!"

Melody grabbed her arm. "What the hell are you doing?"

"Cheering her on," came the reply.

"What for?" Melody retorted. "Anybody could have done that."

"You don't have to be so jealous, Mel. Let it go."

Melody folded her arms and looked away. "I'm not jealous I … I…"

Vanilla raised her eyebrows.

"Screw you," Melody sighed.

She sat on a bin as Vanilla began chanting again, along with a group of people.

Skoobie sat next to Melody.

"Chanting not your thing either, huh?" she asked.

Melody glared at her.

"Yeah, whatever yanks your chain, babe," Skoobie quipped.

The cheers grew louder around them.

Kelly peered down. The streets were growing with people and the news helicopter was closing in on her, followed by another.

She beamed delightedly, stepped onto a small, wooden platform and waved proudly. A loud creak followed, the platform crumbled under her and she wailed as she tripped and then tumbled over the side of the building, hit an outstretched pole, and was left dangling miles above the city.

"Yeah, that'd be right!" Melody scoffed, getting a glimpse of her on Turbo's phone.

Silence fell over the crowd.

Vanilla continued chanting. "Ke-lly, Ke-lly, Ke-lly …!"

"Yeah, doesn't work now, Scoops," Melody retorted.

Turbo turned up the phone to hear the news report.

"*… And things seem to have gone horribly wrong with the young blonde woman now hanging off the building and screaming for help …*"

Melody fell back against the wall, her face in her hands.

"Should we chant 'Melody, Melody, Melody' now?" Skoobie asked.

Melody smacked her wearily.

Nearby, in an alleyway, a young couple ran excitedly along, heading for the party in the distance. The man clutched the girl's hand warmly as they picked up speed, passing two concrete slabs that had fallen from the skyscraper. Joyously, they rounded the corner, leaving the area empty.

Moments later, a glimmer came from between those slabs. Slowly, that glimmer grew into a glow, revealing an object that had fallen neatly between them without a scratch.

An object now known as the Vase of Power.

Despite its fall from the skyscraper's tip, it was intact. What's more, the shell of the cyber virus chip lay beside it, dead to the world.

The Vase's glow morphed into a gentle pulse, almost like a heartbeat, growing brighter and brighter, encompassing the chip until …

Crunch!

A black high-heeled boot stepped mercilessly onto the chip, crushing it out of existence.

A smooth hand reached down, touching the Vase and feeling its tingling presence. Another hand moved near the first, lifting the shiny object into the bristling cool breeze. Steadily, it was raised before a tall woman with short hair, jet-black sunglasses and a long, dark coat. Her hair, however, was blonde.

Platinum blonde.

The Vase pulsated rapidly, as if talking to her.

She gave a wry smile and spoke coolly. "Relax, Demergatron. You're not in any trouble."

It kept pulsating.

She raised a hand, cutting in. "Forget it. The Crossing's turned into splitsville. No one blames you for ditching it. You couldn't have done much anyway."

The pulse slowed, then turned grey.

Her face darkened under the shadow of a passing cloud. "No, it's not good. The Village is knocked for a 666 and the Judges are under heavy fire, literally." She paused as the cloud passed, leaving a glimmer of sunlight to stream through. "At least here's safe. The Vine's path needs to be clear. It's already infected enough and the last thing it needs is one of its tendrils snapped off. That's down to you, me and …" She paused again, listening to Vanilla chanting Kelly's name in the distance "… my dream-team who've given me nightmares since day one."

The Vase flickered yellow.

"No, I *tried* to train them," she corrected, "but they threw the rulebook out the celestial window. Mel even pushed to call them the Crossing Operative Periphery Squad, or COPS. Luckily that name was vetoed. By everyone."

The Vase pulsated in golden beats, as if laughing.

"Still, they work," she conceded. "It's all down to their dynamics which somehow turn into operative dynamite, blowing us all away. No one can understand it, but their rolling ball of chaos hits the mark every time." She inhaled sharply. "How that party-patrol works is a mystery, even to them, I think. Still, they help keep the bad guys away from my covert operations …" Her lips pursed " … despite the global chaos they cause doing it." She looked up at the chopper moving in for Kelly. "Blondie was a good choice too. The best we could have hoped for." She looked back at the Vase. "We'll grab Sandi and lie low. The Crossing's about to be blown to hell by the Death Syren's wail which is mounting for a final screech. We need to be prepped."

The Vase turned dark blue.

"Yeah, I know. It's big. Still, you did good work infiltrating the Delirium. Keep this up and you'll be promoted to a human in no time."

She patted the Vase, it flickered brightly, then she turned, strode away, rounded the corner and was gone.

"*… And yes, our mystery girl on the skyscraper's climbing into a news chopper as we speak. From what we can see, she's being aided by a cameraman and … oh! She's fallen onto him in an awkward position. Their limbs are flailing everywhere and they're struggling to untangle themselves and … whoa! She's smacking him now …*"

Melody grabbed the phone and hurled it away. She got ready to boot a bin when …

"Mel!"

She turned to see Darren running around the corner for her, followed by Charley and few of the Delirium's survivors. Without a thought, she ran in, leapt high and landed on him, with both her arms and legs wrapped around his body. He hugged her tightly, holding her up as she grabbed his face in her hands, kissing him over and over while wolf-whistles rose behind her.

Nearby, Skoobie felt a gentle tap on her shoulder. She turned to see Turbo, grinning sheepishly.

"We made it, Skoob," he said, as if expecting something.

She rolled her eyes and sighed. "Fine then, reward central. Here goes …"

She clasped his face in her hands and kissed him long and hard. To her surprise, he kissed back. Slowly, they parted, and for once she was taken aback.

"Wow," she floundered. "You got stronger."

"Yeah," he replied. "Or maybe your heart's melting, Skoob. Did you think of that?"

Skoobie fumed. "You have no idea who you're messing with, buddy …"

"Yeah, I do," he cut in, "but I'll risk it. I've thought about it a lot lately, and y'know what?" He inhaled sharply. "I … uh … and I don't believe I'm saying this." He paused. "I'd give up everything for you."

She blinked. "Give up what? You don't have nothin.'"

"Nor do you," he pointed out. "Does that make us even?"

She pursed her lips and looked away, unusually riled. "Mother of a b…"

He peered at her. "Are you blushing?"

"No!" she retorted, for once losing her cool.

"Yeah, you are – you're blushing." He grinned. "Look, there's nothing you can say that'll embarrass me …"

"Isn't that your mum?" she asked, looking over his shoulder.

"Doesn't work, Skoob."

"No really, that's your mum."

"What?" He looked back. "Oh crap …!"

"Irwin!" came a cry from nearby.

A few people were pushed aside like ninepins as Mrs Newcombe ran at him, her arms outstretched.

"Mum!" he wailed in horror.

She grabbed his face in her hands, kissed him repeatedly, then pulled his head down into her bosom. A laugh exploded from Charley and the others as he cringed, "Oh, Mum! Get off …"

"Irwin!" she cried. "What did they do to you?"

"Enough already!" He broke away from her and stepped back.

She stared at him astounded. "Now you don't even want a cuddle from your mother anymore?" She pointed at her chest. "You used to love it there!"

Charley and the others burst out laughing again.

"Shut up, Mum!"

She raised her hand angrily. "Don't you speak to your mother like that, Irwin Newcombe!"

"Mum …"

"Say sorry!"

"No!"

She pointed at the survivors. "Show them you're a good boy. Say sorry!"

Turbo sighed as their laughter grew. "Okay, I'm sorry, I'm sorry …"

"Say it like you mean it."

"Oh geeze, Mum …"

Skoobie cursed under her breath and stepped up.

"'Sup?" she asked Mrs Newcombe wearily.

The older woman eyed her suspiciously. "Oh, hello." She looked at Turbo. "Who's your friend, Irwin?"

"Skoobie," he replied.

Mrs Newcombe nodded and addressed her. "That's an interesting name. Are you Catholic?"

"Nuh," Skoobie answered.

The older woman frowned. "So what are you, dear?"

Skoobie shrugged. "Nothing."

"Oh," Mrs Newcombe said simply. "Well, it's very nice to meet you. Let's go, Irwin …"

She reached for him.

He pulled his hand away. "No, Mum. I'm staying with Skoobie. She's my girlfriend."

Skoobie groaned and looked down, running a hand through her hair.

"Her?" Mrs Newcombe asked, shocked. "This … this … girl who's not even Catholic? Do you know what she does?"

"Yeah," he replied, clutching her hand. "She saves the world." He paused. "That's why I love her. Completely."

Skoobie clenched her free hand into a fist and, for once, lost her cool and muttered, "I *hate* this crap …"

Mrs Newcombe stared at Turbo aghast. "But … but … she's no good for you, Irwin – can't you see that?"

"Actually," Skoobie began, "I'm not the one controlling his every move in life. It's not him that's the problem. It's you, lady."

Mrs Newcombe gasped. "What …?"

Skoobie continued. "You're stuck in a nostalgic past that never existed 'cause you're too scared to change. You're highly insecure and trying to control him to prove your self-worth since you have no identity without your son. You need to go with the flow instead of clinging onto him like a rock that's dragging you both down to crap central. He's just helped save the world, lady, and if he'd stayed home listening to you we'd all be dead. Now high-five him and go fix up your own life."

Mrs Newcombe was too shocked to speak. Her jaw dropped in horror, then opened and shut several times.

"My son the juvenile," she whispered. "I didn't raise my boy to end up this way."

Turbo's head rose and he spoke confidently. "See ya Mum, for now anyway."

She was about to reply, then stopped and relented. She gave a small nod, before reaching in and clasping Skoobie's hands in hers.

"Take care of him," she pleaded.

"Nah, I'll make him take care of himself," Skoobie replied.

"You'll be good to him, won't you?"

"Don't have a choice," Skoobie answered simply. "See, universal law throughout the whole of space time states that love is merely a peak frequency spike of high energy that's around to keep the whole of reality flowing in a reproductive cycle in a heavenly body. Severing that connection only leads to static that leads to decay and the forming of dark matter which evolves into …"

Vanilla and Melody slapped her from either side.

"Give it away, why don't you?" Melody huffed.

"Sorry," Skoobie mumbled. She saw Mrs Newcombe's confused look and sighed wearily. With a deep breath, she glanced up at the sky, looked back down, and, for the first time ever, spoke from the heart. "Yeah, I will 'cause …" She squeezed his hand and looked at him. "I … oh hello--rama … I want to."

Turbo's face lit up like a Christmas tree and he came in for a kiss.

"Yeah, not now," she said, putting her whole hand on his face and pushing it back lightly. "That'd make her volcanic sexual repression blow in instead of out, leaving us with a *real* mother of a mess."

"I'm sorry, what?" Mrs Newcombe asked.

"Forget it," Skoobie said, looking back at her. "You just be good to yourself. Go live a little. Get out there. Try helping people as much as you can, but have some fun too. Can you do that … Mum?"

Mrs Newcombe recoiled hysterically. "Oh my God … !"

"What's the prob?" Skoobie pressed "… Mum?"

The older woman turned and hurried away. "No! No, I've got to go talk to Father Pablo! This is too much! I'll be back!"

"Don't hurry!" Skoobie called after her. "Mum!"

Mrs Newcombe wailed and fled.

Turbo wrapped an arm around Skoobie. "What have I done?"

"What have *I* done?" Skoobie mumbled, sitting on a bin.

"Guess you'll have to open up a bit more now," he said, sitting beside her.

The bin lid gave way and he yelped as his backside dropped into the squishy remains of a meat pie.

"Look what happens when you do," she pointed out. "Your brain goes and your butt suffers for it." She took a deep breath. "Okay kid, let's get this right. I'm the boss. What I say goes."

"Kid?" he asked, baffled. "We're the same age, right?"

"No, I'm older," she stated firmly. "A *lot* older."

"Can't be that much," he said. "We look the same age."

"Cheers."

He nodded. "As long as I haven't found someone just like my …"

She glared at him.

He backed right off. "Got it."

"Then *she* has no part in you and me," she pressed. "You got that too?"

"Yeah," he replied, "but instead of this kid's stuff, how 'bout we try to work things out together, as adults."

She looked away, seething. "Oh, this is bullshark …"

"Skoob?" he cut in gently. "Isn't it time we both grew up?"

She sighed wearily and looked back. "Whatever, but I'm still the boss."

"Whatever you say … boss." His hand rose, brushing her hair behind her ear. "So how 'bout a kiss?"

"Oh, Jehovah …"

Unable to resist, they both came in and kissed gently. Slowly, they parted, and he hugged her warmly as she muttered, "I am not attached to you; I am a free spirit, repeat, I am a free spirit …"

A gust of wind swept in as a helicopter hovered over them and Kelly descended on a rope. Once on the ground, she freed herself and stepped away as a cheer rose from Charley and the survivors.

Vanilla ran in and hugged her. "Sweetie, you did it! You actually did it!"

Kelly smiled. "Thanks Scoops. We all did."

Vanilla kissed her cheek, hugged her again, then stepped aside as Melody approached, smacked Kelly's shoulder and said, "Yeah, well done, yada, yada, yada …"

She moved on.

Skoobie watched her go, frowning. "I didn't know she could speak yada." She looked at Kelly. "Nice work."

"Thanks, Skoob," Kelly replied.

"Welcome. You into hugging?"

"Yeah, I am."

They hugged.

"You into kissing?" Skoobie asked.

"Yeah."

They kissed each other's cheeks.

Skoobie spoke cautiously. "You're not into hard mouth kissing, are you?"

"No, Skoob."

"Thank the stars."

"Kelly!" a voice cried.

Kelly turned back. "David!"

He emerged from behind Charley's group and ran at her, while she did the same. They met halfway, she leapt into his arms and they fell backwards, kissing in mid-air. A large garbage bag broke their fall and his eyes nearly bulged out of his head as he winced in pain. She broke away, horrified, as he removed a piece of junk from under his back and threw it aside where it clanged onto the street.

"You okay?" she asked.

"Better than ever," he replied. "More importantly, are *you* okay?"

"Better than ever," she answered, grinning. "Is your back alright …?"

"It's fine, Kel."

She nodded. "Guess you saw that stumble I made on the world stage."

"Forget it," he told her.

"I can't, David. God, it was humiliating …"

"No, not really …"

"I mean, it's on the news and everything forever now and I …"

He placed a finger on her lips. "Kelly?"

"Mmmmmf?"

"Don't ever shut up."

He pulled his finger away. The garbage bags crunched beneath them as they kissed again, then parted and smiled.

Melody took Darren's hand as she, Vanilla, Skoobie and Turbo, all stepped in.

"Well," Melody said, "I don't know about you guys, but I could sure use a coffee right now."

Vanilla grinned. "I know just the place."

"The café?" Kelly asked.

"Café," Melody agreed.

"Café," Skoobie confirmed.

"Café it is," Vanilla said. "Best place in town. Let's make tracks, guys."

"Hang on, wait a minute," David cut in. "The whole world's just seen Kelly here save it from a nuclear apocalypse. It was all on live TV. Now she'll be flooded by cops, federal police, spy agencies, the works. She's just made history, which is great, I wouldn't think anything less of her, but her life'll be crazy from now on."

"Wish it were me," Melody muttered.

Kelly frowned. "I don't think it'll be a problem, David."

"What do you mean?" he asked.

She paused. "When I was coming down in that chopper, they were saying something about all their footage being wiped. They called the other chopper who said the same. I don't get it."

Turbo beamed. "Oh that was me."

"You?" Melody asked, aghast.

"Yep," he replied proudly. "Used my tech to modify the Immunity Circuit's signal. Gave it a boost to wipe out any digital footage in the city's radius. Hey, we don't want Kelly as an enemy target for years to come. Now no one'll know about anything she's done here today." He grinned proudly.

Kelly shrugged. "Thanks, I guess. Kinda sucks but thanks."

Melody, however, stared at Turbo in disbelief. Her jaw opened and closed several times, then her eyes welled with tears before she suddenly lunged in. He yelped as she grabbed him in a tight embrace, kissing him over and over on the cheeks and wailing, "Oh thank you, thank you, thank you …!"

She kissed him rapidly as he gasped for air.

"What are you so happy for?" Kelly asked.

"'Cause now she can claim the glory for herself," Vanilla answered.

"You're welcome," Kelly muttered. "Gee, don't make a fuss."

Skoobie indicated the struggling Turbo. "I won't. Saves me the trouble."

Melody released Turbo, turned to Darren, grabbed his arm and hoisted him down the street. He yelped and stumbled after her.

"Café, café, café …!" she called.

Vanilla smiled and followed.

Kelly and David hugged each other tightly and headed after them, while Turbo interlocked his fingers with Skoobie and they walked hand in hand behind her, with Skoobie swinging their arms back and forth casually.

Nearby, Vertigo glanced at Sandi in the van and then turned to an officer.

"S'pose we'd better get this one to the station," she said.

"Uhhhhhhh …" the Officer began.

"What?" she asked.

"Can't do that, Sarge."

"Why the hell not?"

"'Cause it got hit pretty bad by a load of petrol bombs. It's mostly okay …"

"Like the cells, right?" Vertigo pressed.

"Not really," he replied. "All the doors are blown off."

She drew a sharp breath. "Fine. We'll keep her in my office."

"Yeah, about that, Sarge," he said, somewhat hesitantly. "That's not there anymore either. It got flattened. Although we did find a letter from a judge thanking you for a hotel stay …"

She smacked the car roof and got in.

Kelly looked back at Vertigo.

"What's up with her?" she asked.

Melody waved her away. "Ah, she's just cranky 'cause she doesn't get to bang her judge's gavel."

Turbo snickered.

"What?" Melody asked, then realised what she'd said. "Oh right." She led them along. "Forget it, this party's ours." She kissed Darren. "You know guys, we really are the best team ever, even if I do say so myself."

Beaming, she led them through the streets amidst the growing celebrations of the day.

Chapter Eighteen

Kelly's heart tingled as she entered the café. True, it was dark, and everyone who'd set up base here was gone, and taken their stuff with them. Despite this, the café was pristine and seemly untouched, which she found full-on bizarre. Sure, the resistance would have left in a hurry when the bomber swept in, so surely there'd be a huge mess, or at least *something* left behind. Nuh-uh, she realised. The whole place was clean to the point of sparkling.

She stopped by the door, her heart aglow, as she recalled when she'd first entered here, and the many joyous times after that.

David entered and stood beside her. She rose, kissing his cheek and rubbing his arm as she leaned her head on his shoulder.

"Welcome home," she whispered.

He rubbed her back warmly.

Vanilla locked the door, closed the blinds and turned on the light. "Oh, yeah. There's no place like it." She looked around, gave a small smile and listened hard. "Everyone's still worked up outside and will be for a while. We'll lie low until things settle. Gosh knows we need a rest after all that. Saving the world's darn tiring."

"Nah," Melody scoffed, pulling out a chair and sitting at a table. "Piece of cake. Still, power nap."

Clunk!

Her head hit it and she was out like a light.

Darren sat beside her and gently raised her up. Her head rolled onto his shoulder as he took her in his arms and kissed her forehead.

Vanilla made for the kitchen. "I'll get us something to eat. You'll all be hungry now."

She went out the back.

Kelly yawned and took a seat at the table next to Darren. Skoobie and Turbo came in too, sitting beside her.

Turbo watched Melody and Darren cuddling lovingly and raised his arm to do the same with Skoobie.

"Can I …?" he began.

Skoobie rolled her eyes.

Kelly grinned. "Go with the flow, Skoob."

Skoobie sighed. "Fine. You did a good job today, nerd boy."

"Thanks, hippie girl."

He put his arm over her shoulder and moved in so she could lean on him.

"Uh … no," she said. She reached up, grabbed the side of his head and placed it on *her* shoulder. "Take it or leave it."

He grumbled under his breath.

Kelly nestled against David.

He kissed her cheek tenderly. "How does it feel to have saved the world, Kelly Morrison?"

She blinked in disbelief. "Surreal. My brain's blown after all that. Who'd have ever thought that I'd stop World War Three? Me? Seriously?"

"Bite me," Melody mumbled in her sleep.

Kelly ignored her. "You guys do know that it's down to all of us, right? God, you lot really are the best. You've given me everything I ever wanted."

"Except a house," Skoobie pointed out. "You lost that."

"Well, yeah Skoob …"

"Your job too …"

"Yeah, I know …"

"You also got arrested, nearly killed more times than we can remember, and what was that about nearly having a threesome with a pirate?"

David raised his eyebrows.

"There was also …" Skoobie continued.

Kelly slapped her lightly, making her shut up, then took a deep breath and said, "What I'm *trying* to say is, you guys have been great. You've been …" She composed herself, then spoke straight from the heart "Better than my own family. They … uh … weren't easy to get along with. You're *way* better than them." She bit her lip. "That's how I'd like to think of you from now on. As family. Always."

The kitchen door opened and Vanilla emerged with tears in her eyes, having heard the whole thing. She sniffed hard as she raised her arms and approached her. "Ohhhhhhhh …"

Kelly knew what she was up to and rose. "Oh Scoops, no! Please don't. Don't you dare …!"

"Only if you don't …" came the blubbering reply.

Kelly's heart bubbled and she swept in for Vanilla who did the same. They met halfway, collapsing into each other's arms and weeping from the depths of their hearts while swaying from side to side.

"We love you too, sweetie," Vanilla sobbed, stroking Kelly's hair tenderly. "Forever and ever. Don't you forget it. Never ever, ever …"

Kelly hugged her back, weeping just as much. "I won't, Scoops. Same goes for you. All of you. Thank you so much."

"Anytime, sweetie. We're always here. Always."

Skoobie inhaled sharply and spoke, for once revealing the honest to god truth, if a little restrained. "Same goes for us, muchacho. We … devas to hell … love ya."

Kelly sniffed. "That means a lot, coming from you Skoob."

"Name of the game," she replied.

Turbo looked up from her shoulder. "Can we swap places now?"

"No," she flat-out answered.

Kelly gave a choked gurgle, laughing and crying at the same time.

Melody snored loudly.

Vanilla reached out, smacking her.

Melody snorted and awoke, rubbing her eyes. "Can't a girl get any sleep 'round here?"

"Say it," Vanilla ordered.

"It's okay," Kelly said, wiping her tears away and stepping back. "She didn't hear anything."

"She heard every word," Vanilla replied, wiping her face too.

Kelly was baffled. "So she was only pretending to sleep?"

"No, sweetie, she saw the whole thing. She doesn't switch off when she zonks out. She dreams of what's really going on. Says it keeps her on guard. The more interested she is, the more vivid the dream."

"Like hell," Melody muttered.

Kelly shook her head. "You guys freak me out."

Vanilla pushed Melody. "Say it, Mel."

"Oh no," Melody cringed. "No, no, no. Hell no …!"

"Clinchy!" Skoobie sparked up.

"Love ya, kid," Melody said quickly.

"Thanks, Mel," Kelly said back. "What's a clinchy?"

"Believe me honey, you don't want to know," Vanilla answered. "Mel found out the hard way. Now …" She patted Kelly's shoulder, strode into the kitchen and returned with a steaming pot of coffee. Skoobie leaned over, grabbed some cups from the next table and laid them out as Vanilla poured. When all the cups were full, Vanilla raised one and said, "A toast."

"Oh no, please," Kelly protested, choking up again and waving her hand. "This is too much …"

Everyone except Melody raised their cups.

"To you, sweetie," Vanilla announced. "To Kelly Morrison."

"To Kelly Morrison," everyone minus Melody chorused.

Kelly choked again, embarrassed to all hell, and sobbed loudly. "Oh my god …"

"Yeah, yeah, whatever," Melody said, moving in to grab her cup.

Skoobie reached for her, fingers curled and ready for a twist.

Melody recoiled, then quickly grabbed her cup and raised it. "Love ya, babe."

They all took a sip.

Kelly was speechless. "I-I don't know what to say …"

"Don't say anything, please," Melody moaned.

"No, I want to," Kelly replied. "Thanks for making me into a better person. Guess I can finally be proud of who I am. So, to me." She raised her cup. "To Kelly Michaela Morrison."

"Michaela?" Vanilla asked.

"That's me," Kelly replied. "Prefer Mickey though."

Melody, Vanilla and Skoobie exchanged glances with a smirk.

Kelly took a sip and sat down. "Wow, that coffee's good."

"Made it myself …" Vanilla began, then suddenly went quiet. Slowly, she raised her hand to her ear, gazing at the roof.

"What's up?" Kelly asked.

"Music," she answered.

"Where from?" Kelly wondered.

"In here," came the soft reply.

Skoobie listened too. "Oh yeah. I'm on your frequency, babe."

Melody looked up. "Got it."

Kelly was about to say something, then stopped, feeling a familiar presence. The golden aura that had called her here now blossomed inside her, brighter than ever, making it seem like this place was open again. She could almost see it teeming with customers lost in the bliss of flowing conversations.

"I get it too," she whispered. "The whole vibe's back. Did we do that?"

"Partly," Vanilla answered. "In a roundabout sort of way."

Kelly was confused. "Huh?"

"We've got a link with back home," Skoobie said. "Makes us the ultimate chain-gang."

"So we're hooked in with a distant vibe," Kelly concluded, "That means …"

"*The Crossing's won!*" all three girls suddenly cried.

Melody leapt up, diving on Vanilla and hugging her tightly. Vanilla struggled to hold her up and kissed her cheek before Melody broke away and kissed Darren long and hard. Skoobie, too, kissed a confused Turbo, then rose to hug and kiss the other girls.

Kelly also rose and was hugged by all three of them in return.

"Crisis blown to hell," Melody said, breaking away first. "Glad somebody shut that Death Syren up. Ooooh, that was close."

Kelly nodded. "So your village is safe? What's the story?"

"A long one," Vanilla answered.

"Who cares?" Skoobie added. "We're on totally the right vibe so we're good. That means …"

The kitchen phone rang.

"Right on time," Vanilla finished. She turned and headed through the doors.

Melody pulled her pants up, satisfied. "That's another notch in our victory belt. You know, I think we need a holiday after this. How does Saudi sound?"

"Cool," Skoobie replied.

Kelly sipped her coffee while clutching David's hand warmly and listening to Melody go on about Saudi.

Shortly after, Vanilla returned to the room happily.

"Report, soldier," Melody stated.

Vanilla slapped her playfully and said, "That was our Gold-Class Platinum call. The Crossing's bounced back, everything's *Vine*, and we'll get a full debrief tomorrow. Not only that, our NUTS have been rounded up and are totally out of business."

Turbo shifted awkwardly. "I would have preferred better terminology …"

"Big Jack's in solitary too," Vanilla continued. "So all's good. Everywhere."

"Least until Karmageddon," Skoobie piped up.

Melody and Vanilla glared at her.

Skoobie gulped.

"Karmageddon?" Kelly asked.

Melody looked ready to blow.

"Oh, you mean like in the Bible?" Turbo concluded.

"Uh … yeah," Skoobie replied. "Totally."

"Who's for cake?" Vanilla cut in.

"Me," Kelly answered. She took a seat, along with everyone else, and wrapped David's arm around her.

Vanilla went into the kitchen and emerged with a plate of sliced chocolate cake which she served eagerly and prompted them to eat up. The cake was delved into hungrily and was soon gone, leaving them all satisfied.

More food was brought out and their chatter turned into laughter which morphed into banter. Kelly relaxed to the max and was soon laughing to high heaven. This was nothing like the Delirium, she realised. No one was trying to suck her into a hypnotic trance for mind-probing. Here, the music was real, and she felt … special. Yes, that was it. More than that. Her friends, her family, were bringing out the supreme best in her.

Their banter flowed freely until it glided into her life story and before she knew it, she was pouring her heart out. Her friends hung onto every word as she spoke deeply, revealing more than she ever had to anyone about anything. Bit by bit, the world faded away, until it was just her and her besties in the sanctity of a café, with a steaming pot of coffee and plenty of cake.

Shortly after midnight, Skoobie casually slapped the jukebox which let loose with a cruisy pop song. Kelly squealed delightedly as she leapt up, pulling David with her, to the joyous chorus of one of her favourite hits. The others rose too, with Melody, Vanilla and Skoobie pushing a few tables away. Kelly beamed as she led David into the middle of the floor, swirling with him as she sang. Skoobie joined them and began teaching Turbo her funky moves.

Nearby, Vanilla glided with Melody and Darren in a triangle. Soon, they were all lost in the moment, twirling, spinning and changing partners at least once, with even Melody ending up with Turbo.

Together, they partied as one, laughing, singing and dancing into the early hours of the morning, leaving Kelly to finally realise that she'd, at last, completed her path into sheer heaven.

A path, she realised, that came from a Crossing.

Chapter Nineteen

Months later

"Sweetie, I really wish you'd have let me drive," Vanilla said loudly, rocking from side to side in the backseat as the car jerked awkwardly. "There's no need to make such a fuss."

She lurched again as she sat blindfolded. Skoobie sat on one side of her, Turbo on the other, while Kelly drove with David by her side.

"That'd kill the surprise, remember?" Kelly replied.

David rubbed her hand. "She can't hear you, *remember?*"

Kelly sighed. "Duh, to me. Least those earplugs are working."

"Welcome," Skoobie said. "Knew we'd need 'em for her one day and the Russians won't miss 'em. High-tech security, pfffft!"

"Just walked right in and took 'em, huh?" Turbo asked.

"Yuh-huh," she answered.

"Turn here," David prompted.

Kelly turned the car into a small car park, entered a bay and switched off the engine.

"This is it," she announced.

The doors opened and they all got out, with Skoobie and Turbo helping Vanilla. They guided her for a short way, then Kelly reached up and pulled out the earplugs. "Surprise, Scoops."

"I don't see what the big deal is …" Vanilla began.

Cries rose ahead.

Children's cries.

Vanilla tensed. "Oh no! You didn't … did you … you didn't …"

She ripped the blindfold off.

A park lay before her, stretched out between bushland and a hill. A junior baseball game was in the middle of it and there, batting, was her son. Nearby, her daughter was seated on a picnic blanket with her father and his new girl-friend.

Vanilla gasped and put a hand to her mouth, watching her son lovingly. "Hit it hard baby, hit it hard, come on …"

Pop!

The shot dribbled a short way as the other team scrambled for it. Her son, however, was faster, and he ran to first base, then second, then third …

"Home run, baby!" Vanilla cried, leaping up and down. "Keep running! Bring it on home …!"

He picked up speed, leapt, and slid smoothly into home base.

Vanilla yelped and grabbed Kelly's arm excitedly. "Did you see that? He did it! That's my son! He hit a home run! He scored a homer! Did you see it, did you see it …?"

Kelly laughed. "I saw it, Scoops."

"Yeah, I wish I hadn't," Melody said, jogging out from the bushes. "What the hell kinda shot was that?"

Kelly looked at her. "Should you be jogging? Your kid's almost due."

Melody stopped and patted her tummy. "Yeah, but who can tell? Look at that. Flat as a pancake."

"There's a bulge right there," Skoobie pointed out.

Melody made a face and grumbled under her breath.

Darren jogged in from behind, puffing and panting like mad, and fell to the ground in an exhausted heap.

"Thought … you were gonna make … shorter runs …" he gasped to Melody.

"That was short," came the reply. "Well … shortish."

"It was uphill all the way," he panted.

"Hey, you didn't have to tag along," she replied.

"Somebody had to keep an eye on you."

"Forget it. I can take care of myself *and* our kid. Toughen 'em up early — that's what I say."

Vanilla ignored them and watched her son run up to his father.

"Did you see my home run, Dad?" he asked excitedly.

"Sure did, Jamie," his father replied. "It was great."

The girlfriend rubbed the boy's shoulder. "Good shot, Jamie."

Vanilla's eyes welled with tears. "I did too, sweetie. I saw it too." She shuddered and looked down to wipe her tears away. Then …

"Mum!"

She looked up with a start.

Her son was running towards her.

She knelt without thinking, he swept into her arms and she hugged him tightly. Her daughter followed and she hugged her too, before kissing them over and over and weeping.

"Why are you crying, Mummy?" her daughter asked.

Vanilla sniffed. "Only because I'm happy to see you, sweetie-pie. Look at you two. Gosh Sophie, you've gone up an inch since I last saw you and … Jamie, did you hurt yourself?"

"Yeah," came the happy reply. "From that slide. It's okay."

"I have a tissue here …"

She scrambled in her pocket, pulled one out and dabbed the small cut.

His father and his girlfriend rose and came over.

"You see the shot, Scoops?" he asked.

Vanilla nodded. "Yeah, Andy. It was great."

"Nice of you to come along."

"Didn't know I was coming, but I'm glad I did."

Melody glanced at the girlfriend. "So what's this bimbo's name?"

"Don't start, Mel," he warned.

"Hey, I don't start; I just finish …"

Darren stepped between them, pushing Melody back.

"What have you got against me?" the girlfriend asked.

"Nothin'," Melody replied, "but if you had anything against us I'd say it'd be silicone."

"Hey …!"

"Social anxiety," Skoobie concluded. "Comes from being overlooked as a kid. What you're really craving for, lady, is parental attention to give you a sense of self-worth. That's why you're propping your chest up to your father figure here."

The girl raised her fist. "That's it …!"

Melody's shot up too. "Let's rock!"

"Guys!" Vanilla cut in. Everyone stopped as she took a quick breath and composed herself. "I didn't come here to fight. I came here because … because …" She frowned. "Come to think of it, why am I here?"

"Same reason we all are," Andy replied. "From what I hear you helped save the city from being nuked to kingdom come. We'd all be dead if it weren't for you."

Vanilla put her arms around her children as he continued.

"I had a talk with Sergeant Vertigo. We did a bit of jiggery-pokery with the courts and …"

Vanilla's eyes lit up. "You mean …?"

"You can have the kids for school holidays and every second weekend for now, pending an investigation …"

"Legal crap," Melody muttered.

Skoobie pretended to spit. "*Pfffft!*"

Vanilla was overjoyed. "You mean it, right? You're serious?"

"Totally," he replied. He indicated Kelly. "Your friend put up quite an argument. She came and told me everything you did. Did the same with the cops too."

David put his hands lovingly on Kelly's shoulders.

Vanilla stared at Kelly, amazed. "You did this?"

Kelly nodded. "Yeah. Guess when I can talk, I really can talk, especially for my friends."

Vanilla pulled her kids in tightly. "I don't know how to thank you, sweetie."

"Don't," Kelly said. "It's fine, really."

"Yeah," Skoobie piped up. "'Specially when we put the hard word on Vertigo, saying we'd expose her affair."

Melody elbowed her. "Shut up."

"So-rry." She indicated Kelly. "Doesn't matter. Blonde-stuff did all the talking with him over there. She brought him 'round."

Vanilla pushed her children forwards. "Kids, go say hello to Aunty Kelly."

"Oh no …" Kelly began.

She stepped back but was held fast by David. Now, with no choice, she knelt as the children came over.

"Hi, Aunty Kelly."

"Hey, Aunt Kelly."

"Hi, guys."

Sophie came in and hugged her. "Thanks for bringing my mummy home."

Jamie did the same.

Kelly hugged them both tightly.

Vanilla looked at Kelly and mouthed, "Thank you."

"Anytime," Kelly mouthed back. She gently pushed the children back to her and stood up.

"No hard feelings, huh?" Andy asked Vanilla.

Vanilla put her arms around her kids. "No. None." She kissed each of them lovingly.

Pop!

A kid on the field sent the ball dribbling away.

"Oh, what the hell was that?" Melody cried, storming onto the pitch. She threw an arm up to the coach. "What are you teaching them? To be wimps?" She grabbed the bat from the boy. "Gimme that!" She called out to another kid, "Throw the ball at me! Hard!"

The boy was wary.

"Today!" she ordered.

The ball was tossed lightly at her.

Bang!

She smacked it out of sight.

"There!" she bellowed. "That's how you sock it! You wanna play, you play right! Don't be fair; don't be nice. You gotta crush the other team into friggin' dust! Rule one in life – don't take garbage from anyone. You're tough; you're strong; you're heavy-duty; you're … AAAAARRRRRGH! OH MY GOD!" She fell to the ground clutching her stomach. "Dammit! Not now, kid! I'm busy! Come back later!"

"Mel!" Kelly called. "Did …?"

"Yeah!" Melody called back. "My waters just broke!"

Kelly ran onto the pitch. The others ran after her, save for Skoobie who strolled behind everyone else.

"I knew it was time," Vanilla said, running eagerly alongside Turbo. "That baby's crying to get out."

"Mother's instinct, huh?" he asked.

"No seriously honey, I can hear it."

Kelly reached Melody and knelt before her. "Okay, I got this. I did the course. I know it all …"

"Get away from me; I'll do it myself," Melody retorted.

"No, you won't," Kelly replied. "Come on, let's get you into the shade over there."

She helped Melody up and the small group made their way off the pitch and into a cluster of trees and bushes. Melody lay down with a groan while Kelly knelt before her once more.

Vanilla quickly motioned to her children. "Kids, go get some towels from the car over there. Oh, and scissors from the glove compartment too. Be careful with them though."

Jamie and Sophie ran off.

A siren wailed as a police car with a broken window rolled up. Vertigo got out angrily and stormed over, pointing to her window with one hand while holding the baseball up with the other. "This is yours, right?"

"Yeah, thanks for bringing it back," Skoobie quipped. She grabbed the ball and tossed it over her shoulder to the coach.

Kelly looked up at Vertigo. "Better call an ambulance."

Vertigo saw Melody and hurried off.

"Okay, I'm up," Kelly said cautiously. "Now just relax, Mel. This is gonna be exactly like we practiced …"

Melody winced. "I hope not. You broke the damn doll's head off."

"Only once," Kelly replied. "We've had a ton of lessons since then and I did real well. So, we'll do this one step at a time …"

"Tell that to the kid; he's coming at his own speed! Oh mamma! Argh! Geeze …!"

"Breathe …"

"You breathe! I want this damn thing out!"

Sophie ran up to Vanilla. "We've got the scissors and towels, Mamma."

Kelly turned Melody around so that she was side-on to everyone else. "Now, Mel, I'm gonna take off your …"

"Yeah, yeah I know. Just do it."

Kelly reached down and removed everything, keeping her eyes averted.

Melody looked up, horrified. "What the hell are you doing? You gonna deliver my kid without seeing it?"

"Well, I don't really wanna look at your …"

"Get over it!" Melody cried. She reached up, grabbed Kelly's head and pushed it down close.

Kelly nearly gagged and recoiled.

Skoobie caught a glimpse and nodded.

Turbo did too and fainted dead away.

"Some Dad you'll turn out to be," Skoobie muttered.

Vanilla raised her head, listening hard. "Oh good. Vertigo got through to the ambulance. It'll be here in a few minutes."

Vertigo ran in. "I just got through to the ambulance. It'll be here in a few minutes."

"Yeah, we know," Skoobie said.

Vertigo was baffled. "How?"

Vanilla tapped her ear. "The roadblock on Duke Street's just cleared. They're heading along it now."

Vertigo stared at her in disbelief.

Melody groaned, trying to ride the pain.

"Okay," Kelly said, "when I give you the word, I want you to push …"

Melody's eyes nearly popped out of her head. "Push? I've been pushing for the last five damn minutes! What, is that kid pushing back?"

Skoobie indicated the fallen Turbo. "I bet he did."

"You're only meant to push at certain times," Kelly told her.

Melody made a face. "Screw that! I want this thing out of … arrrgh! Arrrrgh! Arrrrrrrgggghhh …!!!"

"Okay," said Kelly, "here we go. One … two …"

"Arrrrrrrgggghhh … !!!"

"Push!"

"ARRRRRRRRGGGGHHH … !!!"

"Give it all you got, Mel!"

"Get-out-you-little … AAAAAARRRRRGGGHHHH … !!!"

Pop!

The child flew out into Kelly's hands like a cannonball, almost sending her reeling as she caught it. She steadied herself and then …

"Waaaaaaahhhhhh …!"

She gazed in wonder at the tiny, helpless infant in her arms. Her heart melted as she stared at it in awe, completely blown away, while listening in sheer joy to its first shrill cry.

"Let's go, kids," Vanilla said. She grabbed her children's hands and they hurried over.

Kelly looked up, grinning. "Congrats, Mel. You have a son."

Melody gulped, scrambled up against a tree and looked away, shaking.

Vanilla held the scissors out to Kelly. "Do you wanna do the honours?"

"It's fine," Kelly replied. "You've got this one."

Vanilla raised the scissors and cut the umbilical cord. She was about to drop it when the sight of a tiny dot on its side made her stop. She stared into it, realisation dawned, and she looked up happily and said, "Oh! You're Kelly! Kelly Morrison."

Kelly stayed focused on the child. "What, Scoops?"

Vanilla beamed. "I remember you now. I mean, I really remember. You know, when I was mind-wiped in the Delirium and you were the missing five per cent? I just got everything back."

Kelly frowned. "How?"

Vanilla held up the umbilical cord.

"*That* reminded you?" Kelly asked amazed.

"Uh-huh," Vanilla replied. "See, if you wipe the goo away, that bit there looks like your face."

"I don't wanna see it," Kelly grimaced.

Skoobie peered over. "Oh, there she is. Deformed, but she's there."

"Yeah," Vanilla said. "It darn triggered my memory."

"Not uncommon," Skoobie told her.

Vanilla's free arm reached out, giving Kelly a quick hug. "Good to see you again, sweetheart." She ruffled her hair.

Kelly shook her head, confused.

Vanilla stepped back and handed the cord to Skoobie who raised it and peered in, seeing who else she could find.

Kelly grabbed the towels from Sophie and wrapped the child up.

"Here," she said, leaning in. "Your son, Mel."

Melody quivered, keeping her eyes averted.

Darren knelt beside Kelly and took his child. "Here, come to Daddy, little fella. Come on." He raised him to Melody. "Here, Mel, take a look at our son. See what we did."

Melody shuddered. "No. No, I don't wanna. I can't …"

"Honey, it's okay …"

"Can't …"

He brought the child in closer. She felt his soft breath, a cry in her ears, and then a small hand rose, brushing her cheek.

She turned her head, stared right into his tiny eyes and trembled. "Oh hell …" She gulped, choking hard. "Gimme my kid."

She reached out and took him, feeling his little body against hers as tears of pure joy flooded down her face, knowing that this tiny miracle was the only thing in her life that she had no defences against. Ever.

"Oh, he's so perfect," she gushed. "Look at him." She clasped his smooth hand warmly. "Who'd have thought we did this, huh? Who'd have thought?" She kissed his forehead. "Hey, little guy, I'm your mamma. That's me. I'm not perfect, your Dad even less so, but we'll be good to you. I'm gonna take you on hikes, bike rides, the works. We'll go skateboarding, mountain climbing, skydiving – you name it. Your mamma loves life. You're going to as well." She looked up tearfully at Kelly and whispered, "Thanks, Junior."

Kelly smiled. "Anytime."

Melody sniffed. "Hey, Scoops. We're both mothers now."

Vanilla hugged her children. "Yeah, Mel, we are."

Melody pulled Darren in, kissing his wrist. "Love you, babe. You and him more than anything."

"Same goes," he replied.

She nodded. "Thanks for putting up with me and all my garbage. Don't know how you do it."

"Because it's you – that's why."

They kissed, before slowly parting and grinning at each other.

She looked up at everyone, then saw David.

"You're a good friend too," she told him.

"Congratulations," he replied. "Uh … guess that's about all I can say, really. I was never one for words."

Kelly rose and held his hand.

"We'll help in any way we can," David said. "Just say the word."

Melody smiled. "Guess things turned out alright, huh? The world didn't end. Hey, we all ended up with families and people we love. Well, not the Sarge there …"

"Married guy must be busy," Skoobie figured.

Vertigo rolled her eyes.

"Hey," Melody wondered. "Where's the Turbster?"

Turbo groaned from the ground and sat up.

"Toughened up yet?" Skoobie asked.

"What'd I miss?" he asked back.

Skoobie reached over, touched the baby and then his face. "Here. Baby goo."

Thump!

He passed out yet again.

Melody grinned. "Good stuff, Skoob." She glanced at them all. "This is the best. Look at us. Me, Darren and my kid. Scoops and her kids. Skoobie and the Turbster, blondie and David and ..." Her jaw dropped as she looked past everyone in horror "... the entire junior league baseball team. What the hell ...?"

The baby gurgled.

"Sorry, kid."

The coach motioned to the baseball crowd and they all clapped and cheered, with the adults gushing, and the children, just curious.

"Well done," the coach called. "We saw the whole thing."

Turbo sat up groggily. "Wish I had."

Melody looked back at her son. "Well, this is embarrassing." She kissed him. "Not that *you* have anything to worry about. Just remember, never say sorry ... except to me and Daddy at times, and I'm not sorry for you – that's for sure."

Skoobie knelt beside Turbo.

"You okay now, bud?" she asked, slapping his shoulder.

He put a hand to his temple, feeling queasy. "Yeah. I think so. Hey, whatcha got there?"

"Umbilical cord." She held it up to him.

He peered into it curiously. "Is that Kelly?"

"Uh-huh," she confirmed.

He nodded, then stared at the baby, spellbound. "God, look at him, he's awesome." He took her hand in his. "Doesn't this just make you wanna have kids, Skoob?"

Her jaw dropped. "Uhhhhhhhhhhhh ..."

Melody wiggled her child's arm.

"What are you gonna call him?" Kelly asked.

"Sam," Melody replied. "Darren and I agreed on it. Short for Samson, and that means strength. He's already got the hair for it." She held him out to Kelly. "Here, you did a good job, blondie. You can be the first to hold him."

Kelly was taken aback. "Oh no, really, I delivered him, remember ..."

"That's different from holding him," Melody pointed out. "You brought him out, you get him first, but if he ends up calling you Mamma ..."

"I know." She knelt, took him carefully and rose. "Uh … hi Sam Hill. Welcome to the world. I'm Kelly."

"*Aunty* Kelly," Melody corrected.

Kelly paused and looked at Melody whose gaze was resolute.

"Aunty Kelly," she repeated, looking back at the baby.

David stroked the child's head gently.

"Good stuff," Melody said, and took a deep breath. "Well, it's been great." She motioned to Vanilla's daughter. "Hey, kid, go get that bag over there. I'll need that strap on the ground too."

"What for?" Kelly wondered.

"To make a satchel out of it," came the reply. "It'll hold Sam in place."

"As I said," Kelly pressed, "what for?"

"Hike time," Melody answered. "Gotta show him the world, and God knows I have to wind down after that."

The crowd laughed.

An ambulance wailed as it drove up.

"Forget it," Vertigo stated. "You gotta get to hospital."

"Screw hospitals; I hate 'em," Melody scoffed. "Just a quick walk, hey?"

Vertigo dismissed this. "Aunty Donna says no."

"Lady, you are so not an aunty."

The paramedics ran in.

"Duke Street's a pain, huh?" Vanilla said to the nearest one.

He frowned curiously and hurried past.

Melody groaned. "This is such a waste of time."

Kelly handed the baby to Vanilla.

Vanilla beamed. "Hey there, I'm your Aunty Scoops. I'm going to teach you how to cook – yes, I am. We're going to make lots and lots of yummy dishes together. You bet we are." She touched his nose lovingly, kissed him, then handed him back to Melody as the paramedics knelt beside them.

Kelly grinned as a cool breeze swept by. She blinked dreamily as it picked up, feeling like a giant ghostly hand was slowly embracing her. She raised her head blissfully, relishing its touch, then suddenly sensed a presence inside it. Her skin tingled and her heart leapt as the presence grew, overwhelming her. She gasped at its sheer awesomeness, never feeling more alive. The sunlight blurred in her vision and then …

***

Kelly opened her eyes and looked up from the café counter to see her empty cup and saucer being taken away, while feeling like she'd just woken up.

"What the …?" She saw the clock on the wall. "God, I'm late!"

She grabbed her bag, hurried to the door and ran out into the morning, just in time to see her bus heading off into the distance.

"Oh great!"

She threw an arm up and turned around with a groan, thinking what Melody, Vanilla or Skoobie might do. With a sigh, she looked down, and suddenly realised what she was wearing. The exact same clothes she'd worn on the day when she'd first entered the café. A glance at the clock inside told her it was roughly the same time too.

She froze in fright. "What the hell? No way …!"

The café door opened.

"Here, sweetie," Vanila said, holding out a packed lunch. "You forgot this."

Kelly went over and peered inside. There, on the counter, stood a framed picture of herself, Melody, Vanilla and Skoobie, all on the beach, right before the turtle exploded.

Kelly sighed with relief. "Oh, thank God!"

She hugged Vanilla tightly.

Vanilla was startled. "What's this for?"

"Is it hug time?" Skoobie asked, walking past.

"Yeah," Kelly replied, breaking away from Vanilla and taking the lunch.

Skoobie turned to a table, leaned down and hugged an old man. He jumped, surprised.

"He needed it more than you," she told Kelly, and strode away.

Vanilla smirked at Kelly with raised eyebrows. "Looks like someone enjoyed our first anniversary friender-bender a little too much last night. Must have been the extra herbs in the ginger beer."

"Must have been," Kelly agreed with a grin.

A horn beeped from the road as David rolled up in his car and called, "Hey, sleepyhead, you miss the bus again? Want a lift?"

Kelly glanced back at the clock. "Hey, you know what? It's okay; I'll walk. This boss is cruisy."

"Suit yourself," he said. "We still on for dinner?"

"You bet." She went over to the car, leaned down and kissed him. "See you tonight."

"Bet on it."

He drove away.

Kelly turned to Vanilla and tapped the packed lunch. "Thanks, Scoops."

"Anytime, sweetie," Vanilla replied. "Now go on. Face the world." She came over and squeezed her hand warmly. "Just remember, we're always here."

"I know. Same goes."

Kelly squeezed hers back, then smiled and walked away with her bag over her shoulder, her thumb under the strap, while holding her lunch with her free hand. She hadn't gone far when a bike whizzed past and her arm was slapped.

"See ya round, kid," Melody called, with Sam strapped into the baby seat.

"Yeah," Kelly called back. "Soon!"

Melody turned the corner and sailed smoothly away.

Kelly crossed the road and headed along the street. Happily, she pushed her glasses up, pulled her bag higher on her shoulder and strode into the early morning light.

Behind her, Vanilla watched her go, before retreating into the café with a satisfied smile and closing the door, all while the laughter inside grew ever louder.

About the Author

Sam Silver is an up-and-coming and yet-to-be bestselling award-winning author. He has three university degrees, all in the interests of literature, education and information management, but puts his writing first in the interests of his true legacy.

He has been part of various literary festivals, writing groups, and stalls, and has written daily for the last twenty years.

Incipience is his third literary firework after his first two novels, Burning Embers and Meltdown.

He lives in Perth, Western Australia.